T0304846

even
beyond
death

Also by Fiona Melrose
Midwinter
Johannesburg

even beyond death

FIONA MELROSE

corsair

CORSAIR

First published in Great Britain in 2025 by Corsair

1 3 5 7 9 10 8 6 4 2

A CIP catalogue record for this book
is available from the British Library.

HB ISBN: 978-1-4721-5876-5
TPB ISBN: 978-1-4721-5877-2

Typeset in Baskerville by M Rules
Printed and bound in Great Britain by Clays Ltd, Elcograf S.p.A.

Papers used by Corsair are from well-managed forests
and other responsible sources.

Corsair
An imprint of
Little, Brown Book Group
Carmelite House
50 Victoria Embankment
London EC4Y 0DZ

The authorised representative
in the EEA is
Hachette Ireland
8 Castlecourt Centre
Dublin 15, D15 XTP3, Ireland
(email: info@hbgi.ie)

An Hachette UK Company
www.hachette.co.uk

www.littlebrown.co.uk

The Personal Recollections of The Marquis Jehan de Baudelaire

on
The Year
1657

To Beate Schulter-Brader
Interpreter of Ghosts

'Betrayed and wronged in everything,
I'll flee this bitter world where vice is king,
And seek some spot unpeopled and apart
Where I'll be free to have an honest heart.'
— Molière, *The Misanthrope*,
translated by Richard Wilbur

Contents

VOLUME 1

Salutations

My name is Jehan de Baudelaire. I am, by birth, a nobleman, but more than that, a gentleman.

Notwithstanding my nobility of spirit and self, I hope that you will find me an honest confessor and where I err, I can assure you that my scribe, the damsel Melrose, will be quick to complain.

I will relate, for the purpose of my legacy and your amusement, the events of my life, and those around me, as they unfolded in the year 1657.

It is my most heartfelt intent that, having taken you into my confidence, you will return the favour by reading this document with a forgiving heart. I confess that, in retrospect, I may from time to time have been impetuous or misguided. Granted I have been vain and, some would say, jealous, for mine is a tender, doting heart.

A smattering of politics might find its way into our document in so far as it is relevant, but your amusement will be our highest aim; for while I am a gentleman, I am in addition a poet, dramatist and raconteur, and both my scribe and I are minded that we must not become distracted by a treatise on administration. No publisher would stand for it.

Thus, we will try and limit your exposure to the tedium of the royal House of the Bourbons and to papal machinations, unless I feel it adds a meaty sense of drama or my scribe feels it is important for reasons of clarity. She can be a little tedious in her demands.

But do you see how well she and I work together?

Furthermore, I have promised my scribe that in the telling of my tale there will be a good deal of passion, intrigue and carnal pleasure to have you flapping your fans and pawing at your lover for attention. But love is not all panting assignations and insoluble desire, and so we offer too a substantial application of tender devotion. An additional measure of chemise-shredding misery should bring the balance a good story requires.

To date, my scribe's heartfelt fictions, though emotionally subtle and quite devastating in execution, simply do not offer the weary reader a sufficient supply of sword fights and fornication and that is where the weighty purse lies. It has always been thus. Some will say a damsel scribe is not the best choice for this tale. I disagree. A scribe may learn as much about themselves through the writing of a story as those who read it and he who tells it.

But I digress.

In 1657, one was practically encouraged to frolic in Cupid's arbour and allow oneself to be tossed about on the horns of love: to secure dynasties, provide heirs, entrench advantage and, in general, pass a discreet afternoon. It was a dangerous time to be alive – swords were drawn for less than an off-flavour glance or the slightest intimation that one's lady was a swine. So an afternoon spent supplicant to the charms of an alabaster bosom was an afternoon during which one was much less likely to foment an uprising or consider a military alliance with a distant Spanish cousin.

No. We are not for such ugly squabbles. Rather, our story concerns itself with love. And given that love is the house in which we all are born to abide, I trust you will now lean a little closer for its telling.

Eternally yours,

The Marquis de Baudelaire

1

The Game

Avignon, 1657

You find me, *raquette* in hand, on my *jeu de paume court*. Picture it. I am the very embodiment of agility, virility, grace and speed as I rush and swoop upon the net. So dazzling. My opponent scurries after the ball this way and that, on at least one occasion colliding with the wall with such force that his newly acquired lover somewhat exposes herself by being the first to rise suddenly to her feet and gasp aloud.

The galleries were packed. Every lady and gentleman of quality and all their servants jostling for space. The noise was tremendous. From the side of the court, I managed to locate my beloved sister, Hortense, and her husband The Toad, as well as the cousins Cherbonne and my most adored Comtesse de Montmorency, with her implausible allure. Her bull-faced husband was not in attendance.

My friends and cousins were notorious *jeu de paume* obsessives. It was the wine we were raised on. One dear cousin, Camille, long since sent to a convent, was frequently in confession after having worked herself up into an unseemly state of arousal during a gentleman's game: the sight of sweat-drenched flesh through an open chemise, combined with muscular lunging, arching and thrashing, rendered a young lady of such a hot disposition entirely ungovernable. I was told by the sisters of Sainte-Thérèse that she found great comfort in prayer and needlework. Poor, dear, Camille.

But I digress. Let me describe my exquisite *court*, built by my father before my birth.

The court resembles a large marketplace with a beautiful, vaulted ceiling spread grandly overhead. A cathedral to my sporting mastery, a theatre in which to display my physical prowess and, above all, tactics and cunning.

On the day in question, my opponent was the Marquis de Vermont, a visitor to our city. He had shown himself, on our previous meetings, to be skilled, occasionally excellent, but my estimation was that he was a predictable player. I knew I could beat him.

I was magnificent. I lobbed the ball from gallery to chance line over and over again, each time to roars of approval from the crowd. I was the very embodiment of supple, masculine thrust.

It was thus with great dismay, after a display of such extraordinary sporting guile, that I found myself on the cusp of losing, the game suddenly poised on a single point. If Vermont took it, he would then take the serve and gain advantage. On my own court! Unacceptable.

Hortense gestured to me, tapping her head to indicate that I should concentrate. The crowd, sensing a change was near, began to call and stamp, ladies' fans whipping and flapping as if a fox had been let loose in a flock of starlings. The noise and heat were immense.

Readers, I am the epitome of grace in situations of enormous pressure. In battle I have un-seamed a man from crotch to crop without so much as a blink. So, as you would expect, barely a flicker of discomfort passed my face as I took the ball. I lobbed it high and deep into Vermont's court. But it fell poorly,

allowing him the space to send it back over the net like a musketeer's grenade and past the deepest chance line in my court.
The crowd was on its feet, cheering for Vermont.

Then, as if my misery could not extend further, one of
the side galleries began to jostle; calls to arms were made, a
trumpet sounded and in strode the King's own cousin, Conti,
making his way towards Vermont's end of the court. My humiliation was complete.

He was a man of questionable temperament and loyalty, un-
balanced in both the saddle and the head. Furthermore, I had
it reliably reported that he was an unmitigated flop in the bed
chamber, most likely on account of being in love with his sister.
And so, while ladies flattered and fawned and gentlemen of
quality deferred to his every opinion in the hope of attracting
favour from the royal house, I treated him as I would another
cousin of more or less my age.

It is to this day my assertion that Conti waited until I was on
the brink of defeat before making his appearance.

Of course, the customary greetings would now have to
be made. He waved a wrist in my direction and I replied by
making so great a show of my supplication that I practically
stuffed my nose in the dust of my court. I was a demi-breath
away from base scullion.

What a charade ensued. Conti applauding Vermont even
before I was beaten, the game disrupted mid-play, and every
face in the crowd – from marquis to mouse, comte to cat –
turned towards Conti and Vermont when I had conspired the
entire day for *my* glory, my victory, my amusement.

There was only one possible remedy.

I looked at the ball fallen just over the chance line. With the
disruption, it had not yet been marked.

I cast my eyes around the court. The entire crowd was
distracted.

I extended a toe, quickly glanced up, and then nudged the ball forwards, just slightly towards the more advantageous line.

You will know the feeling. The chill prick of hair around the neckline. I was seen. I tilted my head and saw, on Vermont's side of the net, a man, younger than I with short, cropped hair. Our eyes met, directly. Too, too bold, for he was outfitted as a valet, and not of any house of Avignon. I lifted an eyebrow to query his impertinent intrusion into my business, which had the desired effect of a hasty lowering of his eyes and a subtle deferential bow. He retreated a step or two to better hide himself in the shadows. He had been too presumptuous by half.

After an interminable amount of time had lapsed, and a laboured marking of the ball in its new position, the referee (who, when not adjudicating, was my sommelier) announced the game would resume. He briefly consulted on the score and called *avantage*.

This demanded we change ends so that my opponent might serve. I allowed myself a quick glance back up at the *fils* who had so brazenly caught me tampering with the game. He stood now beside my own valet, Bobo, and another young man.

I must admit to some not insubstantial trepidation at this point. I was banking a good deal on Vermont not querying the mark and risking a scene in front of the King's cousin.

As it transpired, I was incorrect.

As I took my place I noticed Vermont stalling. He had found the mark, but not, it seems, where he had expected to. I ignored this and made an extravagant display to ready myself for his serve. He made no such preparations and instead called out clear as a trumpet on a saint's day in summer, 'The mark is incorrect.'

Well, friends, where earlier all heads had turned to Conti, they now all turned to Vermont.

'The mark has been moved.'

Hortense, I saw, gasped, covering her mouth with her gloved hand in horror.

I replied, 'Dearest Vermont, I can assure you that it has not. I was the only man on the other side of the net and I saw no intruder while I enjoyed my residence there.'

The man would now either accuse me outright or retreat.

Sensing an unseemly scene was about to unfold, the referee cleared his throat.

'We must, *Messieurs*, defer to the marks as we find them as we have no other way to confirm. The eye is deceptive and in a game as quick and skilled as yours, Monsieur Vermont, as exceptional in speed and strength, I can think of no other recourse we have unless there is one who can without prejudice say he knows otherwise.'

A hush fell across the court.

Then a voice from the galleries. 'Here is one, here is a man who says he saw exactly where the mark was.'

Again, the throng turned in unison and out from the shadows came the young man. He stood exactly over the line where I had placed the new mark.

'And who are you?' asked the referee.

'I am Jonathan Kryk, Monsieur.' He bowed.

'What is your station?'

'I am a valet, sir.'

'But whose valet, boy?'

'I have no master.'

'Good, good, then we have an impartial eye.'

Applause from the stands and even more calls to hush.

I did not take my eyes from this Jonathan Kryk, the valet who had no master.

The stillness and strain were so immense that I could have sworn I felt the very rafters of the roof begin to creak as if we were trapped below deck in a great galleon. I could see every individual hair on his head, eyelash, mole. It was as if his face were a map on which I could read my entire future.

'Then did you see where the ball fell?' said the sommelier-referee.

'Yes, sir. Clearly, sir.'

'Where then?'

This servant, in the presence of a royal prince and all of Avignon, turned his head a fraction and brazenly, without impunity, held my gaze; as he did, he allowed a near-invisible smile to extend to the corners of his mouth. Then, he returned his eyes to the referee, extended his palm, cleaver-like, and dropped it, indicating that the ball had fallen where I had decreed.

An explosion of cheers. A cacophony of stamps, applause and calls of, 'Play on, play on, play on.'

You must understand, readers, the spectators do not favour one player over another; they may admire the speed of one, the elegance of another, but in the end what they live for is *the game.*

It was still *avantage* to Vermont. He could not claim he had been outdone. That was the trick. I had still allowed him the advantage so that any complaint would merely seem petty and un-gentlemanly. Which was exactly how it was reported for weeks to come in every salon, alehouse and lovers' bower.

There was no idle chatter that the Marquis de Baudelaire may or may not have moved a mark. This was never uttered. Not once. Rather that Vermont, that inelegant outsider, had arrived in Avignon and cast aspersions on our families of quality, had embarrassed himself and his hosts in front of a Bourbon prince. For shame! They should send him to a colony was the retort. And indeed, I believe he left soon after.

Before he could scamper away, his immediate humiliation was brutal and swift as I finished the game victorious, trouncing the swine conclusively.

I was lifted from court to rafters on the cheers alone. My entire body sang like a fiddle bowed for a forbidden love serenade. I was planetary. So much so that three ladies fainted, a priest fell to his knees in prayer and, it was said, a whelping bitch in the stables immediately gave birth to her pups.

2

Bobo

'A stupendous effort on the court, Monsieur. And now so elegantly attired, the ladies will tremble to see you approach!'

He was, of course, correct, for I did look very fine.

Not so Bobo, who had begun to take on the appearance of a Camargue marsh sheep. Inherited from my dear departed father, my *valet de chambre* was well advanced in years. His bow legs and craggy spine made him a somewhat inelegant spectacle considering his high rank as my manservant.

'Bobo, a question. Who was that man, Kryk, who stood beside you? For he saved my game. One should perhaps offer him a few *pistoles* for his purse.'

'I thought you'd never ask, Monsieur.'

'You could have offered, Bobo.'

'Oh, not I, for I had some small hand in his arrival.'

'Indeed? His hair is cropped very close. He is not one of us.'

'He is a valet not long from Angers, by way of Paris. Originally of Amsterdam I believe, Monsieur.'

'Where is his master?'

'Dead, Monsieur, poisoned by a rival in love.'

'That, Bobo, is why I do not involve myself with love and instead play *jeu de paume* and write verse.'

'Yes, Monsieur. Very wise.'

'What does this Kryk want with us?'

'He seeks employment.'

'But we do not need a valet, do we, Bobo?'

'Not exactly, no, Monsieur.'

'Bobo?'

'Only, Monsieur . . .'

'No, no, I cannot hear it, Bobo. No. You cannot desert me. I forbid it. No.'

After my father's death, Bobo became my one true anchor and *confidente*. The subtleties of my position I learnt from Bobo, not from my Uncle Hippolyte, who had a more heavy-handed, politically expedient approach – despite or because of being a man of the cloth. Other elders in the family were full of advice and I was instructed for hours on the military exploits and daring of my forefathers. Legacy is a tedious and weighty thing.

But in the end, it was Bobo who taught me all I needed to know about honour, duty, elegance and proper behaviour. All that he had taken from my own father. I cannot say I took it all in; he was in constant dismay at my attire, which he considered at one moment too undone and the next too extravagant.

His true name was Beaumont. Immediately on my father's passing, when I was still a boy, Bobo announced himself at my chamber.

He said, 'I was your father's servant to his death and if you will have me, so I will be yours.'

I remember the words as clear as day. The fact that he had begun to suggest that he was too aged to work was unacceptable.

Yes, his fingers did tremble with the laces and fasteners while he dressed me, and it was also true that I had to hoist him off the floor with increasing frequency when he got himself stuck after arranging the florets on my shoes.

Yes, he had collapsed twice – but I think perhaps 'collapsed'

might have been an exaggeration. I suspect it was closer to his
having misplaced his foot as he walked, for he was prone to
chatter while he went. It made him most inefficient and my
winter drinks were often brought to me cold, a natural consequence of so large a *maison*.

I did not mind it on the whole, for I had such deep and
tender affection for him.

But in truth, only that morning my new and very fine clock
told me it took him a full forty-five minutes to get himself from
the kitchen to my writing desk. That he should raise it while I
was still so flushed with victory was a blow.

'Bobo, I am desolate.'

'Monsieur?'

'Bobo, are you truly decrepit? You must be honest with me.'

'Sir, I am.'

'You *are* very slow. This morning you took just under an
hour to make the journey for my ink pot and *tisane*.'

'I apologise most profusely, most, most.'

'Is it the legs? You have always had excellent knees.'

'I was the fastest running footman there was in my youth.
Overtook the horses!'

We said the last part together, for it was his oft-repeated trope.

'Yes. But Bobo, how are you now?'

'Oh, I must not say, Monsieur.'

'But you must, that I may assist you.'

'It is no happy tale.'

'Well, it isn't the knees, we have established that. Do you
shake? A palsy perhaps? Are you in any pain?'

'Well, no, sir, no pain, only some discomfort that requires
terrible and immediate remedy. I was delayed by it on my way
with the *tisane*.'

'A small note: *tisane* and ink pot, Bobo. You did forget the
ink pot.'

'No, sir, I did not forget it. I simply left it where I stopped.'

I had the sense that this tiresome *comédie* might continue well into the afternoon if I could not extract from Bobo the source of his unhappiness.

'You must tell me what is wrong so that I might get you a physician and we may see an end to your discomfort. It is of course self-interest. I will die without you. You do know that.'

'Well, sir, it is most delicate.'

'Oh?'

'It is my pipes below you see.'

'Oh?' Oh.

'I get an awful burn all the length of my man's yard – please excuse me for mentioning, Monsieur – and then I must relieve myself with great haste or there will be an unseemly mess. And, Monsieur, if this were to happen in your presence, then it is I who would rather die.'

'*Pardieu*, Bobo. This is a dreadful thing. And most inconvenient.'

'Most, sir. There's a swelling of the testicles that goes with it. I was struck with the pangs when I was already halfway up the stairs to your writing chamber and had to retreat as fast as I could.'

While I loved Bobo as my own father, I could not have my valet pissing himself as we sat at the barber, or discover, on leaving an entertainment, that he had wet his breeches while in the gallery of a lady of quality. We Baudelaires had standards to uphold. Our reputation depended on it.

'So I may indeed be in need of a new valet.'

'Yes, Monsieur.'

'And if I do not like Kryk?'

'There are two that might please you and another six or seven whom I have taken the liberty of sending away.'

I daresay even before Bobo's predicament was terminal, the

wicked little network that seemed to run between pages, foot-men, valets, lackeys and the rest, would have found me at least fifty of them. Both the valets Bobo had in mind for me were, he said, young and energetic. This was hardly helpful, for that is only part of a manservant's role, but it did bode well for the prompt delivery of ink pots and *tisanes*.

My valet was always to represent me, accompany me on every occasion and in all company. He had to be perfectly at ease and attend to all my intimate needs. My dress, clean-liness, barbering were all under his remit. He needed to be educated, honest with money, handsome and discreet. A sur-prisingly complicated balance. Especially the last two. The rule of thumb was, the more handsome the less discreet. One gentleman, whose name I will not mention, had a valet who was nothing short of ugly: pocked complexion and most irreg-ular in feature. It reflected very poorly on the family. Still, a valet who was too handsome was likely to cause havoc in the household and send scullery maids swooning. It was one of the reasons I liked Bobo so well. Though he was now decrepit, he had a most attractive face and was ever the favourite of the households we visited. His advanced age meant there were never any problems with maids losing their minds or petticoats to his charms.

'Dear Bobo, you are a parent to me. I shall die without you.'

An inelegant snort emitted from my man as he tried to re-strain his tears.

'Do take your time to ease your broken heart, Bobo. But when you are once again in possession of yourself, might I, eventually, have my carriage?'

3

A Spaniel for a Wife

I was expected at my cousin Maurice's *maison de ville* for the continuation of the festivities. Maurice was hoping to gain favour with the Prince of Conti, cousin to the young King. Dear Maurice. He had the odd distinction of being attractive when approached in profile, while the frontal revelation was, at best, startling. But I had no cousin more loyal nor more willing to drink himself under a petticoat or table should the occasion demand it. And occasions did, it seemed, frequently demand it.

We found him in the *grand salon* of his *hôtel*, still sober enough and triumphant, toasting our royal guest.

I was mildly dismayed by the amount of wine being consumed. My cousin had fallen on lean times after ill-advised skirmishes in both marriage and merchant ships and I was carrying the purse for this latest extravagance.

The toast completed, I was able to extricate myself from a tedious discussion on horsemanship in war and seek out my sister Hortense, hoping to convince her to feign exhaustion within the next hour so that we might escape and begin the exodus home.

Disappointingly, I found Hortense in animated conversation with other ladies, being kind and honest-hearted.

'Oh, there he is. Jehan, we were just speaking about you.'

'Favourably, of course?'

'We were speculating,' said a little viper of a comtesse, 'if this will be the year when Avignon's most handsome and eligible gentleman will finally choose himself a wife?'

'Ah well, I choose myself a wife every other day, only to discover they are invariably married. It does not dissuade me, though their husbands do prove an inconvenience.'

How amused they were.

'I have a sister,' said one. 'Lucille is very pretty. Will she not do?'

'I remember Lucille very well. She was, disappointingly, more enamoured with her spaniel than she was with me.'

'Though in her defence,' said Hortense, sensing my ability to tolerate the conversation was reaching its zenith, 'it was a most delightful and engaging little pup.'

'Well then, perhaps I should apologise. It appears that all along I should have taken a spaniel as a wife.'

I took my leave as they tittered and flapped. *Mon Dieu*, give me salvation. Then, like a blessed miracle, the Comtesse de Montmorency appeared.

We stood side by side as dear friends might. I circled her pretty wrist with my hand and we stood in silence, watching the scene become more unmoored as the wine took hold.

'Jehan, you are disconsolate.'

'I am besieged. Trapped by the rapacious laughter of little girls.'

'They claim to be ladies.'

'They still smell of nursery milk.'

I was suddenly overwhelmed by the wish to demand that she take me to her and let me hide my face in her bosom.

You may judge me, but in truth, I had no dearer *confidente* than she. No friend I had in Avignon, and thus the world, could match her mind and wit; converse on all matters political, literary, fantastical. More often than not, I would hazard her husband and his boorish spies to be with her, for she filled my mind with fresh ideas, stirred my ambitions to write better, seek better company, study more widely, swear off drinking. For all her beauty and poise, her more than ten years advance on my age, she gave me harbour where I could be entirely without artifice. And it is true that, from time to time, we lay together. For I needed solace in many ways, as did she. Her chief role in my life though was as friend and companion.

'It seems Conti has redeemed himself,' she said.

'I cannot imagine it. First, he sides with an insurrection that would have us all murdered in our beds – against his own cousin the King, no less – and then that unspeakable lunacy about being in love with his sister. Was there a witch too?'

'Oh yes. All true. But he is now a reformed man, we hear. He will not redeem himself with action, rather his inaction and, it is said, increasingly obsessive piety.'

'How obsessive?'

'Rapacious.'

'Rapacious piety? And he comes to live among us. We will all be dressed like friars and eating a dry crust to act as his fig leaf for insurrection and incest.'

'I fear so. It is said that he will withdraw his patronage of Molière and his players.'

'Oh, I cannot hear it! That they arrive in Avignon this summer is what allows me to survive these exhausting soirées.'

'Noted,' she said, bristling.

'I apologise, but I am in distress. No players this summer?'

'You are a fool. Can you not see? Molière will come to Avignon simply by necessity of route. What he now lacks for the season, though, is a patron sympathetic to his art and – critical to his enterprise – a theatre.'

'Oh! Were it ever possible to adore you more? I will invite the players to perform on my *court* and in so doing I will rid myself of having to pander to Conti *and* gain the opportunity to add Monsieur Molière and his troupe to my accolades.'

You see how clever she was, my comtesse; how invaluable to me.

Festivities continued late into the night and early morning. Gallons of claret, music and carousing. Later the comtesse found me for a quiet, personal farewell.

'Well, *marquis*, for a man so obsessed with the theatre of Molière, your performance at *jeu de paume* produced the drama of the year. I commend you.'

'We could have Molière too, if you agree to seduce Conti and advance my cause. He is the critical hinge in this enterprise. Without him, Monsieur Molière will never be released to play at my theatre.'

'My charms are manifold, but I confess, seducing a hinge may be beyond my capabilities.'

'You did not even try. In seduction, the application of both fantasy and feigned enthusiasm is all.'

'You speak from experience?'

'I do.'

By the time carriages were being called, I had drunk a few gallons more of *hippocras* and had to be taken home tucked in between Hortense and her husband, The Toad, whom I may or may not have tried to kiss.

The day had been an unmitigated triumph.

When eventually Bobo undressed me and dispatched me to my bed a few hours later, I was still groggy with wine, its effects being amplified by the heat of the fire in my bed chamber.

I lay back in a dreadful fog, my head aswirl: vague images of the ladies and their talk of marriage, the intimacies of the comtesse, my sister's sweet embrace as she handed me over to my household for safekeeping, Bobo arriving behind us, the climb up to my bed chamber, the echo of the stone underfoot, the height of the ceilings, the depth of the rooms, Bobo, again, rustling ahead with a trident of guttering flames, muttering about sullen scullery maids. It occurred to me, terribly, that I had never felt so lonely and desolate in all my life.

4

The Game Reprised

I sit at my scribe's right shoulder. She writes at her desk or in a coffee house. She takes a deep breath to let me know she is ready and by the time she exhales, I have begun to narrate, leaning so close she feels my breath on her skin. What sumptuous intimacy. We work daily and with great enthusiasm. She reminds me frequently that she is encumbered by her corporeal burden. She must sleep and eat whereas I am free from time and its constraints. I confess that I forget she is earthbound and must attend to the tedium that involves.

Let us return then to the monotony of life in Avignon in 1657. A year that began with no significant war between foes, nor any mention of plague, was a rarity for us and as such, something to be celebrated. My life was seamless. My chief joys were *jeu de paume*, writing, hunting, carousing, playing at cards, attending to my collections of curiosities for my seclusory, the comtesse, and of course most importantly, my sister.

Hortense and her Toad lived on one of my estates, outside of Avignon. While the house had a beautiful aspect and good trees, forming a lovely avenue on the approach, I found it too large and awkward to inhabit on my own and thus I preferred to pass most of my time in my *maison de ville*. My *maison*. The noise of the streets and proximity to life was a spark to my veins. I had always been prone to a melancholic state and the noise of a drunk stable hand rollicking in the hay store with a fishmonger's daughter was always good medicine for that. The years before 1657 were for me not uncomfortable ones but had the flatness and pallid consistency of the marshlands that extend between Avignon and the sea. Having once again sworn off wine and wives, I had been working studiously on a new story that I hoped might impress Molière. But if the King gave Languedoc to Conti to reward his new piety, libertine Languedoc would soon be quashed and in its place, a stringent reverence which would not allow Conti to support a band of players. Notwithstanding this about-turn, I hoped that subtle arrangements for Molière's future could be made by directing his troupe my way.

I was deep in thought, trying to perfect a pretty rhyme, when Bobo arrived at my desk with the news that Hortense had decided to assist me in interviewing a new valet, despite my protestations that I had scant time or interest in the matter. She was, apparently, on her way to my chamber imminently. Insufferable.

You will notice again and again as you read this document that I was constantly being undermined by all in my household. My sister would come and go from my *maison* without warning or announcement. Bobo was a bag of nerves from trying to corral her. She barged into my house, my salons and, until very recently, all my private rooms. It took a mortifying embarrassment for all involved before she demurred from the last.

But I adored Hortense with every fibre of my being. On the day she married The Toad, I wept. Though I could no longer see her every day, she was ever loyal to me and I continued to dote on her as my life's true companion.

Back to the ordeal of the valets. Hortense announced herself in my salon and kissed me.

'My sweet, you were so gracious and wise to invite me to help you make your choice.'

We were to interview two candidates. One French and from Paris (perfect) and then the man from *jeu de paume*, Kryk. Bobo assured me that though he was Dutch, he was fluent in French and had passable English and even Latin. Both came with good references. I had decided that the most elegant response to the Dutch boy would be to simply ignore the fact that he had lied, bare-faced, in front of the King's cousin to protect my name. There could be no awkwardness. To do otherwise would mean I owed him a debt and, given he was a servant and an unknown one at that, this was quite obviously unacceptable.

The first to arrive was the Dutch. He was modest in a simple black and white collar. His hair was short and he was clean-shaven, which made him hard to age. Hortense made approving noises as she sat next to me and showed no sign of recognising him as the man who had called the line.

After his display at *jeu de paume*, he did absolutely nothing to endear himself and stood entirely still. He looked not unlike a man with some sort of palsy, pale and rigid. It occurred to me that he was terrified. Hortense proceeded to ask him all manner of questions about matters in which I had no interest, other than that they would take place without my knowledge. Things to do with armoires and chains of command. The Dutch valet answered most politely and clearly and I noted (to myself, of course) that he had a good chin for a valet but he did border on dull. I wondered if I should like to wake every morning for eternity to see his face.

I concluded that I should not.

Being a valet, he was attractive. Of course. Light honey hair, good skin tone, clear, slim and would represent me very well in my household livery. But for all his bravado on the previous day, he seemed to lack any energy or charm. It was so terminal that I began to wonder if indeed he was the same man.

'I should like to ask some questions if I may, Sister?'

'Of course.'

'Mister Kryk, is it? This is not the first time I have made your acquaintance.'

'No, Monsieur.'

'You did me a service.'

'No, Monsieur.'

'No?'

'My service was to the game.'

'As it should be.'

Hortense swung to look at me and then to him.

A perfect answer, which had in an instant absolved us both of any debt or obligation. Still, my discomfort remained.

'Can you mix ink?' This would be a quick way to root him out. Then we could end the discussion and bring in the next candidate. 'I do not always like to buy ink and it is good to know that someone about me might be able to make it should the need arise.'

Hortense lifted her eyebrow to express her displeasure.

'My brother is a writer. He likes it almost as much as he does raquette and ball. He sometimes writes through the night and should his pots run dry, it might put him in a sulk.'

'I do not sulk, Hortense. Please. But I should like to know if you have experience with ink.' There was scant chance he did, but perhaps he knew enough to bluff.

'Yes, Monsieur. I can mix all colours, paints and washes too, and can prepare gold leaf and whatever else you might require. I have also had occasion to assist with the stitching of volumes.'

Silence.

Well, I was routed. Hortense was thrilled to see me so roundly bettered.

'How so?' I did not believe him and affected a cool disinterest.

'My father was a map-maker.'

'A cartographer?'

'Yes, sir. In Amsterdam. He was commissioned to provide volumes too.'

'He is no longer with us?'

He paused. 'No, sir, he died while travelling. At sea.'

'My condolences.'

'Thank you, Monsieur.'

'Right, well, that is enough. We have another to see. You may go to the kitchen to meet Monsieur Benoit, he is both my *maître d'hôtel* and my chef. He will speak to you and we will let you have a decision by tomorrow.'

As the door shut behind him, I turned to Hortense. 'I want Bobo back. Can we not fit him with a pig's bladder on a strap?'

'You are being silly. That was an excellent candidate.'

'I will die of boredom before he has fastened one button. The son of a map-maker is not a jolly companion.'

'He is your valet. Not your companion. If we were interviewing companions, Brother, you would have arranged for a row of wine-soaked poets and troubadours to visit.'

'Related, Sister – I am trying to have Monsieur Molière to visit but you insist on detaining me with this dull exercise. Let us hurry this along. And you know that I am prone to melancholy. I cannot have a Dutch misery shadow me around the world. Where is Bobo? Let the next one come.'

The second was perfect. Charming, very good-looking, very energetic and from Paris, so that he knew all the new ways and I dare say could have me looking half my age in one sweep of his barber's blade. His previous master had died after an ill-advised duel left a festering wound. I had already made up my mind. The *Parisien* was perfect.

'Can you make ink?' asked Hortense. She was being very naughty.

'Ink?'

'My brother is a writer and should his ink pots run dry, he would require you to make him a fresh supply.'

'In my previous household, the *chef d'office* prepared such things, it being too messy an employment for the valet.'

'My sister is testing you. Please do not worry about making ink.' I dismissed him and the door had hardly shut before I turned on my sister.

'He is a valet, Hortense. He is not meant to make ink.'

'You asked the Dutch one if he could do it.'

'That was to throw him off and give me a reason not to hire him.'

'Are you pleased with how it went?'

'Well, I could hardly be expected to know his father was a cartographer. In any case, I am planning to hire a *chef d'office*.'

'For a household of one? That is frivolous, even for you.'

We sighed in unison, something we often did.

'He is perfect,' she said. 'So subtle and understated, not too showy, just as a valet should be. And I sense a great seriousness in him. He will be a most devoted manservant. I have always admired the Dutch.'

'What? Sister? You are quite mad. Why would I have him when I could have a proper Parisian valet who clearly has excellent taste and discernment?'

'Because the Parisian valet will bring you no end of trouble and shame. He is all fluff and no substance. He is far too fresh and he will not have been here two months before the scullery maid is with child and he has overslept three mornings in a row.'

'He will not. Though, speaking of scullery maids, I should mention that Marielle is a terrible harlot. She tried to catch my eye just this morning. She is a highly disreputable girl. I would rather have a new scullery maid. I am quite sure she has syphilis. Do you think she does? How can one discover these things?'

'Marielle does not have syphilis, Jehan, and your language is quite unrestrained. You are trying to distract me. The Parisian valet thinks making ink is below him.'

'Well, it is.'

'You are making a grave mistake, Jehan.' It was so rare that we disagreed that we were both agitated. 'That Dutch boy has already proved that he is loyal to the very end of the earth. Do not think I am ignorant of your shameful cheating on the chance line. Once that man is contracted to you, he will die before he leaves your side.'

'You are so dramatic. I must stop bringing you my romances to read.'

'And your Parisian will sell you down the river for less than half a bag of gold and a soft bosom.'

'Now *you* are being fresh, Hortense.' I stood to give my words emphasis. 'I thank you for your assistance in this matter, but this is my household and I will have who I wish to attend me. If I desire a well-looking Parisian valet, then I shall have one. Your work today was to endorse my choice, not inflict your dull-faced Dutch boy on me. You have overstepped your role in my household, Sister.'

'Quite so, my love.' She kissed me so sweetly. 'Please forgive me.'

5

My Valet-Spy

The Dutch map-maker's son moved in to take up position as my manservant the very next day. You will no doubt find this almost as amusing as my scribe, who seems to enjoy recording each and every detail of my multiple humiliations. I will keep her awake for a few nights and play mischief with her dreams. That will teach her a salutary lesson.

He was not, as it turns out, quite as young as Hortense and I had both supposed and was already twenty years old. Still, I did feel a little aggrieved at not having a smart Parisian to tend to my closet. Additionally, there was some awkwardness around the tournament. Obviously, I would not thank him for his intervention, but he had seen me manipulate the game and I had experienced him step entirely beyond the bounds of his place. As a result, and by way of restoring balance to the situation and establishing myself quite firmly as master and he as a servant to whom I owed nothing, I may have been a little off-mooded for a few days. Or possibly weeks.

There was also the matter of my Uncle Hippolyte who, against my better judgement, and how it irked me to admit it, had planted an unsettling seed of doubt regarding the miraculous arrival of this particular valet and the events that transpired.

Uncle Hippolyte had, of course, received word of the goings

on at the tournament. He knew too the fact that I had moved the mark and that my new valet had lied for me. You may well ask yourself how my uncle was privy to these details. As our story progresses, more will become clear. After she challenged me, I had admitted the extent of my indiscretion to Hortense as it was with great difficulty that I ever kept anything from her. Surprisingly, my uncle seemed privy to the same information when he had not even been present at the game.

He announced himself at my *maison* one afternoon when Hortense was visiting, a large trunk of feathers and related fancies for both of us having just arrived.

'You are exposing yourself to charlatans and spies, Jehan. What will Clusy de Marcilliac say?'

Uncle was obsessed with the happiness of every hair on his patron's body and more so his opinions. It is true that Marcilliac was powerful and ambitious. As the power of the papal legates declined in Avignon, his ruthless grasping to hold on to whatever was left of his access to Rome grew ever more calculating. That he had Uncle Hippolyte as his puppet was a source of endless bother.

'Conti is vulgar, Uncle, but to call him a spy may be going too far. Marcilliac is, as ever, paranoid.'

'Jehan is correct, Uncle, he can hardly be called a spy,' my sister agreed.

An extravagant eye-roll from our tedious Uncle Hippolyte. 'Not Conti, your new valet.'

'Oh, Uncle,' said Hortense, 'I helped Jehan choose him myself. A very sober and intelligent man. He is a cartographer's son.'

A sigh to upend a mule. 'I despair that neither of you has asked yourselves the most central question to this whole affair. Three questions, really.'

'And what might those be?' I was keen to hurry things

along given that Hortense had yet to begin unwrapping the
pretty things I had ordered for her. It fell to me to buy her
gifts as The Toad could not be relied upon to remember,
nor choose anything Hortense could be expected to wear in
public.

'Firstly, this valet appears from nowhere at the exact
moment of the Prince of Conti's unexpected arrival. We know
nothing of him except what he tells us. He arrives in Avignon
and at the door of the man who is about to receive the prince.
Secondly, why did this manservant lie for you when he stood
to gain nothing?'

'Quite simple, Uncle. He wished to display his unwavering
loyalty to me and as such gain employment. He was, I discovered, one of two valets whom I was to interview for the
position. As it turns out, all arranged by dear Bobo so that
I need not be bothered by it and could concentrate on the
tournament. The Dutchman demonstrated this loyalty and
I obliged by hiring him. There is no question here. And the
first is circumstance. Spies do not loiter around *grandes mai-
sons* on the remote chance that an ageing valet will suddenly
develop an awkward leak and be forced to take an early
retirement.'

'I will concede that fact, but here is the third and most
important question, which when combined with the other
two should give you pause. Why, when all of Avignon had
their eyes trained on none other than the King's cousin, *the
King's cousin*, recently returned to the fold, why, Jehan, were
the eyes of this apparently innocent valet trained exclusively
upon *you*?'

To this I had no answer. Nor did Hortense, who then spent
the afternoon in a state of high agitation and did not enjoy her
pretty gifts nearly as much as she might have. The prospect
of being responsible for spies and plots related to Bourbon

princes such as Conti, who themselves only recently plotted against the nobility, does rather dull the thrill of a new fan, three hats and six pairs of silk gloves.

It was directly after this conversation that I decided a period of hermitage was required, not least to let the dust settle around the scandal of the game.

In truth, I was in need of solitude. I had not felt myself since Bobo's very recent departure. The night after he was sent home to his family was one of the most desolate of my life. I found myself alone in my bed chamber, no sound of him clattering around talking to himself, no muttering nor chiding at my drinking or attire, no cheerful call of, 'G'night to you, Monsieur, and may God bless y'while y'sleep', as he pulled the drapes closed about my bed. I will admit to you here – though you will, of course, not repeat it – that on that night I cried myself to sleep, exactly as I had as a boy for weeks after my father died.

And so, the instinct was to seclude myself awhile. I had bought some new volumes and was making yet another close study of the work of Petrarch, his glorious Avignon poems in particular. Readers, he fell in love with a pretty maiden he could not have and pined for her for years in his hermitage in the hills. Such elegance in his desolation!

The upsetting episode with the game, dear Bobo leaving and the business of finding a new valet had all interrupted my efforts to complete the rather complicated story I was working on. My tale (another of unrequited love) was not too surprising in chronology, but it was an emotionally complicated one and I was keen to return to it, fearing my own internal weather had shifted since I last sat at my desk for any length of time. If this was so I would be unable to complete it with the same tone and temper.

I immersed myself fully and I cannot tell you the relief it brought. The space between quill and page held for me the most perfect sense of wholeness. It was the one place where I could give myself an honest name and speak of the things no one wished to hear mentioned. It was as if in the fraction of time between the thought and the motion of the quill across the page, I was never more fully understood. I could feel my mother, my father and all the parts of myself I seemed to have mislaid gather around behind me, leaning in about my desk saying, 'Yes? And what is next?'

Of course, on re-reading I would realise that they were mocking me and that I had produced the most incoherent jumble. A rat's nest, no less. But at least for a moment, I was godly.

I spent at least six days in this place between godliness and rats, much as my scribe is doing now, immersing herself in the telling of my tale. She is most loyal and would have made a wonderful valet. She does lack humour though. I suspect it is the absence of a *grande passion* in her life. Well, I will set about seeing what I can do for her. Perhaps I could lob a young cavalier her way. Ah, she bristles, straightening her spine. Where cavaliers are concerned, I see I will have to be clever.

I digress. I promise something meaty soon. In the meantime, back at my humourless hermitage, it was only when a folded *billet* was passed under my door, followed by a loud clatter that nearly stopped my heart, that I realised I had disappeared into my fable of thwarted passion for too many days.

I pulled the door back to reveal the Dutch boy, bent very low in apology.

'What is this?'

'Monsieur, forgive me. I was leaving a note for you but dropped the pitcher I held.' I let him stay bowed that I might better appraise the sincerity of his gesture. I noticed his hand trembled terribly as it clutched the empty vessel. If he was a spy, he was a very unpractised one.

'Never mind that, what is the note?' I had for some reason almost forgotten I had a new valet. It is possible I had found it all too troubling, found *him* all too troubling, and had banished him from my mind by way of self-preservation.

'From the Comte de Villette.'

'Ah, let us see how it is with my most lecherous cousin in all of Aix and Avignon combined. Mister Kryk, we forgive him all his whoring in Aix for he is very well-educated in the arts. You may come in now. I am hungry and probably look like a bear. Do I look like a bear?' (I had just included a bear in my story.)

'No, Monsieur. Not a bear. But some grooming might be in order. That is, if it pleases you?'

'You are being polite. I look like a bear.' I almost threw wide my banyan and made a noise like a bear and a big claw with my hands (Bobo would have liked that), but then remembered myself. 'Let me read this note while you fix my writing desk. Do not disturb the papers.'

I settled on a low chaise with a pipe to read and noticed out of the corner of my eye that not only did Mister Kryk not disturb the papers, but that he carefully weighted them down before opening a window a small crack to let in some air.

'Mister Kryk, in a week's time the comte returns to Avignon and I am invited to join a hunt followed by an evening of music at his home.' I watched as he brushed fallen rose petals from my desk into hand. 'It says here that no bears will be permitted.'

'Of course not, Monsieur.'

It was dry, but it was, I suppose, a hint of humour. Dutch humour, I surmised. I could not make him out. He unsettled me, made my hair prick. Again, I cursed my sister for not allowing me the French one.

'My uncle thinks I should have you interrogated.'

'Monsieur.' He looked up from his work at my desk, visibly frightened.

'He thinks you are a spy. Are you a spy?'

'No, Monsieur. I'm just a valet.'

'My uncle wants to know why, when all of Avignon was watching the Prince of Conti at the game, *you* were watching *me*.'

'Monsieur, I cannot say.'

'Cannot or will not?

Silence.

'Well, my uncle would like to know.' I took a deep puff on my pipe. 'And, in truth, a part of me would like to know too.'

Additional silence.

'I see I will need to get used to these vagaries of what passes for conversation in Amsterdam.'

'Monsieur, I will collect oil and towels for your grooming.'

And with that my valet-spy bowed and left the room.

6

The Hunt

It is late morning. A hunting scene in winter, the year still a suckling pup. The sky is grey and the earth barren. The linden trees are bare and silver, like ten thousand swords thrust into the hills that surround the city of honey-coloured turrets and ramparts. You will be hoping for the romance of a snow. There will be very little this year. It will be seen in the distance, an unpromising little shroud over the peak of Ventoux. Snow falls infrequently in Avignon.

A monstrous boar, quick and fierce, had been chased, cornered and garrotted. Its blood a hot spill on the ground, pooling quickly and sending the dogs into an even more carnal frenzy.

That the boar was caught or not did not interest me, rather it was the speed of the chase, the immensity of the passion I felt as the pace quickened, trees thrashing past, the labour of the horse, the cold of the air in the breast, the sense that one had, even if only momentarily, escaped the bounds of the city, duty, obligation.

And what bliss that was.

Let us return to the scene. Our party had arrived back at the lodge, where all of Avignon's families of quality were represented. Immaculately coiffed ladies drifted outside to greet us. So many were our number that their husbands and lovers

became a single masculine ideal. Over the throng, I managed
to offer a greeting to Hortense, knowing she finds the hunt
truly unpleasant, suffering as she does from the cold and a misplaced affection for beasts. (I shall resist the urge to mention
The Toad in this regard.) She had, as we find her, not been
well, suffering in the last weeks the loss of an unborn babe.
She had succumbed to this agony before. She bore it elegantly
but I, who understood her heart as my own, knew the rack
over which her heart was stretched. She would not, despite my
pleas, hear the suggestion to stay at home, warm and closeted
with her maids, saying the company of friends and cousins
would do her well.

I tried to get to her side, for she did look weary, but the
noise and general excitement of the hunt's return made it
impossible. In addition to the ladies and their gentleman,
now in the forecourt of the lodge, there were also a few dozen
boys to see to the horses, a few more to control the dogs, still
baying for their prey, and another retinue of men to see to
the weaponry.

My sister accounted for, my eye began to seek out my dear
comtesse.

Having lavished praise on her husband (his bravery, his
daring, his horsemanship), she managed to slip behind the
leathers and furs and beckon me to a convenient stable where
she offered me a delicate kiss and a saucily placed glove; with
it, I expelled a gasp of delight.

'I have news,' she whispered.

'You will flee with me to Paris?'

'You are being naughty, Jehan. And to punish you, I will
now not share the tidbit with you.'

'Then it could not have been very valuable, for you tell me
everything.'

'You are very confident.' With a cursory glance for spies,

she rearranged her plumes and set across for the festivities. She turned back.

'Such a shame, I had thought you enjoyed base gossip from the house of the King.'

'What? What news?'

I was about to chase her when a late arrival, an unparalleled dunderhead whom we had lost at the first leap, came clattering into the yard.

'Ah, Baudelaire. D'you know, I'm always surprised to see you here. You don't strike me as, y'know, a man for the hunt.'

'A man who is not a man for the hunt and the kill may still be a man for the game and the chase.'

'Do you mean ... I don't ... or ...?'

A skein of geese hooted across the sky.

Oh, empires were conquered, dynasties fell. Time replaced her swaddling clothes for a crone's corset and still, still I waited. At last, even the horses fell silent to support our dunderhead in his confusion.

'Dear chevalier, you will come to it, one generously assumes, eventually. In the interim, I have developed a full winter's worth of appetite. Good day.'

I can report that he died a month later after a misadventure with a musket. He was not missed.

The comte's hunting lodge was a delight. Balance, refinement, repetition. It was perfect. I could have designed it myself. An elegant facade, an extravagance of high glass windows, candles reflected in every pane.

Despite the cold, its interior glowed with a golden air enhanced by fire and fur for warmth, musicians, footmen, a few cooks. My own exceptional Monsieur Benoit had been enlisted too, taking command of the dishes as the comte's own *maître d'hôtel* had died of an ague two days before; the assistants could not be trusted to bludgeon an eel, let alone cook it. There were a few more cooks to assist, and, naturally, a wagon-load of wine. Additionally, a valet for each man, and at least two lady's maids for each lady.

Eventually, my comtesse and I were reunited. I handed her a cup hoping it might loosen her tongue. 'I demand satisfaction.'

'You have had that already.'

'But now I would like the rest. What news?'

'It is less news and more the best and tastiest sort of secret. It is not to be shared. Do you promise me?'

'And yet you share it. And if you have heard it, I will assume all of this unscrupulous assembly know it too. Who does it include?'

'None other than the King's brother.'

'Our Petit, the Duc d'Anjou? No doubt another improvident indiscretion?'

'Oh much, much more.'

'Has he been caught kissing his own hand?'

She leant as close as possible. 'He has been corrupted.'

'What?'

'To completion.'

'*Dieu!* This is too rare. Who did it?'

'Promise you will be quiet when I say it?'

'Tell me at once, who, who did it?'

'Mancini.'

'No!' Friends, I confess I did shout out and at least three ladies turned to stare.

'Shush, Jehan, you promised.'

'How can I? Our glorious Cardinal Mazarin's own nephew? Are you certain?'

'Of course I am.'

'I am dumbstruck.'

'You are delighted. As are we all.'

'Will he be sanctioned?'

'I cannot say. Word is that Mancini will be sent on a distant commission and the Petit Monsieur is to begin his military career immediately.'

'If he was one of us, he would be for the stocks, the rack and the pyre.'

'Who was the last?'

At this point, Maurice joined our party.

'Who was the last what?' he asked.

'Sodomite of Avignon,' the comtesse replied.

Maurice winced. 'The one we know about or all the others?'

'The last to burn.'

'Oh, it's been a while. They did a cook's help near Orange the other day though.'

'How basely you speak. "Did." The comtesse is present. Are you drunk?'

'I am so far in my cups, Cousin, I require a mule to drag me back to shore.'

'I heard about the cook's help from my wigmaker,' the comtesse said.

'It is well known,' said Maurice. 'Rendered him a eunuch first, I think, then a sword from crotch to crop so his guts spilled out and then to the pyre. They say he was still alive on the flames. Can't say how.' Maurice drank deep from his glass.

'This is not jolly at all,' she sighed.

'Well, when our newly devout Conti installs himself over the Rhône from the Palais, the legates will have to keep a pyre going day and night just so they can lob on a fresh one every now and then.'

'Maurice, indelicate of you.'

'You are the dramatist, Cousin. You well know that when one theatre closes another must open. Uncle Hippolyte tells me we are due it.' He drained his glass. 'Is this about Mancini railing the Petit Duc?'

The comtesse retreated behind her fan to hide her delight.

'How do *you* know about Mancini? Why am I always the last to hear anything?' It was infuriating.

'Everyone knows.'

'I did not.'

'You've been locked in your tower writing your clever little love ballads.' He was being fresh.

'I have been busy.'

'Keep that up, Cousin, and Mancini will have you next and then toss you to Anjou. Uncle Hippolyte will be most conflicted. On the one hand, you will, against all expectations, have gained entry – is that the correct term? – to the House of Bourbon, on the other hand . . . Hmm. Pray, Cousin, when will you take a wife?'

At this, the comtesse near split her sides with glee and Maurice laughed so hard he began wheezing.

'I hope you choke. You are both insufferable. I see I am not among friends.' That I was constantly hounded on the matter of taking a wife was becoming the source of my most desperate melancholic states.

'No, please, Jehan, let us know when you choose a wife. But know too that there are other routes to good fortune.'

Friends, it took all my mettle to resist pounding Maurice clean across the head with my cup. 'Perhaps I will take a wife tonight and neither of you will be invited to the church.'

'Oh, do you spy something pretty here tonight? I fear you have already dismissed every lady in this room and now that you are wanting one, none will have you,' said the comtesse.

Utter wretches. Even as I swung away, I could hear them descend into undignified mirth. I collected my pretty sister and took her home to rest, resolving to return to my desk and eschew my cousin's vulgarities.

7

My Eternal

Preparation for the night of music that followed the hunt required much bathing and shaving, during which the near-invisible and strangely silent Mister Kryk twice nearly sliced my nose clean off. He was far more blundering assassin than subtle spy. After I had rejected all wigs (too big, too pale, too ridiculous) and three ensembles (too colourful, too dull, too desperate), I was finally able to make my way to a modest but charming chateau for an evening of musical entertainment. I had myself sent spies and had been assured that accompaniment of the singers by the infernal lute would be at a minimum (*pardieu*, the head-jangling noise haunts me still) and thus felt it safe to attend. I had always admired my host's taste.

My damsel scribe has instructed me to qualify my use of the word 'modest'. She considers the Comte de Villette's home a fairly vulgar baroque construction with three salons, a ballroom, a music room, an *orangerie*, two libraries, a peacock house and a small zoo, among others, and she fears, dear reader, that you will dislike my judgement.

She is incorrect.

My sister, her toady husband, the brothers Cherbonne, at least two Villeneuves, a clutch of Clusy de Marcilliacs and all the usual suspects were there. I was unhappy to notice some of my more ambitious cousins were also in attendance.

Notwithstanding their bristling presence, I cheered up immediately to see the Comtesse de Montmorency arriving with her husband. She was luminous.

The painter Nicolas Mignard was there. You will know him by his portraits. In Avignon, he was my rival in *jeu de paume court* theatre rentals. Molière tended to prefer Mignard's court and had yet to knock on my door. I hoped that this would be the year things changed in my favour. It occurred to me that I could ask Mignard to execute an extravagant and thus expensive portrait of myself – a sufficiently elaborate commission might dissuade him from challenging me when I made advance to Molière. I would suggest a handsome demi-profile at my writing desk. Intelligent, philosophical.

(My scribe's eye-rolling is noted.)

I had the sense that the evening would be a delight. It was my first outing to a *grande maison* with my new valet and I was pleased that he looked so well in my livery. These were the things that were noticed. He was slim, marginally shorter than I (you do not want a valet who looks down on you) and his face was neatly set against the blue and silver of our crest. He had nothing of the lively countenance and good cheer of Bobo, who I missed desperately, but he would represent me well and I knew my sister would be very smug to see him.

As ever, our host had produced the perfect evening. He was a man of very refined taste and I frequently found myself looking to him when I was unsure how I wished to proceed on matters of discernment, particularly in the household. It was true that having a gentle, refined wife would be more useful. As I rounded the room in search of my favourite ladies, it once again occurred to me that I should, by the end of the approaching summer, make at least some effort to secure one for myself. It would certainly keep my uncle from pestering me. I would ask Hortense to remind me: a Mignard portrait and a wife.

The problem with finding a wife was that the ones I admired for their sharp wit and clever conversation (such as my most dear comtesse) were invariably considered too old for me and were, like her, married. And the ones that were considered a good age and could still be relied upon to produce children, were, on the whole, so dull and mindless that they could also reliably be put to work as a sleep aid.

How many excruciating afternoons had I spent in my sister's *salon* trying to make conversation with some girl who only wished to make a good marriage so that she could please her father and buy even more dresses and hat plumes to match? Which is not to say I was not partial to a good clutch of plumes myself, but there must be more to one's wife or, failing a fortunate strike of pestilence (recalling Cousin Maurice's fortunate release from his ghastly marriage), one has nothing but a lifetime of silent dinners to look forward to. Some of you reading this document are perhaps even now contemplating the silent repast you have just endured. Well, let me assure you there is yet another tomorrow, and another after that.

After every meeting of the sort, my sister and I would enjoy a variation of the same conversation.

'Well, how was she? Did you find her beguiling?'

'I can confirm that she has all her limbs intact and can speak most eloquently on the subject of picnics, plumes and spaniels.'

'But she is so pretty.'

'That is all that she is.'

'You could get her a spaniel.'

'Then, as I repeatedly point out, I would rather marry the spaniel.'

This conversation was enacted so often I felt we were rehearsing for some great stage. And indeed, I did use it to great effect in another piece of theatrical magnificence which would be included in my folio for Monsieur Molière.

I was too old to not be married, being twenty-four, and too eligible, being in possession of land, title and robustly healthy coffers. (Not a euphemism, but euphemistically, also correct.) Still, the prospect of marriage raised in me a not-inconsiderable nausea that I had never managed to dispel. I had consulted astronomers, soothsayers and priests, all of whom advised me that love was an illusion and I should simply make a financially expedient match. I found this realistic but abhorrent. I understood that while it may not be possible for me to fall in love, it should at least be possible not to die of boredom within the first five days of the union. Still, it was conceivable that this was the last year that I could avoid marital constraint. Uncle Hippolyte would not stand for it.

The more I was pressured on the matter, the more melancholic I became. It was my disposition. I had in me a solitude which announced itself unbidden when least I expected to find it. It had come to me that evening, just as I had handed my hat and long cape to Mister Kryk and stepped from the cover of dark into the brightly lit room. As he stepped away and I made the single step alone towards the throng, I had the most desolate sense of a soul abandoned by itself.

The salon was stuffed to the filigree and there were more guests than there were places to sit. I found Hortense a chaise (her husband being too coarse to assist her in this) and took my place standing at the back near the side service door, through which the staff were bringing wine and sweets and where I could be assured of a little air. Though it was still winter, the room was febrile.

The music was sublime. A small ensemble and two singers, soprano and tenor. They sang such songs as could break your heart just for hearing them. The first taken alone was enough to set a man's wig to fire. I glimpsed my sweet sister and saw that she leaned forward so intently, as if being closer might allow her to hear even more. There was great applause after the first *chanson* and as the musicians rearranged themselves in their seats, I turned a little to look through the servants' door for some cooler air. Along the wall of the corridor, I could just make out the shape of two valets, standing together waiting to be called, and then closer towards me was my own, Mister Kryk. The other two seemed to whisper together conspiratorially, but mine knew no other to call friend and so kept to himself.

The music began again, this time a lighter melody and less prone to crushing all hope of survival by sheer force of its beauty. More applause and both singers bowed. Our host himself was delighted and placed a hand on the knee of the Comtesse de Beaucaire to celebrate. The Comte de Beaucaire looked down and noticed the offending hand on his wife's knee but simply turned away again. That was the moment of scandal, of course – not the placement of the hand, rather her husband's indifference. I noted this exchange as an excellent moment to commit to a story. The music began again.

There is some music that you enjoy, some that you love, and then there are those rare pieces that transport you right out of your body so that you hover just a few measures above it, becoming a celestial mass made of nothing but starlight and cool water. And this was such a piece. Soaring and dipping as each voice overtook the other and then came together again only to go their separate ways once more. I thought I might drown in the beauty of it. To save myself from being permanently stripped away from my mortal self, and to save my dignity for I was suddenly entirely overwhelmed with tears, I looked away from the *salon* out to the corridor.

There was my valet, Mister Kryk, leaning back against the corridor wall, his cap in his hands, face turned up to the light, eyes closed against the music and his cheeks an exact mirror of mine, entirely awash with tears.

There was in that moment the briefest split in time: a bee's breath, a single drop of rain. The in-breath before the song, the whisker on the cat, the first drop of wine, the last star still visible before dawn. All of these tiny, half-born moments were suddenly numinous and alive, part of my very being. There began in my body a great roaring as if a momentous tide approached the shore. As I watched Mister Kryk, he unaware of me, of anything, only subsumed by the beauty of the music, I felt another great spill of tears overwhelm me, so that I fear I was submerged in them.

My breath came only in desperate, drowning gulps even as the air around me went silent and the only thought I held was *Yes, there you are, I know you and have known you and will know you now for eternity.*

Then the music soared again, voice over voice, the two so perfectly entwined that they became one song. My heart beat faster and faster as if it might explode; more tears, gasps for air, my skin alight to every note, every candle that reflected here and there, dizzying flashes of fire and sound and I knew without any doubt in my heart that Jonathan Kryk, the cartographer's son, was my one, my true, my eternal love.

8

Over a Barrel

There was a tempest in me, grievous and beautiful. He stayed as he was, listening, his face lit on the one side. I turned away quickly. I dared not look at him too long. How I yearned to. I was twenty-four years old and until then had more or less managed to hold myself in order, restrain my impulses. And yet, there in the poor light of a service door and in the space of an in-breath, I was stabbed through to my core, upended even as I stood trembling, while shock and then panic began to choke me. It was too dangerous, I had to leave the *salon*.

The clearest way was out through the door beside me, past Kryk and through the service corridors. But I would have to explain to him why I was leaving. He would rush to assist me. And everything in me wanted him to do so. I was trapped. No longitude nor latitude could help me navigate myself free from that room and I could not – I must not – make a scene. I had to wait for the music to end. So, when it finally did and the applause began to echo, it was all I could do to stop myself leaping over the other guests to get out, as I pushed along the rows of feet and skirts to be free.

Why had he wept? Perhaps a moment caught off guard. Was it the music? Was he melancholy? *Pardieu*, his face.

Why, despite efforts and vigilance, did I find myself feeling as I should not? Lack of air. Perhaps the room had simply been too warm and the music too rich. An excess of emotion. That would certainly explain it.

I clawed my way outdoors, thinking perhaps a few deep breaths of the night air might settle my tempers, but I soon realised my predicament was more fundamental.

Mister Kryk of Amsterdam.

I decided to leave the evening with urgency, unattended and with as little attention as possible.

I would return to my *maison*. A fast horse would see me there in less than an hour. I would leave a note with my sister's lady to alert my servants and my sister. I could send my apologies to my host in the morning and explain that the music had been so lovely as to entirely overwhelm me, and that I had felt unwell. All true.

My scribe does not believe me. She does not believe that anyone can fall in love in an instant and with such force. She denounces it as the stuff of verse. And I confess, perhaps I too had refused to entertain the existence of such a madness.

Yet there I was, shaking right through, my clothes so burdensome that I had to unbutton myself. I eventually managed to tear my collar right off simply to breathe.

All I could see was his face, drenched by tears, eyes closed against the sorrows of the world.

How was it possible, to love so completely where the moment before one had not? How could love announce itself as hot and joyful and yet bring with it the icy chill of fear? They were eternally one and the same.

I borrowed a horse from my sister's man and told him he could ride home on the carriage with the rest. He might normally have resisted – to allow me to ride alone was reckless – but I suspect the urgency in me made him rethink. I swung up and was soon away.

Twice I slowed. I felt I was being followed, that I had some-how betrayed my own feelings. The freezing air though acted as a sobering winter's slap. By the time I was back through the great gates of the city walls, my hands were cramped with cold. The tremendous panic had reduced to a stub.

Though it was getting past late, Avignon's wine houses were as noisy as ever. As I re-entered the city's bounds, familiar streets, battlements, the sound of hooves on cobbles, all these offered some reassurance.

And yet, I could not shake the sense of horses, riders, eyes that followed me as I went. I turned again but saw no one.

I stopped at the doors of the church, Saint-Pierre. I would pray, absolve myself. I could hear singing coming from inside and my nose pricked at the scent of frankincense that sat so deep in the wood and fabric. And just as I let my mind settle to a moment of calm, and I shut my eyes, I saw his glorious face again.

I took one last breath of absolution and I turned away.

The wine house was rank and seemed to be filled to the roof with every last reveller between Lyon and the stink holes of Marseilles. I spotted the Chevalier Levesque in a dark corner with his hand down the bosom of some or other wench. His usual posture. A pair of grub-minded musketeers arrived soon after me and sat a bench away. I ignored them and ordered a large measure of *hippocras*, my truest friend. I then remem-bered I had no coins, that being my valet's remit. After some negotiation with the landlord, it was agreed that I could send payment in the morning. With such a happy amnesty I took order of another and then another and was soon feeling much the better.

It occurred to me, as I placed another convivial cup on the table, that I must have mistaken my earlier heightened emotion. The music had been so dangerously arousing that anyone of a romantic nature would in the moment be prey to a wayward Cupid's arrow. I dare say I would have fallen in love with old Bobo had he been propped up there with his eyes closed and his britches damp, leaking like a drain. I ordered another cup. My mind began to return itself to order and balance. It was quite clear that the excellent music, the intense closeness of the room and the great crush of bodies had worked a mischief on me. I would complain to my host about his arrangements for ventilation when I sent apologies for the disruption I caused with my hasty departure.

To prove my regained health, I would find a willing lady to lie with me that very evening. The wine house was just the place for it. Over in the far corner was a group of younger lads and some maids too. Alas, even through the delicious *volupté* produced by the *hippocras*, I could tell they were a poxy lot and would raise no pleasure.

Almost as soon as hope had returned, it left me. I was melancholy and shamed. Casting about wine houses for eager bosoms was not acceptable behaviour for Baudelaires. We were no Levesques. I took another measure from the innkeeper – which I swallowed in one – and with nothing more for it, conceded it was time to find my way home.

I would have to be clever and quick as I had a long walk home and had mislaid my sword in my earlier haste to rush away. I nearly collided with the musketeers who were just ahead of me and for a moment I thought I might hire them to walk me home. I thought better of it.

I had a memory of a horse. Had I had a horse? Nothing was clear.

I would walk. If a bandit's sword found my heart, I was unlikely to feel it. It was bitterly cold and I had lost my cloak too. I felt another layer of misery descend.

'Monsieur.'

It was a woman's voice. I could not surmise from whence it came.

'Here.' I could just make out a form in the side door of the wine house, where they took delivery of all the barrels and jars.

'Who are you?'

'Thérèse. I work inside. I've been watching you.'

'Ah-huh.' I turned to see her sitting on top of a wine barrel.

'You don't look too happy, Monsieur, if I may say.'

'Well, Mademoiselle . . .'

'Thérèse.'

'Thérèse. I am not happy.'

'Oh. Is it love?'

'It is always love. It is a cruel teacher.' I could not remember having seen her before at the inn, but then I could hardly remember my own feet. I liked her. She had an open face. Gold hair, round plump shoulders and soft.

'Come in,' she said. 'You will find it warmer. You can pull the door behind you.'

'You should work, *non*?'

'This is work. I mean, not you, Monsieur,' she waved her hand. 'This.' She leant back a bit on the barrels, patting the side with her hand and kicking her legs about. 'Do you want to kiss me?'

'Oh?' Eager. I admit that soaked as I was, I was rather surprised to hear it. She did not have the look of a whore at all.

'I have seen you in town. At the wigmakers, at the booksellers. You are always at the booksellers.'

'Indeed I am.'

'You must be very learned. Have you a lady?' Even wine-house wenches wanted me married. 'You should have someone to love and someone who can look after you.'

And then I could see Jonathan Kryk, his head to the light, his lips slightly parted, eyes closed to the music.

'That prospect is not unappealing, of course, though I am on my way home now.'

'I could look after you—'

'I do not wish to affront you. I should leave.'

'—for tonight anyway.' She pulled me a little closer to her, up against the barrel where she sat. 'Don't you want to take some pleasure? There's no one here.'

She was touching me and pushing my bands to the side. She was too forward. I was confused, stupid even, and yet did nothing to stop her. She unfastened me and continued with her work, arranging her skirts and taking my hand to her. I understood where she was leading me with her hand and mouth, whorish now, and I felt myself respond to her. I thought, this is very useful, a good remedy. I felt as if I were about to commit some base adultery and yet could not name against whom.

All at once she arranged herself to help my way and then guided me inside even before I knew what was about me. I could not stop yet felt such terror too, such repulsion at myself. And then with it a base, vengeful anger. Some darkness.

I took the girl off her seat and turned her face away, so she bent forward. And I took her that way. It pained her and I did not care for her comfort. And with my release, which came so soon, but which she seemed to echo with her own, I felt a surge not of pleasure but of horrible, devilish clarity.

It was him I saw and him I wanted.

There has been such shame in recounting this. I do not want my scribe to think less of me – though she inevitably will as we progress. But when we began our work, I did commit to reporting honestly the events of this tale, no matter how she might respond. She can be an awful scold and this is such a miserable, inelegant telling. She would never let herself be so rudely humiliated, erring as she does on prudish. Even if she allowed herself an infatuation, the object of her affections would be the very last to know. She might snap at him or humiliate him, this being her awkward and ineffective manner of flirtation. I, of course, hoped the same level of decorum and cool detachment might adhere to me. In poems and stories, even of my own writing, love is seamless, joyful. Even in the tortures of anticipation, there is such a delightful thrill; a charge, yes, but with a lightness to it.

Instead, what had I done? A fast and rude release, initiated by this maid but roughly taken by me. When I woke some hours later, propped up outside the barrel-room door like a sack of wheat, cold and in some pain, I could not recall her leaving me, what had been said between us or how I came to be left there.

It was still dark and I knew I had to find my way home before anyone was about to see me there. It was a miserable walk. I could not remember where I had left the horse and the thought of looking for it and then dragging my body up to ride the poor beast was too awful. I was an unholy mess. I knew as much. I remembered I had wanted to go to pray. Instead, I found myself no more than a half-frozen, wretched gutterling.

By the time I found my gates, marked by stately trees in the forecourt, the sky was considering its resurrection and houses were stirring with servants making fires. My guards and doorman rattled themselves to life to let me in. I like to think I managed some posture to mask my dishevelment as I passed by them, but any man with a half-functioning nostril would know my state. I cast a mad, pulsing eye about. No Mister Kryk. I told a footman to make sure I was not disturbed, that

I would undress by myself. Never was a man so happy to find he was alone in his bed chamber. The maids had at least seen fit to keep a fire alight for me. I slept.

9

Hercules

I woke to a rumpus.

'Madame, he is not to be disturbed.'

'He might be ill, stand aside.'

'Madame, he is not ill.'

'I will judge that. Open the door, please.'

It was Hortense. She pushed past a wide-eyed page, nearly knocking him clean over with the force of her skirts. She and my scribe have much in common: a degree of forthright focus that can be somewhat overwhelming. But if she had come to save me from myself, she was too late.

'*Nom de Dieu,* Jehan. I have been up half the night worrying about you. Oh. Oh, no. What a stench. You have been drinking. You are beyond hope.'

She swatted my face with her plumes. Quite unnecessary, I thought. She went on, 'I have been awake in the cold waiting for my lackey to come home with word that you are safe and well, only to have him arrive back this morning to say that you returned without the horse you stole. Where is my horse? No cloak, the lackey reports, no sword, no collar and that you had clearly been beaten and robbed.'

'Sister . . .'

'Were you beaten and robbed?'

'No, Sister.'

'I did not think so. And I had to hide all of this from my poor husband who would be ashamed to know it. You set a very poor example, Jehan. This is all most inelegant.'

'I am sorry.' My head was dry and aching. I felt I wanted to have her hold me and let me tell her all of it. All of it. But how could I?

'You left because you did not feel well and then you did not arrive home. What was I to think? I now find you were sufficiently well to drink enough wine to turn the Rhône to claret. How could you? Shame.'

'I am sorry. I could not say why I did it.'

She finally stopped flapping about and came to sit on my bed.

'What is the matter, Brother? This is not like you at all. We cannot have this. It will not serve us. Do you think your exit went unnoticed?'

'I did feel unwell. Truly. I thought to come home and was headed that way, but alas was most grievously distracted en route.'

'You must not drink to a stupor, Jehan. It will not help you. It will not help us. You know my predicament. And I worry for you. You are my true love, though you do not smell very well. It is most lamentable.'

She leaned against me. It took everything in me not to confess, not to tell her all that I had suffered; that the drinking was the least of my woes and the wine had saved me from my own mind that was brimful of wickedness and wanting.

She sat up smartly. Bristling again. 'And where is my husband's horse?'

I sent word for the horse to be found and returned and made it clear that I should not be disturbed for the rest of the day. The thought of Mister Kryk arriving in my bedchamber was entirely too much to bear.

I was comforted that Hortense would announce that I was indeed unwell and that would give her an excuse to return later. I hoped she might be persuaded to stay a while. I did not want to be left alone in case my mind began to busy itself too much with things it should not. Additionally, she would act as a shield and save me from seeing Mister Kryk.

Nothing was clear for me at the time, but my scribe assures me that an effort at some clarity is required, as much for herself as for readers. She continues to be obstinate, refusing to believe in love at first glance. It is true, Mister Kryk was not the first man to arouse these feelings in me. Far from it, but they were flashes, passions that flared and eventually passed and were, shall we say, entirely corporal. I learnt to distract myself. I would hunt, pray, retreat, work and after a while I could feel whole again, though as the years passed my melancholy became harder to lift. There were weeks, even months, when life felt entirely hopeless, so deep was the sense of being adrift on an island, remote from the hope of true companionship. It was my sister's patient love that saved me each time, even though she never knew the true reason for my despair.

Obviously, I would never do anything to compromise my reputation or that of my family. A dynasty, centuries of kinship and allegiance, depended on it – and so too the lives of my family. It was impossible.

Legacy, lineage, reputation, these were the things that bound me to my history and my station. The region, its marquisates, estates, the seats of its power, its proximity to the papacy, all relied on each one of us, inheritors of the burden of the first-born son, to make practical application of these ideals. These estates held no home for love. And let us not forget the pyre, the tortures, trials, the banishment. Hortense would lose her marriage, her home. Our good name would be expunged and everything related to me – titles, deeds, records of birth – burned as if neither I, nor my name, nor my family, had ever existed.

You will remind me of the King's brother, the Duc d'Anjou, and his own now-known corruption. But though we were of noble blood, we were not Bourbons and there would be no such leniency. Some sanction would need to be taken. Examples made.

One might be permanently exiled, if one was very lucky. But even if I survived, the other would not, certainly not if he was a servant. He would die the most unholy of deaths, dragged through the city in stocks before being tied to a stake in the square and burned, still breathing. And this after a public trial during which evidence would be offered in detail for all to hear.

This was Avignon, the seat of the papal legate, and soon to be the new home of the Prince of Conti, enforcing his obsessive newfound piety. The punishment for those inclined to wickedness, to sodomy, would surely be death.

Who would choose that?

So, instead, hunting, *jeu de paume*, retreat, writing.

Hortense returned and brought food to my chamber.

'I could not let the servants see you in such a state.' She was being prim with me. 'What is your new valet to think?'

'Oh? I had quite forgotten about him.' I watched her closely.

'You must treat him better. He was in a turmoil thinking he had let you go off unattended and then that some harm had come to you, knowing that it would be his fault entirely. He has been with you hardly a month. And already this.'

'I hadn't thought.'

'I have sent him off with a boy to retrieve poor Hercules and pay any outstanding debts you may have incurred. You see what I must do for you?'

'What? Who is Hercules?'

'He is my husband's horse.'

'He is no Hercules.'

She sighed with enough vigour to uproot a venerable cypress. 'Did you incur debts last night?'

'Yes. I had no currency. Not a solitary *pistole*.'

'I thought as much. We must settle all of this before anyone knows of it. Your manservant will arrange it.'

'Thank you, Sister. You are much more cunning than I have ever given you credit for. There is one other thing.'

'Yes?'

'It is a delicate matter.'

'Yes.'

'It is that ...'

'Yes, I understand you.'

'I'm not sure you do.'

'I understand you.'

'Only ...'

'I am not a novice, Jehan. I cleared your clothes away this morning. I could not have a new valet do it. Bobo was at least half-blind.' She lowered her voice.

'*Dieu!* You mortify me. Leave me.' I hid under the covers.

'It is too late to be shy, Brother. Does this, this *lady*,' she made very heavy work of the word, 'require a courtesy call, a small gift? We cannot have a scandal in a few months' time. Uncle would turn puce.'

I peeped over the top of my bed covers. 'No. No. Only, I can't much remember. Yes. Maybe a small token. I did not take what was not offered, I should like to say, Sister. No. No token. It seems like an admission when no wrong was done. You see, I was taking myself home, feeling unwell. I had lost Hercules ...'

'I do not wish to hear any more. I feel my day has already taken an irretrievably base turn.'

'My whole life has taken a base turn.'

'It has.' Another nautical sigh. 'What happened to you?' She was tender. 'Never in all our time have you done something as rash and public. At home is quite a different thing. I know you are impetuous, and you are always naughty, it is why I love you. But there was quite some chatter as you launched yourself out of the salon. It was most immodest behaviour, Jehan, leaving like that. And this morning, winding your way home half-paralysed with drink. Could anyone have seen you?'

'I cannot say. And I do not care. I am so unhappy.'

'Jehan, whatever it is you can tell me. I am your sister.'

'Some things are better not said.'

'What is it?'

I shook my head. 'You are more than my sister. You are my everything. You are still and always all that I have.'

'Then you are melancholic.'

'Of course. I do feel most strangely solitary sometimes, but more than that. Sometimes it is as if I were quite split apart from my nature.'

'My dear.'

'Abandoned even. You will call me dramatic. But I feel it. In a way I cannot describe to you.'

'Yet I see it in you. You will find someone, my love.'

'Will I?'

'Of course.'

'But will they be acceptable?'

'What are you saying?'

'Nothing. I am saying nothing, only it is perhaps difficult to find someone to love who will be correct for the role prescribed.'

'Jehan, do you love someone who is not, shall we say, of quality?'

'Quality is no issue, you know I have excellent taste. Never worry, what is love anyway? It is all as air.'

'Please hear me when I say that we were joined before we were born. I know your heart.'

'I do not think you would like to.'

She leaned close, taking my face in her lovely hands, her rings clicking as she did. 'Listen to me. Listen to what I am saying, Brother. I love you. And I know your heart.'

I could feel my eyes sting hot to see hers brim bright.

'I do not love well, Sister.'

She kissed my forehead. 'Well, I believe you do. And I love you still and always.'

10

Kissing Madame Benoit

The following days were dark. I passed them in solitude in my private quarters, which comprised my bedchamber, a small antechamber, writing room and my curiosities cabinet. The perfect seclusory for both lurid fantasy and the chastity that needed to accompany it, both of course related to Mister Kryk.

After some deliberation, my sister thought it prudent to at least send a spy to the inn to find out who the maid was, and her provenance, so that we might intervene should there be any awkwardness. If my only true heir was illegitimate there would be a dreadful scandal. Or at least a considerable complication. I could not bear to put Hortense through it.

In the end, and after much subtle enquiry, no such girl was even found. I could not have imagined her. I did remember her name was Thérèse. Despite the wine, I recalled the whole incident and in particular the moments when I might have made another choice. It was clear that among unsalvageable souls, I was peerless.

To add to my despair, there was still the matter of Mister Kryk. At a certain point, to deny him access to my rooms would become awkward. To exclude him would become its own scandal. What was I hiding, they would ask?

*

After a time, I had to relent, allowing him to attend to me and resume at least a semblance or normality. He became for me an all-consuming fear. His approaching step like a distant church bell on a saint's day, his quiet way of moving about my chamber arranging clothes and moving drapes aside each morning, how he waited in silence as my page added logs to the fire. If I pretended to be asleep, he would crouch down to the grate for warmth, waiting for the logs to take, his face lit and warm, breathing slowly, his eyes always a little weary, blinking. All of this brought with it such tender terror as I hid under the bedclothes, adoring him. When he left my chamber and I heard his steps recede, my desolation was complete – nobly borne, of course, but complete.

I wanted to take this Dutch map-maker's son into my arms, to kiss him, have him. In my fantasy, he would tell me all the secrets of his heart as I held his hands in mine. It is also true that in my imagination our ravishments had with each passing day, and with increasingly theatrical elaboration, become prolonged and thunderous.

My scribe, whom I grow to love, is this morning looking particularly pious and disapproving. She reminds me that we are working together on an elegant yet emotional memoir and not a tawdry romance. She reminds me that we are not writing a codpiece-popper. I would submit that the one should never exclude the other. I do enjoy the thought of her falling in love with such force that she can neither eat nor sleep, in a daily torture of unrequited passion. It would be perfect punishment and I shall set about getting the stars to align the very moment we finish our work.

While I reject her accusation of tawdriness, she is correct to accuse me of being dishonest, for much of my discomfort around Mister Kryk was not exactly related to his soul at all, but rather entirely related to my prodigious thirst for him. And so, I should relate the daily torture of my dressing.

The first occasion on which I decided that I might brave the world outside my chamber was a full six days after I had disgraced myself. I required fresh ink and books and though a lackey could have fetched them, a need for fresh air and release from melancholy forced my hand. I required urgent remedy from my own mind, which was so turned in on itself that I felt as a serpent gorging itself on its own tail.

Days had passed and with the assistance of prayer, tears and pleading to my higher conscience, I felt the panic subside enough to risk seeing him. In addition, if I was to ever leave my house again, I would need him to attend to me. No man of my station had ever been reduced to dressing himself. Unthinkable.

The only times I had ever dressed myself were as a child after swimming (and even then, my nurse would help me) and once or twice after some sort of indiscretion away from home that required me to be present and correct almost immediately afterwards. Most laces and buttons were entirely impossible to fix without the aid of one's manservant. Clothing was designed with the assumption that someone would be there to attend to the fastenings, of which there were invariably hundreds. Not to mention the fashion for slashed sleeves ... Without someone to guide your arm it could take three or four attempts before your glove finally found itself poking through the correct piece of fabric. I attempted it once. It was a disaster.

I awoke, ready. I cannot say how long I sat there. Mister Kryk had already come to raise the fire and had brought oil and water for my shave. I had, as was my new custom, pretended to sleep as long as was feasible without raising alarm. To feign sleep was a tactic I realised I would be employing a good deal. Mister Kryk would find me a most slumberous master.

I had surveyed my armoire to see if there was anything I *could* manage on my own. There was none, but I did take the precaution of choosing an ensemble and then getting myself into my drawers and breeches before I rang for help. This would at least do away with the usual necessity of being patted and tucked and neatly buttoned up at the front below one's waist. *Nom de Dieu*, I missed Bobo terribly. As much as I loved him, he could never provoke any kind of flourish in my blood.

I should mention that my scribe is finding this all hugely amusing. She should not. It was an agony and to mitigate it, very cunning preparation was required. Or so I thought.

Soon after he was called, I heard Mister Kryk clipping among the corridors. (A small heel on limestone floors is an excellent combination for an alert system, should you ever require one.) I took a good breath to steady myself and stood at the window facing away from where I knew he would arrive.

'Enter.'

'Monsieur.'

'I am ready for you now.'

'Yes, Monsieur.'

'I have already chosen. I did not wish to waste time.'

'I beg your pardon –' I turned to see him and was surprised to see him looking at me with some amusement, for he had always seemed to have a great seriousness to him, being Dutch. '– but, Monsieur …'

'Yes? Is there a problem?' I was affecting my most commanding stance. Rather well I thought.

'Monsieur, if I may, you have forgotten your legs.'

'Mister Kryk?'

'Your hose. You will need to remove your breeches again that I might first attach your hose, or your legs will be bare.'

My humiliation was complete. Not only did I realise that I was standing like a buffoon who clearly could not even dress himself, not only had he seen it and been clearly amused by my absolute stupidity, but I was then required to undress again, with slow and deliberate agony. He then stood in front of my near-naked form, a breath away, leaning around my waist so his pale, honey hair brushed my skin, sending a flame all through me. Oh, it was terrific. Running his warm hands down my back to smooth my chemise, tucking it cleanly into my breeches, which he then with fast and clever fingers buttoned closed; then my doublet, starting around my neck, each button all the way down towards my belly. All the while I stood imperiously, eyes closed, arms outstretched like a perverted goose ready for slaughter, trying as well as I could to imagine that I was kissing Madame Benoit, wife to my cook, Bobo's sixty-four-year-old sister, and a woman who was possessed of many warts and few teeth. It was effective enough, but I realised with horror that I would be beginning every day, for eternity, imagining myself in the pungent embrace of Madame Benoit.

Also, I resolved to eat more meat. I was perhaps too thin to be considered a good and virile specimen.

11

The Strumpet!

Eventually, I made my way into the city. The initial humiliations now behind me, I felt freer than I had in days. Mister Kryk, as was customary, trailed by a step or two. I tried desperately to think of something amusing to say to him, but in the end, it was too enervating. Behind us skulked a couple of my lackeys. Miserable boys.

The sun had come out after a few days of grey and the air was warmer. All about us the noise and bustle I enjoyed. Few ladies of quality were out, instead their maids and cooks stood around chatting as they waited for chickens to lose their heads and eggs to be counted. A particularly plump-looking goose was putting up a good fight even as the chopper was coming down on his neck.

I greeted the Marquise de Marcilliac as she rode past. She was a cousin, of course, and wife to our uncle's overbearing backer. We were all multiple cousins and half-cousins. Entrenching our kinship through marriage and lineage was what allowed us to prosper and survive. At this hour she was probably off to visit her lover, about whom everyone knew though no one mentioned. She was officially the patron to this man, a painter of some talent. The lady was so impressed with the masterful strokes of his brush that she found herself weekly visiting his studio, in need of a new painting. (For clarity, I should say that it was not Nicolas Mignard.)

The deliberation would take hours and the chosen piece would then, of course, require the artist to deliver it personally to his patron's residence while the rotund little marquis was out, usually hunting a hapless boar. I admired the marquise enormously – such *élan*.

'Mister Kryk?'

He came forward. 'Yes, Monsieur?' He looked at me with such clarity.

'It occurs to me that you have not been with us very long and I have not been very helpful in offering instruction.'

'Monsieur.'

'You are far from home, yes? I will ask Monsieur Benoit to give you more attention and careful instruction so that you will very soon feel more included in the household.'

'Thank you, Monsieur.'

I could hardly bear to let myself look at him.

And yet for the smallest moment, despite the market – geese, pigs, fruit sellers, bakers shouting their prices, carriages, lackeys, cooks, all jostling and calling – I allowed myself to glance sideways at his face. Earnest, professional, framed in his golden hair, like an ancient shepherd god. Seeing him like that, his proximity, it was as if a perfect moment of calm descended. Avignon receded and a stillness I had never known but always reached for was suddenly between us. I wished so terribly to tell him.

'It seems to me, Mister Kryk, it seems ...'

Right at that moment I saw her. The wine-house wench.

'Mister Kryk, hide!' I leapt sideways between two fruit stalls. Mister Kryk, a little slower to understand the panic, joined me.

'That girl, the one in the blue dress, standing with a basket at the fishmonger, do you know her?'

'No, Monsieur.'

'Is her name Thérèse?'

'I don't know her.'

'We must find out. By which I mean, of course, *you* must find out.'

'Yes, Monsieur.'

'Discretion is everything.'

'Of course, Monsieur.'

'I need her name, her full name, and where she is employed. There, she is going. Off you go.'

'Yes, Monsieur.' He was full of alarm. And rightly so.

I held my position, nestled between the vegetable sellers, wishing I did not have such ostentatious plumes attached to my hat. As I recall, they were peacock blue and must have waved about like a great tournament flag as I dashed to hide. I observed Jonathan Kryk pick his way towards the fishmonger and with a well-practised and casual air, strike up conversation with the man. I crouched down between the onions to obtain a better view. I made a lengthy note of his calves which were very well shaped and held great promise.

My scribe mocks the erotic importance placed on a man's calves at the time. She should not, and would find her daily life greatly enlivened for casting her eyes twixt knee and ankle, particularly when such a calf is encased in a fine stocking and ending in an elegant heel, the shoe festooned with florets and ribbons, again, to highlight the ankle and calf. Oh, I shiver to remember it.

But, back to the market where the fishmonger and Mister Kryk appeared now to speak more conspiratorially. My valet looked so fine in his livery; it suited him well. And his fine thighs should not be omitted from the spectacle. They were loosely encased in his livery breeches and from what I could see, their relative strength and shapeliness as they ascended would best be described as immensely reassuring. I would make sure he had another livery as good.

The fishmonger rolled out a hearty lascivious laugh and then made lewd gestures indicating a woman's chest. Mister Kryk laughed in turn, and I felt a kind of revulsion at this. I knew him as sober and serious and obedient, not a lusty young scamp discussing women's breasts with street traders. It was invigorating. I was jealous too, wildly so, of the ease he showed with this stranger, compared with the stance he took with me, which was decorous to a point of subservience, never betraying even a glimpse of his private self. And the ease too with which he showed his desire for conquest, whoever that girl might be. All of this jostled for space in my mind as I hunkered among the piles of turnips and cabbages. It was a tumultuous few minutes. He turned back. I scrambled upright and straightened my cloak to assume a posture appropriate of nobility.

'Monsieur, her name is Marie.'

'Marie? She told me Thérèse.' I realised as I said it that I had been indiscreet and yet even as quickly, I felt a satisfying, even cruel joy that he now understood what she was to me. He betrayed something with his eyes, something I could not quite identify. Surprise. Repulsion too, no doubt. We were still hiding between the wagons.

He continued. 'She is a kitchen maid at the big *hôtel* just below the Palais.'

'What? This is not right.'

'It's the truth, Monsieur. The fishmonger is a vulgar man, but an honest one, I think.'

'He certainly is a vulgar man.' I cleared my throat a little to show disapproval. 'Are you sure about the house?'

'The man sends fish there later today.'

'That is my house. She feeds my uncle?'

Mister Kryk looked a little startled by the sheer force of my response.

'I apologise, Mister Kryk. I did not mean to involve you. Only she has been dishonest. She, well, let us leave it there. Let us to the booksellers.' I noted how pretty his lips were. 'And I am being dishonest, it is not exactly my house. I gave it to my uncle. To keep him further away. She works in his kitchens you say?'

'Yes, Monsieur. That is what I was told.'

Then, to punish Mister Kryk for his merry exchange over a kitchen maid's bosom and perhaps hoping it would give me some alibi after ogling his calves, I added, 'The strumpet!'

My scribe would like it noted at this point that so wildly jocular and vivid is my telling, my readers will half expect three musketeers to arrive henceforth in the market. Absolutely not a sober *mémoire*, she complains again. She mutters about smut and codpieces and hopes this reprimand will temper my tone towards sobriety. On the contrary, it only encourages me further. It is my assertion that would she turn her mind more actively to codpieces, she would find her days – and dare I say nights – greatly enriched. *Mon Dieu*, that has struck a nerve. Well, I can only relay what happened. That it becomes a caper is the product of my impossible situation, not a flaw in my telling.

Back to the cabbages. I was unsettled. Why had Thérèse, who was Marie, been at the wine house, approaching me with a false name? Avignon was not so large that I might not eventually discover her. Could she be a spy? But for whom? This was ridiculous, but I was prone to anxiety. I always had the sense I was being followed about, though I knew it was my conscience that stalked me and nothing else. I resolved that she had seen me at my uncle's (I was summoned there quite often to be chastised), had taken a fancy to me (who wouldn't?), but in order to protect her position had used a false name. Or could my uncle have sent her to me? An odd gift from a man of the cloth and I remembered that I had only been at the inn by chance and did not frequent it regularly. She would not have known to find me there. It was with some relief that I realised it was unlikely she would seek me out again. Not after that performance.

I make light of it, as is my habit, but underneath it all sat a polluted, complicated yearning. To love another in the way I did raised the most intense isolation. He did not see me. He could not.

The situation was without hope.

Suddenly, standing surrounded by the peal and babble of the town, I felt worsted and miserable. I regretted my decision to venture into the world and felt that any further proximity to Mister Kryk might suffocate me entirely.

I sent him off to complete my errands – books, ink, paper – pretending I had not seen the leather baron, Scipio Le Gratia, trying to catch my attention as I went. It was enough that I was trailed by a pair of sullen lackeys who would rather have spent the morning flashing their swords at chambermaids rather than attend to my safety.

Once home, I hid in my cabinet room, my seclusory, sur- rounded by my collection of shells and gems, bones, pods, creatures and feathers, all from places I would never see. I reclined in my large, cushioned chair, watching the light bouncing off the mirrored panels, comforted by the slightest aroma of juniper and pine that had been left to warm near the fire. Thus, I felt I could survive this fresh assault of madness, this ill-advised ardour and wretched paranoia. I resolved to retreat once more into my mind, by far the safest and most pleasant place.

And yet, his face stayed with me.

12

My Marquisate

Some weeks passed and with it the days became longer, and the winter eased a touch, though on occasion the far, high mountains were still snow-capped and the wind bitter.

There was a knock at the door. Just the sound of it set me on edge. He had so disrupted my ways.

'Enter.'

Even before he was in my chamber, I felt myself begin to unfurl at my edges.

'There is a letter. Your uncle's man brought it early.'

'Thank you. I will read it now.' It was always with dread that I received any sort of missive from my uncle and on this particular morning, after a fitful sleep and lurid dreams that left me feeling I could not breathe for rancid air, it felt all the more foreboding. I read.

Meet me at your sister's house this afternoon at two.

His quill seemed always to be filled from a most presumptuous ink pot.

'Monsieur, will this do?' Mister Kryk arrived back from my armoire. Even though I felt weighty and tired, to see him so tidy lifted my spirits a touch.

'I am afraid not. Something more funereal. I am summoned

by my uncle.' He turned back to fetch me something and I surrendered to the familiar panic, realising that my daily agony of having him dress me was about to reprise its torturous pleasure.

'I will need to shave but perhaps a quick visit to my barber will suffice. He has such good blades and you may find more balsams while we are there.'

I was visiting the professional barber more regularly. The process of having Mister Kryk shave me, his hands working around my face with hot oils and water, leaning so close to my mouth that I could feel his breath on me, was increasingly impossible. To the barber and then on to my sister.

Hortense's house, I felt, was not pretty enough for her, even though it was my gift to her. The park was pleasing but the house was unexceptional in style and it seemed to have a weighty air to it that other houses did not. It must have been on account of The Toad living there with her. He was not as grand as the Villeneuves, but liked to emphasise his proximity to their family and in so doing only exposed his distance.

Hortense and I were born in the house I still chose to occupy. According to our wet nurse, from the day of our birth Hortense would wiggle around in her swaddling until she was free to put an arm across me and keep me safe. This never stopped being true. If ever I was in trouble with my tutor or our father and later, our uncle, she would use her sweet ways to convince them of my innocence. I remember once running away up the grassy banks of the hills, where the windmills turned, to eat mulberries. Hortense refused to come with me, being a good child and knowing the consequences. Though I returned with my chemise dyed red and black from all the berries I had eaten, and Hortense remained pristine, she swore, with straight face, that she had not only accompanied me but had made me pluck the tree bare so that she could eat the juicy fruits. It was our father she had cajoled then. He died less than a year later of a fever.

It was a tumultuous time. Weeks of feeling our father might be well only to hear he had declined again the next day. Fear of contracting the plague meant we were not permitted to sit at his bedside. I wrote him excellent stories though, to cheer him, and sent them to his chamber that my uncle might read them to him. It was shortly after my father died that I discovered all my efforts stuffed into a large urn in the long gallery. My uncle had not given them to him and I never overcame the cruelty of his deliberate withholding. From that day, my mistrust of my uncle began and though I was nine years old, I took it as truth that I could neither love nor trust him and would simply offer him false affection in exchange for peace and quiet. Artifice in emotion has always been my most accomplished skill – perfect for a writer, of course, to conjure an emotion, a persona, even as the need arises. Less perfect for a happy life and true connection to those you love and those you might wish to.

Hortense was my one refuge. My place of safety where I could let the mask slip enough to feel understood. We never spoke directly of my proclivities though; this would compromise her too greatly. If she ever suspected, she remained silent and, I assume, trusted that I would never act but simply harbour them with stoicism and restraint. For the most part, I had.

After each fresh heartbreak (an unrequited passion, a new mark for my infatuation), I knew I could go to her and without explanation, I could lie in her lap and have her comfort me. She has never known it, but in my twenty-four years before meeting Jonathan Kryk, she saved me from myself, saved my life even. Knowing I would break her heart if I succumbed to death allowed me to survive my own devastation.

Have I described Hortense to you? My scribe reminds me I

have not. I expect they would have been fast friends and probably taken sides against me. My scribe suggests that in many ways, Hortense is the true hero of this story and, as we progress, I dare say there will be those of you who wish it was she who had told it. She may well be more qualified for the rigours of the work my scribe was expecting. Perhaps more nuance would have been included. My scribe tells me too that these days it is very common for stories to be told by female characters. How very wise. I cannot disagree with this development. Men are at the very least conceited in their storytelling and Hortense would have made a much better witness than I. By the end of this story, I know that you will adore her almost as much as I do.

Hortense was the prettiest woman imaginable. Though we were born twins we did not look exactly alike. Her hair was always much fairer than mine and her skin whiter. The style of the day was to wear her crown curled about her face, decorated with ribbons and pearls. From our mother's portrait, it was clear my sister inherited her beauty and grace. I was always darker, like our father. Hortense was unblemished and when she blushed, which was often, her cheeks would flush all the way to her ears. She had the loveliest neck and posture and she never succumbed to all the foul paints and potions of her peers.

She had lost three children by 1657. Some wives in similar positions were declared useless – the marriage annulled and the barren woman sent to a convent in disgrace. While there had never been any suggestion of this indignity being forced on my sister, I would, of course, be forced to defend her position, with arms if need be. My uncle would object and try to dissuade me, but I felt nothing for The Toad and indulged his presence only as a necessary alliance.

But, on that day, the day of my uncle's summons, I found

my sister still married and cheerful enough, though bristling a little, no doubt because of our uncle.

'Is he here?' I handed her the posy I had my gardener pick for her and leaned to kiss her.

'Yes.'

'Let me kiss you longer. You look so pretty. How is the book I gave you?'

'Oh, I like it. It is so clever.'

'Did you laugh?'

"'Til my corset burst, sire!' She quoted the book and we both laughed.

'You are so naughty, Sister. Come, let me rest here with you before we see what this is all about.'

'It is about you.'

'Oh? What now?' Such a misery. An immense burning came about my chest.

'As ever, dearest, he is concerned about you lacking a wife.'

'He should be more concerned about your having a husband.'

'Jehan. That is enough. My husband is a good and generous man.'

'I have offended you. I am sorry, Sister. But you will admit that he has never, ever laughed until his corsets burst.'

We laughed again, both imagining The Toad in corsets.

'That is enough you two.'

'Uncle. Good day.' The unmuzzled, dog-hearted, bladder-sucker.

My scribe reminds me to temper my language. Quite an admonition considering the blasphemies she herself utters fewer than ten minutes after rising. I will ignore her. She is in poor spirits today, very bad company and complains of backaches and other maladies. I have learnt that this is her way of saying she is lonely and burdened, but this is something she will never admit. Until she is willing to so do, she should cease her incessant whining or we shall never complete our task.

My uncle stood before us, nothing short of imperious. I bowed with such extraordinary flourish that I hoped he might at least intimate some mockery. I made sure to stay bent, my hat and cane held out to the side in ostentatious display.

'Jehan, come. Hortense, you too.'

Please note that our uncle had invited me into a room that was not his, in a home that was not his. Even by your own lax contemporary standards, you will agree that this was a boggling level of intrusion. He then bid me and Hortense sit in the smaller salon like naughty children. Staggeringly vulgar and discourteous, and quite usual.

Uncle Hippolyte's face was particularly ruddy that day and did not look good against his robe. He was no doubt testing his complexion against every shade until he found the one that he felt would suit him best: cardinal red.

'Jehan, are you well?'

'Very well, Uncle. You look well too.'

'Quite. Jehan, how old are you?'

'Ah, straight to business, Uncle. How efficient of you. As you well know, I am just twenty-four.'

'So, a man of some advanced years. And let it be noted of considerable means and a lineage of some influence.'

I noted he did not suggest that I personally had any influence.

'Quite so, Uncle.'

'These are complicated times. As you know, the legates have, over the years, been in some disarray. And while Rome makes life difficult for us, we are still under their banner.' He hardly drew breath, so rehearsed was this soliloquy. 'And Villeneuve and others seem to have done well in spite of all that.' He made his fingers into the shape of a steeple. A decoy gesture, for he was clearly imagining a dome.

'They have.'

'Why do you suppose that is?'

'I couldn't say.' It was useless to swat at him in this way, but it was the only protection I knew.

'The Villeneuve family has made sensible decisions around matrimony. Each one of them has chosen for themselves a partner that will ensure their continued influence across the region, no matter the foibles of the legates.'

'As expected.'

'But what of the Baudelaires, Jehan, what have they done?'

'Well, Uncle, our Hortense has made a fine match. And she is so happy with it.'

'Hortense,' he turned his head slightly to her. 'Though, my dear, you are most assuredly always in our hearts, you are no longer a Baudelaire.' He fixed me in his sight once more. '*You* are the last remaining in that line.'

'I am quite aware.'

'If you do not produce an heir, the name dies with you and with it the influence that name still holds. Not to mention the fate of our marquisate. What will happen to that? Will it be bought by some spice merchant from Marseilles?'

'A point of clarity, dear Uncle Hippolyte. It is not *our* marquisate, but rather, *my* marquisate.'

His lips pursed to a hard knot.

And then, for the first time, and I cannot say why it took so long, I understood. I had all along assumed that my uncle had simply wanted the respectability of my marriage to some or other woman of name and wealth. But that was my own preoccupation. I understood the need for an heir, but I now perceived with brutal clarity that his name, his family name, was my family name, and if my line was to cease to exist, in a sense, so would he. He existed because I existed. My refusal to marry and produce a male heir meant that he was permanently on the cusp of extinction.

This, then, was the bitter nub of his hatred. A priest with no dynasty is a monk, not a bishop, and certainly not a cardinal. He feared that if I did not make a good marriage and produce a male heir, he could disappear without trace. I had known it, of course, but as an abstraction. There in that moment when I asserted my own status over his – *my* marquisate, not *our* marquisate – the frailty of his position suddenly became real for me. Every year that I did not produce an heir led him another step closer to oblivion. My heir, my name. And now I had pronounced it, *my* marquisate.

'*Your* marquisate. Thank you for making that so plain.' He steeled himself a little. 'Jehan, I am loath to mention this of course, but there is also the matter of gossip that surrounds a man of a certain age who does not marry.'

'Uncle, I am still present.' Poor Hortense. I was grateful for her interruption.

'I apologise, my dear. I am being indiscreet. Perhaps you should leave us for a spell. I will call for you. Thank you, my dear.' Hortense stood but held my eye long enough that I could see the tears in hers. The door closed. 'Now we are men I can speak more freely.'

'I wish you would not, Uncle.'

'But Jehan, people do talk. Not that I am suggesting for a moment that this sort of base sin applies to you. Obviously, there are no sodomites in our family.'

The ease with which he had let the word slide off his tongue sent a deathly chill across my body.

'Uncle, for shame. You will find that I behave with utmost modesty, chastity even, and certainly not in the manner to which you allude.'

'Of course. Of course.' He affected an unconvincing shake of the head. 'And there is no suggestion whatsoever ... only, people do talk and from time to time it would not go amiss to let it be known that your tastes are impeccable and your proclivities beyond reproach.'

'What are you saying?'

He sighed as a martyr might before they face the pyre. 'I work tirelessly for you, Jehan. You have no idea the labours I make on your behalf.'

'I am not sure I understand.' There was that feeling again, of someone out of eyeshot, a snapping twig, breath under a bridge. Always eyes that followed me across a room or an ear waiting for me to misspeak. You may say I only imagined them, but the effect on me was the same. I early on learnt to speak in riddles and jokes and innuendo so that any misjudgement could be soon explained away. It made me a passable writer and a very good dinner guest.

Back to Uncle, who was near smirking.

'I have taken the liberty of occasionally putting in your path a woman who can be relied upon to gossip a little, elaborate on her experience.'

'What? What are you saying?'

'Your reputation is safe in my hands.'

I felt a sickness rise. 'Tell me what you are saying, Uncle.' I was on my feet.

'I have sometimes found it necessary, though it was with heavy, heavy heart, to produce evidence to counter the rumours. You might recall a pretty thing you met in a wine house? As expected, she could not hold her tongue.' He smiled as he said it. 'Any suggestions that you might have any awkward tendencies assuaged in the instant.'

'What?'

'Do not pretend you cannot remember her.'

'You disgust me.' My voice had left me, nothing more than a hiss escaped. 'You sit here as a man of God and yet trade in whores and gossip.'

'You are ungrateful, Jehan. And, as she helpfully reported, it is you who trades in whores. You ignore what is said about you. That Baudelaire has a taste for masculine love, that he is a true Socratic. We should send him to Paris and see what the King's brother makes of him. And let us never forget what they say over and over: *he lacks a wife.*'

Anger, panic, shame all raged from nowhere, allowing my voice to return.

'Who? How? I have never heard it spoken, never. I have done nothing, let me pronounce it: nothing to attract this gossip.'

'Gossip needs no evidence. It exists beyond evidence. You have no wife and you have no heir. A man of twenty-four.'

'And yet you see fit to provide evidence in the shape of a whore whom you thrust into my path? How did you even know where I was that night? Even I had not known I would be there. I am dumbfounded. Uncle, I cannot fathom your thinking. I cannot begin to excuse you.'

'Pfft. Women's talk. She tells the other scullery girls, they tell the cleaners who tell the lady's maids who tell their ladies while they curl their hair. It is the way of the world and it is what we must use if we are to garner advantage. Gossip has its profits too. I suppose it is at least some small comfort to me that you can do what is necessary to produce an heir.'

My head was alight in a kind of terrible pain that can only come from the soul. A flame set to bare skin, a brander's poker, a witch's stake. 'I am leaving. You will prostitute your own family for your tawdry provincial politics?'

'You are too naive, Jehan, this too is what worries me. You left the salon in a hurry. I made sure to find where you had gone.'

'You followed me?'

He waved a hand casually about himself. 'Not I. Obviously. It was executed by others.'

'You have set spies on me? I cannot, I will not believe this.' My chest was tightening, heat began to rise, crushing the air from my lungs.

He stood and fixed me with his eyes once more. 'And you, Jehan de Baudelaire, bring shame upon your family. Paterfamilias in name, but not in nature. If there is so much as a whiff of indiscretion, any minuscule suggestion that you will let your untrammelled passions overrun to unspeakable sin, then I will unleash my wrath, and that of my office, and you will never draw another breath in Avignon. Do you understand me?' He was spitting. 'What would your father say? God rest him.'

I managed to hold myself straight. I did not flinch, nor lower my head, and somehow, I cannot say how, I held his torching gaze.

'I am my father's first and only son and as such *I* am still the head of the Baudelaire family. Do not ever, ever invoke the name of my father to insult me.'

'Of course, of course,' he was quiet, the menace of a serpent. 'And I am as ever most, most aware of your position.' He turned away, pacing as he continued. 'But Jehan, with that comes responsibilities: lineage, alliance, kinship. An heir is all that is required. You could produce one inside of a year were you so inclined. I raise these issues out of concern for you and nothing else. A good marriage would cement your future as well as your good family name. Have you no one in mind?' He had become strangely simpering, conspiratorial even. It turned my stomach.

Hortense reappeared. An angel.

'I apologise for interrupting, Uncle, only I felt some more

refreshment might be in order? I have called for something to tempt you.' Her voice was as cheerful as a midsummer song but, oh, she was burning. I knew she had been listening at the door as she always did when we were young. She would creep down to hear what my punishment would be.

'My dear,' Uncle returned to his paternal stature. 'How thoughtful you always are. We were just discussing how many beautiful young girls there are and which ones your brother might find most appealing.'

Hortense managed to affect great jollity, feeling her time for inclusion in the conversation was due. 'Uncle, our Jehan is a most desirable, most gallant man that there might be many candidates. Was ever there such a handsome man as my brother?' She came to my side and slipped her arm through mine, squeezing my wrist as she did. It required every last ounce of fortitude I had not to fall into her arms and weep.

She looked up and kissed my cheek. I could hear her breath was short. 'I fear, Uncle, it is I who has been remiss in finding him a suitable lady of quality. Were he to be too aggressive in his pursuit it would be most unseemly. Look at him, Uncle Hippolyte. He is so elegant and accomplished. I shall make more effort, I promise. I am sure it is all the fault of my idle ways. And no doubt my hope to be greedy and keep him all to myself.'

Dear Hortense knew just how to cheer me up.

'He need be neither elegant nor accomplished. He has wealth and standing. This is more than enough and that is why it troubles me that he has not yet made a good marriage, or indeed any marriage. And that is why we are gathered here. I pains me to raise it, but should anything occur, God protect you, there will be no heir. Time does not favour abstinence.'

'I am sure he does not want to rush his marriage, given that there are so many who would be quick to have him, simply to take advantage of that wealth and good standing.'

'I couldn't care less what a woman hopes to gain from him, all we wish from her is a son. There are candidates. The girl from Orange, the one whom I brought here. Both her uncles and her older brother have made excellent careers in the service of God and the military, and her father is a good cousin. What was wrong with her, Jehan, I cannot recall?'

'She did not laugh. Not once during that interminable afternoon.' I tried to be glib, for Hortense's sake, to act as distraction for myself and steady my hands, which were shaking with rage or fear.

'Brother, she may have been nervous. You can be a little, shall we say, dramatic. She may have been overwhelmed. She was very young.'

'I do not think that a lack of laughter should disqualify a girl from marriage. Particularly as she comes from so fine a family. And laughing can be vulgar in a woman.' He caught Hortense's eye.

'Well, Uncle, the girl who would not laugh is now dead from an ague. Surely that disqualifies her? Or are you undeterred?' I hissed this last.

'Mind your mouth.'

'And those sisters Beaucourte? Did neither of them catch your eye?' Hortense was trying her best to act as the perfect distraction.

'Sweet Sister, they both looked as if they had been struck with a permanent pox. To produce an heir with either one of them would require extraordinary fortitude and an affliction of blindness.'

Hortense was greatly tickled by this.

'Enough. You are both shameful.'

'Well, Uncle, I did tell you I continue to find the Comtesse de

Montmorency most charming. She is intelligent, well-read and most, most beguiling. Breasts like sun-warmed alabaster . . .'

'For shame! Quite apart from still being married to the comte, she is more than ten years your senior. And I do hope that you are not suggesting I should prepare for a different sort of scandal involving her?'

'You are being difficult, Uncle. She has always been my natural choice and you do not approve of her, so, I have heard enough. You would like me to marry. I understand you. I will set about finding myself a bride at once. Perhaps even tomorrow. I shall start by scouring the wine houses and taverns of all Languedoc. In fact, I know just the place. The wine house next to the Palais will be my first port of call. There are plenty of very ready, eager wives to be had there.'

My uncle adjusted his posture. Hortense ignored my last comment, as best she could. She always pretended not to hear that which was hurtful or vulgar and instead chose to look very pleased.

'Oh, Brother, that is encouraging. Better yet, I will have a party, a great dance and lots of pretty girls to tempt you. Or a salon. It will be very amusing, my love. I should like something to amuse myself too.' She rubbed her flat hand across my shoulder in her mother's way. 'What good sleeves you have on this. Is it new?'

'Yes. The pearls are from Paris. Look here.' I lifted one of the slashes to show her the lighter grey silk underneath.

A groan interrupted us.

'Come, Uncle Hippolyte, let me escort you on your way,' said Hortense, taking his arm. 'You are looking so well. Will you come and stay with us a few days, if it pleases you? I know you are so busy, but we so miss your company.' She began to lead him away.

'Uncle.'

'Jehan. I look forward to some development on this matter.'
'I am sure you do.'

Even before the door had closed, I was overwhelmed with nausea, faintness. Spies. He had me followed all the way from the comte's salon. A fen-sucking viper in a cassock. I could have kicked his legs out from under him and had my lackeys beat him senseless as he lay swimming in his robes. I would gouge his eyes out myself. I sat, stood again. Oceans of fury and frustration engulfed me. Spies, traps, accusations. My only escape would be to have him killed. Easily arranged, Avignon was overrun with slubbering thugs. Or Marseilles, far away and known for its bootless assassins.

I had wished my uncle dead forever. Quite a few years before, he had gone off to Rome to ingratiate himself with anyone who could be bothered to cast their spit upon him. He travelled with a party of twenty or more. They all were struck down with fever and plague (though he denied it was that) and only he, his two lackeys and the abbé survived. I received the news with great sadness, wrote a poem about the Devil and then was so struck with guilt I went to confession twice for three days and made a large donation to the almshouse.

I left Hortense. We said nothing to one another. Nothing could be said. Every footman and page boy suddenly had the look of a shadowy villain about them. I even caught Mister Kryk glancing at my tear-drenched face as I shambled to my carriage, trying to affect some semblance of calm, though clearly failing to do so. I had eventually banished my tears, but nothing could disguise that I had wept like a child and I did not have the energy to care that he saw it.

By the time I was home, I was inconsolable.

It was conceivable that I could find a woman whose company I would find agreeable and amusing; I might even love her with some filial affection. But I would always love another no matter how I laboured to curb my desires. I had seen astrologers, physicians, even a woman who was closer to a witch than I ever dared confess. I longed to put an end to the yearning for comfort, to have my life witnessed and given safe harbour. To know that I might not die alone and if I did, know I was loved and had loved another.

13

Endymion

In the days and weeks after that episode with my uncle, I struggled to stay whole. I could not find a way to be in the world that did not elicit shame and the sensation that every lackey and stable hand was watching my every movement. Some days, the moment of waking delivered a blow so powerful that the mere shock of being alive was almost too much to absorb.

I had forgotten Molière, Mignard. Nothing held any promise or hope.

I tried to invent ways to dismiss Jonathan Kryk, to remove him from my life without scandal or speculation and simply retreat, if only temporarily. This was an appealing option, to be unbothered by his face, his voice as he quietly offered instruction: 'Thank you, Monsieur, please turn around now. If you will, Monsieur, please sit down now.'

Each day I resolved to dismiss him on some fatuous grounds and each day he would appear around my door and I would realise that for all the misery it brought, he was still, in every way, not only the source of my pain but also the balm that made my life possible.

I considered going to Paris and taking a house for a few months. The promise of salons, coffee houses and entertainments gave me great energy and I began to make enquiries as to what was available and for what price. Of course, any hopes of this were scuppered early on when word reached my Uncle Hippolyte. He sent a note. It read:

Jehan, I understand that you are considering taking rooms in Paris. Allow me to assist you. As you know, I have so many friends in Paris who will be able to welcome you and provide you with the correct introductions to families of quality and, of course, keep a close record of your happiness and well-being. Our esteemed cousin, Clusy de Marcilliac, also most keenly aware of your plans to travel, looks forward to assisting you in this matter.

A shot over the bows of liberty. A threat to have me watched and stalked, my every breath recorded and reported back to antechambers and offices in the Palais des Papes in Avignon.

And so, to pass the time and distract my mind, I set about rearranging and cataloguing the contents of my cabinet and the treasures it housed.

My scribe now interjects, complaining that I seem to have had any number of cabinets and to spend a good deal of time skulking in all of them. Not so. My cabinet of curiosities was an antechamber off my private rooms, to house my collections from the natural world. Shells, specimens, magnificent creatures in bottles and the like. It was a panelled and painted seclusory, dark and private. By contrast, my *cabinet*, dear readers, is an artefact of great significance and intended for public view. I dare say you may visit it today in the Victoria and Albert Museum in London. I sent my scribe to find it, accompanying her of course, for we travel so well together. (I dare say she grows to love me, in spite of herself.) At the museum, we trembled together to see it still so beautifully kept, each pretty detail and clever hidden panel so well-preserved.

It was such a remarkable piece, and a source of such great

pride for me, that I installed it in my *grand salon*, in a position where guests would see it as they arrived. It was made in Paris and though there were other gentlemen in Avignon with pretty pieces, none was as fine and detailed as mine. People spoke of it, tried to get me to open it up that they might be able to report that they had enjoyed a private view. If I held an evening's entertainment (cards, wine, music), my guests would beg to see it and I would take great delight in affecting a near-lethargic interest in revealing it. When eventually I did – showing the mirrors, angled and faceted, each layer opening further and further to expose yet more and eventually, at the centre, a small stage for miniature players, the wings mirrored to exaggerate the effect, displaying each little treasure, gem, figurine and fresh facade – I felt as loved as any man.

All across the dark mahogany doors was engraved the story of Endymion, the most beautiful man that ever was. Some recorded him as a king. For others, myself included, he was a shepherd who tended to his flock on the grass slopes of Mount Latmus. His story of endless sleep and long-preserved beauty was immortalised all along the panels and when the cabinet doors opened, further layers of the narrative revealed themselves, carved most finely: the moon who loved him, the flock, the sleeping dog, landscapes. And, of course, Endymion himself, the naked sleeping shepherd, its own tremulous delight. How I gazed at his beauty, alight and luminous as he stirs and imagines himself in love with the moon. I had been writing my own version of his tale for my own pleasure, and liked to revise it if only to spend more time alone with the shepherd. At least three other compositions were being written alongside the piece, as I could never quite manage to complete the story.

Dieu, I break my heart afresh, just remembering it and the cabinet which inspired its telling.

Soon after the arrival of the piece, I ordered new figurines made to bolster the cast of six I already had and which sat on the central inner stage. The additional six figures included, for the first time, a chevalier and, I admit (and given my specific instructions sent to the cabinetmaker), one who wore a valet's livery, soft curls about his bonnet which even in static miniature gave my heart a thunderous jolt. The addition of these figures added some depth to the detailed tableaux on the stage where I liked to act out my stories, thus imagining how they might unfold with Molière's players, and then return to my desk to adjust the tale.

I would write Endymion's story one day, then grow weary and return to a jester's tale (more unrequited love) the next, then another entirely. But all were played out in detail in my cabinet.

Candles could be lit to illuminate the surfaces and mirrors in an elaborate display of trickery and sophistication. My cabinet was a magic box of reflections, deceptions, layers and locks. Then when I had exhausted all narrative possibility I could unlock another tiny door and out came yet more screens, a secret wall behind a wall and in it, minute drawers each to contain treasures: in one a ruby, in another a unicorn's tooth and in yet another a small gold box containing a tendril of my own mother's hair. Secret keys and more secret compartments. To disappear into this labyrinth of fantasy and beauty was my heart's true solace.

I seem to have diverted into something of a rapture describing this to you. But in the early spring of 1657, it was my obsession. I moved between my seclusory, my desk and my *jeu de paume court*. I managed to drag myself to a few social engagements, enough to keep my sister and Uncle happy by making great display of flirtation with any number of tedious girls. I even managed to muster some masculine vigour for my cousins the

Cherbonnes, by accompanying them on an ill-advised hunt after a night of carousing and playing cards, too much wine and too little sleep. Dear Maurice missed his mark and shot his lackey.

It was relaying this tale of dundering idiocy to Mister Kryk (me in a practised and inviting recline on my chaise, he organising my writing desk), that for the first time since I had known him his impassive, monkish face began to twitch most peculiarly. First the nose, then the nose accompanied by a few rapid blinks, then those combined with the mouth. He seemed to be in some distress.

'Mister Kryk?'

Alarmingly, he spun for the door with barely audible, '*Pardon*, Monsieur.'

Within seconds of him disappearing around the corner, I heard him erupt, nay, reel skyward in gales of unfettered laughter. I had never felt so light, so filled with everything that I had imagined love was. His laughter had so moved me that for days after I had only to think of it and I was brimful of childlike joy.

How it sustained me, how he sustained me as I simply sat at my desk and wrote.

14

A Perennial Cocke-Pivot

I was installed at my desk early one morning, labouring on my retelling of Endymion to send to Hortense for approval, when there came at my bedchamber a furious tapping, unheard of at that hour. Behind the door, a wild-eyed footman, quite out of bounds for his station. I would have beaten him then and there for the impudence, but his urgency suggested I should hear him out before I lashed him.

'Monsieur, you must come at once.'

'Why? What is it? And where is Mister Kryk?'

'That is the trouble, sire. Marielle asserts that Mister Kryk has tried to lie with her.'

(Even my dolorous scribe sits up in her coffee-house chair to hear this.)

'And I suppose I am called upon to expose the truth of this matter?'

'Yes.'

'Are you aware of the hour?'

'Please, Monsieur. There is a scene. Please.'

This was a labour well below my station, being the remit of Monsieur Benoit, but the alarm on the footman's poxy face forced me to conclude that some urgency was required. I exited my chambers in haste and had to try and fasten my banyan together as best I could to mitigate my state of undress. Even as I approached the kitchen along the many halls that preceded it, I could hear the shouts and shrieks – Marielle most obviously, but for some reason my entire household was adding their opinion.

The footman opened the door and revealed Marielle on the kitchen floor, wailing like a dying sow, Monsieur Benoit standing over her in foul temper, holding a large cooking pot in his right hand, and all the scullery maids clucking around the scene. Then, off to the side, Mister Kryk in the most tremendous passion, something I would not have thought possible in him, accusing the prostrate Marielle of being a liar and (thrillingly) 'a perennial cocke-pivot'.

Dear Lord and all the saints together.

Notwithstanding his truly invigorating use of language, I did notice Mister Kryk was somewhat *déshabillé*, in an open chemise that hung quite low in the front, exposing a neat collarbone and smooth, strong chest. It occurred to me that I too was similarly undressed. It was immensely stirring and it took great fortitude and a vision of Madame Benoit in her corsets to quell my brimming animation.

Still, the magnitude of the situation was obvious. I immediately wished I had simply pretended to be asleep.

'What is this? I have had to leave my chambers at this ungodly hour, your screaming is so wild.'

The room fell silent. Not for long. Marielle whipped around from her position on the floor, then facing me, extended an arm and accusatory finger at Mister Kryk.

'He has molested me!'

And again the kitchen began to shriek and roar.

'Enough! Monsieur Benoit, please accompany me to my hall, now.'

'Yes, Monsieur.'

Even as I turned with Monsieur Benoit stepping after me, the din continued.

'Silence! I should dismiss you all. I cannot abide this infernal noise. You, Marielle, go to the pantry and stay there until you are called. Mister Kryk, that is enough, I have registered your protest. Out here in the hall if you please and the rest of you go to your cots. You have ruined my day before it has even begun.' I wished for all the cotton in India I had stayed in bed. 'Mister Benoit, come into the salon. Mister Kryk, please remain where you are.' I noted he was raging all through: steely face, jaw clenched in fury. It was a revelation. I retreated with Monsieur Benoit and affected calm. 'What is the story, please?'

'Monsieur, you know I do like a good sleep and I sleep well for the most part, I prefer a harder cot and it does help with the aching. But this morning—'

'Monsieur Benoit. I can certainly appreciate the benefits of a good night's sleep. As you can tell, I have been rudely roused from my own efforts. Might we cut ahead to the important details of this matter? What has Marielle said, what has my valet said and what is your opinion, please?'

Monsieur Benoit cleared his throat. 'Marielle, who is, if you will excuse me sir—'

'A perennial cocke-pivot?'

'Nom de Dieu . . .'

'Please continue, Monsieur Benoit.'

'Yes, yes. Well, Marielle says that your manservant, Jonathan Kryk, tried to lie with her in her cot and, excuse me again, molest her. Mister Kryk denies this, saying he was asleep in his own cot and he woke to find her lying naked beside him and with – apologies, sir – his hand on her breast. He leapt up shouting and chased her to her cot, where she turned back on him and began to scream foul.'

'Oh, *Mère de Dieu*, this is so weary-making.' My head slumped into my hands.

'I arrived to find Marielle still undone, weeping and shouting, and Mister Kryk in his underclothes calling her a liar and a ... that. As you can appreciate, the household woke and then, Monsieur, you intervened.'

'I wish I had not. I wish you had beaten them all with your saucepans.'

'Yes, yes. Yes, Monsieur.'

'What is your opinion?'

'Marielle is trouble, sir. She has been fresh with your man since he arrived. I do wager she fancies him something wicked. The other girls do not like her and say they saw her just last week try to – excuse me, Monsieur – handle Mister Kryk in the crudest manner.'

'Oh?' This was interesting. 'And what was his response?'

'He pushed her away most smartly.'

'Do we trust him on this matter, Monsieur Benoit?'

'Yes, Monsieur. Most assuredly. I have it from the other girls too and they tend to gaggle together.'

'The matter is settled. But let us call in Mister Kryk.'

He was called and as he rounded the door, tried to pull his untucked chemise about him in modesty. He was still in an acute state and was shaking. I admit I found that seeing him so undone produced, again, suddenly, a hot and unwelcome distraction beneath my banyan. Entirely inappropriate, given the circumstances. For discretion, I pulled the cloth closer to myself lest any protuberance betray me.

'Mister Kryk, Monsieur Benoit has given me his opinion. But I must hear it from you. Did you go to Marielle's cot and attempt to molest her?'

'No, sir.'

'Why should I believe you?'

'If I was to molest a girl, I would not go to them when they lay asleep with three other girls lying head to foot, not inches apart.'

'This is a most logical and yet strange response, Mister Kryk, for you do not rule out your desire to do so.'

'Monsieur, I do rule it out. I have no desire to touch Marielle or any of her sort. I was simply pointing out, Monsieur, if you will allow me, that Marielle is not alone where she sleeps. I am. My cot being well apart from all the rest in a different corridor. It was she who found me alone and without witness.'

Very sound reasoning, I thought. Mister Kryk's cot *was* well apart from the others. As my valet he was required to sleep nearer to my quarters so that he might access my rooms quickly and discreetly should I require it.

'Monsieur Benoit?' He nodded to me and I was satisfied by Mister Kryk's response. 'Please call Marielle.'

Along she came, all wet-faced and trembling, and had not, I noticed, taken the trouble to lace herself up her front and repair her dignity. No doubt for my benefit.

'Marielle, I have had the account of Monsieur Benoit and Mister Kryk.'

She began to cry again.

'Please, Marielle, I cannot abide weeping, it is most unseemly. Will you please compose yourself for a moment? Thank you. Now, you say Mister Kryk molested you in your cot?'

'Yes, Monsieur. Most rudely.'

'In the same cot you share with the other three girls?'

She shot the merest narrowing of an eye at me then smartly redirected it to her side, where Mister Kryk stood.

'Yes. He is a crafty thing.'

'He would certainly have to be. Now, if I might, where did he, on your person, Marielle, seek to molest you?' I asked this last part more quietly.

'You are a brute, Monsieur.'

'Yes, I appreciate that. And you are not the first to mention it. Let me be more delicate. In relation to your stomach, Marielle, was it towards your knees or towards your chin?'

'My knees,' she whispered.

'Your knees. And yet, Marielle, it is your near-naked bosom that I am now being forced to look at.'

'Monsieur?'

'Go away, Marielle. You are dismissed. Monsieur Benoit, see that she is gone by noon. You may have a week's pay and take your clothes and blankets.'

So, she left, not without a cat's bagful of shrieking and wailing.

My scribe would like it noted that all of this would never pass muster in the eyes of contemporary readers: to have a jury of men ascribe crude assertions about Marielle and then shame her into silence before dismissing her from her employment. Incorrect again, dear scribe. I ascertained the facts, those being that Marielle was an appalling person, be she man or woman.

And I could not have my valet embroiled in scandal. It would reflect very poorly on me.

15

A Catalogue of Desire

A few days later, Monsieur Benoit came to me with news from Mister Kryk.

'He wishes to leave your household, Monsieur.'

I felt as though a vicious old carthorse had hoofed me through my gut. Part shock and panic, part indignation. 'Why? What is his complaint?'

'No complaint, Monsieur. He feels he has been shamed by the incident with Marielle and would not want to bring disgrace on your household.'

'Preposterous. The fault was hers. It has been established.'

'I have tried to convince him. He will not have it.'

'Then he is ungrateful. And I would have no valet.'

'No, he has assured me he will stay until a replacement is found.'

Here was the perfect opportunity to rid myself of Mister Kryk. But the very thought of him leaving was enough to break my entire self in half and render me no more worthy of life than the muck in a chicken's claw.

'Monsieur, I fear that only your intervention will dissuade him, for he is quite set on it.'

'Why must I, Monsieur Benoit? I leave these messy quandaries in your capable hands, do I not? Why should it fall to me?'

(I was conspiring already of ways to trap Mister Kryk in my employ.)

'Indeed, undoubtedly, and many apologies, yes, but he is determined to leave us and as valets go, he is quite exceptional. He has many friends but is not over familiar, he gives me no trouble, takes no advantage so that – and I admit this in the hope you will not punish me, sir – I am able to leave him alone to get on with himself. I hardly pay him mind, whether he is here or there. I know he will simply get on. He's a fine one.'

'Yes, isn't he?'

He was exceptional in all possible manner of ways and all at once I was overcome by a lurid and most delightful reverie of quite how exceptional Mister Kryk might be if we were trapped together alone during a long harsh winter, with no hope of rescue until the new year . . .

'Monsieur? Monsieur? Are you well?'

'Monsieur Benoit. I apologise, I was simply reminded of our dear friend, Bobo, and was momentarily overcome with emotion. Another exceptional valet who is still much missed.'

'Indeed. But back to Mister Kryk. I like him, I will be honest. Not the same with all these other young ones. You know what happened with that one up the way last week, I dare say?'

'Indeed. I was entirely affronted just hearing of it.'

In truth, I had spent an afternoon with my beloved comtesse two days previously and we had both near expired laughing to hear that Valle-du-Pont's new valet had been caught with his daughter, Valerie, and her chambermaid simultaneously. All three. Can you imagine it? Valerie was only just of marrying age and had been promised to one of The Toad's nephews. I myself had passed her up as a prospective wife after yet another dull picnic, but on hearing the news of her passion for an unholy trinity, I was immediately overcome with remorse. She might have been a very jolly life's companion. The comtesse chastised me, saying I could have married Valerie and we could all three have been friends. Now she was off to the convent for the rest of her living years. The valet had run away in the night and though I couldn't say what happened to the chambermaid, she would never be seen again.

'I suppose, Monsieur Benoit, I should speak to him and demand he stay. But in so doing, might I not lead him to think he is indispensable to me? We cannot allow him to become self-important.'

'Of course not, a disaster. Perhaps you could demand he stay, Monsieur, but offer a small punishment for the disruption with Marielle.'

'A small punishment? What constitutes a small punishment when the man was innocent?'

'I cannot think, but I will contrive something, as must you, Monsieur. A small sanction is all it will take. You might simply say that you understand he wishes to leave and as punishment you will not release him of his position, since you yourself have already suffered enough inconvenience.'

'And continue to suffer. Daily.'

Monsieur Benoit went to call Mister Kryk, who would meet me in my *grand salon* before the hour was up.

I was in a frenzy of conflict. I needed him here, calmly moving about me, ordering my chamber, handing me wine as he attached the ribbons to my shoes, agreeing to my questions; just speaking out loud to someone and having one's thoughts acknowledged, a balm in its own right.

How had I come to rely on him so? Simply his ordering of my life, my physical environment, gave me such comfort. I looked forward to it. When I could write no more, he would bring a maid to change the flowers, open the windows, spray orange water all about; I trusted him to look after my work, keep it neat without disturbing the pages, simply give some semblance of stillness to the usual chaos I created after a session at my desk. A few minutes of his presence about my rooms and suddenly all manner of reverie was possible again.

When in melancholic temper, his attention to my person (shave, coiffure, attire) immediately gave me a feeling that things were brighter than I had first imagined them. The proximity of him, his hand on my body as he dressed me, his fingers as he turned my face for his blade, filled me with passion on some days but, for the most part, simply offered me the perfection and comfort of a chaste caress of kindness. I had begun to feel I might exhale into his arms, find harbour there. It was not simply that I desired him – and, oh, how I did – but that I loved him, tenderly, and hoped that he might love me too. That, I found to my surprise, brought its own higher order of need.

I tried to engage him in conversation, reaching towards a more intimate companionship, but he unfailingly replied with, 'Yes, Monsieur, no, Monsieur, thank you, Monsieur.' For the impediments to intimacy were many. He was not simply another man but my servant too. And let us not forget that if caught, the punishment was death.

He stood waiting in the salon, his back to me and his face illuminated on one side as the light came through the large windows on either side of my cabinet. Deep shadows fell about his eyes. It was as if the master painters had alighted in my room to present him in this light. Endymion in front of his life's tableau.

How my heart leapt from my breast. How carefully he moved, as if he knew he might forget himself.

The doors to the cabinet were open, for I had earlier been moving about some of the *maquettes*. The facade lifted out, exposing the scene inside, the stage and all the mirrors facing this way and that, reflecting the light. On the extension, some shells and gems.

I wanted to alert him to my presence, I should have.

He lifted a conch from the shelf, ran a finger along its underbelly. I hid like a fool, a mute reduced to some shameful leering from behind drapery. I felt terror and thrill; at once consumed with joy and the horror of its concealment. I had to make myself known before I burst out of myself in some unholy and unseemly display.

'Mister Kryk, I am present.'

He started and immediately replaced the shell. He had a look of terror.

'No, no, please. Continue as you were.'

'I did not mean to intrude. Apologies, Monsieur. Had I thought you were here, I should not have entered. Please, Monsieur, my apologies.' He bowed low.

'No. Do not apologise.' I was too hasty, shrill, too panicked. 'You admired that shell. It is, I am told, from the West Indies. Islands where it is warm and verdant the year-round.'

'Yes, Monsieur. It is beautiful.'

'Quite so. It still smelled of salt when I received it.'

'It is out of the sea then?'

'Yes.'

'And this?' He lifted a small flat dragon that I had hung from one of the drawer handles. It was S-shaped, ribbed, and had a perfectly formed face with two protruding eyes.

'We cannot say what it is, or where it lives, though it is a dragon of sorts, of course.'

He began to smile a little, unusual to see. Did he blush? His eyes were so clear. I tried not to scrutinise him too closely. I felt I might shout out 'I love you', so full was I with the moment. I contained myself to say, by way of exploration, 'I should like to know its true nature though. It is important to know its nature.'

'From land or sea? I cannot see that it matters,' said Mister Kryk.

'But it does matter. People like to know what they are faced with. It offers a level of comfort.'

'Yes, it is true they do. But I do not. I do not care.'

'No?'

'The dragon is beautiful. That is all that matters.'

'Though you cannot name it?'

'That is its beauty. It does not need a name.' He looked directly at me as he spoke this. The same eyes that had held mine on my *jeu de paume court*, as I moved the ball across the line.

'No. No name is necessary.'

'And the name given would not describe it. The name would contain within it its description, its place, but nothing of its beauty. That is what my father said of maps. Even though he made them.'

He spoke more words in the past moments than he had in the previous months combined. It occurred to me he had made up his mind to leave and that this made him bold.

'There is no beauty in classification, Mister Kryk. That is true.'

'No.'

I lifted the shell he had admired before.

'There is beauty here too. May I give you this shell?'

'Monsieur?'

Had I misspoken? He did not offer much on his face, so that he was impossible to decipher, but he did not look reproachful.

'So that you might know it better and keep it safe.'

'Thank you, sir. I will have it.'

I placed it on his palm and with my own hands closed his fingers around it. I felt as if there was tremendous boldness, even in this. My heart was galloping.

I said, 'And we'll not name it. Let it keep its beauty.'

Nom de Dieu! What was happening?

He betrayed nothing but said, 'Monsieur, I know why you have summoned me.'

I was trembling all through. 'Will you stay, Mister Kryk?' My voice had lost any authority, it was barely a whisper. I felt I might begin to weep. My throat burned. I needed him to stay, more than anything. I would beg him, implore him to stay, tell him I would surely die if he left me.

'Monsieur, I will stay.'

Dear God, the reprieve. 'Monsieur Benoit will be pleased to hear it.'

'Thank you, Monsieur.' He bowed again. And left.

Immediately, overcome with terror, I felt as exposed as a beggar at court, ragged and mocked. Had he understood me? Had he replied and what was that reply? He gave nothing away. Utterly polite and decorous. If he denounced me, I would have to return the accusation. After all, I could have had him lashed for being in my *salon*, my treasures unattended, and he, rifling through them.

Oh, the thrill that he might one dark night rifle through my treasures. His proximity, the moment of quiet. Nothing was tangible around him; everything, all elements, light and air, were rendered rhapsodical. He was all that there was in any room that he occupied.

There was the possibility that he had not received my meaning, that I had been too veiled. For him to be so presumptuous as to assume I had feelings for him when I may have simply been kind or well-mannered would be a disaster for him.

But a worse option presented itself: that he understood full well my feelings and shared my inclinations, but not with me. It was possible that he found me repulsive. If this were so, then I would have to discharge him of his service and condemn him as a lazy, dishonest valet. It would be a pity, but it would be necessary. I am sure you agree.

I spent some time examining my aspect in the mirror of my curiosity cabinet. Was I not a handsome man?

I took an inventory. My forehead was a noble one, wide and smooth though not so high as to suggest disproportion. My nose was lean and straight and my hair was good and full and fell in long waves well below my collar. My eyes were green – a good green, though prone to murkiness after too much wine. I resolved to drink less wine.

He should be honoured that I would look at him.

But everything about him made me feel wholly inadequate. He had a kind of confidence in his body, an ease of movement that was at once energetic and entirely controlled. He had balance and poise, strength, agility. Even my scribe admits that he was the very embodiment of a desirable man and she understands entirely my extensive passion for him.

I slept badly, rewriting the events over again until I became convinced that I had exposed myself most terribly and I would be summoned in the morning for some or other trial. I had not touched him though and I would denounce him as having misunderstood me on account of being Dutch. The fact that his French was perfect and his Latin passable would have to be overlooked.

And yet through all my restlessness, I still dreamt about his hands over the conch, his softness, his stillness.

My dearest scribe would like it recorded that, notwithstanding her appreciation for the lithe form of Mister Kryk and her sympathies for my predicament, what was announced as a serious and studious memoir of my life in 1657 is now veering dramatically towards 'Romantic Melodrama', and any minute she expects one of us to flounce across the page in petticoats. If anyone is going to flounce in petticoats it will be me, and I see no problem with a historical romance at all. She reminds me that this is my memoir and not what she calls a 'bodice-ripper' for English ladies, to be read while drinking wine on their French holidays. I have no objection to this either, though these ladies are in for a rude shock and should rather think along the lines of a 'codpiece-popper'.

Why must only the history of war and misery be recorded as serious and the history of desire and love be rendered less valid? My experience of love to this point had been no less merciless and devastating than any of the skirmishes I was obliged to join. As if a wound to one's body were more valid than a psyche in turmoil, one's very being contorted in pain.

This is the memoir of a man in love. You may have your kings and your generals too; catalogue their battles and body counts. In this memoir, we catalogue whispers and sighs. We immortalise longing and make index of our passions and fancies.

And so, back to my *mémoire d'amour*, my catalogue of desire.

16

A Rutting Stag

Fate intervened in the form of duty. I was only awake a few minutes when I recalled I was due at a local Estates meeting later in the day. Uncle Hippolyte, Clusy de Marcilliac and even Scipio Le Gratia would be posturing their way around the Estates halls. I was inclined to hide away and prolong my reverie, but this was a treacherous path given the scrutiny I was under. I would need to prepare from my office and make representations concerning tax and security, when really my mind was still drifting across the plains of Mount Latmus. Oh, Endymion.

The other great misery of the meeting was of course that I would be unguarded. I had no Hortense nor any other friend who might act as a distraction should my uncle try to extract from me some information or promise. My cousins were unlikely to make an appearance as they would simply never manage the final part of the journey from the wine house to the meeting. Wisely done, cousins.

And so, the daily torture of dressing. My increased spiritual ease with Mister Kryk's proximity did nothing to quell my physical discomfort. You must understand, dressing could extend to an hours-long ritual and could not be hurried lest one's valet take insult. Some gentlemen would receive guests in their private chambers to watch them dress and shave; it was a great honour to be invited. I refused such absurdities of course. Upholstering me in my finery was not a public performance. Much of the day could be dedicated to its preparation. My impatience with this theatre was the reason I was so often dismissed as *déshabillé*.

This even before you can imagine being naked and trembling in the presence of your life's greatest desire – heart and loins in a torrent of longing. I was one part tortured moon, one part rutting stag.

There is no more excruciating pain than that of an unreleased ardour. Fervid does not come close to describing it and after the preceding day's awkwardness, I felt I should be even more restrained in language and manner than usual. A nod here or there had to suffice, and sobriety was essential – a glass or four of *hippocras* while at my writing desk before Mister Kryk's arrival in my bedchamber might produce such a jolt of corporal approval that I was likely to sing out: *Have all of me now!*

Inelegant.

So, to the Estates council I eventually went: vexed, unsatiated and painfully sober. On arrival, a nose through the drapes confirmed no friend was present. Uncle Hippolyte saw me but made no effort to acknowledge me, forcing me to approach him and his cabal of sycophants, all of them in turn agreeing with whatever Clusy de Marcilliac might announce. Mewling loiter-sacks all.

'Uncle.'

'Jehan. I am surprised to see you.'

'You should not be. I so look forward to these meetings, and all the better for your presence.'

'Baudelaire. You surprise me.' Clusy de Marcilliac seemed even more gaunt than at our last meeting a few weeks before. No doubt the vinegar he used for blood.

'Sire. I am pleased to find you looking so well.'

He said nothing, did not return the compliment, which one would have thought was the very minimum of requirements. I sensed a chill and all my paranoid fears of exposure reared in the instant.

'A word, Jehan.' My uncle led me away from the rest and I felt their terminal disdain as we turned from them. Had Mister Kryk exposed me? Spies at the doors of my *salon*? 'What are you doing here?'

'Uncle, I am fulfilling my duty and representing my estates. I would have thought it would please you.'

'It does not please me.'

'I assure you, if I had not made an appearance, you would have been even less pleased. You are very clear in your constant and, might I add, uncalled for commentaries on my lack of engagement at these conferences.'

'You have no idea, do you?'

'I confess I do not.' My cravat was doing its best to throttle every last bit of air from my throat.

'You are the source of no small scandal and you claim you to know nothing?'

'Uncle, I assure you I know nothing. And I cannot imagine how I am involved in scandal when all I do is work and, when the heat abates, take monkish walks along the riverbanks. I do not even have a spaniel to call friend.'

'You are either an imbecile or you believe me to be one.'

'Then I confess it is I who is the imbecile, Uncle.' My heart began its gallop.

He leaned closer, forcing a retreat deeper to the darker reaches of the room.

'Do you deny that you sought to smuggle from your house the Comtesse de Montmorency? Both of you in a state of undress and – the true scandal – *through the kitchen* for all your household to see?'

It was all I could do not to laugh and dance swirling about my stupid po-faced uncle. A joyous reprieve!

I was emboldened.

'Well, Uncle, would you rather I send her out the front where *all the world* could see? I am a gentleman, and she a lady of exceptional modesty and breeding. She was required to leave on very short notice. Her lady's maid, a most loyal charge, sent word that the comte would return early from his hunt. As such her departure was both hasty and, for my part, deeply regrettable.'

'Are you insane?' He was puce. 'Have you lost your mind entirely? The comte is our most loyal ally, he has sent his young sons into battle on our behalf.'

'Well, Uncle, now we owe him nothing. Your own nephew has fulfilled a different, though no less vigorous conquest, to repay that debt.'

There was nothing he could say, he was burning with rage and would have taken a hand to me right then had we not been surrounded by the twitching plumes of the great and good. It pleased me hugely to see him thus.

'Jehan, with God as my witness—'

'No, please, Uncle, do not thank me. It gave me enormous, nay, thunderous pleasure to do it. I am, as ever, your servant.'

And with it, I bowed, spun on my spurs, made sure to flick my cloak in the direction of the parliament and strode towards the exit, summoning a lackey as I went.

'For God's sake, quick, my carriage, waste no time.'

Of course, almost as soon as I had turned my back, the great bulking ships of shame and terror began to assemble.

I could barely get my hands into my gloves I was trembling so violently. I cannot say what it was, fury or relief, but whatever its name it left me feeling cruelly exposed – a cloak stripped off in a gale – and all the while the terrible knowledge that I had done the Comtesse a dreadful disservice when she had never been anything less than a most dear friend and *confidente*.

I was lower than a scurvied knave and you may judge me as such.

17

The Promise of Salvation

I was in a tender and awkward mood. At least I had one source of comfort: I had made repair with the comtesse. She forgave me immediately, reminding me that an exit through the kitchen had been her idea, but I knew I had been indelicate and regretted it deeply. It did mean she would not be able to visit me for a while, nor I her, and that was another blow. We had passed such a happy afternoon in my bedchamber, a reprieve of intimacy in a long line of solitude. I had read her my rendition of *Endymion* and she had been most approving, suggesting only one or two improvements. I so longed to tell her about Mister Kryk, unburden myself of my secret, take her advice even, but I knew it was an impossibility. I organised at once to send her some garnets for her hair.

My temper was highly erratic even by my own standards. So much so that I considered consulting my astrologer, but then decided that even he could not be tolerated. My every mood depended on how I found Mister Kryk. He brought fresh flowers for my desk and mentioned that he remembered that I favoured the darker jewel colours? I was elated. Was he too brisk, did he not acknowledge my clever witticism? Utter despair. One minute airborne but the next felled so low it took all my courage just to put on a good face for the servants. *Yes, Monsieur Benoit, your partridge is most excellent, it is quite the finest I have ever tasted. I was entirely enraptured with it. The bird positively regained its fledgling wings upon finding my tongue. Yes, indeed, your cakes are so sweet and delicate I can hardly bear to bring them to my waiting lips for fear of blushing. And if you would not mind, Monsieur Benoît, a small hemlock* digestif *so that I might never have to endure another day of this lonely gastronomic torture.*

Or something along those lines.

(My scribe would like it noted that she makes a point of buying darker flowers for her own writing desk for our time together. Burgundy roses at present. She is fishing for gratitude of course, very unseemly, but she is needy and so I will this once acknowledge her attention.)

At my Avignon household, I became a sullen degenerate, creeping in all the darker shadows. I watched as Mister Kryk assisted a cook's help untie her apron ribbons that had become tangled behind her and in one moment went from jealousy to intense tenderness at the patience he showed in unpicking her stubborn knots, his soft smile as they spoke. I let my eyes glance at him from under a low-drawn *chapeau*, as he joked conspiratorially with valets from other households before drawing himself into a perfect sober posture on seeing my approach. His laugh alone could cure an entire city of pestilence. Once, on a tour of the topiary with Monsieur Villet, my head gardener, I saw him teaching some children to turn cartwheels. He could turn five without drawing breath. I was so devastated by such an effusive display of youthful pliancy that I had to retire to my bed immediately thereafter.

On a cooler day (and even now this image fills me with such a soft ache of love), he hid himself away on top of a low wall and lay in the warm sun, his cap under his head, his hand occasionally swatting a passing beetle. I was at a gallery window looking down. I cannot say how long I stood there, watching him sleep, a lithe, easy animal, oblivious to the world, oblivious to me. I put my hand against the pane, a cold and thwarted touch; said, 'I love you.' How I wished that he might hear me.

And yet, the thing I feared most was the possibility, the eventuality, of a first touch. Not the brush of his hands as he buttoned and fastened, not the slightest graze of his fingers on my wrist as he removed my glove, all of these were nothing but a wild thrill of hope in an otherwise bleak forever. Rather, the touch I feared the most was the one that might come with purpose. If ever it were possible that he would extend his hand across the void between us, extend so much as a fingertip with the intention of letting it rest on my face or hand or hair ... that I feared. And in fearing it, yearned for it.

So it was.

I was deep in one of my reveries when my sister arrived without warning. Not unusual, it is true, but she did startle me.

It was then that I remembered that I had sent her a story I had been working on, though not my *Endymion*.

'Poor darling, this story is even more devastating than the last.'

'You do not like it.'

'Not very much. But there is hope for it. The idea is very good and you write so well. You could write it all again but use the jester's voice as the main and put the chevalier in the background.'

'I could.' I may have let out a dramatic sigh. I was prone to it that spring. 'I lack the energy.'

'Well, why not write it again until it is perfect and I will hold a salon for you. You may read it out – you are so good at the voices – and then everyone may enjoy it.'

Hortense was so clever at cheering me up.

'I love you, Sister. That is a wonderful idea.'

'How long will you need to make it right? You tell me and

then I can set about inviting everyone we would like to hear it. We must invite the recently arrived principessa. I hear all the gentlemen are in fine flutter over her. It might be, well . . . you might like to make her acquaintance too? You have not been naughty for weeks and weeks. You have been so sad.'

'Yes. I confess though that the thought of an ebullient and wild-eyed principessa does not stir me. If I so much as offer a salutation, I will be barrelled down to the cathedral in a new ensemble and a fresh nosegay before I can even replace my hat.'

'I am sorry. Uncle is very hard on you.'

'I regret his existence.'

'You must not say that. I *am* sorry though. Can we not contrive a plan to make it happy for both of you?'

'I must marry a stupid girl, principessa, lady, any moneyed wench of laying age with land, lineage and a small army, or he will never be happy. If she is half-mole and lives in a tunnel she has burrowed straight to Rome, with a lengthy stop at court en route, then even better.'

'It might not be so bad. It is possible, Jehan, if not to love the person one is married to, to at least find in your heart an understanding of them, a kindness that recognises their own struggle to find satisfaction. Sometimes it is we who disappoint them.'

I realised that she spoke of her own life, her own struggle to find any kind of love for The Toad, who had been always too old and too miserable for her.

'*Pardieu*, Hortense. I am so sorry. I am so preoccupied with my misery I did not see your own.'

'Oh, don't be silly, I am perfectly happy. I am very lucky.'

'Sister . . .'

'He is very nice to me, very patient.'

'You will have beautiful children, my sweet.'

'I am sure you are correct. And I am so lucky. Other men might not be so kind.'

'You are wrong. It is he who is lucky. It has always been so.'

She wiped her eyes, 'That is enough. Let us plan a salon to cheer ourselves up. It will be a beautiful night.'

'Your dreadful little Toad will be so proud of you.'

'He will. And I will be proud of you.'

18

Commedia Alla Maschera

Early summer came with multiple intrigues. The first was the confirmation that Philippe, Le Petit Monsieur and younger brother to Louis XIV, had indeed been corrupted to completion. From memory, he was seventeen or eighteen years old that year.

I must confess I received this news with immense delight. I even allowed myself to become hopeful that this would herald the start of a new more lenient dispensation. A more useful defence in the courts, perhaps, and an atmosphere in which allowances could be made. Perhaps Uncle Hippolyte would send me to make merry in the court of Le Petit Monsieur. Fantasies all, and preposterous ones, but after a glass of *hippocras* on a cooler evening, the mind is vivid with possibility.

Not so, was the report from the *salons* in Avignon, Aix and Orange. Wiser cousins, and those I considered savvier and more cunning than I, had a more nuanced view and one I took to heart. The previous king's younger brother had caused him great political peril, and been such a destabilising presence for the crown, that to have Philippe as a confirmed Socratic was politically expedient for the Bourbons. It made it impossible for him ever to aspire to the throne. Should he overstep his position or seek advantage among allies opposed to Louis, his crime and sin would provide a useful and public sanction. More subtle and yet more devastating was that his proclivities exposed him as morally weak, a libertine and an aesthete, incapable of holding serious office. They rendered him ridiculous.

Then came word on Conti. The scoundrel had indeed become a zealot in his piety, so much so that he *had* dropped Molière, who was suddenly without patron. He and his band were poor but free to play wherever they pleased as they made their tour of Languedoc and all of France in the coming months.

With so much intelligence to absorb, I resolved to recommit to my story, *The Lonely Jester*, and another I was working on which would serve as backup should the *Jester* not be to my liking. A salon was a fine idea.

My longing for Mister Kryk had not abated. I was becoming jealous and obsessive. I would spend hours in a day simply trying to ascertain with whom he spoke and for how long. Did he spend too long at the stable with any of the boys there, when he was sent to tell them when the horses would be required?

My obsession was darker still: allowing myself to imagine that he had understood my meaning when I had given him the small shell and that he was, at every moment, deciding when and how to expose me, even so far as to imagine him in cahoots my uncle and his spies. That there were spies in my household was clear, the incident with the comtesse leaving through the kitchen exposed as much. My despair was deep.

But salvation was at hand. A few days later Scipio Le Gratia sent an invitation. A group of Italian players would soon be his guests and he extended a personal invitation to myself and a small retinue to enjoy their performance. They would perform at Mignard's court.

*

The night was perfect. The warmth seemed to arrive earlier in 1657, the merest hint of summer in the early weeks of spring. Avignon's walls were golden and over hung with a lapis lazuli sky. Even the starlings sang a pretty song. The troupe comprised *commedia dell'arte* players or, as we called them, *commedia alla maschera*, for they all wore masks to denote who they played. The piece was magnificent. It had within it cleverly written vignettes and *lazzo* (little jokes), as well as much of the *improviso* for which they were admired. Masks, farce, characters that we recognised and adored, all collided on the stage so that the joyous mayhem it created seemed at any point likely to tip over into complete annihilation. I had a sense of watching something on the very edge of the known world, the thrill and the pace of it made me laugh until I cried. It is true some of the verse lacked refinement, but it was a magnificent entertainment.

Hortense and her insufferable husband attended too – he after much protest. Hortense enjoyed the piece as I did and shrieked with delight as she always used to when we were younger. I was greatly obliged to Mignard for the entertainment and forgot entirely that we were rivals. I asked that I might personally meet the players after the performance and thank them. I cannot tell you, friends, the humility I felt before them. This ragtag assortment of men and women into whose ranks I could only dream of being embraced. I expressed to them my thanks, that I was their eternal servant, and managed not to betray my excessive and childish delight when the leader of the troupe presented me with the mask of the *Capitano* of the piece. Hortense tied it in place immediately and I affected a superior posture that they would know how much it pleased me.

Mignard and his family provided a marvellous feast for his own and Scipio Le Gratia's guests. I drank a good deal of wine and made a pact with God that I would recommit to my writing, infusing it with more daring and making space in the lines for audacious *improviso*. I also resolved to stop wasting my days in idle swoon over Mister Kryk. There was a moment between my third or fourth glass of *vin de Dieu* and some quite exceptional sweetmeats that I even considered a life of chastity. (Undignified guffaws from my scribe here.) I could retreat to a monastery. But, by the end of the fifth glass (a glance to my scribe), I decided instead to take the more punishing route of writing, so that I might still drink an excess of wine. I dedicated myself to that too and may have had as many as eight brimful. Certainly enough that my sister sent her lackey to follow me home.

Mister Kryk was preparing my chamber for the night, the room scented with rose and neroli, a small fire in the grate. It took some effort to straighten myself up and hide the effects of the wine. I did not want him to think me a vulgar wine-soak.

'You need not have waited for me. I have been at the painter Mignard's court. The play was a delight. More than a delight. I am a changed man for having seen it.'

'Yes, Monsieur.'

'It was exceptional, the scenes and words combined were transcendent. It was audacious, so brave.'

'You are very taken with it, Monsieur. If you please, your cravat, Monsieur.'

'More than taken. I am in love with words again. I am resolved to work harder at my own writing. Tomorrow, you may accompany me to get new ink and quills and I will need my bureau rearranged. It will need a new *tapis* on it perhaps and fresh flowers. I can already see dark pink and claret roses. Is it too early for roses?'

'Yes, Monsieur. But I will see to it, Monsieur. Please extend your arm.'

How sweetly he attended me. He was so close I could count his eyelashes, each the tiniest imitation of an angel's wing.

'Mister Kryk, I am quite alive with life. I have, it is true, had a good deal of wine, truly, a good deal, but I feel that tonight there has been a great change in me. Oh. What is the matter? I cannot get my arms to come out of this sleeve?'

Did he smile? I know that he did. That he was mocking me in my drunkenness I did not care. He had smiled at me.

'Monsieur, it is best that you stand still and allow me to attend to you.'

'See? It won't come off; I might have to sleep in it. I am so beside myself. The *improviso* was exceptional. And later this year we will have Molière. It can only be better still.'

'You are agitated, Monsieur. If you will please stand still, I will be able to free you from your doublet.'

It may be true that I was toppling a little this way and that. Agitated.

'I would be very pleased if you would free me from my doublet. But please, Mister K-kryk, I will continue to wear my mask, given to me by the players.'

Free me from my doublet and all the rest! Ravish me now! I began to feel a familiar tension twixt my loins. Oh, dear heaven, I was on dangerous ground.

He took some effort to reverse the tangle I had made of myself.

'Let me sit here so you can help with my shoes. I have scuffed them. I may have fallen over.'

He knelt to remove my broken shoes while I continued to gabble most inelegantly. I had become a riot of fervour that threatened to consume my entire body. The fact that I would soon be released from my britches became suddenly worrying.

'Have I ruined my shoes? There is no praise high enough for

the piece. The pathos and humour were so well aligned that I did not know whether to laugh or simply allow my heart to be broken in two. Do you know the feeling? Just speaking about it raises my blood again. I am determined to work so that I may impress Molière and have my own band of players to present my work.'

'Yes, Monsieur.'

And with no more than a breath between us, I leant down to Jonathan Kryk of Amsterdam, took his face into my hands, and kissed him quickly, gloriously, full on his soft mouth.

He did not respond. Even through the haze of wine, I could tell he had not anticipated my mouth on his. Then again, nor had I. His eyes were wide with shock. Yet no one was more stunned than I by what I had done.

Nom de Dieu.

I had no idea what to do next.

'Well. There.' I added great flourish to disguise my abject fear. 'You have been kissed by the successor to Molière.'

That he most likely had no idea who Molière was did not deter me.

'Thank you, Monsieur. A great honour, I am sure.' He kept his head down so that I could not see his face. I was suddenly both sober and terrified. Rigid with horror at what I had done. He removed my other shoe, then stood to place them. 'I will leave you now. I will see to your desk in the morning.'

What had I done? I had put myself at such great risk by exposing myself to his rejection but worse, exposing myself to a extreme censure. He was my servant. He could be my uncle's spy. There was nothing at all that he had ever done or said that might lead me to believe he had the same needs as I.

These elements combined caused an immediate sobering effect, as I began to think of how I might remedy and explain the situation. For, while I *had* kissed him, and on his mouth, should he report it or complain I could claim drunken fraternity.

It was not unusual to kiss a friend, possibly not quite so fully on the mouth. My hands around his lovely face were, it is true, a misjudgement, but again, I would have to make recourse to the wine. Hortense could support my claim to being an amorous drunk. I am not unconvinced that I had not tried to kiss both her and her Toad in the back of a carriage on any number of nights. (I should like it recorded most emphatically that I have never, ever considered her Toad an object of attraction. My manhood droops to think of it.)

I may have fallen asleep immediately, stunned by the effects of the wine, but woke through the night, my mind composing pieces of verse and snatches of conversation all on the theme of 'grieving lips' and 'aching ardour', as if possessed by a most needing Socratic incubus. It was nightmarish and wonderful all at once.

19

Billet

The morning dawned with thunderous sobriety. My head and heart were both in a state of some dishevelment. Wine is no friend of mine. The swill of Lucifer himself.

Oh, but the shame. The shame of having finally taken his perfect face into my hands only to be rejected so swiftly and wordlessly. It was more than I could bear.

All my passions were doomed to rejection, chastity or women. I was the jilted marquis. (It did occur to me that it would make a very good title for a story and my scribe will write it down again so that I remember it.)

Apart from the extreme humiliation, my immediate problem, as I lay in my bed, was that I was both hungry and exceedingly parched and in the absence of my valet, I had no idea how to remedy these problems. Even as this thought arose, another came: he was being very remiss, even impertinent, given the hour, in not bringing some refreshment to my bed. The cord to my bell was too far from reach and I was about to fall back into my pillows in a miserable sulk when footsteps approached the door and under it came a folded *billet*. For some reason, I did not know what to do. Partly because he should have been there to retrieve it for me and partly because I was not sure what it might be and so had no desire to read it. I shut my eyes against the light.

On opening them I found the letter was still there. With great effort, I roused myself from bed and went to retrieve it. My body told me I had most certainly fallen over on my return journey. And while I had demanded that Mister Kryk not accompany me to the theatre, he should have insisted and been there to protect me from such things. It was his duty. I was getting too lax with him and he was taking liberties.

I was relieved that the note did not bear my uncle's seal. Perhaps it was a summons to answer for my sinful immersion in the theatre. I opened it.

Monsieur, I took the liberty of letting you rest. I have left a small refreshment on the bureau outside your chamber. JK

Was there ever a more thoughtful and discreet valet than my Jonathan Kryk? Literate and with such skilful penmanship. Oh, my loins! Being a cartographer's *fils* had given him refinement and education. I opened the door and there was a shepherd's repast: bread, butter and conserve, milk and a pot in which I discovered a most restorative *tisane*.

I concluded from the note and the meal that despite the daring of my kiss last night, the planets were this morning undisturbed. I was overwhelmed with relief and despair in equal measure. I could not bear to see him. I turned the page over and scratched out a reply.

I will be writing from my bed all day today. Leave refreshments as before.

I posted it back under the door and returned to my bed to eat and write. If I was to be the next Monsieur Molière, I would need to make serious purchase before I slumped back

to sleep. But slump I did, shortly thereafter, upending my ink
pot all over the bed linen.

I woke again much later to find Mister Kryk had come and
gone unnoticed. My chamber was tidy, the offending ink pot
removed to a safer place along with my quills and paper. He
had left water in which to bathe, straightened my bedclothes
as well as he could given the lump that lay there, and had left
another small meal.

It concerned me that this was how we would be from now
on. It was untenable. For one, I would never be able to dress
in anything other than my nightclothes.

I would have to dismiss him. He could go to Arles or Orange
or as far as Lyon. He would easily find employment there – he
was handsome, educated and utterly discreet. The perfect
valet. I knew just the gentleman to take him on. I would tell
Mister Kryk in the morning. Or get Hortense to do it. That
might be better.

I fell asleep again and woke the next day to a tempest of light
as someone pulled back my drapes. I pretended to sleep but
eventually, inquisitiveness got the better of me.

'Monsieur, I have laid out your blue and gold linen and your
new one too so that you might choose.'

'Oh. Yes. On reflection, I think neither. Something darker I
think, less fussy. I will be writing here all today.'

'Home, all day?' Even as he said it, he realised his indiscretion. 'I apologise, Monsieur. Only I remembered you were due
at your cousins' this afternoon.'

'No. Do not apologise. You are right to be surprised. And
I was due, but we will send a note explaining my poor health.
For as you see, I am a reformed man. I may have had a good
deal of wine the other night, but I intend to dedicate myself
to writing this whole month. And Mister Kryk, I should like
to impress upon you *just how much wine I had.*' I tried to say this

slowly and most deliberately so that in hindsight he must have considered that my speech had been permanently harmed after my night of excess.

'I have already laid out your desk and, if I may, I will go and fetch you some new quills and ink to replenish the ones you have.'

He seemed even more focused and attentive than usual, which it hardly seemed was possible. It was as if he was more interested in supporting my quest to become Molière than I was. It crossed my mind that, in light of what had passed, he feared for his position. Given my resolution the previous night, he was probably correct. I was cruel, I knew it; of course he would not go anywhere.

He returned the clothes he had brought out for me and returned with a perfectly sober ensemble, positively monkish.

I let my eyes drift to his mouth. I could not help myself and immediately lost my hearing. I cannot describe it beyond that. Even the haziest and most impaired memory of our kiss raised my blood. I pulled the heavy bedclothes up around my loins.

'On reflection, let me rest a few minutes longer, alone, and then you may help me dress for the day's work.'

20

A Debt

My scribe and I have had a conversation which bordered on the disagreeable. She feels that Mister Kryk is more and more the object of my lusty gaze and little else. What a notion. She is not telling this story, I am. It is mine to tell. The scribe's job is to be in service to the story and this story is mine. It is not for her to interfere and, quite apart from anything else, anyone would be delighted to be mentioned in such flattering terms.

Against all expectation, including my own, the next few weeks passed in a happy haze with my pen. I was encouraged by my new routine, which involved rising early, dressing for the day and going straight to my desk, which my perfect valet would have already laid out for me. I taught him to sharpen my quills properly and he was sent back and forth to retrieve ink. I showed him how to make it with soot from the fire should we run short.

So strange and deep was my immersion in my work that he began to fall to the background. My first thought on rising was not to arrange myself artfully on the pillows, eyes shut, and await his arrival (for this is the madness that I had succumbed to, I still blush to remember it), but rather my mind was immediately upon the progress of my work. I had included a musketeer in my new story. He was a perfect balance of opposites: masculine prowess and refinement, action and reflection, elegance and adventure, seduction and restraint.

I modelled him after myself. Naturally.

Mister Kryk would come and go from my chamber – beautiful, subtle – and I viewed him now with the endless and familiar sadness that I had rehearsed so well over the years. That solitary desolation that is akin to being separated from God.

It was in the middle of my misery that something quite unusual occurred. Mister Kryk came to me at my desk. An unusual event as I was not to be disturbed except at appointed hours. He was agitated, which for him amounted to no more than a slight twitch around the eyes and a restlessness with his hands. He had removed his cap and clutched it in front of him.

'I am sorry to disturb you, Monsieur.'

'You do disturb me.' It was hot, I was weary.

'I must beg your indulgence. It is most important.'

'What is it? Is it my sister?'

'No, sir. It relates to ... It relates to my family.'

'Your family? Oh. It never occurred to me you had any.'

'Yes, sir. And normally I would not ask, but I must beg for this afternoon off. I must see a man who will take money to my mother, who is unwell.'

'Ah. Oh, but of course.'

He handed me a letter. 'My brother writes that she is ill and in light of, well, there is no money and I must send help. They must not incur a debt.' He said it so softly. 'Monsieur, this shames me. I apologise.' He bowed almost to his knees. 'I can arrange for Jean-Baptiste to attend to you this one afternoon, Monsieur. I will return by five in time for your meal.'

Seeing him there I was distracted by an unfamiliar sentiment in me, which was sympathy, or concern, nothing I had felt for him before. You must recall that a debt was a grave shame. My Molière had been lobbed into the debtor's prison over unpaid rent for a *jeu de paume court* in Paris. It was nearly the end of him.

'Stand up, stand up. Your mother is sick and it must be done. Can this man be trusted? How much do you send her?'

'100 *pistoles*. It is what I have for her.'

'Is it enough?'

'Yes, Monsieur.'

I knew it was not enough, given it would likely be a long while before he would have the opportunity to send more.

'Here is the letter. I am honest, Monsieur.'

I took it from him. He wanted me to read it.

Monsieur, please find here a letter from your mother that I have transposed to French, should you require it.

My sweetest child, my sweet Joe, I would not burden you with this news were it not so necessary. We have fallen on bad times since the passing of your father, as you know. All the help you give us is so well appreciated and without it we would surely be done for. I am unwell and the pain is much worse than when you last wrote. I require weekly visits to Dr Horst for bloodletting and tinctures. Edvard has written and by reply he learnt of my troubles and has assisted in some small way.

'What is Edvard's employment?'

'He is a tutor. Mathematics.'

'You are called Joe?'

'Yes, Monsieur. By those who know me.' He bowed his head as he said this. He may have blushed a little on his ears. All the angels in heaven. *My sweet Joe.*

I stood to go to my bureau. I doubt he knew what it held.

I unlocked the doors and reached into an inner drawer, unlocking it with a separate key, to retrieve one of the pouches hidden inside.

'Here. Take this. Make sure it gets to your mother. It is five hundred.'

'Monsieur, I could not.'

'I command you to.'

'Monsieur, I could not pay it back for many years.'

'You will not be paying it back. It is yours to take. A gift. And it is nothing. I have no mother so I will have to have yours. Is she kind?'

'She is the kindest woman there is. And courageous.'

'Would she like me as her son?'

'Monsieur, I am sure she would be most honoured.'

'You are a liar. She would think me vain. Just as do you.'

'Monsieur, never.'

'You are not wrong. I am both vain and stupid. Even my stories are ridiculous. A good and strict mother would perhaps have made a better man of me.' Unexpectedly, hot tears rose as I said it. My effort to blink them away was futile and he saw them fall. I wished he would hold me, I wished for some harbour.

'Monsieur, I apologise. I have intruded where I should not have.'

'The apology is mine. I have been unguarded and now you are uncomfortable. Please, take the money.'

'I apologise for the shame I have brought.'

'The shame is mine. I buy rose-coloured plumes for my hat and all the while your mother is ill and you are in distress. I had not even thought you had a family. That is how vain I am.' I handed him the pouch. 'Take it and we will not speak of this again. From now on, you will also have double wages on the assumption that half goes to your family. Then you will still have yours to enjoy.'

'Sir, I cannot thank you enough. My family is forever in your debt.' He came to me, took my ink-blotched hand in both of his, bowed down and with the smallest of hesitations, kissed my signet ring. My heart was in chaos, my tears still wet on my cheeks and now this, a perfect kiss. But of filial gratitude, servitude? I could not bear to speculate. I was exhausted by it all.

He straightened up to look directly at me, unblinking.

'Monsieur, I am forever your servant.'

'I will never speak of it. And nor must you.' My voice had all but evaporated. A whisper. Not of conspiracy but of defeat.

'Yes, Monsieur. Thank you, sir.'

'Might you be back by six?'

'Much earlier if I am quick.'

'Be quick then. And send Jean-Baptiste.'

21

Reasons to Whip
a Footman

A few weeks later and after many hours scratching pen across paper, I felt *The Lonely Jester* was ready for my sister's salon. The satisfaction was enormous.

I knew I had written a good story and I was sure Hortense would be proud. I would send it to her to read and then have it returned to me that I might practise reading it out loud before the salon. I tied the pages up quickly, but in my haste I did not, as I usually would, take care to number each folio. It was a risk – dear as she was, my sister had a habit of throwing pages to the ground one by one as she read, with no concern that someone would later have to rearrange them into their correct order. Bobo used to assist me and he was very good at it. Only once did he make a mistake, resulting in my chevalier mounting a pretty horse to visit his lady love at the end of one page and, according to Bobo's new ordering, on the very next whispering wicked suggestions into his mare's ear and stroking her flaxen mane suggestively. I know how surprised I was to read of it and can only speculate as to how the mare received these advances. The chevalier's human love made no return for another three pages.

The footman disappeared with the bundle of pages, with

strict instructions to wait until they had been read and to
return again that evening. If Hortense found any of it jarred
or was not good enough, she would write a note and attach
it to the top with her suggestions. I used to sit with her as she
read, but the torture of watching her face go from a smile to
a frown, and then a deeper frown, was so excruciating that I
would end up quarrelling with her and she would then refuse
to read further, saying I should not ask for her opinion if I was
not brave enough to hear it. This happened so often that we
agreed that her reading it alone was a better option.

I was weary after the endless days and nights of effort and,
the days being warm, I spent much of the morning talking to
my gardener, who was planting another very smart hedge, and
in consultation with Monsieur Benoit about what he might like
to try for the kitchen. It was happy distraction and I remembered for a while how well I like the sun on my skin.

In the evening, I heard the footman arrive and I was ready
for him in the entrance.

'You have it?'

'Yes, Monsieur.'

'And a note from my sister with it?'

'Yes, Monsieur.'

'Good, give it over then.'

He looked strangely reticent.

'Here, Monsieur.'

The bundle he handed me was unrecognisable. The pages
were frayed and torn, the topmost, which showed my sister's
note, was brown with mud.

'What in God's name is this?'

'Monsieur ...'

'Did you do this?'

'Monsieur, I tripped up and could not stop it from falling.'

'How did you trip up? Who were you distracted by?'

'No one, I was distracted by no one.'

'You imbecile. Look at this. It is weeks of work, weeks of work and you ruin it in moments.' I could feel my temper begin to overwhelm me. It was all I could do to stop myself beating the lackey right there. 'Monsieur Benoit? Come at once!' I caught myself bellowing the last, which was not considered good form. Monsieur Benoit came quickly, followed by an alarmed Mister Kryk.

'Monsieur Benoit, see what this pathetic boy has done to my manuscript.' I waved the pile of rumpled pages at the chef. 'Ruined, filthy, torn.' I turned back to the footman. 'Are all the pages here?'

'Yes, sir.' He was cowering. It annoyed me further.

'How do you know?'

'I did not leave any behind.'

'If it were not beneath me, I would whip you right now. This is my work. Do you understand? It is my work, days and nights of it! Monsieur Benoit, you will take a horsewhip to this useless laggard 'til he bleeds. I should clean my spurs on your balls, you useless fen-sucker!'

'Yes, Monsieur.'

'Halfwit!' I shouted. 'You will be beaten and you will deserve each strike, but what will become of this? What?' I lifted some of the pages. They were all, without exception, creased or torn, the ink had run on many of them and there was no telling what order they were in. I felt my spirit leave me, my voice had gone too. 'It is ruined,' I gasped.

'Sir, I will fix it. Please do not whip me.'

'How will you fix it? You cannot even read.'

I handed the bundle to Monsieur Benoit. 'It is no use. You may dispose of it in the fire.' I wanted to weep and as my face began to burn hot, I turned away, heading for my *salon*. 'Bring a carafe and my pipe.'

Devastation. Weeks of work and nothing to show for it. My sister's salon was a week away and I had nothing to read. She would have to cancel it of course. It would be humiliating for her.

The wine arrived and was poured. Once the door had closed and I was again alone, I poured myself another more sensible and medicinal measure. Nothing was going quite as it should. The whole lengthy misery over Mister Kryk had exhausted me to a point of high anxiety. I had tried to retreat into my work and literally ended up in the dirt. I could do no more. My despair was complete. With no hope of finding solace in love or work, only wine remained. I drank deep and it went down very well. I inhaled long and slow on my pipe and my chest eased. I had finally failed and perhaps there was some relief that came with that. I was alone and any hope of proving my worth to Molière was by now fuelling the fire, warming the toes of the scullery maids. I had another measure and with it allowed myself a great whimpering exhalation of tears. I was beyond redemption.

My scribe here accuses me of melodrama. I could not help it. It was a dark, dark hour and she well knows the tears she has shed for similar defeats. I wept not only for the lost pages but also for my desperate loneliness, the cruelty of my love being placed in front of me and yet not being able to have him. This madness was the punchline to some vicious comic mockery and I was suffering it daily.

22

He Dies

I do not remember falling asleep but woke at some strange and even darker hour. The fire had been refreshed and I was under my favourite banyan. A large carafe of water had been left too. That would have been my Eternal Beloved. He was so considerate that it was no wonder I could misinterpret it as affection. He could break my heart just calling for my chamber pot to be refreshed.

It was a miserable waking. Yet again I resolved to stay off wine. I drank all the water and decided I would sneak along to the kitchen to see what I could find there to eat.

You may all find this peculiar, but there was hardly any reason for me to walk through certain areas of the *maison* at night, or indeed at all. So to steal along to the kitchen left me feeling as though I was an intruder. I realised how much darkness the halls and rooms could hold. The corridor was lit by candles, but they had sunk low. They reached high without even the smallest suggestion of light and all the furniture lay barren, like boats on a great cold sea waiting for passengers who never came.

The kitchen was large enough to hold all the staff at work and had two antechambers and additional rooms and cupboards, dry larders, wet larders and on and on. This on the left for pastry, that to the right for mixing tinctures and infusing wine. I made it my business to know very little about all of this except that I always appreciated what it produced. Monsieur Benoit, the maids, the lackeys and so on all had rooms that lay out the back of the kitchen along a deep corridor. The girls all slept together and the boys shared a space too. Mister Kryk had his own cot away from them all, as the incident with Marielle attested. Setting the valet apart from the others, even in his sleeping quarters, oftentimes made him the subject of some abuse from the rest of the staff. Combined with easy access to and personal attention from their master, a valet was prone to ideas above his station. It was a common topic of discussion where staff were concerned: the problem with valets.

As I approached the kitchen door, I noticed that there was good light coming from under it though no sound could be heard. After a small concern about unattended candles, it crossed my mind that the silence was a good thing – I could not bear another vulgar encounter involving lusty lackeys or, heaven forbid, the impressive corpulence of Monsieur Benoit going about some intimate business with nothing but a jar of pomatum. I felt quite ill suddenly, but a cautious ear to the keyhole still revealed no sound and I felt bold enough to push the door open.

Mister Kryk leapt to his feet almost as I came through the door. He was shocked to see me.

'Monsieur, I thought you were asleep!'

'You thought I was drunk.'

He said nothing but appeared sheepish. I let my eyes fall to what was in front of him. Across the table, in neat rows up and down, were the remains of my manuscript, *The Lonely Jester*.

'What is this?'

He looked panicked.

I could feel a dreadful sickness in my stomach. 'Did you steal it to read?'

'No, Monsieur, no. I meant to mend it.'

'I wanted it burned. I gave orders.'

'Yes, Monsieur.'

'I do not follow, Mister Kryk. And as you can see, I am a little weary.' It occurred to me that he had seen me looking drunk and in partial undress a good deal. It was no wonder he found me repulsive.

'Monsieur. I apologise. I should not have read your manuscript without your permission. I should not have.'

I was suddenly overwhelmed with exhaustion. I went to sit at the table across from him. 'No, you should not have.' My head was thunderous.

'Only, you have been so kind to me, and my family, and when I saw the state of the papers, I knew I could repair them. My father was a cartographer and I was often charged with cleaning the page where there had been a mistake or the ink had run.'

This was interesting. 'Tell me more.'

'I knew that if I could make out the words where the pages were dirtied and torn, I could write them back in, even do so to resemble your own hand. I had a notion I could leave the manuscript at your door for you to discover in the morning, without knowing who had done it. Once you had seen it, you may still choose to throw it on the fire, but at least you would have a choice.'

'I have known you for months and you have spoken in the last minute more words than in all those months placed end to end.'

He bowed his head. 'But, Monsieur, please, look at this page. See how well it has come out.'

He handed me a grubby page. Some of my words were original and intact and then where the ink had ruined or run out entirely, he had inserted in careful mimicry of my own hand the missing words.

'Ah, well, here is the work of a magician. This is stupendous.'

I looked up at him. Quite uncharacteristically he was smiling.
I felt a warmth spread from my heart all across my chest and
into my head.

'Monsieur, if you will please come around to this side you
will see what I have done. I have not got as far as I hoped but
if you could help me, I can make a quick job of it.' *Dieu.*

I went around to him. He was pointing out this page and
that, explaining how this page was nearly done and that one
was going to be very difficult.

'Mister Kryk, you are most enterprising. I am beyond
pleased.' I was instantly energised by his enthusiasm and the
urge to embrace him in shared delight was immense. 'Shall we
get food and more candles and set about it then?'

'Yes, Monsieur. Are you not weary?'

'No! I am reborn. Some cheese and cakes might complete
the resurrection. Can you see what Monsieur Benoit has left
for me?'

He went off. He had laid out the pages as best he could, but
I could tell a few were out of order and I rearranged those. He
had cut himself a quill as I had taught him and had made a
good pot of ink to help in his work.

I sat examining how his hand had gone over the pages,
how he scratched his mark over mine, squinted at the ob-
scured words and tried to make sense of them, one at a time,
deliberately and, I hoped, with tender care. I noted that the
blotting was to the left of the script, not the right. Could he be
a left-handed man? Almost as scandalous as sodomy and often
equated. One who uses their devilish hand must be degenerate
in all manner of ways. It only made me love him more. That
he carried this secret with him as I carried my own. That we
two were not made to fit the world as it was constructed about
us and were forced constantly to make adjustments so that we
might not be discovered and shamed.

I heard him return and a plate was placed on the far side of the table.

'Thank you. You have done a most excellent and careful job. Truly. I cannot say how pleased I am for the attention you have given.'

'I was pleased to do it, Monsieur.'

'Come. Let us sit together and work through it.'

We worked without stopping. He reached across, with his right hand, and rearranged the pages as I found them misaligned. As he read out the lines, I replaced missing words from memory and he scratched them in. Candles were burned and replaced over and over, the ink was replenished and slowly each page came out of the shadows.

'We are missing the last two pages,' I said.

'There were no more.'

'He claimed he retrieved them all before they scattered away but I knew even as he said it, it was not true. The fact of a great hoof print across the back of at least three pages suggests he was not as quick as he would like me to believe. Those pages had sat in the road long enough for at least one horse to ruin them further.'

Mister Kryk chuckled at this.

'You enjoy this work, Mister Kryk.'

'Yes. It was my childhood.'

'I forgot to eat.'

He handed the forgotten plate to me.

'Here, Monsieur.'

'Where is yours?'

'I, well, I did not think to bring one.'

'You must. Fetch one at once. We have worked hard and are not yet done.'

Now, in some households of, shall we say, less discernment, it was quite customary for the servants and the family to eat together. Not so in my household nor any of those I knew. To eat with one's servants was unacceptable, an awkward blurring of the boundaries leading the servant into confusion over his status. I was committing a significant faux pas. But what of it? It was at some dark hour between dinner and morning, we were alone, and I felt nothing but easy friendship after the levelling function of shared work. Why should we not eat together too, to celebrate our labour?

He returned, a little sheepishly, with a plate of much more modest fare and in more meagre proportions than mine, indicating most subtly that he understood his place even if I had forgotten mine. Again, he upstaged me with his subtlety.

'It is a pity we do not have the last two pages, but they can easily be written again. You have done me a huge service. And my sister, who would have had to cancel her salon.'

'Yes, Monsieur.'

'How is the cake? Monsieur Benoit makes very good sweets.'

'Very good.'

The sudden realisation of our casual proximity seemed to have made him awkward.

I patted a page. 'Yes. I am most pleased.'

A horrible silence fell. Suddenly we were a master and his servant eating cake and staring at a table of pages in the middle of the night. Centuries of convention meant that neither of us had the language nor the gesture to navigate that wide and treacherous sea.

'How does it end?'

'What?'

'The story. I do not know how it ends.'

'Oh.'

'I am sorry, Monsieur. I have intruded.'

'No, no, you have not intruded. I should have thought. You have worked so well to resurrect these characters and you should know their fate. You already know that the jester is isolated, he likes to make riddles about islands and towers. He is in love with the queen but cannot speak it, obviously.'

'What happens to the jester?'

'He dies.'

'Why?'

'Because the jester is a poet and the poet must always be the one to die,' I said.

'Why?' He seemed unsettled by this.

'He knows the truth.'

'The truth is a good thing.'

'Ah, but if you are the poet, it will kill you.'

Our eyes met. And for the merest grain of a moment, I felt I was falling away from myself and into a well of cool, cool water. He looked down at the table again.

'Let us continue, Monsieur. We can finish before morning.'

'Yes. Let us continue.' Oh, I was in shifting sands again.

We worked together, with shared energy and intention, until the manuscript was completed. In the end, only four pages had to be physically reconstructed, by neatly securing each torn page onto a fresh sheet.

'How do you know how to do that?'

'My father owned a vicious cat. She would claw at his charts and walk her dirty paws across his freshly inked pages.'

'Why didn't he just get rid of the cat?'

'He loved her.' He looked surprised that I had even suggested the cat be dispatched. I felt a brute for mentioning it.

'It is done.'

'Yes, Monsieur. It is. I will fetch some ribbon to secure the pages.'

'It was good of you to add page numbers.'

He went to find the ribbon. Our hours together were over. I would climb the stairs to my bedchamber and he would return to his cot and the next day it would be as if we were never even here.

He set about wrapping the pages together.

'I will leave a note for Monsieur Benoit that you need not be disturbed tomorrow morning,' I said. 'A deep sleep has been earned.'

'Thank you, Monsieur.' He handed me the precious bundle. 'Here it is.'

'Well.'

'Yes, sir.'

'I will retire now.' I did not know what else to do, let alone say.

'I will get your light.'

'Oh, you need not. You are weary and I can make my own way.'

'Yes, Monsieur.'

Did I sense that he felt rebuffed? I had meant to be accommodating, only perhaps I had denied him his duties.

'Good night. Thank you for your labours.'

'Yes, Monsieur.'

It occurred to me that I had never wished him a good night before and it seemed an awkward parting, but it was too late to retract it. I turned and as I walked over the threshold of the kitchen and out into the corridor, I knew that he was gone and my heart broke again.

23

Oh, Holy God

As expected, the rest of the week passed as if our candlelit night had never happened. I played it over and over in my head, trying to remember every word that was spoken, every moment of shared involvement. Mister Kryk arrived in my chamber each morning with the same punctual calm as ever. He never mentioned the story, the kitchen, the cake. I could not decide if this was a result of discretion or awkwardness. Possibly it was both.

The day of Hortense's salon approached and she reported that everyone of quality and discernment was attending. She was in a flutter of excitement, had a new dress to wear and even The Toad was showing signs of looking forward to the night. Monsieur Benoit and my girls had been sent over to help with the preparations.

I too was greatly anticipating the salon, though I should temper this by adding that I had not slept for the preceding two nights and had practised reading my tale out loud so often that I feared I might lose my voice entirely. I also took to performing it to myself in front of my cabinet, as the mirrored panels helped me to realise when I was being awkward or was prone to strike an unflattering pose, which was often.

I kept the manuscript safely locked in my bureau, but on the morning of the salon I took it out, ready for the evening.

I called Mister Kryk earlier than usual, as I wanted to be at my sister's on time and had taken what I felt amounted to an audacious decision.

He brought the shaving tray and began to warm the balsam.

'I have added neroli to your oil today.'

'Good. Good. But before you begin, in relation to our work the other night, I have something to share with you.'

He stood upright from the tray, prim, hands at his side. I had a horrible moment when I thought that perhaps *he* thought I was about to give him some coins, payment for the work on the manuscript. It had never occurred to me to do so.

'Yes, Monsieur?'

'Well, nothing, well it is not substantial. It is ...' My command of language was dissipating fast. 'I have completed the story again. I thought you might like to hear how it ends.' I hardly spoke the last aloud.

'Yes, Monsieur, I would.'

I instantly regretted having said it but was now committed.

Reader, do you understand my motivations? I do not.

I would normally have stood to perform the piece, but feeling no wind in my sails and the immense silence in the room around me, I took my place on my chaise.

My hands were shaking and I felt a nauseating clammy heat rising around my temples. *Pardieu*, he must have thought I was infected with an ague.

He sat on the floor a few feet away, leaning forward on his knees in polite attention. His effort to appear interested made it all the worse. My instinct told me to feign choking or even a faint so that he could leap to action and I could escape the whole miserable scenario. I was too confused and upset even to think how to do it elegantly and instead, trembling like a lamb before the chopping blade, I started to read the last pages. '*The Fool, though he was the greatest Fool in all of Foolery, understood that greatest in all of* comédie *was to love another who would never see him without his mask and bells, without his exceptional Foolery . . .'*

I read right through and managed to lose myself in the words, so that I feel I may have even delivered them with some dignity, in spite of my trembling.

'*Fin.*'

'Monsieur, he lives.'

'Yes.'

'You gave him reprieve.'

'I did.'

He looked pleased.

'I felt that perhaps the truth should not be a death sentence. The pyres have had enough fuel these years.'

'Yes, Monsieur.'

'Of course, it will not be taken seriously.'

'No, Monsieur?'

'No. For literary work to be taken seriously it must involve gallows and pyres. It was ever thus and I daresay will be for hundreds of years hence.'

'I prefer that he lived.'

'Yes. He survived the truth. We will see how they like it tonight.'

'Yes, Monsieur.'

'Now, I must have my shave.'

He stood quickly, bowed a little, and then went to my toilette and began to mix the oil again. I sat and let him cover me with cloth. If it was possible, he seemed even quieter than usual. Bobo would have been jabbering away like a chicken looking for scraps.

'Please set your head further back, Monsieur. Thank you.'

The oil was fragranced and warm and he rubbed it across my beard and face. It was a comfort simply to shut my eyes against the world for a few moments. I regretted reading him the new end. It was an uncalled-for encroachment. My scribe here suggests I am too harsh a critic of my decisions, that even she might find herself in love with a man who helped fix a manuscript that she thought was lost. She is kind to try and console me, but in truth, the familiar emptiness began to rise. I resented it on this night when I needed to be confident, brimful of voice and verve. Solitude is never the worst in times of misery – one is already miserable. Rather it is the inability to share one's joys and triumphs with anyone that exposes one's solitary way in the world. One's quotidian glories, if left unwitnessed, become meaningless. This is the cruellest cut.

I could hear him preparing the blade.

'To the left first, please, Monsieur.'

I turned my face from him. The bristles gave but small resistance as they stood prime before the blade, sliced through. Water fell like blood along my face and down my jaw to my neck and into the cloths, warm and slow. This was the favoured time for servants to kill their masters. Many more masters were killed by their servants than the other way around. One is in complete and virgin surrender as the blade is stropped and swiped around one's throat. It might not be the worst end, and one worth considering.

Mister Kryk completed the one side and instructed me to turn again, this time to my right. In so doing my face turned towards his chest. Through the oil I could still smell his familiar scent. Where it was usually a torture of delight, in my misery and the exhaustion the last week had produced, it was rendered simply comforting. His hands worked neatly but slowly across my cheek and neck. He had a habit of running his still-oiled fingers warmly across the skin he had just cut, to soothe its surface.

Around my mouth he was always careful and precise in order to make the shape I favoured, but was even more

deliberate than usual for tonight's performance. He understood the importance of the occasion. He leaned in so close, so
immediate. My eyes stayed closed in supplication to his blade.

Then, I felt his fingers lift from my chin for less than a
moth's breath and, as lightly as was ever possible, touch and
then trace the outline of my lip above. I opened my eyes. His
fingers retracted. His face was as close as it could be without
touching. He did not move. I could feel the heat of his body.
Our eyes locked. I could not move, staked through with his
gaze. I tried to speak but could not. He then lifted his fingers
back up to the side of my mouth and kissed me, once, slowly.

Oh, Holy God. I flinched – not for anything but exquisite
agony – but it made him immediately retreat a moment, lifting
his lips from mine.

'Mister Kryk?'

'Monsieur.' He had lost his voice and he was shaking, from
fear or emotion I could not tell.

'You may repeat the process. Especially the last.'

He did. And I, underneath the cloths, burning and yet
strangely immobile, as if each touch of his mouth delivered
another drop of some divine opiate. I had dreamt of it so often
that in order to absorb its sublime reality, I seemed only to
be able to feel it through a veil. My hand reached to his hair.
How I had longed to touch it, take it between my fingers, let
it curl around.

He pulled back a moment. His breath was shallow. His heat
was up and I reached with hand and mouth and pulled him
back to me. He felt me quicken too and his mouth became
more vital. Then he bit me, by design or accident I cannot say,
and I near fainted from the charge it sent through my yard. I
could hardly breathe.

'Mister Kryk, you are eager.'

'I cannot help myself, Monsieur.' He had pulled away the

cloths and had his hands and mouth all down my neck and chest. *Nom de Dieu*, was it real?

Suddenly a great rumpus from the entrance – dogs, hooves.

'My carriage. Dear God.' I stood up with haste, done and undone all at once. 'Quick, I must dress.'

'Yes, Monsieur.' His lips were red and he had the look of someone rudely roused from the deepest slumber.

'There, the other chaise, my clothes, the rest is there too.'

'What? Monsieur?'

'You have forgotten where you are.'

'Yes.' He seemed to have forgotten his own name too.

He was completely rooted. He was dumbstruck. I went quickly to him and grabbed him to me and let my hands run the length of his back, trying to feel the shape of his body underneath the livery and all the while kissing him with acute desire. I felt not tenderness as I had earlier but overwhelming, raging lust. I should like to demur, naming it otherwise, but that is all it can be called.

The bell sounded. The carriage would soon be ready to depart. Confounded swines! I had been in an agony for months, I had my answer and now, I must arrest my love for a fat, impatient carriage-driver. (They are always fat.)

What followed was an exuberant chaos as both he and I tried to get me clean of oil, into my clothes and sufficiently buttoned to make my way downstairs.

'Is it front ways on?'

'No, no it is the other way, Monsieur.'

'Look what you have done to me.'

'I, yes, I am sorry, Monsieur.'

'Never be sorry. Only this is still facing about ways.'

'Oh.'

'Might I see you later? In this manner, the manner of what has passed?' I said it and then thought I should not have.

'That will depend on you, Monsieur.'

'Then, please ... Oh, wait, lace this quickly, Mister Kryk, if you might.' I had suddenly lost my language. I only had words of command for him. *Come here, go there, leave me now, never leave me again and let me have all of you naked and breathless.* Despite loving him from afar for months, I did not have a romantic word I knew how to use with him.

'Monsieur, you are ready to go.'

'I assure you, I am more than ready to go, Mister Kryk.'

This made him smile with ridiculous honesty. Oh, he was so sweet to do it and with the panic and fever we had both felt, I know he too would feel the burn of this intimacy.

'I must leave you now.'

'Yes, Mister Kryk.'

He was ill at ease. He bowed slightly, as was his custom, before he left me and was gone.

Against all logic and circumstance, I remembered to take my manuscript from its place and made my way down. Quite apart from the dreadful discomfort I had from not finding any release, my entire body felt unfamiliar. My mouth was dry, my hand damp against the pages they held. It turns out that love does not make you immortal, rather it renders you a terrible and uncomfortable assortment of most unfamiliar symptoms.

By the time I reached the door (perfect early-evening light, long shadows, a light breeze to cool the persistent heat, birdsong, a thrush, a robin, oh, I shall never forget it), my two lackeys and Mister Jonathan Kryk were waiting in a neat row. Mister Kryk had on his cap and wore the brim lower than usual, avoiding my face. The driver (who was indeed a dreadful man), was muttering something about tardiness. I shot him an imperious look to tell him I had heard it and was not impressed with it. I resolved to release him from his duties.

24

Tonight, I am Immortal

To my sister's. And all the way burning with tremendous passion and anticipation, knowing that just through the carriage, next to the driver, sat the man who had kissed me not moments before. I cannot even say the road we took, I saw nothing and cared only that this dream might continue.

The night was perfect. The skies were clear and warm, carriages came one after the other to the entrance and soon I was moving though rooms swaying and shifting with swathes of plumes, silk and gold, silver and jewels, all shining and glowing. Music floated through the air and glasses were filled and refilled. I felt in myself a desperate, frightening sense of hope that I never dared to dream of before.

I found Louise, my sister's lady.

'Make sure my valet is allowed into the salon for my reading. He may stand at the back to hear the proceedings.'

'Monsieur?'

I made it clear that her question was impertinent. A disparaging flick of a glove does wonders to remove unwanted persons from your proximity.

'It is my instruction to you. He saved the manuscript from ruin after an accident. He should hear it read.'

'Yes, Monsieur.'

Hortense looked perfect, if a little flushed.

'Oh, Brother! You are late. Isn't it lovely? It is going so well.'

'A night already better than either of us could have imagined.'

'Look at you, my love.'

'What is the matter with me?'

'Nothing, only you look a little bright. And you are in your own hair.'

'Ah, yes, well . . . I did think to wear a nice piece, but you see, my dear, tonight I am not the Marquis de Baudelaire, rather I am but a humble scribe. I thought a piece might be immodest.'

'Oh, you are so, so dear and thoughtful. And what sweet humility. I adore you.' She kissed my cheek. I am quite sure I had never received so many kisses and professions of love as I had in the past few hours. 'Now, Brother, I must leave you and attend to our guests. I might enjoy another cup on the way. If you can bear it, there are two sisters standing near one of our uncle's *confidentes*. If you make a fuss over them, the little spy is sure to report back to Uncle and you will be immediately in his good books.'

Hortense was as ever the consummate hostess. She always knew who was standing near whom and of what they spoke. If someone so much as blinked too slowly she would whisk them away and find them more stimulating company before they even knew they were tiring of the last. She was so gracious and kind in a way I never could be, lacking as I did any of her patience. Even The Toad was civil and managed to say that he looked forward to hearing my tale. It was a lie of course, but I was pleased that he had said it.

'My dear, it is now time for your story,' said Hortense with the sweetest squeeze of my hand although given she had begun to sway a little it was possible she required a little anchoring herself.

'I am ready.'

'You must not be nervous.'

'I am not. Tonight, I am immortal.'

'Silly. Come now, I will get the musicians to call everyone together.'

It was true. I felt immortal. I delivered my performance perfectly and on taking my bow to the assembled guests and great applause, I spied Mister Kryk in the darker recesses of the room. I was desperate that he had been impressed too and would feel some pride at his part in the proceedings. I sought his face again through all the fans and plumes flapping back and forth, like a great flock of swans trying to break through the stifling air, but he had gone.

I was pleased with the crowd's generous reception, long hoped for. But as usual, unable to enjoy anything for more than a moment, I allowed my old anxiety to creep back in. In an effort to hide myself from potential entrapment, I retreated to a quieter corner. I shut my eyes and reprised the events in my chamber.

We had kissed, but what now? How would we be? Was I expected to make some demonstration to advance matters? I sensed I may to some extent be led by my baser nature rather than my ideals of love. And yet – and you will please recognise the humility it takes to admit this – despite my advanced years, I was not well-versed in the intricacies of what I longed for. Not in that way. This is not to say I had not imagined it. But my experience had not been wide. An unrepeatable encounter with a dastardly Italian in Marseille, years before, had rendered me chaste and terrified.

A valet had arrived in Avignon to attend to me. He was twenty years old and had been with me since the beginning of the year. He had a mother and a brother and his father the cartographer was dead. He had left Amsterdam for France and eventually landed in my household, but of his life before I knew nothing. Uncle Hippolyte thought him a spy.

His kiss had been unspeakably daring. He could have found himself already in the stocks for lewdness, for insubordination, for an entire catalogue of crimes and sins, and be banished from Avignon. The boldness in him had quite overcome me. For months I had calculated his everything; I was so minutely versed in how much space he occupied in a room (which was all of it), how light attached to him, air moved around him and how vast the void he left when he closed a door behind him. More than the exquisite sorcery of his kiss, I was ablaze with thoughts that he might think of me too, that he might dream of me as he lay sleeping, extend a hand across a lonely cot, hoping to find mine. With that came the rare and dangerous hope that he might hold me in his heart.

Was I the first man he had kissed so sweetly? It seemed possible and yet to look at him, his beauty and poise, the tenderness of his mouth, I felt there must have been others who loved him. Had he belonged to someone else?

'You have been avoiding me.'

'My dear, my heart, my exquisite comtesse. How radiant you look.'

'Yes, I do, which makes your avoidance all the more unforgivable. Or is it that I am so exquisite and so radiant that you simply cannot bear to be near me?'

'That exists as a very plausible possibility.'

'You have always been an excellent liar, though only a passable if brazen cheat.'

'I cannot deny it.'

'So, do you avoid me?'

'I do not. My mind is distracted. I apologise. Will you forgive me? I would never wish to hurt you.' I kissed her hand and her brow. 'I have of course been forced to keep a discreet distance from you. And I am still humbled by the disservice I did you.'

'Pssht. That is gone. And it was a trifle.'

She was ever my dearest friend. I felt quite suddenly that I may have betrayed her. Does one not tell one's dearest friends all the secrets of one's heart?

'What distracts you? Your theatre I expect. Your ambitions know no end.' She was so bright and playful.

'There is much to distract an old heart with a quick mind.'

'You talk in riddles.'

'Because it is a nothing.'

She frowned.

'Jehan, you cannot look at me. You blush like a boy. It is not nothing at all and furthermore, it is not what distracts you but whom.'

'Is it?'

'You know it is. And as your closest friend, I cannot but admit that I am suddenly flushed through with envy.'

She was. She was as I had never seen her. Gone was her playfulness, her jest, her flashing eyes and easy touch. In its place a multitude of confusion and something which I had not anticipated, given the nature of our involvement: she was hurt. I had been callous. It had not occurred to me, possibly stupidly, that she might feel slighted that I share affection with another. She had a ruddy-cheeked husband after all and nothing could become of us. She knew I would have to marry eventually and often suggested suitors for the role. As for Jonathan Kryk, she knew nothing of him.

'Will you say who she is?'

'I assure you there is no lady who distracts me.'

'Why do you demur? Do you deny that you are in love? Your bridegroom eyes tell me that you are.'

'I deny nothing.'

'Well. There is the rub. I see your sister. I will congratulate her, though I see that she is in her cups and will not remember my thanks in the morning.' With a swish of her skirts, somewhat too theatrically, she left me against the drapes. I did not appreciate her unkindness about Hortense, when clearly her anger was aimed at me.

Well after midnight, the upended day began to work its way to my bones. I may, in hindsight, have delayed my departure, for in truth I was somewhat unresolved as to what might occur next.

'Sister, I must leave you.'

'So soon?'

'It is not soon. You are the worse or the better for the wine and look quite ravishing for it.'

'I should like to be ravishing, my love, but I do not think there is anyone to produce the ravishment.'

'You do not imagine yourself in the grips of a lusty Toad?'

'Oh, you are awful.' She tapped my nose with her plume, wrinkling her own as she did.

'May I leave you? I will tell Louise to make sure you are kept from the cups until you are steady again.'

'Pfft.' She leaned on me a little. 'It was a triumph, yes? And you were quite sublime, my sweet.'

'I adore you.' I kissed her.

'And I you.'

'I will leave without mention.'

25

Thunderous Good

The relief of the fresh air. I allowed the night to wash over me. With my sister's festivities still a few hours from being over, the lackeys were caught somewhat off-guard and had to scramble to alert my driver and *postillion* to ready my carriage.

It was late by the time we returned home and, after we had parted at the door as was custom, Mister Kryk was nowhere to be seen. This was quite proper, since it was my custom that if I was home beyond a certain hour, I need not be attended. I found it tedious – Bobo could take a full hour to ready me for sleep – and preferred to simply slump to my bed. I simply kept up the habit with Mister Kryk, partly because if I was home so late it was likely I was also full of wine and vanity prevented me from allowing him to see me like that too often.

I sat in my *salon* a while, my thoughts hot and unruly, before turning to my bedchamber to sleep – if it were ever possible. Though the chambermaids had made efforts to reassemble the shaving tray and cloths, the room was still in some disarray. I lifted a cloth to my nose, inhaling the neroli scent. I lay down on my bed and closed my eyes. My entire body had become something I could no longer inhabit with any confidence or ease, its every sense alert to the faintest breeze or sound. A frog in Lyon could have pierced my ear with his song.

A familiar tap.

Dear God. I was on my feet in one.

'Enter.'

Never had I been more elated to see him come through the door bearing water and cloths for me. He put down the vessels and turned to me.

'Mister Kryk, I thought you had gone to your cot.'

He shook his head. Now, his eyes were on mine. I did not know what to say or how to be with him, in this audacious gaze. He took a step towards me and, instead of matching it, I retreated.

But I needed to be nearer to him. I only knew our usual ways together and so, after a good deal of self-chastisement and encouragement, I managed to approach his side. I stood, as I always did, straight-backed with arms slightly lifted out to the side, ready for him to undress me as he had done every night for torturous months.

Still his eyes did not leave mine.

He began his work. Collar, bands; with every button and fastening, my core shuddered so I felt I might lose my footing. I tried to rearrange myself to get myself free and so that I might inhale.

'Please, Monsieur. You must wait.'

I wanted to kiss his lips, take him to me. But he would have none and told me so by simply continuing to work his way along the rows of fastenings. At last, I was out and in my chemise; the relief of the air allowed me to try to breathe.

'Will you not have me?' I managed to whisper.

'No, Monsieur. It is you who will have me.' And with it his hands were in my clothes, around my waist, moving down my skin, which had found itself a new language for expression and it was the language of birds, winds, tempests. Such terror and excruciating delight as he then continued down to take me in his hand.

My delicate scribe is all but fluttering her fan and clutching at her choker as I tell her: there was *thunder* in his touch.

He was bold. Without releasing me he steered me to my bed, where I fell back. He took no time removing his own doublet and undoing himself below, that I might see what he had.

Oh, sinners, saints and all the heavens, I shall never forget it, a most prodigious gift.

Might you enjoy a description?

Ah. My scribe reminds me that my indiscreet narration is already entirely ungentlemanly and that it is not my place to offer details of other men's bodies, exquisite as they may be. I can reassure you that there is a good deal more ungentlemanly evocation to come, so let me continue at once.

Mister Kryk became more and more intent on his purpose. I wished to speak, felt I should, but knew nothing to say. I can admit now, and confidentially, that he was entirely my master. I no longer had language, had lost all natural control of my body, I simply allowed him to decide what would happen and how.

It was the most exquisite revelation. And I was terrified.

He was no longer the servant but the man I had seen in the market, the young charge lolling on the wall, cartwheeling down the lawn, at the kitchen table surrounded by inked pages. He was his full self. He smiled as he lunged at me with his mouth. He was beguiling and charming, easy and confident. It is possible he sensed my hesitation. I could not admit to my lack of courage, certainly not, but it is conceivable that despite my best efforts to appear assertive and assured, my inexperience may have betrayed itself.

His passion was mounting yet he allowed me to lie on him, to face him and see his pretty face (how lovely it was!) and feel him taut underneath me. He ran his hands along my back and bit my mouth like a young wolf teasing another. Oh, it burned me to rapture. Yet still, I felt I was being hesitant, even amid this longed-for love-making.

Suddenly the source of my apprehension became clear. If I was novice, then he was surely most practised.

It raised something akin to anger in me and so I wrapped my own hands around his yard and let him breach them until he was done. He did not suppress anything. He then sat across me, his one hand pinning mine above me as his other did its last with me, using his mouth to stifle my cry. After, we lay together, his face resting on my shoulder.

'Mister Kryk, I have no words.'

He lifted his head to kiss me. 'Oh, that was but the flint. We've still the fire to go.'

Dear *heaven*. This was surely witchcraft.

I tried to stay awake to let myself feel the bliss of this terrifying, perfect intimacy. It felt as if my life-long desolation had been banished for the first time. To sleep with the warmth of love and skin stuck to my own filled the human core, made replete the tempers, allowed them their full life and sustenance.

Outside: crickets, frogs, the rustlings of night. Surely comets traversed the sky that night, the moon held its phase, Venus herself forbade the stars to fall. There would be nights enough for that, but for this one divine chapter, the heavens desisted their usual antics allowing only we two to shine.

When I woke, he was gone.

As you will have gathered, easy intimacy and confidence in chambering were not my most apparent virtues. My mind was prone to filling in the spaces that I could not witness. In the time between waking and the relief of Kryk's footsteps along the hall, I had already imagined he had either run to report me, or would return to deliver a letter of blackmail, or had simply left, never to be seen again. Obviously, I could never let

THUNDEROUS GOOD   165

him know any of this and made sure to affect a casual recline among my bedclothes.

The drapes that surrounded and cocooned the bed were pulled back.

'Monsieur.'

The room seemed unreasonably bright and I uncommonly underdressed. 'Oh, ah, you are here.'

'I will prepare your bath for you.'

'Will you?' My resolve to be more confident in love-making was not going quite to plan. 'Or, a suggestion, you could assist me right here and in so doing go some way to fulfil your employ as this particular gentleman's gentleman.'

'Yes, Monsieur. I could.' His initial reserve gave way to a most wicked look.

'And I note that you call me Monsieur. That is not what you called me last night.' I was suddenly feeling impatient to have him.

'No, Monsieur, it is not.' He began to remove his collar, carefully, thoughtfully.

'Should you not latch the door?'

'I've already done that.'

'Oh?' I charged to hear it. 'What foresight. You would make a good soldier. In any skirmish, preparedness is all.'

'To that end, Monsieur, I have brought you this.' He placed down a small jar of pomatum.

'Well, then.'

With that he fell onto me and we resumed the previous night's play with great spirit and a venturesome exploration of one another.

I was a little bolder and more ready and soon felt myself needing a new conclusion, but hesitated. As he had done before, he anticipated my reserve, taking command. It was immensely stirring. He faced me, standing on his knees. His hands were so clever that I thought it might already be the end for me, but seeing this he slowed. I too hesitated, fearing my commodious passion now threatened to drown me and unsure how to proceed.

Sitting over me, he leaned forward to kiss me. 'You need only lie back. I will decide the rest.'

'If you insist, Mister Kryk.'

'Oh, I do.'

With word and hand he guided me in. (Oh, I died five times before I was halfway there.) I knew I could not be long, so good was the rush. His panting told me he did me great service, even as he chose the pace. I tried to reach for him as he rode but he refused me.

'Don't move.'

'I must.'

'Don't move.'

Then with what felt like a single swoop, he slid his hands under my back and grappled my waist to himself and he took me into him full. *Nom de Dieu*, it was bold and dangerous and thunderous good.

My mind was, for the first time in my life, wiped entirely clean. We lay awhile, he strangely curled in on himself but with his head resting on my shoulder so that I could cup his face in my arm, our faces near touching. I kissed his eyes. I would have had him no matter what, but, oh, he was so beautiful.

'I have longed for you all my life. Where have you been?'

'Waiting.' He bit my mouth and kissed me.

'Don't leave me.'

'I have duties. I must.' He sat up and swung off the bed. He looked so young with his cropped, light hair, no beard. I was relieved he had misinterpreted my pathetic plea, which might well have seen me throwing myself at his feet and whimpering that I would die without him.

'You are beautiful.'

His ready smile told me he was pleased, but he washed quickly and began to dress himself. As I watched him, I felt as if a ribbon of light connected my heart to his, my mind to his, my body to his. I felt I had known him for centuries, as if we were born under the same horoscope, our stars having long ago decided that we would find one another. It was always he who would arrive in Avignon just when Bobo took leave, he who would come through the door before the *jeu de paume* tournament. There could be no other who would be the most intimate in my household and it would always be he who would save my story and sit with me through the night until it was written. Every constellation had for eternity ordained that our fortunes entwine. There would never be anyone nor anything other than he.

'Might you come later?'

He nodded. 'This afternoon.'

'I will be here. When you are here, simply enter.'

'If you will allow me.'

26

My Father

All day I was in turmoil. I wrote my sister a note to thank her for the salon. Some notes of congratulation arrived for me in turn and at least two invited me to offer new stories at various evenings of entertainment. All of this was too rich an accomplishment for this same day. I must confess to being something of a quivering jumble. I slept too, and made some effort – which will surprise you, for it certainly surprised me – to arrange the disorder that seemed to have descended on my bedchamber. I knew it would be taken care of, but somehow I felt the chaos might betray me. To whom I cannot say. Doubt had set in. Guilt too, and she is a punitive mistress.

After washing, I thought I might walk to affect a degree of ease about myself, but it was too hot and my mind remained agitated beyond any reasonable calm. It being summer, a few minutes out in Avignon with the screaming cicadas and the pulsing heat of the day was enough to drive me half to madness. I had to retreat indoors to my seclusory room and the darkness it offered. It was the only remedy. Had I been a braver man, known what I now know, I would simply have sat in my chemise and breeches in my moss-covered fountain until I felt cooler and my mind was settled. But this would only invite rumour and worry.

Related to matters of propriety, my scribe and I have

discussed at length why I include private moments and lurid details in this tale of my time with Joe. I do so as they are the natural expression of our desire which, when properly respected, is a powerful aspect of our devotion. This *mémoire*, this secular confession, is one that will record all that could not even be named, let alone recorded. To tell it has taken nearly 370 years and there are those even now who will have it not spoken.

Additionally, we include it because it was precisely that expression that might lead to our demise. It was the act of our desire and our love that marked us out as demonic. Well then. The exact act of love that was then unspeakable, indescribable, will be the thing that is described to you here in breathless detail.

Notwithstanding this small sermon I have just delivered, I am also entirely aware that there are those who will take immense personal pleasure in the reading of these scenes and I would not wish to deprive a single one of you. After all, I so enjoy conjuring a feast. To this end, I will insist that my scribe offers a detailed index of all rumbustious coupling, tender kisses and other less specific moments so that you might easily find them again in these pages for a more intimate reappraisal.

Do not think that our conjugation was entirely without concern, that even in my impossible rapture I, a more secular man than most, did not feel the eyes of God upon me. Once I was alone again, Mister Kryk departed, I felt a heat rise, my neck began to prick, my breath uneasy. I reached for a glass, but my hand trembled so violently that I quickly replaced it.

And I saw it.

I saw myself, naked, a beastly collection of limbs and sounds, and I understood what had been done, that it was I who had done it – and he too. I saw its baseness, its crude wickedness.

I stood, as if that might dislodge the image. I returned to my bedchamber. I had not done enough to return it to order and cleanliness. The water that had been brought earlier was still there. I washed my face again and again and around my neck. I knew what was required.

I managed to get downstairs and beyond my *salon* unnoticed and thought to flee past the fountain again, across the courtyard and down the park to the gates. I knew that at this hour, with the heat as it was, the household would be slow and lazy. I would be near assured of a safe escape. I reached the gates to find my sentries half-asleep. I glanced left and right. Behind the great pillar, I spied one of my lackeys, his hand most deftly finding its way down the front of some girl's bodice. I must have made a noise trying to speak. He turned and looked to see me, rigid with fear; her face red and hidden.

'Monsieur . . .' He knew he would be whipped.

I looked at them, shame all across her body, exposed as if fully stripped in front of me.

'Monsieur, I am . . .'

I lifted my hand to silence him. 'I am going to Saint-Étienne to pray. I may be some time. I wish to go alone.'

He looked puzzled but I knew that had I not said it, duty would have compelled him to call someone to accompany me – and I could not have that.

My mind was broiling and unquiet as I made for the church. I can scarce remember getting there. I entered through the side door I always favoured, finding the main entrance too grand for a sodomite – not just that day, always. You may find my attitude to God a little out of step with the era and even then, this was apparent to me. I rarely attended on the Lord's Day for that seemed a day for sermons and public gathering, none of which suited me. Many, including my sister, attended not once but twice on that day and it was (another) constant source of concern that I was not seen ostentatiously seated near the pulpit in our family pew. If Uncle Hippolyte himself gave the sermon, he made great pains to show his offence, though in truth he did it rarely, preferring instead to burden us in our private chapels.

If I did attend a public mass, I would loiter about the back with the merchants and gamesmen. My regular companion was a man who kept a few pigs and a cow near the river. He made the journey twice a week with his two hounds and each time stood in the same place so that they might not cause offence. I found him very good company and a useful informant on things to do with crops and weather and any discontent that might be brewing.

My business in church had nothing to do with anyone but myself and my God. We had an awkward relationship, in the most part because I was not there to receive instruction from on high. Rather, I had, since a boy, used the time there, enforced upon me, to talk to my beloved, departed father, whose counsel and guidance I sought at every turn.

It was cool and dark inside Saint-Étienne, balm for an unquiet mind. I could feel my skin and heart cooling even as I knelt. I thought of my father, the prayer he had taught us in childhood. He would gather me and Hortense to him and we would all three kneel in a row before our bed, and he would say: 'Be still. And know God. Let nothing and no one intrude on the sanctity of this prayer. God alone knows the truth of your heart and he alone knows that you are loved.'

I could almost feel him now beside me, and my eyes began to brim with tears. 'Father, I have sinned, forgive me. I do not know who I am become nor how to find remedy.'

I stayed there and let the quiet settle across my shoulders and with it came the voice of silence.

'*Be still. And know God. God alone knows the truth of your heart and you are loved.*'

'My true heart loves whom it should not.'

'*God knows the truth of your heart and you are loved.*'

'I am a sinner and a criminal.'

'*You are loved.*'

It was my prayer, my answer and my absolution. My heart was known and loved and from that moment on, it was all that mattered. The sin was mine; it was known and I was loved by my father.

I wiped my eyes as subtly as I could, overcome and drained of any vigour. I crossed myself and stood.

Home. Even before I had removed my hat, Monsieur Benoit came clattering towards me along the hall.

'Monsieur Benoit.'

'Monsieur, are you well?'

'Quite well.'

'Your man was left worrying about you.'

'He should know better than to worry.'

I had not intended to be so short. Constant intrusion and the need to explain oneself even to one's household had always irked.

'He had thought you would be in your private rooms all this afternoon and not finding you there, he was concerned for you.'

'I went to pray.'

'Of course, Monsieur.'

'I should like to be left alone now. Have some wine and water left outside my room.'

'Of course, Monsieur.'

I felt I should say something to Monsieur Benoit that he could relay, something to comfort Mister Kryk – who, I now dared to hope, could be my Joe – but there was nothing I could think of. Language seemed to have become so insubstantial.

'Tell my man that he has done no wrong.'

I went to my seclusory, dark and comforting, church-like too, and cool. I knew Mister Kryk would be in terror by now, but I wished to remain as I was. Just for a moment. I stretched back in my chair, thought of his long back and how he had felt in my hands. I was stirred.

I felt the first great breath enter and exit my mouth almost at once and with it great and weary heaves of tears. The relief I had been seeking all these years was finally able to exist. It was the greatest exhalation I could remember, as if I had been holding my breath my entire life.

There was a tap at the door. I had asked not to be disturbed. I knew it would be him. I hesitated and wiped my face.

'Enter.'

He was wide-eyed and pale, holding a tray from Monsieur Benoit.

'Monsieur . . .'

'There is nothing the matter. Put down the tray.'

He did, closing the door, and then stood rooted in front of the wall, holding the *herbier*.

'I went to pray.'

'Alone, Monsieur?'

'Yes. That is the best way.'

'Because you had sinned?'

'Yes. No. I required some clarity.'

He was breathing light and shallow. 'Why turn to God when he will not have you?'

'I required solace. More than solace, understanding.'

'And what did you find, Monsieur?'

'I found that I am loved.'

'By your God?'

'By my father.'

He had straightened, perhaps to prepare for some blow. 'What does he make of me?'

'I have no hesitation in thinking he considers you very fine indeed.'

'And you, Monsieur, what's your opinion?'

'I am deeply, deeply enchanted.'

He smiled, through relief or joy I cannot say.

'I must rest now, but not because I wish to be away from you. Only when I am with you, I am over-agitated, as you might conclude.'

'Shall I attend to you later?'

'Yes.'

He bowed in his usual way. We had not yet found a middle register. He was either entirely supplicant or so far abandoned in the boldest of intimacy that he might be on the brink of death. And in all, it was not quite a full day since we had first kissed.

He looked as if he might come to me, wished to, but did not. He left and that was good.

27

The Prentice and
The Novice

The sun was down a full hour before he knocked at the door and I was by then long over my need for solitude. I had returned to the heights of virile anxiety.

He was hardly through the door when I grabbed him and pressed myself to him up along the wall, sending the tray he had brought crashing to the ground.

'You must be quieter,' he said, as his hands pulled away my chemise. 'We must not betray ourselves.'

'I cannot help myself.'

'You must.'

We made our play, my yard in his hands.

'Ssh. Quieter.'

He then, Oh Heaven, covered me with his mouth in a manner so torturous with delight that I thought I might be the next in line for immaculate conception.

Near delirious with pleasure, I had him in for the first time. He helped and coaxed as I tried to hold my voice, finding it hard to breathe. I was both drowning and floating. But when he eventually filled me full and hot, his hands and body pulled at me so desperately and, despite his own earlier warning, he shouted his pleasure. This thrilled me, the understanding he was mine.

He lay on me, limp, cherubic hair against my neck, his arm across my chest.

'Thank you,' he said.

I took his hand in mine, curled his fingers around my thumb, gently outlining the gold band of my emerald ring.

We slept awhile, though the heat of the night made it restless and we woke from sweat and thirst. It was not yet midnight.

'Are you well? I asked.

'Very well.' He stretched himself. Looking at his supple form I again resolved to eat fewer cakes and more meat. I remembered I still had wine and some water on my desk. I brought them both and gave him water. As he took it, I saw the faintest of smiles that acknowledged the strangeness of this service.

We lay, replete, hours of night still ahead. For all the months I had been near him I had never looked so clearly at his face. A small scar, nearly invisible across his left eyebrow. I ran a finger across it.

'My brother threw a bowl at me when he was only four, no more than that, and he threw so well he cut me smartly.'

'That is Edvard.'

'No, Jacob ...' He paused. 'Who is dead. That Edvard of whom I spoke—'

'The mathematics tutor.'

'He was not my brother.' His eyes met mine.

'Ah. Your lover?'

He nodded. 'He is not a mathematics tutor. He was my father's second assistant.'

'So he lived in your household.'

'When my father died, he stayed on and completed all the work that was still outstanding. It allowed my mother to receive still the money owed. She loved him for that service. And because he was kind to her.'

'She did not know your secret?' I immediately wished I

THE PRENTICE AND THE NOVICE   177

had not asked. By now you know me as a jealous man who will demand information and then torture himself with it for years.

'No. Yes. She may have.' He shrugged. 'She never mentioned it if she did. But the house was small.'

Pardieu.

This was more than I could bear. My very heart was speared right through with a dagger.

'Well, quite.'

The thought of his ecstasy with this prentice cartographer was too egregious to contemplate.

'Where is he now?'

'I don't know, though he passed through recently to see my mother and asked for me. But I do not wish to see him. I am certain he assisted my mother in writing her note to let me know he was back.'

'You broke with him?'

'He left. We were discovered. The house should have been empty, but the maid came in and found us on the stairs.'

On the stairs? I could not even fathom the mechanics. Quite apart from the undesirability of that level of discomfort.

The stairs? 'I assume she betrayed you?'

'She ran wailing to her priest. Edvard left the next day and after lying low for a time, I had to leave too. To spare my mother.'

'You came here?' (My mind was still very much preoccupied by the stairs.)

'Eventually. I worked as I went. I hoped Edvard would contact me, send for me maybe.'

'But he did not.'

'No. He was not kind. I have not forgiven him.'

'Understandably.' I wished to tell him that this Edvard was the vilest sort and he should never think of him again, that I would through spy craft and retribution send an assassin to his door. But even I was wise enough to know this would expose me for the weak and desperate man I was.

'Were there, have you had others?'

'Not like him. I mean, not really … well, you should know better than to ask me these things.' He said it laughing and, out of mercy or pity, kissed my neck. But it was too late.

Nom de Dieu. I did not dare speculate nor ask what he meant by *not really*. There had been encounters. But how many? And what should one consider an *encounter*? A glance? A kiss? A hand down one's front next a haystack?

Oh, it was all too dreadful to contemplate.

I looked at him and remembered our lovemaking that morning. His hands had been so assured, his mouth, his tricks and way of holding me back and leading me forward, touching me in such a manner that I forgot whose body I was in. And I, by comparison, an unadulterated novice. 'Well, it is nothing, a passing thought.'

'It is my day off on Sunday.'

'So it is.'

'I may go to Vaucluse for the *papegai* tournament.'

I was silent a moment too long. 'Yes. But of course.'

'You're unhappy.'

'No.'

'Will you forbid it?'

'How can I?'

'You know that you can.'

I knew this was a test. I wanted to forbid it, as his lover, demand he stay. And yet, being his master, I would never be able to do so, for I would forever reduce him to a transaction – and myself too. Inelegant, you will agree.

'I would not dream of it. I will miss your sweetness, that is true, but the tournament is always fine.'

'If I do not go, it will not look well with my friends.' This was his apology. And the truth.

I dreaded the day of the tournament and was already jealous at least two days before. The night preceding it, I made sure I was even more attentive to his pleasure, encouraging him to instruct and guide me to do his bidding. As it transpires, there was a good deal to learn. But as my law professors would attest, when adequately engaged by the material I had always been a very good and willing student.

Eager to see him before he went off but trying to hide my despair, I tried to remain indoors. This failed as a ruse. Instead, like a sad little puppy looking for its master, I found myself stalking around my gates on the pretence of wanting to show Monsieur Villet the hedging, feigning concern for its health.

'It does look quite fine to me, Monsieur.'

'Are you sure? Does it not require another cutting?'

'All I do is cut the thing.'

'And so well, you have preserved it so bravely against the mistral.'

'It is the plant that preserves us from that devil.'

'A devil but a good one.'

'True, Monsieur, true.'

'Oh, and what have we here? A gaggle of lackeys on their way out for the day.'

The two footmen, two of the maids and Mister Kryk, my Joe, made a pretty group. All five happy and free. It made me miserable. They all stopped to bow, the maids reluctantly curtsying in an embarrassing display of weary duty. I waved my hand.

'Never mind that. Are you for Vaucluse?'

'Yessir,' said the newer lackey whose name I never remembered.

'It is *papegai*, Monsieur,' said one of the girls.

'So I hear. Mister Kryk, might you be back by seven? I know it is your day off, but I require some help with—'

'Sharpening your quills,' he offered. Wicked.

'Just so. I will receive you at my writing desk tonight.'

That caught him, even with his lowered chin I could tell that he lifted an eyebrow just enough to tell me to stop being naughty. I had given him enough to keep him honest while he was gone. Was I not audacious? My scribe agrees that I was adapting very well to my new role as illicit lover and taunter of men. She should commit some of my more daring lines to memory should she ever find herself in such a situation with whomever I conspire to send her way in the future.

He did not look back as they left. I wished he had but knew he could not, and I knew too he would be mine for the day. And as it happened, the night too.

28

I Have Captured the Moon

While Kryk was gone, I made quick work of getting myself to my sister's – though you should understand the time and effort involved. If I was to arrive back at my *hôtel* before the roads were too dangerous, I would, by my calculation, have less than the hour with her before I had to leave.

Nevertheless, the effort was important. I had been unkind. I was so distracted by the lawlessness of the past few days that I had not yet gone to thank her for the salon which was, after all, held in my honour. She had two days previously sent a note asking if she had offended me, saying she had only had three brims of wine. (She had not. It was considerably more.) To my eternal shame, I did not even reply to that. It was Mister Kryk's job to take my letters to the footman for hasty dispatch and though I penned a letter with hearty apologies, the sight of him when he came to collect it meant I immediately forgot what he was there for, other than what I needed of him.

So, hastily to my sister's house by horse to thank her for her kindness. I had sent for a pretty gift the day before. I always took care to visit her when her stuff-bellied husband was sure to be out.

Unusually, she did not come out to greet me, but waited for me in her *salon*, indicating that I was out of favour. She sat a little haughtily as she forced me to walk to her. The approach was typically an arduous one in that it was a very long room. Some would say too long, though I would argue that it was proportionate but suffered from inferior light.

'Sister.' Instead of rushing forward to kiss her, I flung out my hat to the side and bowed in desperate subservience.

'Oh, stop. Come to me. My sweet, do you hate me?'

'How could I? You are my most dear. It is I who should apologise. I have wronged you greatly by not coming sooner.'

'Do you forgive me?'

'It is you who should forgive me.'

(My scribe finds that our mutual adoration and constant fawning borders on the ridiculous, but I assure you, we were most sincere.)

She let me kiss her beautiful cheeks.

'Jehan, I have missed you dreadfully. And we still have so much to talk about. Wasn't it wonderful? What a night. You were sublime.'

'That night and indeed the next morning too, the very stars coursed through my entire body in ways I had not dreamt possible.'

'Yes?'

'Truly.' I kissed her. 'Thank you, my love. I can confirm, Sister, that it was the best night of my life. I have floated on sighs of ecstasy ever since.'

'You exaggerate. Silly.'

'No. Truly. It was without precedent. And, to that end, I have a gift for you.'

'Oh dear, have you written me a poem? I grow suddenly weary.'

'Ah much, much better than a poem, for while mine are quite lovely, none can be as lovely as the thing I have in this pouch.' I revealed the little pocket.

'Oh, how exciting.'

'Yes, very exciting. For you, dear sister, I have captured the moon.'

'The moon?'

'The moon. Each step it took across the sky left a mark so that now,' I drew a line of great pearl orbs from the pouch, 'I have captured each one on a string.'

'Oh! They are magnificent! I have never seen such pearls, the size of them. Can they be real?'

'You may call them pearls, Sister, but know that they are moons. And of course they are real. *Dieu*. What do you take me for?'

'Oh, I love them and you.' She clung to me. It was just the response I had hoped for.

'Come, you must wear them.'

I fastened the pearls around her neck and faced her again to see how well she looked.

'There. You are so pretty. Though I do regret not getting you some of the same size for your ears. If you are good, I will do that. Pretty.'

'Pretty? I think not.' She found the pearls with her fingertips and bowed her head for modesty.

'Yes, pretty. You always have been and most alluring too, without being pert.'

'I should hope I am not pert. I am a married woman.'

'True, but there are those who are in their nature so naughty that married or not, they will be pert.'

'Nonsense. I have not met these women.' She was lying.

'You have not only met these women but are related to them. Have you forgotten your cousin Caroline? Pert as pert can be.'

'She can be a little ... open-hearted.'

'Ha! Open-hearted. You are being kind. Pearls for you but a chastity belt for her.'

'Brother, you are being too naughty now. What has come over you?'

'I may be naughty but there is truth in it.'

'Yes, there is truth in it. Poor Caroline.'

'I would not feel too sorry for Caroline. She has a very merry life. I saw it myself last week. She is merry and she is pert. She and her alabaster bosom.'

'And what of you?'

'What of me?'

'Is your life merry? You seem in very good spirit.'

'But of course. Merry as merry can be.'

'You are being clever, Jehan. You know what I mean. Is there someone you care for? Someone new who is pretty and pert?'

'There might be. Though you would be the last to know. I couldn't bear to suffer the teasing.'

'There would be a great deal of teasing, that is true.'

'Do you mind?'

'About what?'

'That I have someone to care for?'

'You know I do.'

'Well then there is. There is someone I care for quite deeply, passionately even.' I could not meet her eye.

'Oh, sweet, I am so pleased.'

'I am not sure you should be, but thank you.'

'Do you ... Are you in love?' I adored her optimism. We fell silent as I felt the maelstrom of the past few days, suddenly too much to hold any longer. I heard Hortense dismiss the pages and ladies.

'Brother, oh my dear, you are in love. Desperately so.'

'Yes.' I looked directly at her. She read my face as no one else could and as I let my tears fall, I saw in her the intimacy and comfort that only she could offer.

'Come and sit here with me. Come closer. Why the tears?' Her hand, so white and lovely, was set against the deep reds of the chaise.

I went to her. She smelled sweetly of orange water, so that I lay back and rested my head in her lap and let her run her long fingers across my forehead, smoothing my temple as she had always done, always the mother to me. The pearls were perfect around her neck.

I wanted so much to tell her everything. To keep a thing as important as this from her, any of it, felt like a cruel betrayal.

'Oh, love. Jehan ...' She had begun to weep. We were incapable of seeing the other in distress without registering it ourselves.

'I apologise, Sister. I had only meant to bring you a string of moons. Even for myself, this is excessively sentimental.'

'It is. Which is why I am pleased to have you here so that we might be excessively sentimental together and spare all others this *comédie*. We will keep our excesses to ourselves, shall we?'

'Yes. Always wise.'

'Jehan, this person that you love, whom I suspect you do not wish to name, have you expressed your love to them as you have to me?'

'I have not.' I considered that she addressed a *person* and not a lady in her question. But she could not know.

'That is perhaps for the best.'

'I expect you are correct.'

'My love, you will ... exercise some caution ... over this person for whom you feel so deeply?'

'I'm not sure I understand, Sister.'

'But you do. As do I. I understand you, Brother.'

'I see.'

'Do you hear me, Jehan?'

'Yes.'

'You must exercise great care. These are difficult times. Conti comes to sit in our midst and is declaring the end of libertine Languedoc and the return of piety and sobriety, neither of which are your most prominent attributes. And our uncle seeks promotion. You know that.'

'He seeks power.'

'He seeks Rome. And it is not just his reputation he considers; there are powerful men who have staked their own reputations on backing him. So, my love, the greatest care, promise me that.'

'I promise.'

She leant to kiss my brow. 'You are so handsome.'

'Am I? I hope to be.'

'And vain.'

'Of course. It is to be expected when one is so handsome. But am I still loveable?'

'To me you always are.'

Her pearls picked up the late-afternoon light coming through the window.

'Might others find me loveable though?' She made no move to reply. 'Hortense?'

'Only a fool would not love you.' She was near voiceless.

'Dear, are those now your own tears?'

She leant to kiss me again.

'The greatest care, Brother.'

29

I Am Your Servant

It is with some despair that I now relate my clumsy attempts to woo Mister Kryk, who at night became Joe and in my heart was always my beloved. My scribe finds it charming and encourages me to share the worst, saying it will encourage all others. I daresay she begins to fall in love with the idea of love.

Over 350 years have passed and still I squirm with shame at how ridiculous I must have seemed. I confess that I employed every trope at my disposal to attract his attention.

Now, I would not go so far as to say I arranged my person in, say, doorways and on furniture to show myself in a better aspect, but I may perhaps have had occasion to let my tunic fall casually open. (In my defence, Avignon and indeed the entire region was unusually warm in the summer of 1657, you will find it recorded.) I may have arranged my hair and allowed myself to recline somewhat more languidly than I might normally upon hearing his approach along the corridors in the late evening, but I like to think I retained an assured, masculine dignity at all times, despite my raging heart and thundering loins.

My most loyal scribe protests and is threatening to hang up her quill. She would like it recorded that 'thundering loins' is expressly *not* the temper of language of serious *mémoire*, nor is she happy to have her name attached to a work that employs it. Furthermore, she accuses my style of being baroque – but how could it be anything else? We are in 1657, after all. She assures me modern readers will find my effusive descriptions as distasteful as she does. We shall see.

Nonetheless, it is difficult to convey to you what Joe meant to me then, when we first began to know each other. He woke me each day, climbing onto my bed in his full livery to lie atop the sheets and enfold his arms around my torso. Before he settled, he would move my hair to kiss my neck. A moment of such sweet perfection I felt *adored*, and there can be no rarer gift than that.

We were careful, of course. Always the doors were latched, always one ear on the corridor, and although there was some game, we were careful to not speak out of turn in company. We addressed each other appropriately, he never lingered about me nor did I offer him special favour.

In truth though, we may have erred. We may have allowed an eye to rest where it should not or for too long, a wry smile to escape when one was not appropriate. I was prone to watching him too carefully and if his eye then caught mine, I would flush all through. And he, far more than I, was prone to outright boldness. His was an eager but affectionate appetite and it was clear that I was more afraid of Monsieur Benoit and the maids than he. Waiting for my carriage, I would suddenly find myself pinned against my gate, the guards not yards away. The peril that his brazenness brought made me want him more.

Any decorum was done with the moment he came around my door each night. We would lie for hours and talk in easy companionship. He was for a while obsessed with Barbary pirates and would bring me every fresh report of their plunders. French and English, he would say, all taken into slavery in Tunis and beyond. This horrified us. We lay together in the dark facing one another, our hands entwined.

'You would make a very bad serf,' he said.

'I would. My hands would be ruined in a day.'

'And you would be dead within the week. Flogged for affecting regal ways.'

'You are impertinent.'

'I am a very good valet.'

'It is true. The picture of decorum. All those many months.'

'And you did not know I craved you from the very first.'

'All those months?'

'From the first game of *jeu de paume*.' He was shy to admit it.

'I don't believe you.' I thrilled to hear it.

'I could not take my eyes from you. And then you cheated, in front of the King's cousin.' He was chuckling to himself as he recounted it. 'I mean, who wouldn't want to be plundered by a man as bold as that?'

'Why did you not act then? Did you not see how I craved *you*?'

'I did, of course. I am not blind. And I do dress you every morning. It was hard to ignore.'

I died for shame. '*Dieu*. All you ever did was affect your icy ways and go about your work without so much as a sniff in my direction. It was agony.'

'You think it was not agony for me? You think, seeing you like that, feeling you as I tucked you in, was not impossible? I would have done anything to rail you.'

'Heaven above.'

'A few times I was so heated from seeing you like that I barely made it down the stairs. You recall I even tried to resign my position.'

'My agony was worse. I am quite sure.'

'Of course, marquis, Monsieur, your agonies are always worse.'

'They are. You were not the one being tucked into your

breeches each morning and then being stripped naked each night. It was a recurring torment.'

He was laughing. 'It is true, it is true. But what you took for coldness was my effort to be done and gone before I betrayed myself. The evening you kissed me, after seeing the players, I didn't know what to do. You were so drunk, and ...'

'I thought you detested me – or worse, rejected me. I tortured myself so long after that kiss. Even then you could not see how I desired you?'

'I couldn't risk it for a passion. I had to be sure it was not just vanity.'

'Never.'

He was quiet. 'You were, are, my master. I had to be sure I wouldn't simply be your whore to be thrown aside once you had tired of me.'

'What?' I was horrified to my very core.

'It happens. I have heard it. It might still happen. If things soured or if after a few days you dismissed me to rid yourself of the shame, then what? Then I am workless and homeless again and still my family is in need. I could not, cannot be your plaything.'

'You are never that.'

He shrugged. 'I am still your servant.'

'No. You are my love. The rest is happenstance.'

'But it is truth.'

'I cannot hear this.' I turned onto my back, so I did not have to look at him. I felt ashamed.

'All sin aside, I am not only a sodomite but one who tampers with his master. It's forbidden in every way. My very presence here, in your noble bed, is against the order of things. If we are found and sanctioned, it will be me for the rack and the gallows. You could negotiate reprieve.'

'Do not say it. Do not.' I was angry. 'Why do you raise this?'

'Because I must. The truth is I thought you vain and hollow. I feared you wanted me for nothing more than amusement, but then you were kind to me, my mother, I read your stories, I read your heart, and I felt bold enough to test that. I knew you could be more than my master and I your servant, I felt you could hold me in your heart.'

'I can and I do.'

'Then you must also understand my position.'

He was uncommonly sensible in all of this, wise. As usual he made me feel selfish and unkind.

'If you love me as you say, you will understand that it costs me more to love you than you me.'

'You should know I love you. You should know.'

'I do. I do. But then I must ask that you honour that love by showing me that you understand what I may lose.'

'I understand it.'

'You do now. And even knowing it you can cast me out tomorrow.'

30

Even Beyond Death

I will say that what I did next was an act of pure devotion. My scribe suggests it was a product of my jealous heart and my attempt to mark Jonathan Kryk as my own. I do not employ her to have opinions, though she seems to offer a prodigious number of them. But we are both eager to continue our story. I woke her quite early today, before sunrise. I had been whispering in her ear and feeding images into her dreams, so she woke with urgency and focus and wrote at her desk for a full three hours before repairing to the coffee house to continue. And so, let us to it.

While looking for pretty trinkets for myself in the crates that Mister Gambaccini, the jewel merchant, had brought to me, and finding none that moved me, I did spy some rings that would suit themselves to devotion. I picked up a few things, a pearl in the shape of a tear for my ear, a pretty bracelet for Hortense, but my eye kept returning to the poesy rings.

'You would inscribe these for me?'

'Of course, Monsieur.'

Gambaccini did a rich trade in Avignon. Hortense bought my very fine emerald ring from him and since the day she gave it to me, I had never removed it. Much of his custom came from the Palais, where the legates and their sycophants amused themselves with mistresses. Mistresses who required constant reassurance: garnets, rubies, emeralds.

The poesy rings were heavy and had a demi-circle dome which allowed a delicate light to play over them.

'Monsieur, I need you to understand that this inscription will require some discretion, a trade in which you are well-versed.'

'But of course.'

'And I would be willing to pay an extra ten per cent if you personally would see to the engraving. I would not like even a prentice to do it. Your work is so fine.'

'But of course.'

'Then it is done. I will write the inscription for you that you may copy it well.'

'No doubt for a very rare companion.'

'Oh, more than you can possibly begin to imagine. But, as I said, discretion is essential and you must give me your word that you and only you will see these rings and inscribe the poesy?'

'I give you my word.'

'Good. I will pay you when you bring them.'

'Did you want the bracelet?'

'No.'

'Perhaps your lady would like pearls?' An image of Joe posing puckishly in nothing but a lovely necklace of sea pearls popped into my mind's eye.

'I think not. Not yet. Might the rings be done today? You could bring them back?'

'Well . . .'

'For an additional fee.'

'I am sure it would be possible.'

Gambaccini left with his instruction and the promise of a full pocket. I was sure I had financed a new house for him in the preceding hour, but I did not care.

Before the day was done a prentice from Gambaccini returned the pocket with the rings and I sent him away with the weightiest pouch of *pistoles* he had ever seen. I sent two lackeys with him, both to protect him from thieves and the purse from himself.

The Cherbonnes had come to call, and Monsieur Benoit had conspired to get a lark to rise out of the top of a pie, head and wings, while its body and feet lay submerged beneath the crust. I shall never forget it and congratulated him heartily. I then filled the brothers with sweetmeats and *hippocras* and sent them on their way as quickly as was reasonable.

Upstairs as fast as I could. I had only just rearranged myself according to how I would wish my lover to look when the latch lifted on the door.

He rushed in. The door had hardly closed and he was kissing me.

'Bolt it.' He ignored me and I had to reach behind him to do it.

'I thought they were never leaving.'

'*Pardieu*, what is this?'

'I haven't seen you since early this morning.' He tried to grab at me.

'I am sorry, truly, but if you will stop molesting me for just a moment you will see what has had me so busy without you.'

'It had better not be this.' He grabbed my loins. How I adored his indecorous ways.

'Stop that. No. Stop, you are being pert and I have a gift for you.'

He feigned petulance and slumped into my chair. 'What is it then?'

'If you are going to be horrible you shan't have it. I am regretting it already.'

He could see I was serious and sat more neatly. 'I'm sorry. I am listening.'

'I bought you a gift.'

The pouch with the rings was hidden in my hand.

'Well, what is it? I am waiting.'

I suddenly felt ridiculous. I had halted his play and now he sat looking at me, rendering my offering an awkward ceremony.

'It is nothing, it can wait. Let us drink instead.'

'I have my day off tomorrow. We may drink to dropping.'

I had two cups in quick succession to stave off an accelerating melancholic slump.

(I suspect my scribe judges me. A coward and a drunk combined, an ignoble pairing. She is a coward but a sober one. She will not drink and she will not love.)

Joe and I had our wine cups full and I read him some bawdy verse I had been composing for amusement. My clever rhyming of 'aesthetic' and 'pricke' amused him greatly.

'What else do you have?' he asked.

'I have a new story and the start of a play. Let's to bed and we'll not play, only lie together and you will rest.'

'Read me the story first.'

'To bed and I will read.'

That night and so many more, I read to him until he fell asleep. I regretted not giving him the poesy ring and instead kissed his head as he slept.

He woke early as usual.

'Will you wait?'

'I must go.'

'It is the Lord's Day, the others will be slow. Stay a moment.' I went to my bureau – still groggy but determined – and retrieved from it Mister Gambaccini's pocket. 'Here is the gift I wished to give to you.' I felt I was erring on ceremony again. 'It is but a token. Put out your hand.'

He did and I dropped the ring into it.

His mouth parted a crack. He frowned.

'It is a poesy,' I offered. My nerves began to jangle.

He nodded.

He read it out: '*JB & JK Even Beyonde Death*'. He caught his breath and looked at me with the tenderness he so rarely allowed. He was chewing on his lips. 'It is the rarest thing.' He kissed me quickly like a bashful child told to do so by their parent. He rolled the ring round and round so that he might read its inscription more. My heart near collapsed on itself for relief and joy.

'You like it?'

'Yes. And more.' He was soft, overwhelmed even. He kissed the ring and then placed it in his coat. His response was even more than I dared hope from him.

'Will you not wear it?'

'You know I cannot. Here.' He came to me and took mine from me and then placed it on my finger. 'It suits you fine. I will conceal my own.'

'But you do like it?'

He said nothing, only nodded.

'Perhaps I should not have,' I said.

'You should. I like it very well. Very well.'

'Then what is the matter?'

'You may wear yours.'

'Ah. And you not.'

He shrugged.

'Why must it be?'

'The gold is too rich. It will attract attention.'

'Oh, Joe, I apologise.' I had been thoughtless again. 'I am sorry. I am sorry.' I tried to make it right with kisses, but nothing could ever make it different. Even in our concealment, we were thwarted.

Even so, that night when he came to me, he wore the ring around his neck on a leather lace, and as he lay over me to face me and slowly moved himself in me, the light caught its sphere like a lovely golden hope. I leaned up to his chest and reached to hold the gold in my mouth.

Even beyond death.

31

Hortense I

A few weeks more were passed in happy seclusion. I had forgotten I was needed in the world and, it is true, may have overlooked a few commitments related to both family and station. I saw no friends and had little desire to. My sister sent letters and I replied to notes from the Comtesse de Montmorency with vague excuses and assurances of my affection. Which was honest. I had on any number of occasions felt that my instinct was to share my upended life with her, but it was an impossibility.

One of the afternoons (which had fast become my mornings given the longer and longer nights I was keeping), I found myself being rudely roused from my bed by the noise of dogs and horses. Joe was asleep in my bed, as he often was at that time. As we let our precious hours together reach well into dawn, he often went straight from my bed to his cot, which he rumpled a bit, moving things around his table and changing his livery, before immediately starting work. Where I was free to rest during the day he was always fatigued, and so in the middle of the day when my staff were allowed a break, he came to my chamber to sleep.

I went to my window to see what the noise was and just caught sight of one of my sister's lackeys rounding the house.

I dashed to my bed. 'Joe. Quick, you must rouse yourself.'

'I cannot.'

'My sister is here.'

'Oh, heaven is cruel.'

'I will go down to greet her, you must dress. You, oh dear, your ... You might need some water. Use the looking glass.'

'What?' He could not wake properly and was in foul temper. I threw a cloth at him. 'Wash your face.'

'Sister!' I just about had my arms through the sleeves of my banyan as I reached the bottom step.

'Oh. My sweet. Goodness. What a vision you are. Look at you.'

'You are already looking at me. Most accusingly.'

'Well, you are near naked. And it is gone three.'

'I was writing.'

She tapped a gloved finger to her neck as she looked at my own exposed throat and chest. 'I very much doubt that, Brother.'

'What is that supposed to mean?'

'You have been branded most whorishly.'

I thought to deny it, but being all exposed in gown, and no grooming to speak of, there was no real point. So, I attacked.

'What language you use, Sister. Unappealing in a lady.'

'Are you denying it?' She was feigning anger.

'I do not deny it.'

'Well, then I would ask who this ... oh. No.' She was suddenly overcome, serious. 'Perhaps I would not.' She brought a hand to cover her mouth as if overwhelmed by the need to hold back her words.

She understood, I was certain of it. She had known it before, but in abstraction, and now she faced me half-undressed and branded with another man's lust.

She was immobile and had the look of one stranded,

mid-river, with no way forward or back. I went quickly to
her side.

'Come, Hortense, take my arm. Shall we walk in the
garden?'

'Please. It is very warm.'

'And then we will see what Monsieur Benoit can feed us.'

She was slow to let her hand find my arm. We walked until
we were through the doors that lined the courtyard and out
into the light. Nothing was said between us.

What secret had I asked her to hold? This knowledge was
a death to her. Perhaps I should have been more fearful, imagined her betraying me. But to whom? The shame was too
deep for her to tell anyone. She would be rendered worthless
from the scandal and her husband would be tarnished too. She
could not and would not speak.

And worse than that, I knew she now saw me differently.

We sat under my favourite cypress near to the fountain,
which offered some brief respite from the scream of heat
coming off the sun, the shrieking cicadas making everything
feverish. I struggled to take in air.

'Hortense.' I tried to make her look at me, but she would not,
only bowed her head, cheeks flushed.

'It is unusually warm,' she offered.

'You have already mentioned it.'

'Have I?'

'Yes. Sister, I—'

'No.'

'Yes. Please, please. You must understand me.'

'No. I cannot. I cannot understand you.' She was whispering, yet through clenched jaw and wet eyes.

'You have always understood me. You said so yourself. You
said you understood my heart as you did your own.'

'I thought I did, Jehan. Can *you* not understand *me*? It is one

thing to have a sense of it but now that I see you so *branded* . . .
you must sympathise with my horror. I cannot fathom it. Why
must you? Are you so impoverished in spirit or life's amusement? Is there nothing else for you?' She was gulping through
her tears now.

'Shh . . . quiet, quiet, you are too bold.'

'What have you done to me?'

'I love you, please know I love you. Please, my sweet, tell me
you love me still?'

'Who will I love if I say I love *you*? Who are you?'

'I am not changed, only the same as ever.'

'This crime is too great, Jehan. It will kill you.'

'Let it, only please, please, you must love me still.'

'Do you love me, that you will choose this?'

I tried to kiss her, but she pulled away.

'No. You cannot kiss me when your lips have sinned. I
cannot, cannot accept what you do.'

I was in the grip of a suffocating panic. The light was so
bright as to be disorientating and the noise of the beetles
screaming and screaming was as if hell itself had opened up
to meet me.

And Hortense, who would not say she loved me but had not
said she did not. I held fast to that hope. We both sat, silent
and exhausted. Hortense, my Hortense, shut her eyes against
the light.

'Why must you, Jehan? Why must you be so, oh God, so
wicked?' She opened her eyes to turn to me for the first time
and, seeing my distress, did what love and habit allowed her to
do. She held my face in both her hands and passed each thumb
under my eyes to clear my tears. The little pearls that dotted
the lace of her gloves rolled along my skin like a perfect prayer
of absolution and caused yet more tears to fall.

'Sister, forgive me.'

Still holding my face, she dropped her forehead to mine and let it rest.

'I fear for you.' Her voice had gone.

'But love me too.'

She let her hands fall and sat back.

'I feel so afraid. It is not hatred I feel, it is the hand of fear, here, on my shoulder. You have raised the promise of death in our lives, Jehan.'

'No. It need not be like that.'

'It already is. I can feel it. And we will have to meet it when it comes.'

Hortense repaired herself and I too, as well I could. Her skin was sallow, her eyes were glazed and I could see small drops of sweat about her lip and chin.

'I need some rest from this light. It has the temper of madness today,' she said.

We returned to the dark and cool of the interior and the *salon*. A lackey appeared.

'Ask Monsieur Benoit for some wine and something to go with it,' I instructed.

Hortense unpinned her headpiece and threw it aside. 'It is not much use for the sun, is it?'

She would not sit and instead walked about the room with detached interest in furnishings: a hand over the corner of a chair, running her finger across a vase. I sat like a terrified lamb expecting to be kicked. I felt a chill run across my skin as if a winter's wind had just crossed the valley. By contrast, the longer Hortense moved about the more her temperature seemed to rise.

I could feel her bristle and fight begin to return. 'Sister, will you sit?'

'Do not command me anything, Jehan.'

'No, Sister.'

'I have travelled to see you on this most disagreeable day because my lady's maid tells me that you are ill. I have not heard from you for weeks and you did not appear at the Estates Council. I know this because our uncle complained to me that he had expected you to be there. Thinking you were ill or, as is most likely the case with you, in some terrible, terminal melancholy, I came to see you here today. I do not find you ill or melancholic, Brother; instead, I arrive to have you dance down the stairs entirely naked, like some wanton cavalier in one of your stories.'

'Might we return to the earlier accusation? Why does your lady's maid find me ill? I never see her.'

'Her cousin is your maidservant. She reports that you are locked in your bedchamber these full weeks, only take short walks in the garden and then return to your seclusion. She reports that the only person who seems to have seen you and can even vouch for your still being alive all these weeks is your *valet de chambre*, Mister Kryk, whom she tells me ... is ... he is ...' Her voice had suddenly dropped and she picked the words out one at a time, slowly, as if she were searching a tree for ripe oranges. 'He is required to attend to you.' Her eyes met mine. 'Most carefully.'

I could hear footsteps approaching the door. I moved quickly towards her, my hands at her mouth to try and stop her. 'No, do not say it. Please, Hortense, do not name him.'

Two footmen came in, bearing trays. Hortense was frozen yet her eyes darted left and right as she tried to contain her emotion.

They left the wine and I peered along the hall to make sure they had gone before shutting the door and turning back to her.

'Your servant?' She was incandescent. 'Are you unsound of mind? He has been here not six months. You know nothing of him. How can you trust yourself, your very life to him?'

'That is exactly what I trust to him, Sister. I trust him with my life.'

'Oh, this is beyond reason. And even if he is good and kind then you have abused him, Jehan. You owe him paternal care, discipline, a wage, but this?'

'It is not like that, not in the way you say it. It is nothing like that.'

'What is wrong with you, Jehan? Have you sought any remedy for it? What? Is it a madness?'

'Yes.'

'You admit you are mad?'

'I am in love.'

'Oh.' She shut her eyes again, exasperated. 'No, no. It is not *love*, do you hear me? It cannot be. It is wickedness and that is all. Why must you say these things? They are devilish, do you hear me?'

'Please listen, Hortense. He knows me. And you would love him too. When I came to you and said that I was in love, you believed me then. And now I am even more so.'

'I cannot bear this.'

'I love him.'

'I will not hear it, Jehan. And you must stop repeating those words. I must leave.' She turned to fetch her plumes. 'Do not come to my house. Ever.'

And she was gone.

I stood a while, having to lean on a chair. The chill I had felt earlier began to take me over. She had not shown me anything I did not already know. Secluded in my house those weeks, I had begun to confuse reverie with truth; I had forgotten that outside of my three private rooms, another world existed. I fell to the seat and I gasped for air. My chest felt it was caving. The walls swung left and then right, my ears distorted my own breath so that it made the sound of wind gushing, this way and that. I called out for help but could not tell if my voice went anywhere. An excruciating pain spread across my breast, spirals of agony and terror all through me and then, nothing.

VOLUME 2

1

How is My Brother?

From out to sea, a great ocean, the most perfect turquoise, and in the distance an island from which rose a tall tower, trees I could not name.

I felt a soft hand on my brow. 'Hortense?' There was no reply, or at least I could not make one out. I extended a hand that felt my bedclothes. I opened my eyes, but it was too dark to see.

'Sister, forgive me.'

A cool cloth was applied across my forehead and down my cheek.

'She's gone.' It was Joe.

I tried to lift myself.

'No, better rest.'

'I must see my sister.'

'She's not here.'

'What hour is it? Does she know I am unwell?'

'It's night. She was leaving this afternoon when you took ill. She was near the gates, but Lucie ran after her.'

'And she came? At once?' I managed to focus my eyes somewhat.

'No.' He passed the cloth back across my face. 'She left. It surprised us all.'

'You should not be here. She knows.'

'You aren't well.' He said it clear, but his face betrayed his pain or fear. Possibly both. 'How can she know?'

My breath was strange and difficult. 'She deduced it.'

'And you admitted it?'

'I had to.'

'You admitted sodomy? To your sister?'

'No.' I had to close my eyes again. 'I told her I loved you.'

His hand paused. I heard him immerse the cloth and wring it out again with fresh water. He applied it then to my neck and chest. It felt like plunging my whole body into the Rhône in winter.

He said no more, only continued to douse me. I slept again and dreamt once more of the island. Perhaps it was the Indies, hot and damp, a bright sun that flashed off the sea so brightly that it could blind a man; burning sun and dark storms, with waves that threatened to sink whichever cay I tried to cling to.

Through my sleep and in the distance, I could hear Hortense, herself a formidable storm.

'I will go where I wish.'

'Master cannot ever be interrupted in his bedchamber.'

'I am his sister. And he is ill.'

'He is very proper about such things. I will be whipped.'

'You deny me my brother? Then I shall do the whipping.'

I tried to open my eyes. The drapes were not drawn about the bed. It was light, morning. I tried to move but could not.

'Madame . . .'

'Leave me. I will see him alone. Go.'

I managed to sit half up as she came through. Her eyes were flushed, wide and ready. She looked at me, then to the floor. Joe, still in his livery, lay there asleep, the cloth he had used to cool me still in his hand, the vessel of water at his head. The rumpus must have roused him. He scrabbled to his feet in one move, blinking, disorientated, capless, hands clasped together, head bowed, facing my sister. I fell back to my pillows. The silence was judicial.

'Sister, say what you will.' I could not bear any more.

'I shall, Brother.' Her voice was suddenly less sure. Her determination had given way to something else. She had not expected Joe to be there and now she saw us both caught in our domestic vulnerability, such as it was.

'Mister Kryk.'

'Madame.'

I raised myself again and covered my nakedness better.

'Mister Kryk.' It seemed an eternity had passed. She breathed deep and straightened. 'How is my brother?'

Oh, dear God and for love, what it must have cost for her to ask it.

Joe glanced sideways at me.

'Madame.' His voice was soft, even reverential. 'Monsieur has passed the night fitfully and with great fever, but before dawn the heat subsided and he became immediately more restful.'

'I see that you have attended him well. Thank you for your service, Mister Kryk.' She was impeccably cool.

He bowed to her. 'It is my duty, Madame.'

'No. In truth, it is not your duty.'

'Then, Madame, it is my honour.'

Oh, I was reborn. He had answered perfectly.

'Might you send someone to prepare a bath for my brother? Then you may leave to rest for the remainder of the day. I will attend to him. Tell whoever comes with the water that he will need good soap and more cloths. I will need an apron.' She stood so straight.

'Yes, Madame. Thank you, Madame.'

He left quickly and without looking at me.

Even before the latch had fallen on the door she crumpled, racked through with tears. She howled for all Christendom. I could not hear all of what she said, only that she had thought I was dead and without prayer for forgiveness and it was all her fault for leaving even though she knew I had collapsed; that she had not slept, not one wink and had raced to find me as early as she could. And then the shock of finding him there. But so devoted, on the ground still clutching the cloth. She howled anew. I had never seen such an unholy mess in a woman and certainly never in her. I had seen her stung by bees when we were young and once a scorpion nearly caught her. Both times she simply brushed the incident aside, feeling a shriek was uncalled for.

'Goodness, Sister.'

'I cannot. S . . . stop.'

'It is best not to try. This is my experience.' I wrapped my arm about her and held her.

She clung on and all her adult disappointments seemed to find their escape in great and ugly gulps and snorts.

'I thought you dead, by your own hand even, poison.'

'My sweet. Can you see I am quite well? It is true I was taken very ill, but it has passed. I have done all this to you, can you forgive me? I love you more than you can ever know.'

With that she howled all the more. I resolved to keep quiet. I seemed to extract even more sorrow. My silence was a good balm and after time I felt her breathing ease and deepen.

'I love you, Sister.'

'Jehan,' she lifted her head from my shoulder where she had laid. 'You are putrid.'

'I beg your pardon?'

'You must bathe at once.'

'Ha!' I swiped a pillow at her, but she was practised and caught it even before it was near her.

'Please. Brother. I am too old for these games.' She tried to straighten her bodice and pushed her hair into place. 'See? I wear my pearls. I never dress without them.'

'They suit you well.'

'Are you stronger?

'Yes.'

She took in a deep breath. She was still sad. 'Come. Let us prepare for your bath. I will find where the water is.'

'Are we friends?'

'We are one half of each other. How could we not be?'

'Because I disappoint you.'

She thought awhile. 'Yes, you do. Painfully so. But if I was to no longer love every man who disappointed me, I would have no one left to love.'

'Sister?'

'Men are weak. They must have what they must. And the women who love them, or who depend on them, must endure it or the sun would no longer rise after the moon.'

'What are you saying?'

'I am saying I am practised in forgiveness.'

'I will kill that Toad.'

'I do not think this is quite the time for your righteous anger. Do you?'

'No.'

'I do not agree with it, Jehan. I cannot. Truly, I cannot. And I do not understand you. But I do love you. God will judge me too. My forgiveness of you, knowing what I know, being my own sin. My other being that I will speak no word of it to anyone.'

'Thank you, Sister.'

'No thanks are due.'

'You were kind to him where you might not have been.'

'It was not kindness. It was necessity.'

2

Mister Jonathan Kryk
of Amsterdam

My scribe is minded to note the immense depth of charac-
ter displayed by Hortense on repeated occasions, and I
am not one to argue with this assessment. She was ever the salvation of me and bore the weight of her position so graciously.
It is understandable that she could not give me full reprieve,
but how I wished it from her.

Of course, the consequence of my weeks of absence required
still further censure from my uncle who, not three days after
my fever, demanded to be seen. He arrived early, as expected.
He had always done so. Punctuality, discipline, all of these
things kept the Devil at bay, or at least gave the impression of
a man who cared about such things. He never had more than
one glass of wine and if he thought it had been over-filled, he
stopped short of the measure. He read exactly two pages each
night before sleep and walked every morning for an hour, no
matter the weather. All of this was as death to me.

'Welcome, Uncle. You look most well.'

'Jehan. You do not. Do you ever sleep?'

It was unfair of him to mention it. I was not used to being
up so early and thought I had made an immense effort to look
respectable, even though my eyes may have been a bit swollen.

He knew too that I had been retrieved from the very clutches of death, yet failed to mention it.

'Please, come through.' He had already marched ahead to the *salon*.

He stayed standing. He was shorter than I, though I seldom felt the effect of my height when he was in the room.

'How may I assist you today? Or are you here out of concern for my fragile health?'

'You are being tedious, Jehan.'

'I do what I can.'

'And yet you do not. Why were you not at the Council?'

'I was not well, as you know. I sent representation.'

'You sent a two-page *comédie* on how to secure haystacks against Spanish spies. You fell ill much after that theatric. It is no excuse.'

'You did not find it instructive?'

'No. I found it impertinent and childish and it reflected very poorly on us.'

'You mean it reflected poorly on you?'

'Jehan, I should like you to understand me.' His face had changed, I cannot say how. Perhaps less of the judge and more of the man, if that were possible. 'Your father, may God give him peace, was the inheritor of all of this. He was the eldest son and that is the way it is and should be. He had no excess of ambition, as you know. He did a fine job in his role. He did not extend our influence to acquire more land, but he did not squander it either. He was not suited to public office; he could not negotiate the ways of the world in a manner that might be advantageous.

'I, Jehan, am a natural broker. We both know it. Had I been the firstborn, the name all would know would be Baudelaire, not Villeneuve or any of the others. Baudelaire. But I was born second and so, to the Church.'

'Where you are most comfortable.'

'I have made myself comfortable. I am no preacher. Moreover, I found myself the guardian of you and your sister.'

'You used us well, Uncle. I cannot feel too sorry for you. I will not mention the small matter of the coffers of which you availed yourself during those ten years.'

'How dare you. I was your guardian. There were expenses.'

'Of course. And I have always admired your house.'

The room was silent.

'I will take my leave. You despise me, Jehan.'

'Likewise, Uncle.'

'Yes. I find that I do. And that my life is so cruelly held in your hands makes me despise you more. There is nothing more I can do. You will crush me with your frivolities and vacuous capers – no wife, no heir, nothing. You will die having achieved nothing. Your father weeps for what he knows, marquis.'

'Do not raise my father. He was a better man than both of us combined.'

'Then give him honour. A wife, Jehan, a son. Mend your ways. Restore your reputation. That is all.'

'Good day, Uncle.'

'I will find my own way. Perhaps your *valet de chambre* will see me out. Mister Jonathan Kryk of Amsterdam, is it not?'

His voice cut flat.

I flinched, but before I could muster a reply, he had turned and was through the *salon* door, clicking his fingers as he went to beckon a flurry of footmen.

3

Even Beyond Death II

The wind was stirring, bringing cooler air; a relief, yet the constant whipping and slapping of the clime made for frayed tempers.

The sun had long surrendered and Joe had settled in my rooms as usual. He was tired and in no mood for talk, so sat apart from me. I tried to sit with my book but was agitated. I could not tell him what had passed between my uncle and me. Our conversation had left me overwrought and anxious, that day more than ever. I found myself pacing up and down to help myself think. I wondered if Hortense had betrayed me, but quickly put it from my mind. What was his meaning then, 'mend your ways'? He said it pointedly. He was not a man to waste words. *Mister Jonathan Kryk of Amsterdam.* He had been investigating Joe, that much was clear. He had mistrusted him from the start. A spy.

Joe kept shooting glances my way with increasing ire. 'Must you pace about so much? What is the matter? Shall I . . . give you some relief?'

'*Pardieu!* On the contrary, I was about to suggest that you come with me to church.'

He was beside the fire. It was cooler than it should have been for the time of year. He was slumped low in the chair, my cloak over him.

'Now, to church?'

'Let us go and pray together.'

'Are you mad? It's late, the wind is high. Pray here if you must, is that not the point of having your own chapel?'

In truth, my chapel had become an auxiliary barn. I had found a pile of horseshoes in there when last I visited. I would not be shocked to find a yoked oxen asleep next the altar.

'No. I must go to church. My mind is frayed. I cannot think. Can you not see how upset I am?'

'I can, I can, I'm sorry, but church?'

He did not seem very sorry at all, nor did he leap to comfort me. Irksome at the very least. (Here again, my scribe sides with Joe. I begin to suspect she loves him more than she does me.)

'What else is there? Where else will advice come from? There is no other authority I can turn to.'

'The church forbids us. Have you forgotten?' He was impatient.

'My uncle forbids us.'

'What? He knows?' He stood.

'No. Yes. I don't know.'

'Your sister?'

'No. No. I cannot believe it would be. And you insult my sister.'

'Are you sure?' Now he was agitated. 'What did he say?'

'He mentioned your name. He said: Mister Jonathan Kryk of Amsterdam. I think he has investigated you.'

'He will find nothing.'

'There was the fight with Marielle. She may have talked. If ever I should like to wring a girl's neck.'

'He suspects, perhaps, but if he knew he would have said. He is taunting you. Do not panic.'

'But I do. How can you not?'

'To panic is admission.'

'Then I must pray.'

I began to arrange myself.

'Please, no, Jehan. It's cold and there is nothing we know for certain. He has no evidence.' He pulled the chaise closer to the fire.

There was a most perilous moment when I almost commanded that he join me, commanded as a master might his lazy valet. To my eternal credit, I managed to hold my tongue and ask instead, 'My love, I go to pray. Will you accompany me?'

'No. I will find my answers here.'

The impertinence! He fidgeted with his cuffs, restless in his whole body.

'Very well. I will go alone.'

'How will you go?'

'I will walk, of course.'

'You are impossible.' He sat forward, leaning his eyes into the cups of his hands. 'Now I must come with you. You are so stubborn. What will happen if you are seen out on your own? *He has a lazy manservant*, they will say. *Cannot even arrange a few lackeys to protect his master. Why does the marquis skirt around in the shadows in the middle of the night?*'

'I will tell them I am smuggling Huguenots.'

'Don't be trite. And you forget I am presumed a Protestant Huguenot. All Dutch are—'

'*Nom de Dieu*, are you? Are you a *Huguenot?*' I confess it had never occurred to me I might be harbouring an insurrectionist, a Protestant heretic. I was seized with an elemental horror. He did wear his hair short, it was true. 'This had never occurred to me . . . Are you . . .?'

'On my *life*, Jehan.' He said it with such a tight jaw I hardly heard him. He was seething. A small part of me thought he might smack me clear across my face, he was so enraged. Quite an enlivening prospect, though I would regret any scar I might receive.

He began to assemble himself, straighten his gilet. He did look weary and this emboldened me to think I stood a good chance of winning the joust.

'I am here marooned, trying to dress with no light and you will not help me. I have the wrong coat on, I am sure. We cannot be seen together, that will upset the court, Cardinal Mazarin, the King, God, the very universe. And yet if I am seen alone, without you, society will be upset that I am unattended. Is this my blue coat? Together, alone, never together, always alone. It is impossible.' Unexpectedly, I could feel my own rage building as I often did, across my chest. 'It is enough!' I did not care that I wept.

'Calm yourself. You will be heard. Come here.'

'No.'

'No? Come closer so I can fix you.'

'You cannot fix me. I am upset and tired and I would like to go to L'Église Saint-Pierre for solace. And I will go with or without you.'

'Jehan, you've have laced yourself askew. I need to fix your doublet or you will hardly be able to breathe, let alone walk to church.' He smiled and began to sort out the knots I had made of myself.

'I hate you. And you are a lazy valet, a left-handed devil and, worst of all, most probably a Huguenot.'

'Oh, dear.' He managed to straighten me up and began to re-button the fasteners. 'That's a problem for you then.'

'On the contrary, it is very much your problem.'

'No. It's yours, because you love me.'

'Oh, do I, Mister Kryk?'

'Yes. You do.'

He let his tongue tease my lip so wantonly, forcing me to reach all the way to him, but he then pulled away.

'Shall we to church, Monsieur?'

The hussy.

To church, in the dark and through the roaring mistral. We should not have left without protection, at least two quick swords apiece. It was wild enough for witches. We just needed a heretic and we would make an unspeakable trinity. We walked close, under the cover of our cloaks, and held each other's hands fast, for comfort and safety on the streets. We could mark our way; the moon was high enough behind the scales of cloud and reflected well off the pale grey cobbles.

'Let us go this way, across the square. It will be quicker,' he said.

'The Marquis de Graveson might see us.'

'You are a man going to prayer, there is nothing to hide.'

'Still, they will ask why I did not pray at home.'

'*They* will ask? I asked!'

'Why do you not understand me? I must find my solace.'

'You should find your solace in me.' He had turned away.

Oh, dear God. Again I had managed to think only of myself and had not seen that he was offering me comfort. It was so clearly my fault, impossible to admit. So I said:

'You are insufferable! You do not care for me and you make no effort to understand me.' I swung on my heel, making a clear point of walking right in front of the marquis's house.

By my tenth step (yes, I counted), I was delighted to hear Joe rushing across the square to catch up to me.

'I understand you very well. I understand that you are stubborn and childish and when you are upset, only a grand gesture more suited to the stage than to life will do.'

'Granted.' I took back his hand in mine. 'Give me your dev-il's left hand now, let us to church and to God.'

We pushed through the heavy doors to the side, towards the nave. Saint-Pierre was gold and silver all at once. The high, cool arches, great swoops of stone made somehow liquid with light. Some candles still burned, though there was not much left in them. It was silent, the silence I sought, the kind that even my own unruly mind could not interrupt. My heart tum-bled and soared all at once and I knew that Joe felt it too. He made a small circle with his forefinger so that I knew he would search the outer chapels and altars to see if anyone lingered there.

I knelt in a pew, shut my eyes to all the misery of the day and forced my breath to slow. I could hear my father. I never stopped wishing for him. The comfort of his voice, his pro-tection. I always remembered his straight back no matter the occasion. When he died, I tried to emulate this, standing erect no matter that I was so utterly broken.

Joe knelt one row behind me and a seat to the side, just close enough to whisper. 'We are alone. How are you?'

'Better now. I am better, and sorry too.'

'I know.'

I turned to look at him. His face was fatigued. I asked him to carry so much for me, and he did; all of my awkwardness, my moods. I faced the altar again.

'Jonathan Kryk of Amsterdam, you are my husband.'

'You can't say that, Jehan, not here.'

'I do say it here.' I turned back to him again.

'Then if you will say it, I will say that you are mine.'

'Do you say it before God?'

'I do. I say it before God. I am your husband.'

It was a sublime moment. All my anxieties and hurts, real

and imagined, were immediately expunged. That he had dedicated himself to me as an equal in love wiped away all these nothings to which I had clung. Nothing but love passed between us, our words still in the air, just moments above us. It remains the most sacred moment of my earthbound life and my most perfect prayer.

That night was our true wedding night. We returned to my *hôtel* and parted at the door, guarded by swordsmen; Joe to the service quarters, I to my rooms.

Everything was changed. I sat on my chaise and waited for him to arrive at the door. I no longer wondered if he would. I did not worry how I would find him or he me. There was simply no need.

When we went to bed, he was less playful than usual, he was slow and careful, loved me with such tenderness that it near broke my heart. He lay over me and his eyes only left mine to kiss me. Afterwards, he wept with the same sweet and honest heart that had undone me all those months ago, when I saw him in the dark corridor, listening to the music's exquisite tendrils of devastation.

As we lay pressed together, my head nesting in his neck, breathing his scent and letting him comfort me, I whispered my prayer to him, 'Never leave me. Even beyond death.'

And the answer came in the dark.

'I'll never leave you. Even beyond death.'

4

Swimming

Now follows a miserable chapter in our lives. Granted, there have been many, but in the end, it is possible that our fate turned on this one night. Somehow it comes down to one word, one turn, this way and not that, and everything that might have been begins to spin away from you. So it was with us.

I was due at my cousins Cherbonne for an afternoon of *paille-maille*. (A game in which, naturally, I excelled.) Waiting for my carriage, I was naughty, I concede, and let myself stand too close to Joe. My guards were only a few feet away, one on either side of the archway, and we no more than a few steps under it. He looked so fine in his livery and just seeing him move about – his pretty mouth, the way he would unthinkingly twist the hair that escaped his cap around his finger – oh, it was stupendously energising. It was not for lack of chambering, on the contrary. The more I had of him, the more I wanted, for he had such casual sorcery in his ways. For all the advantage he accused me of having in life (and this confession is strictly *entre nous*), twixt sheet and bed he was ever the master.

There he stood, so close and I so hot; is it any wonder that for passion alone I put my hand about the back of his neck and bit his ear? He responded like a stag hit by an arrow, reeling away from me with wide, admonishing eyes and studiously avoiding me the rest of the day, thus causing me to fluff my chances at winning at *paille-maille*. I knocked the ball every which way except where I intended it. Utter humiliation.

Worse was to come. For the remainder of the night, Joe took it upon himself to remind me, with robust repetition, of the consequences were we to be exposed. My sister already knew. My uncle suspected. The sword would fall on him, whereas with clever interventions and favours called in, I might merely face sanction. And, the *coup de grâce*, I could send him to the fire with less than a word.

Of course I denied this, for it had never crossed my mind to do anything so monstrous. Nonetheless, all of this preyed on his mind and put him in a bad temper. But what could I do? The very fact of our meeting came down to his role as my valet, and should he no longer be employed in that capacity, we would no longer be able to see each other as we did, sharing such intimate space. Only as a valet could he be seen to come and go from my bedchamber and other private rooms at all hours without arousing suspicion.

I could have done more to set his mind at ease, it's true. I was indeed his master. And yet if there was so much as a hint that his heart was waning in its affection, I would immediately be rendered a mere husk, crushed and turned to dust.

My scribe objects. She claims this is overblown and would also like it noted that if Jonathan Kryk was ever disloyal or suggested that he might leave me, I would have immediately conspired to have him shackled to me through indentured servitude, perhaps exploiting the issue of the annual bequest for his mother, or even threatening to expose him. She does take his side over mine a good deal and *her* disloyalty is noted. She began as a supplicant to my story and now has all kinds of ideas she has no place to offer.

But back to the horrible episode.

Joe had overslept. After he had dressed me, we planned when he would return. His rushed departure meant there was no time for kindness. He was to return to my rooms after he had run his usual errands.

Eventually, he knocked. I had expected him around noon and by one he had not yet arrived, so that when he finally did I was already anxious and foul-mooded.

'Where have you been? Lock the door.'

'I have been buying your ink and paying your bill with Gambaccini.' He looked tired.

'How long can that possibly take? Did you bring fresh pomatum?'

'I have brought everything we need, but I was delayed. They are preparing for the boat races. I could not move for drunkards. Physicians and priests will be needed tonight.'

'Anyway, you are here now.' I was being churlish and I knew it. 'Come here. Let me kiss you.' I pulled him to me even though he still held the bundles from his errands.

It was a scrappy, rushed affair. I hesitate to be excessively crude, but it is essential somehow. I do apologise. There was no poetry or tenderness to the encounter. It seemed to be no more than a race to release and I was too rough with him and took him meanly. He cried out but I covered his mouth with mine. I did not let him sit over me to choose his pace. I cannot say why, for it was usual.

After we washed again and dressed, Joe disappeared behind my bureau to repair, something he never did, but then helped me with my garments. All through it, he never said a word. Usually, dressing was a time for softness – as he wrapped me in my banyan, I would kiss his hands and tell him all he meant to me, or he would be naughty as he tucked me into my breeches. But that day, he was like a soldier measuring out rations. As he fixed my band, I tried to kiss him, but he turned away and went to fetch my shoes.

'What have I done?' I said, 'Will you not kiss me?'

'Please sit, Monsieur. I must lace your shoes.'

'Monsieur? You call me Monsieur? What is the matter with you?'

He continued and then set about retrieving a rosette to place over the lacing.

'I have done something. Now tell me what it is? Do you not love me now?' Even my scribe is shaking her head at me and tutting.

'You know what you have done.'

'No, I do not. Your skin is still attached to mine and now I am Monsieur?'

'You have tried to punish me. For being late I suppose; always jealousy.'

'What?'

'I wasn't here a full minute before you started demanding where I had been and why I was late, as if I were dishonest, the lazy manservant. And then before I had had a chance to catch my breath, you set about slaking your heat.' To my eternal shame and horror, he began to shake, tears, his face a knot of pain. 'You have hurt me. I asked you to slow and you ignored me. You have used me as your whore.'

I felt as though I had been kicked in the throat by a plough horse.

'Joe, I beg you, that is not right at all. I hold you in greatest respect. The greatest respect. It is true it was a bit, well, it was not our loveliest union, but ... Will you forgive me? I cannot say how sorry I am, I am appalled.'

He stood arms to his side, unable to move. I had never seen him like it. I went to hold him to me, to comfort him, but he flinched as if I had struck him.

'Please, my love, please come and sit here with me.'

'You took no time at all and all to punish me.'

'I would never punish you.'

'You would never punish the one you loved. But you would your servant.'

'Dear God, you are not my servant. You are my husband. I love you. You must know that.'

'You used me basely.'

'I don't know what to say. Please forgive me, please forgive me. Come here and sit with me. Let me kiss you.'

He eventually came to sit by my side and let me enfold him, and we sat together for as long as we needed to make his hurt subside. 'Forgive me, forgive me.'

He made to move away. 'I have errands to run.'

'More errands? It is too hot.'

'I am meant to go to collect the music you ordered from Paris.'

'Oh, the libretto!'

'Yes.'

'I have waited for that. I am going to have it performed. When you hear it, you will understand why this composer is so much in the King's favour. His arrangements are audacious.'

'Well, I cannot sit and have you love me when I must go and collect your audacious songs.'

I knew it was a well-disguised test, which I could fail so easily.

'No, my love, not a word of it. We will spend the afternoon together.'

'How?'

'Well, we will walk to the pools to swim. Every last knave in Avignon and his pretty maiden is at the race. We will be free.'

In my experience, swimming always seems like a better idea than it is. We had not left the horses and men for more than

ten minutes and we were parched and exhausted. The afternoon sun was bleached to white, making the walk particularly
difficult and the prospect of a swim all the more appealing. Joe
was, as was customary, walking a stride or so behind me but,
even taking that and the heat into account, he was lagging.

I waited for him under a large cypress. 'What is the matter?'

'You have to ask?'

'Yes, I am asking.'

'I told you.' He was out of breath. 'You were too rough, there
has been a lot of blood.'

'What? Why did you not say? Sit here, it is cool.' The depth
of my mortification. Readers, I can barely record this.

'I did say.'

'Well, not as such. *Pardieu*, this is madness. We must go
back.'

'No, it's as far back as up. I should like to submerge myself
a little in the water. It may help.'

'Oh, heaven.' What had I done? 'Give me the bag, sit here.'

'We should go on, the pools are not much further.'

We sat a while and all I could think was what a beast I was,
a shameful beast. He sat so quietly, his eyes shut against the
heat, so still, not complaining at all. I would not have known
had I not seen him struggle with the climb.

'I simply do not have words.'

'Well, that would be the first time since I've known you.'

'I must express my remorse—'

'I preferred your silence. Truly.'

We walked slowly to the pools. The lackeys at the base of the
hill had instructions to sound an alarm should anyone come
along the road. The pools were up a rocky way and then along
a ridge of trees. It was the most perfect place of seclusion and
with a boating tournament in the city, we were likely to be the
only ones there. Joe could not swim, there being very little call

for it in his childhood, but Hortense and I had come to the pools often as children with our nursemaid and tutor, who believed very firmly in outdoor pursuits. When Uncle heard that we were swimming instead of studying, the tutor was dismissed and Hortense was set to sewing. Swimming was in his eyes the pursuit of stable boys and shepherds. Evidently, our tutor did not believe in outdoor pursuits at all, other than those he could pursue with the nursemaid.

I put my arm through Joe's as we went up the last steep climb so that he could lean on me a little. The heat was intense. He resisted.

'We might be seen.'

'What of it? You are protecting me from falling. Anyway, anyone who comes here in the heat of the afternoon on the day of a tournament is surely hiding something themselves.'

The pools were perfection. They were the clearest turquoise, mineral and clean with great grey slabs that protruded into them at a gentle slope so that Joe could sit happily to the side in the shallows while I floundered about in the depths. Now I remember that afternoon in the water as a perfect moment, Arcadia, Eden, innocence, the air scented with the hot pepper of the trees and shrubs. We removed our clothes and, oh, the sun on my skin, I was a child again as I sank into the cool depths.

'Is it a tonic?'

He smiled, 'Yes, it is.'

I had to keep moving or I would sink. 'I am glad. And sorry. Will you swim?'

'You know I don't know how.'

'You have no need, I will hold you afloat.'

'No, no.' He shook his head. 'No.'

'You must not thrash about, only hang on to me and trust that I am keeping us at the surface.'

'Oh, I see. I must trust you?'

A moment passed. I continued to move in the water, watching him as he sat on the flat rock, semi-submerged, carefully removing the pinecones that had fallen down and floated to the sides. He refused to look at me.

'I will not let you sink. Come.' I swam closer to him. There was no sandy bank where he could ease in. He would have to simply drop off the rock where he sat. It was not that deep and, I confess, part of me felt he was being a little theatrical in his refusal. But I could see that he wished to try. That was his nature. 'You need not leap, only shift carefully off the rock and I will catch you.'

'You will catch me?'

'I will. I will catch you.'

'Will you? Will you catch me? Will you? Will—' And with that he did exactly as I told him not to and launched at me like a Spanish cannonball at an English galleon. *Pardieu*, he near knocked me out and then clung at me, laughing.

'You are strangling me, you swine. Joe, kick your legs or we will both drown.'

'No. I will not. I'm trusting you. You kick yours.'

How a man can both drown and laugh at the same time is astonishing, even now, and that he did not kill us both is a wonder.

'God in heaven, you are not sound of mind. But look, you are nearly swimming.' It was a messy effort though and at least twice he near pushed me under.

'Am I?'

'You will drown me, you need to relax. Hang around my neck but relax your body and limbs, it will make you float.'

He managed to hang more lightly around my neck. I moved us through the water, across the pool to the other side, where the rock was a sheer drop from the trees and ferns above it, ending in an overhanging slab. I found a tiny ledge under it where I could just about hold on with one hand and prevent our early demise. He was so close, our bodies so alive in the cool water. He was joy and danger together, his wet hair and face jewelled with the water as it ran down him.

'Do I float?'

'You most certainly do, having nearly drowned us both.'

'Then we die together.'

'Well, something lovers should always aspire to.'

'That was my reasoning. But look, I'm swimming.' His joy took me over as it always did.

'Well one of us is swimming, the other is hanging on.'

Oh, I should not have, but his arms around my neck, needing me to hold him, trusting me to do it. His luminous joy at his own daring, the water, the cool and the heat.

'Do I dare?' I asked.

'Of course.'

I kissed him, there in the water where anyone could see our naked forms pressed together, see how he wrapped his legs around my waist and kissed me back. How I grasped him to me, desperate for his forgiveness.

5

Drowning

What *sweetness* was ours. Even my weary-hearted scribe finds herself melting when reading our tale. I catch her smiling at our love. She tells me she is disarmed by the innocence and bounding joy of it. That was exactly its temper and even she can confess to understanding how precious that is in a world bent on miserable competition and cruelty.

I was due at a musical evening that my precious comtesse was hosting. I am not sure I have mentioned before just how much I detested the lute. An insufferable noise that centuries later can still set my skin on edge. But I had committed. I had been overlooking her and was determined that I should go and make great a show of my affection. I had even bought her a small trinket to apologise for my absence of late.

Joe, still triumphant after his victory over certain death in the water and knowing his friends were over-soaked after the boat races, took himself to the alehouse. He later reported the miserable events thus:

He was enjoying a cup alone on a bench, half-watching a card game at a nearby table, when he felt someone step over from behind. He turned to see Marielle. He had not seen her in close proximity since the horrible night of their altercation in the kitchen.

'Hello.'

'Marielle.'

'You look glum.'

'No. I am tired and I am drunk.'

'No doubt. It's been a busy day, hasn't it?'

'Were you at the boats?'

'No. You?'

'No.'

'May I sit here?'

'If you must.'

'Aren't you going to ask me where I was this afternoon?'

'Marielle, where were you this afternoon?'

'I went for a walk with a friend.'

'Oh.'

'To the pools.'

I can only imagine how this must have felt for Joe, as her words bludgeoned into him with all the force she intended.

''S'nice.'

'Imagine my surprise to see you there. And your master.'

'No surprise. He likes to swim there. I am often called to accompany him.'

'Of course.'

'Are you done? Will you leave me to my cup?'

'That's no way to talk to a lady. Are you promised to another?'

'Perhaps,' he said.

'What does perhaps mean? You either are or you are not. And either way, I don't care.'

'Your ways reek, Marielle. Leave me to my drink.'

'Come, can I not give you comfort?' She reached forward with her hand on his breeches.

'Leave me, you're too fresh.'

'You did not mind being touched in the pool. Your master has ways about him, does he not?'

'Ways? He was teaching me to swim. A master likes his valet to be accomplished.'

'Stuff and nonsense.' She had leaned in too close, so to be eye to eye. 'Why did he hold you so close?'

'I was drowning, you fool. Have you not heard me? I cannot swim.'

'He held you, handsome Joe, as close as a suckling babe to his naked chest. And a fine form he has too. And from what I saw a good long yard. Though I s'pose you know that?'

(I confess I was delighted to have my phenomenal virility acknowledged, but dared not interject.)

'You're disgusting. Get away from me.'

'Why? Will you not have me? Am I not to your liking? Am I not pretty? Your master is pretty.'

Evidently, Joe was now ever the worse for his ale and looking for a way to escape Marielle and her deceits.

'I'm leaving.'

'So soon? We are not yet properly reacquainted, though I dare say I have seen enough to know I should like to know you more.'

'I've already had enough of your acquaintance.'

He was not two feet out the door and around the side to make his way home when she was upon him. She grabbed at his neck and with her evil little claws grappled down his jerkin and grabbed his poesy ring, the one I had given him, ripping it from its leather.

'Give me that, you sow.'

'Make me give it you.'

'I will beat you until you give it back.'

'What is this? Who will you beat?' It was a man who Joe recalled owned some of the dyer's mills.

'This woman has stolen my ring.'

'It is mine, I am sure. Only I cannot read it well in this light.' She turned it round and peered into it.

'Give it back, you stupid sow.'

'Mind your language. Are you not the Marquis de Baudelaire's man? You're not in livery.'

'I'm his valet.'

'I will report this disorder to him. And you are drunk.'

'Yessir. But, sir, that is still my ring.'

'Give it here, girl, and I will judge whose it is.'

He took it from her and held it to the window of the inn to read it well.

'JB and JK. Even beyond death. 1657.'

Marielle gasped in shrill delight. A nasty victory.

'What is your name, girl?'

'Marielle, I am Marielle. I am mistaken, it is not my ring.'

'What is your name, boy?'

'Jonathan Kryk, sir.'

'Then it appears to be yours. Take it and be on your way. I will send a message to your master tomorrow, mind. If you had been in household colours, you would have been whipped.'

By the time he reached my chamber, Joe was sober enough to relate the events but still too far under the draught to be sensible about it. He lay babbling and carrying on and would not hear a word I said to try and make sense of it all.

'She grabbed your yard? Did you respond?'

'*That's* what concerns you? Have you not listened one bit to what I'm telling you? The ring, the ring has been exposed and it will betray us.'

'How?'

'She saw us together in the water and then confirmed it with your declaration. How is this not death to us?'

'She could not have seen us under the rock.'

Joe was not comforted by this at all. The ale was not

helping his cause. The matter of the poesy ring *was* troubling. I had given Bobo a ring but it had simply said, 'Your
service is my debt'. Somewhat more chaste than, 'JB & JK
Even beyonde death'.

'Here, you must take it back.' Joe pulled the ring over
his head.

'Absolutely not. Quite apart from the pain it would cause
me, now that it is known to exist, to suddenly not wear it would
be even more suspicious. We are to act as innocents, as if the
swim and ring and whatever else seems to be the issue are
innocuous. Unless by returning it to me you mean something
else?'

He said nothing but shut his eyes. It occurred to me he was
considerably more inebriated than I had first thought. His eyes
ratcheted open again.

'Are the doors locked? What am I doing here? I should go
to my own cot.'

'You came to tell me about the altercation and warn me
to expect a letter from whatever his name is, Monsieur Le
Teinture, who saw all of this. This is no time to panic.' My
scribe would like it mentioned that I admitted to her that my
panic may have been worse than his, my mind reeling this
way and that.

'I don't think I can do this.'

'You've had too much to drink and the day was long. Go
and sleep.'

'But I don't sleep, I'm tired all the time, I'm always afraid.
I ... you, Jehan, you ask too much of me and for what?'

'For what?'

'Yes, for what?' He clawed himself upright, taking his ring
as he went and wrestling it over his head.

'For what? What are you saying? For love. You are my
beloved.'

He was too quiet, defeated. Tears washed down his face.

'But I will always be a man and your servant.'

The morning dawned with the funereal stench of a plague wind. I must have slept but woke in a bad way. My chest ached and I could feel all the weight of our deception squatting like a fat demon on the bed next to me. There was no sign of Joe and I feared the worst – he had gone.

It was later than I had hoped. The sun was already blinking over the trees.

There was a knock at my chamber door.

'Enter.'

'Monsieur.'

'*Nom de Dieu,*' I rushed behind him and pushed shut the door, bolting it before kissing him. 'I thought you had run away.'

'Where would I go?'

'Let me love you.'

'No. I'm too afraid. That man will be along shortly and everywhere I go I feel watched. The whole kitchen eyes me.'

I ignored him, took him to me and we stood together, arms around each other's waists, for as long as we could, trying to find each other again through the disorder that seemed to be building.

'What are we going to do?' he asked.

'There is nothing to do. We should establish our defence between us, that story must not alter. The ring for filial devotion and service, and yesterday, I taught you to swim.'

'I don't think I should come to you for a time.'

'We are careful, the doors are bolted, no one has access to my rooms but you.'

'I am so afraid. You know I have been discovered before. I know what follows. Let's be careful for a while.'

'Do not fall victim to fear. Should anything be suggested, I will make sure it is quashed. I do have some influence beyond my bedchamber you know.'

He stepped back from me.

'It makes no difference. You will be exiled and I will be executed. Your uncle will make it seem that I conspired to trap you. The stocks are full of people like me and very few like you. How can I never get you to see this?'

'Because I do not accept it.'

'But it is the truth, Jehan, it is the truth.'

'No. It is only the truth if I denounce you.'

'You think your uncle will allow you not to? He will lock you up and write the denunciation for you if he has to.'

'Then I will write another, saying different.'

'Then we will both die.'

'Don't say that. Where can we go? Can we not steal away together? Quebec?'

'Don't be mad. Pirates, remember?'

'True, the smell of them and all those filthy shipmen.' I began to think where we could go. 'So, perhaps closer to hand, Italy and then Tunis. Or Turkey. We would be much welcomed; I hear it is quite common there.'

'Stop it.'

'I am quite serious. Or even Paris.' No one cares for a provincial marquis in the pell-mell of Paris. I could cast off my name, take modest residence and live there, a lowly writer.

In the end, of course, the letter arrived from the monsieur telling me what I already knew. My manservant had scuffled with a former maid. The scene reflected very poorly on my household, though mercifully for me he was not at the time in livery. It was his duty to report it to me as he felt certain I would not approve.

I could not decide how to counter the fire that was certainly coming my way. I knew my uncle would probably know about it already; Marielle would have screamed so wildly on her return he would have been informed before the dawn chorus.

And so it was. Within another two days I received my uncle's summons. He would not have demanded I see him over a servant's spat in an inn.

I made sure to dress in sober colours and arrived early but waited out of sight to get my mind in order. I knew that above all I should try to be sensible, deferential and simply see the summons as a test to endure, nothing more. Joe and I had made sure we agreed on our defence. He was pallid when I left him.

'Uncle.' I kissed his hand.

'Sit.'

'Thank you. How are you?'

'We are not here to discuss how I am.'

'Still, I hope you are well.'

'Jehan, I am deeply troubled.'

'I can—'

He held up his hand. He thought himself the pope. 'I am deeply troubled by your conduct.'

'My conduct? How so? Is it the wine? I have resolved to be more moderate. And I only went to the theatre for Monsieur Molière. I would not go were it any other piece, but he is such a great inspiration to me.'

'Stop with this infernal babbling! This is a serious matter.'

'Of course.'

'There is a feeling, and one with which I concur, that your conduct – in particular your conduct around your manservant – is somewhat over-familiar.'

'I see.'

'I am not sure you do. While of course a good manservant may be in one's household for many years, it would be most unfortunate should he be seen to take advantage of his proximity to his master and, shall we say, exploit that position for his own advancement. In addition, it might be that this close proximity of master and valet may create, and I am keen to put this delicately, the very harmful impression of a bond that goes beyond the strictures of the natural affection a man must owe his master. Do you understand me?'

'I'm not sure I do. Mister Kryk is a very loyal servant and shows a care for his duties that I consider praiseworthy. He is punctual, sober—'

'I will decide how sober he is.'

'Uncle, I am not a child. I run my own household and am perfectly happy with the way they fulfil their duties.'

'Do these duties extend to affection?'

'I would certainly hope so. A servant owes his master a clear duty of affection and gratitude. I am sure you will agree?'

'Are you quite clear what I am asking?'

'Yes. I am quite clear, and I would ask *you* why you ask what you do?'

'Then let me ask again, for my own clarity. It pains me even to have to say it, for some wickedness cannot even be spoken. Is there a – I can hardly think it – a masculine affection between you and your manservant?'

'Pfft, what a notion. Where do you get this?'

He sat impassive in his chair, which might have been a throne for the tone he took.

'Jehan, I must caution you, there are more than a few rumblings gathering about you on this matter.'

'Rumblings? There are no rumblings. This is the word of gossip and speculation. Perhaps you should ask who is best served by this nonsense, for it has nothing whatsoever to do with me.'

'I think not. I have had occasion to hear a good deal of talk. And not just talk.'

'Oh, I suppose you have evidence?' I could feel the skin across my chest burn all through. I knew that if I looked at him too directly, I would betray my terror. I made a point of very slowly picking a piece of dust from my leg.

'Well, you forget how small this city is. It is not difficult to find all manner of information. For example, do not think that a swim on a warm day goes unrecorded.'

'You spy on me? Well, of course you do.'

'Oh,' he held his fingers in a steeple, 'I would not go that far. But I have made enquiries and they have been most instructive.'

'Uncle, please. I have swum for years. Alone and with company.'

'Yes, but it is the company that is the tell, not the desire to swim. Though I would venture that you are too old for it and it is not seemly in man of your name. You are not a shepherd. In addition, there is a ring, a little token, one which your man-servant wears, hidden I might add. And, you also wear such a ring, though you do not today. Why did you not?'

'I am not so bonded to it; I wear it occasionally—'

'Occasionally you say, and yet your finger bears its brand.'

I glanced to my hand, which was indeed circled in red where I had prised off the ring with oil.

'A ring for which you offered Gambaccini's prentice extra payment should he engrave it discreetly and quickly.'

'You are, it seems, mad, Uncle. A man of God who spies on own family?'

'Back to the rings, what was engraved? Ah, I have it here.' He reached into his coat and placed on the table between us the paper I had used to write the inscription: *Even beyonde death*.

'Look at it.'

'I do look at it.'

'You deny it is your hand?'

'No. I do not deny it.'

'So you admit you have bought for your servant, your man-servant, a love token?'

'I admit I have bought my servant a token of thanks for his service to me. I was near dead from fever and I believe he saved my life.'

'These are not words of gratitude for service, Jehan. This is a confession of love.'

'No, Uncle. It is not. It is a token of thanks. I am sorry that your imagination has explored a world of meaning beyond that. I feel that this line you pursue is very much more telling of your turn of mind than of mine.'

'Impertinent, revolting, how dare you? The ring, what of the ring?'

'I am a writer. I may have over-embellished the language, even you accuse me of that, but I can assure you it was not intended as anything more than a token of thanks.'

'Then why did you have it paid for "discreetly"?'

'The discreet payment was in fact for the hasty engraving of a bracelet for my dear sister. As it turns out, the rings were inscribed hastily and the bracelet was not. And you are further mistaken, or at least your spies are, Uncle, for I paid Gambaccini himself and not any prentice spy who would try to make commerce from gossip. That he misunderstood the instruction can hardly be considered my fault.'

'You are speaking in circles. Weaving your worst little fictions. Can you say why your servant secreted his on his person?'

'I cannot say. Perhaps he found the gold too rich for his taste.'

'The gold is too rich for his station, not his taste.'

'Uncle, you are trading in gossip, all your evidence comes from questionable types. These are lackeys and prentices. You would do well not to be turned by their wickedness or you will soon find yourself mired in your own scandal. Do you think it fitting that a man of God, with his eyes on Rome, sends maids out on errands of wanton entrapment?'

'You were not so dismissive of her when you came across her.'

'Well, then I should certainly thank you for her. She was very eager. And I had great sport with her, and roughly too, as you well know.'

'Stop it. You are base.'

'Oh, it is I who is base? Are you sure you would not like more on it? Which way she bent and how well and that she took to panting like a birthing sow while doing it?'

'Enough!'

'I have to wonder if peddling whores to your nephew is the best path to Rome? And to think I was minded to empty a few coffers to assist in your campaign to douse your body in cardinal red. Ah, so that has caught your attention. Well, we all have our base passions it seems.'

'That is enough! Do not try to turn this on me. You have not behaved well. You have been undisciplined. People like to talk and these are complicated times for us all. A scandal involving a servant would not be favourably received. Dutch, isn't he? He wears his hair like a Protestant too. And some have seen him use his devil's hand when he thinks he is alone. He is not made of godliness and by your association, nor are you. You may deny it, but I know what I know and before God, I will see that if you are found with evidence, you will both be punished.'

'What? You will denounce me, have me tried, dragged into stocks and burned?'

He paused. Charging his musket anew. 'There is another way, of course. You must dismiss your man. In light of the talk that is already circulating, it is the only sensible option.'

It was all I could do not to cry out. Instead I managed a more moderate response, though my frustration and fury must have been apparent. 'Uncle, we have this moment established that there is no impropriety. There is no crime. There is nothing for your evidence.'

'Not so. You have simply denied it.'

'I have given you my word.'

'What of it?'

'You insult me, Uncle.'

He turned to signal he had had enough. 'Your valet will go. And that is the end of it.'

'Uncle, he will not. And not because I wish to protect him or myself from an indiscretion, but because I will run my household as I see fit. Sending him away would create a scandal where none exists. It would be an admission of sin where none exists.' I stood.

This had not occurred to him; I saw a moment of doubt flash across his cool face.

'Very well. For now he may stay, but I know your every breath, I know your wickedness and you are playing with fire, Jehan, the devil's own torch.'

I managed a courteous exit as best I could, heat and fever about my brow, my breath again short and difficult. I quickened my step as soon as I was outside of my uncle's view and that of his household, the spies and cretins. I could feel the heat rising up in my stomach and I was only moments through his gate when I had to rush to the wall and my stomach heaved itself full out.

6

Learning to Die

We are disconsolate this morning, my scribe and I. She begins to understand the impossibility of my love for Joe, the cost of it. She slept poorly, unsettled by my desperation and fear. It tends to be that way. Whatever the story needs for its telling, she must hold it too, in order to best express it. I am grateful for that service.

As we sit together now, a silence depends between us. She imagines I slip my arm through hers and lay my head on her shoulder. She feels that I am close. There we remain, absorbed in each other and gathering strength from that companionship for what lies ahead.

August burned its way through the days – wind and sun and dust that could make you mad from constant assault – and came to a miserable end. By early September, the evenings had begun to cool enough to suggest respite was on the way.

Joe and I were in poor form, desperately trying to do nothing to raise suspicion. I was lonely and prone to a terrible melancholy that made waking each day an awful burden, only relieved by knowing that Joe would soon arrive and we could spend some moments together. But he was constantly looking over his shoulder, paranoid and suspicious of all the household. With fear came distance and the grief of it was near crushing. I missed him.

I woke one morning already drenched in tears. By the time Joe knocked, I had curled in on myself, a child in a storm.

I sat up to see him. 'I cannot survive. I would rather burn on the pyre.'

He sat next to me on the bed, his face grey and expressionless. He was depleted. He pressed his forehead to mine.

'We cannot,' he said.

'I die without you.'

'Then we are both learning how to die.'

As the weeks passed and the heat eased, I tried to be seen more: walks along the river when those of quality might be about, cards with Villeneuves on a number of evenings and even an effort to be sociable with ladies at a soirée held by the Marquis de Graveson. I was, of course, the source of great comedy and none would ever have known my true temper. But every effort at humour and levity took such blood from me that after surviving two successive engagements, I took to my bed, drowning in melancholy, and could not be roused for days.

A physician was called. He pronounced an ague and took his money. That night, from deep inside a dream where I was imprisoned in a tower with no door, I felt a familiar weight to my side. When I woke, Joe was there, on top of the sheets in his livery but lying behind with his arms around me, telling me he loved me and begging me to come back to him.

So it was that over the course of these weeks we began to plan our escape. To begin with, more as a fantasy. It was impossible to continue as we were. There was the problem of money. Naturally, I had a good deal of it, but it was not simply sitting in neat bags, ready to be taken. To organise it for escape might raise an alarm. We did not know how far we might go. To Paris first and then on. Perhaps even England, unthinkable as that was, and then to Quebec. It was a circuitous route but one designed to conceal us and pirates be damned. I would leave instructions for my office and estates, and they could be carried out by a legal proxy I would appoint in absentia. I would sell my marquisate. Some merchant from Marseilles could buy it with his shiny new coins.

You will think this an overreaction: to sell one's title, land and reputation – inherited from my father and his father before him – and steal away in the night with a bag of books and some coins. Nothing had been discovered, there was no imminent mortal threat, nothing had changed at all. But everywhere, the walls had eyes and the doors ears. No one could be trusted.

Then came great and joyful news. Now that the heat had subsided, Uncle was to travel for a month rallying support and plumping the coffers for his cause. Which was, of course, himself.

Joe was delighted. 'I shall come back after dark.'

'Earlier if you can. Monsieur Benoit will be out until tomorrow. He visits his sister. I gave him leave.'

'You should give him leave more often.'

'Such freedom! Bring wine too, lots of it.'

He kissed me well. 'Drink this 'til later.'

He had not been so naughty and sweet for a while. He looked happy and his face had relaxed back unto itself after weeks of misery. Stupidly, and yet as you know not without shameful precedent, I made some effort to look more attractive than I had of late. Joe had been greeted, these last weeks, by the saddest man in the world. He had been patient and kind and while I was free to mope and sulk, he had still to be out and at his duties. I resolved to spruce myself to welcome him that evening. And spruce I did, availing myself of nearly a full bottle of oil in my torturous and thoroughly frustrating stab at shaving my own beard. It was a near-surgical undertaking.

'A thing to behold, Husband.'

'Are you appreciative?'

'You know I am.'

He came to me and ran his fingers across my cheek. 'Oh no, did you cut yourself?'

'You offend me. I did not. Not a bit.'

'You mean not a lot.'

'Once or twice.'

'I count at least four.'

'That's enough of that. Instead, let us make merry. Where is the wine?'

We drank quickly and talked and kissed and talked some more, greedy for any information the other had to offer, gossip too. The idle chatter of the dearest of friends.

My cousin Maurice was required to pay an amount to keep silent the pregnancy of a girl in the market. Joe suggested she was not at all with child but rather she and her true lover were cheerfully extorting my hapless cousin. Normally I might have sided with Maurice, but the cunning was so brazen and so clever I was minded to encourage him to give her double the number for good measure. More gossip was that one of the Clusy de Marcilliacs had an unpleasant condition in his nethers and, very new to me, my stable boy who looked about twelve years old had fathered his second child in the past few months.

'I did receive a letter from my mother,' said Joe, once we had stopped enjoying the misfortune of others. 'She is much better. The extra income has made her well.'

'That is excellent then.'

'I'm grateful.'

'Puh, it is only money.'

'It gives her life.'

'What other news from Holland? A pox? A plague? A

colony? I can't even remember with whom you war these days. Is it still the English? Probably Spain too. You are an ambitious place.'

'We are. And you should be pleased for it. We are not deterred by flag-waving and posturing. When we set our sights on a prize, we will have our conquest.'

'I am eternally grateful that warmongering is your national pastime. It has made you a most charming conqueror.'

He paused a while. 'There is other news from home.'

'Yes?'

'Edvard returned.' He looked up through his brows to gauge my temperature.

'Oh?' I was so bland in my response that it practically screamed torment.

'I knew you'd be upset.'

'I am not upset. Merely benignly interested, as you will have judged from my careful and most painfully indifferent delivery of "Oh?".'

'There is nothing to be upset about. He has returned and went to see my mother.'

'He went to find *you*. That much is clear.'

'Yes.'

A sigh had fallen across our merriment.

'He loves you still.' It hurt me to say it.

'No. He never did. It was I who loved him more. He asked my mother if she could recommend him to cartographers in my father's name. Give good reference.'

'He did not ask where you were? I do not believe it, and why do you say did he not love you?'

'Oh, Monsieur, you have *questions*. Well, I was not the only one he had. He was well loved.'

'The brute. If he comes here, I will have him killed. Run through with a short sword or better yet, sent to the bears.'

He looked sad but allowed himself some humour at that.
'Bears?'

'Of course. And that is too good for him. Come, my love, let
me kiss you so that you might forget all this misery.'

'There is one thing more related to the short swords and
bears. My mother says she told him where to find me.'

'Oh. Unfortunate. Why would she do it? She knew what he
did to you.'

'I don't know. But she is old and he is clever.'

'His arrival would be a great complication. Notwithstanding
my honour-bound duty to kill him, if he were to come here and
find you uninterested, might he cause trouble?'

'He would not. It would implicate him. And he will not
come.'

'I will still have him killed.'

'You are very jealous, Jehan. It is your one failing.'

I looked at him and I thought, *I love this man more than anything
else in the world.* And on thinking it I knew I could and would
leave Avignon as a beggar for him.

'Even if he does not come, perhaps we should go. As you
suggest.'

'What?'

'We cannot continue as we are.'

'Are you serious? Is this the truth?'

'Yes.'

'When?'

His face was on fire with joy.

'Soon. Before the end of September.'

Once I had said it and felt the relief that came with it, and
the passion it ignited in him, I knew that it was the best and
only choice. We would be free.

To choose escape was to choose life.

'Freedom!'

'Yes, freedom.'
'We will live as kings together.'
'Well, more likely beggars. But yes, kings.'

7

The Devil

Freedom. It was a perfect night, with wine and hope and possibility. Anything can be endured if only you have the prospect of another life ahead. It is the sense of entrapment that makes life intolerable.

I decided I would not be able to say goodbye to Hortense. Not only would it compromise our secret, but there was no way I could kiss her sweet face and know I would never see her again. I would write from wherever we arrived, and she would have to forgive me.

Joe had clever plans for our escape and it reminded me that he had been in this position before.'Will you love me even when I am desperately saving the scrapings from others' plates for us to eat?' I asked.

'I think we both know it will be I who is charged with that duty, Jehan.'

'No. I will be cunning and find us whatever we need.'

'You may need to steal paper and ink. Or better yet, find yourself a wealthy lady of quality who will be your patron and who, for small, naughty favours, will give you paper, ink and gold too.'

'Ha. I am sure I can manage that.'

'From marquis to man-whore in one journey.'

'Not at all. I would be providing a necessary service that I may be kept in ink and you in apple cakes.'

'You are assuming she will be pretty. She may be poxy.'

'Oh, I had not thought of that. I had imagined my comtesse.'

'Your favoured wife.'

'Quite so. I should have had her husband poisoned and taken her as my own.'

'Why are you so murderous where love is concerned? But even I can see she's beautiful. All the others talk of her.'

'I can believe it. And have hot dreams about her too, I dare say. She has the loveliest skin. Not a blemish on it. And she is near forty.'

'Raphael claims he had her.'

Raphael, though a quick and clever footman and full of cheek and cheer, was no taller than a child and looked the same; freckled and sallow and a child's voice to go with it.

'I doubt he is old enough to have grown the means to do it. I shall miss her when we leave. She has been a good friend.'

'I heard that at least once her face rested in your lap, your breeches undone.'

'But of course. An excellent hostess. She was always most welcoming.'

And with that he finished his glass in one and came across to me.

My scribe suggests that some readers might prefer to skip ahead to the beginning of our next chapter, for what will now unfold is of a dark nature. We make many a jest on these pages. This, friends, is not one of them, and – for those who have suffered – its telling may provoke distress.

Joe sat over me and had me in, full and hot, and it was not long before I could not hold myself from shouting out, freer than I

had felt for many weeks, my lust and the wine conspiring to
release such great joy. He laughed to see it and I knew it would
make him more wanting, so when I felt I could breathe again
I turned for him and stood next the bed. He ran his hands the
length of my back and told me how he loved me, but he was
ready and eager and he pushed as he grappled at my hips to
give him balance. He was hard and quick and let his voice
expend his pleasure. And then, bellowing, a nightmarish voice
as he pulled back. I turned and there ... there were two great
and terrifying masks, hoods black and long and fearsome.

They drew swords. Their great beaks, the plague doctors'
masks, no faces, no hands, nor arms ... only death and the
terrible glint of swords.

'Stand where you are!'

Their voices deep and muffled through the grotesque beak
of the mask. Joe fell from me and with his hands tried to hide
himself. I turned my front towards the bedpost.

'Stand and do not move or you will die.'

Through the haze of wine and love, I knew what they were.
I wanted to put something around Joe to hide his exposure. I
managed to find my voice, but it was not bold.

'Who sent you?'

'God has sent us.'

This was a trap, a plan of wickedness, and base, base cruelty.
I made to move, to retrieve a blanket from the bed to cover us.

'No. Stand as you are. Now face us.'

The horror to stand so naked, to know what they had seen.
How long had they been there? We had latched the door, I was
sure of it. And where were my guards?

I knew Joe was shivering. He would be near to tears. I too
could feel my heart capsize and with it all hope. This was
our warrant and our execution. These monstrous creatures
were sent to be the witnesses who would stand in our trial and

recount what they had seen to a judge and all assembled. I knew as we turned to face them that worse was to follow. The law would require two witnesses and a physician's evidence that one of us had been had and the other had spent in him. These plague doctors would want their proof; seeing what they had would not be enough.

And so it passed. I cannot recount it clearly. Even now – even out here where cruelty, torture and molestation are so distant and strange – even now I cannot recount it well. I will give you the events, but the horror that came with it is still blunted.

One of the masked doctors held Joe at bay with his sword and I could hear poor Joe weeping and protesting, but I could not help him. I felt myself lift a few inches from my own body, separate beyond my physical form, as the other did his work.

It was the cruellest plunder. I was forced to bend myself – he brought candles so close that I could feel the burn of the wax on my skin – and with instruments and tools he proceeded. This, not what had passed before, was the theft of virtue, the brutalising of my own body.

I cannot say how long it took. Perhaps minutes, perhaps eternity. It matters not. I was un-seamed with horror.

Next to Joe, who, with candle held to his middle, was pulled and wiped with the hideous waxed glove of the inquisitor. And all the while my sweet love just wept and wept as he held my gaze, which I gave back to him to offer some scant solace. I said, without voice, *I love you*, but I knew that like me he had, in his soul, left the room to save himself.

We were told to dress and all the while the physicians, so their type liked to be called, abused our names and called us devils and rubbish. Their masks were so deathly. Hat and gloves all covering so that not a single piece of human flesh would show. These plague doctors were Death's own phantasm, the ghouls of disease and infection. As if we two would somehow infect them with our wicked ways.

I managed to find my voice. 'Who sent you? You did not come here of your own accord.'

'You will find out soon enough, Baudelaire.'

'Marquis de Baudelaire. Tell me who sent you?'

'Hurry. We have time to keep.'

'Whose time?'

'You, devil, will discover it when we get there,' said the taller one.

I realised for the first time that we were being taken away. That having their evidence, they were arresting us.

'Joe, take a cloak, we are being taken away.'

'Do not speak to one another.'

'He is not aware that we are to leave now.'

'Quiet!'

The stockier one grabbed my arm and over my shoulder, I could see Joe manage to grab a cloak. I was, perhaps unreasonably given the gravity of the circumstances, suddenly fixated that he might be cold. I was marched down my own stairs, Joe behind me. I tried to turn to see him, but the physician had me cruelly pinned. There was not a soul about. No lackey nor maid nor mouse even stirred as we were taken along and out across my threshold, which was wide open to the night.

It occurred to me that we would be executed right there in the dark night, run through with swords by these death-makers and that would be the end. But instead, under the scant light the moon offered, I could make out a covered wagon. We were both pushed up against it and our hands pulled rough behind us, hard and sharp so that I felt a burn all through my arms and then rope wound around so tight it cut.

I tried to say, 'Joe, say nothing, admit nothing,' and was hit across the back of my head. Then a sack, foul-smelling and coarse, was pulled over my face; Joe's too apparently, as I could hear his protests, saying he could not breathe well.

'Wait 'til the flames begin to lick, then see how well you breathe.'

Somehow, we were rolled into the back of the cart. Inside, I knew Joe was to my left, I could feel his shoe or knee at my own. The two went up front with the driver. Their masks were off, and they sounded as men, not the ghouls they had before. One was gruffer and spoke with an accent. The other was local, I thought I knew his timbre.

The moment the cart began to move I tried to find Joe. 'Can you hear me? Where are you?' I felt him shuffle himself.

'I am here. I cannot move.'

'Do not try then.'

'Who are they?'

'I don't know.'

'We will die.'

I wished I could offer a dismissive joke to encourage him, but I could not. I had no idea who these men were, whom they represented and in whose name they had arrested us.

'Joe, I love you. Do not forget it. No matter what.'

'Yes.'

'And no matter what they conspire, I will never de-nounce you.'

'Nor I.'

'If we die, we die together. I will not betray you.'

'You could save yourself.' He was flayed with sorrow.

'I will not.'

'You could.'

'No. Never. Do not forget it. Do not let them turn your mind.' I tried to listen to the road, to think where we might be. 'I think we are near the Palais.'

'The guardhouse?'

'I cannot say.'

The hooves became clamorous with echo. We were under a portico or a closed courtyard.

'Driver here and whoa!' We had stopped.

'Joe,' I whispered. 'I will not betray you, no matter what.'

'Do not betray me.'

'Never.'

'Get them out,' came the voice I had assumed was the driver's. 'To the Devil with this rubbish. They will burn a good pyre together.'

Through the sack came light, sharp and clear, but I could not see anything around it, no shape nor form to let me know which building we were near. We were pushed and dragged, tripping as we went. Joe was quiet, I heard only his heavy breath and the sound of his feet as he too struggled to find his way.

The sound of metal announced my arrival at a cell. The sack was ripped away.

'Get in.' I was rudely shoved to the floor, a hard landing.

I turned as quickly as I could, but it was dark and none looked familiar. Joe was shaking his head, still under the sack.

'I won't betray you,' I said.

He nodded his reply, but I could tell he either did not believe me or could not, and before I could say more, he was dragged away, the sound of solid doors opening and closing that I had to strain to hear. When finally a metal gate clanked shut, I knew he was locked away. The relief was immense. He was spared his life.

8

Despair

My scribe struggles to recount this episode and I too find its memory greatly distressing. I can feel her breath comes to her in shorter increments and her heart beats faster as she begins to understand our predicament and worries about my Joe. I take her hand in mine and tell her that we must continue. Only by expressing its full horror can the complete story be told.

They had come on commission. They had been given information, access to my house, and knew Joe and I would be alone. I concluded that Monsieur Benoit must have been bribed, though most likely threatened, to take leave of the household, and my guards paid or killed. We had been trapped.

Water dripped from the ceiling, the walls mossy and ancient. Everywhere damp and nasty. I had never slept in such a place. I had seen a cell once when I had gone to accuse a swindler, and again to see a cousin before his execution after an ill-advised plot went awry, but for me to be interred in such rude discomfort was unthinkable. I should like it noted that the straw onto which I was lobbed was not clean and there was evidence that a mouse had left his waste there. If these miscreants were expecting me, and I had every reason to believe they were, I do think a clean bale, at the very least, might have been reasonable.

I called out again and again – 'Joe? Joe?' – until my voice began to give out. With each call, a compounding terror as the silence continued to muffle my cries. Questions and doubts, suddenly certain I had misjudged events and that he was dead or had been taken somewhere. And – God forgive me, how ashamed I am – I even began, for the merest of moments, to speculate that perhaps the one who had trapped me was Jonathan Kryk of Amsterdam, who arrives from nowhere and of whom nothing is known. But, no, no. That was the trick they played, the poison of their play, knowing that in keeping us apart, doubt would set in. I had stumbled early; I was a coward and little more.

Light began to break through the bars at the top of the wall. I heard footsteps approach, two sets it seemed but I could not truly say. They came towards my cell but then, just as I straightened myself and tried to ready my resolve, they passed me by and continued along the corridor. I tried to hear their course. I had lived in Avignon my entire life, knew every inch and cobble, and still could not understand where we were hidden and where Joe was.

I may have slept. Through my drowsiness and the misery of the cold floor, I began to register noise, my name. It was Joe calling out. 'Where are you?'

'Here, I am here. Joe?'

'Jehan?' His voice seemed to be moving and I could then make out others speaking too.

'Jehan?'

'Quiet you!' And then the sickening thud of a fist on flesh and he exclaimed something I could not make out. 'You're next, devil!' came a shout, back towards me. And then no more.

I called and called his name. No reply came. Instead, then, the sound of a metal door closing and again the silence that had been there before.

Dear God, was he to be executed? I felt a heat begin to engulf me. It began across my chest and started to choke me. I heaved once and spilled my belly into the straw.

Then, I heard the door opening and footsteps approaching. I stood quickly and tried to straighten myself, pat down my hair and hide any evidence of distress. Oh, readers, it took all of my will to do it. I had been performing a complicated charade my entire life and this was hardly the situation in which to abandon one's supports: *comédie*, bearing, *élan*. I could not let them see they had frightened me half to death. No matter who they were, until I had been tried – and even after – I was still the Marquis de Baudelaire. The swines would know it.

'Baudelaire, you now.'

'Please, it is Marquis.'

The cell door opened and there were my captors, my abusers, but unmasked and in better light. I felt in my bones that one was known to me. I could not say where from and Avignon was not so large that I might not have seen him about. He produced the sack again and before I could even begin to protest, it was pulled over my head and my hands grappled behind my back so that I had to tip forward to avoid pain.

'No trouble, hear? Don't make me do what I had to do to that foreigner.'

'What did you do to him?'

They were steering me roughly along so that I struggled to keep from falling over.

'Where is Mister Kryk? I demand to know.'

'Quiet!'

'You are thugs. When I am free, I will see to it that you are sodomised by a mule. My own mule. He is a brute and will kick you too.'

The kick I then received knocked me clean to the floor and I lay there clutching at my gut where the boot had landed. I had not yet recovered from the blow, which felt as if it had ruptured my whole side, when another fell and another and then I was dragged upright again. I could hardly breathe for the pain.

They dragged me down around corners, so many corridors, that I lost all sense of direction. A door opened, then another, more corners. Then we stopped. My captor knocked on a door loudly three times and the door opened.

'Here is the other devil. This is the one that had it done to him. Witnessed and evidenced.'

I was shoved forwards so that I fell hard, but even before my face hit the floor beneath me and I had straightened myself, I knew exactly where I was.

9

My Heart Breaks Still

'Uncle. What a delight.'
The sack was pulled from my head, I blinked to try
and adapt my eyes. Joe was not there.

'Here is Satan's work,' said the thug.

My uncle stood impassive.

'So it is.'

'You? You have done this to me?'

'You have done it to yourself.'

'No, no, this is your doing. I have been kidnapped and imprisoned. Your own family?'

'You might reconsider your tone. High-handed morality has
never suited you and given where you were found, the very
stuffing of your skin lacks authority.'

'Why would you trap me? You are so cruel and base. Do
you know what those men have done to me? To my person?
They are nothing but butchers and watermen with new cloths.
Monstrous, Uncle, monstrous.' I was being bold.

'You will not raise your voice to me. I alone stand between
you and the pyre. Do you understand me?'

'I do not understand you though I hear you speak. May I sit
down, please?'

'Let me be more plain then. I suppose you could sit. Though
you have the look of a vagrant. More so than usual, if it were

possible. Filthy. No, not on that one, the other.' He pointed me to an unfurnished chair. Hard wood for the abominable and the damned.

'Might I have a drink? Even vagrants must drink. And I am filthy because your fen-suckers could not be bothered to lay fresh straw in the cells. I shall be making a complaint.'

His annoyance showed. 'Hold your peace, just once!' He filled a cup from his table and passed it to me. 'Again, to continue. The Dutchman. I have had occasion to speak to him already.'

I tried to affect indifference but the relief that Joe was at least where I was, and alive, was immense. 'What of it?'

'He claims you made him do it. That it was your wickedness alone that forced him to conspire and that he, being but a servant, had no other option.'

'You lie.'

'You say *I* lie but not he?'

'He did not lie because he did not say it.'

'You are very sure of him.'

'I am.'

'It will cost you, this faith you have. It is misplaced. He has sold you already and when he stands in court and says the same, you will walk to the pyre alone. What is left of you at any rate. He will be sent to the Americas, but he will live to fight another day. Your carcass will be picked at by dogs and crows.'

There was nothing in his voice. No doubt nor remorse nor any grain of compassion. His mind was set and this charade was simply his process of deciding how best to execute his plans. There was only one way that I might get his heart to ease in its blackened path.

'Does my sister know?'

'She has been summoned.'

'You will break her heart, Uncle. You have no mercy for me, this is clear, but what of her?'

He took in a deep breath and pursed his lips. 'She will survive. And it is you who has done this to her. If she does not know it already, she will have suspected. You think the shameless display you provided for your servant, to catch his eye, did not catch the attention of others? Your lasciviousness was as brazen as day. I shudder to even think of it.'

'Nonsense. No one spoke a word of it. In the eyes of Avignon, I did nothing I should not have. I was never indiscreet.'

'They spoke no word because you are my nephew and my name gives you protection.'

'My father's good name gives me respect.'

'But not protection.'

'But I require no protection, save from you.'

'I understand that no one, not even I, can protect you from your God, if you still have one. The law may set you free, but you have done what is the most sordid and most savage in morality and no one can ever, ever give you redemption from that sin. You are damned and you are unholy, Jehan, and you will burn once on the pyre and again in Hell and for eternity.' He was feverous. 'For months I have watched you. Your extravagant ways, your permanent undress, and then your disappearance into your private chambers for days at a time. I visited your home any number of times and was told, *He is writing, only his valet may attend to him.* Writing. Ha! A ruse for the Devil's work. And your valet, quiet as quiet can be, never a word said out of place, always shuffling here and tiptoeing there. A man who writes with his left hand. I know a manwhore when I see one.'

'Do you, Uncle? How so? Have you vast comparative experience?'

'Enough!'

I admit it was too much. I had riled him beyond my intention. 'Apologies.'

'And now you will not listen when I tell you he has betrayed you?'

'I know it not to be true.'

'Jehan, this is beyond my control. I have tried to protect you, but I can no longer do it.'

'What are you saying?'

'I am saying it is beyond my control.'

'Who else would it concern?'

'I cannot say what—'

There came a knock at the door and even before the order was given, Hortense pushed through. She was ghostly.

'Oh, my love.' She threw herself at me with such passion that it must have stung our uncle more than a little. 'What is the matter?'

'Stand away, Hortense. Do not touch him. You do not know what he has done, but it defiles us all.'

'But I know he is dirty and look, he seems unwell. Were you attacked?'

'In a sense.'

'The fault is not with any criminals, Hortense. Rather it is your brother who has committed the crime. He has been discovered in the most unholy wrongdoing. I am sorry that you may need to hear it.'

A bolt flashed across Hortense's brow as she looked at me. I held her eye. Oh, yet more pain I was weighing onto her already-burdened heart. She straightened and turned to Uncle, affecting sweetness.

'I cannot believe it. Not so. There is some mistake.'

'There is no mistake. There are two witnesses, physicians, and they have taken their evidence.'

'Why physicians? What is their business with him?'

'They are in our uncle's employ, Sister.'

'What? Uncle?'

'Do not question me, Hortense.'

She began to shake; I could see her curl her fingers in on her palms and press them there.

'He is my brother. Whatever he has done, there is always a way to find forgiveness and with it, redemption.'

'He has done the lowest. He has committed the most heinous crime before God and the law.'

She turned her back on him and so that he might not see her face. 'Heresy?'

'He has succumbed to his sacrilegious nature, Hortense. He has already spent a night in cells for it and will spend more. I am sorry that you have to hear it said, for you are a lady and a child of God. But your brother is not. He is the most odious; he is a sodomite. And with his manservant, no less.'

I flinched. Hortense however did not move, but held my gaze and I hers. A single tear escaped her eye and as it crossed her cheek, my own followed behind. I did not care that my uncle saw.

She was my only salvation, my love and my greatest remorse. I wanted to beg her. There was no one else who could sway the course of my fate and perhaps that of Joe too.

She continued to look at me, into me as if imploring me to give her reason to defend me. Her face was written over with grief. I had nothing to offer. Simply myself. Soundless lips offered her my only prayer: 'I love you.'

She closed her eyes, she seemed to stretch her neck a breath to the left and then to the right and when her eyes opened again, *nom de Dieu*, she had the look of a man who had just fixed on the breastplate of his armour before war. She turned away and back to our uncle.

'How are we going to help him, Uncle?' Breathless, plead-ing, sweet, sweet Hortense.

His guard was run through with the assault. 'Help? My dear, there is nothing to be done. He must be tried and he will be found guilty. You know the end.'

Again her hands clamped hard on themselves. 'But Uncle, that cannot be. A trial? What of us? For this is the most dam-aging charge imaginable.'

'Us?'

'Our reputation. If he is to be tried, we will be ruined.'

'He has sinned. He is an abomination. We are already ruined. Look. He sits there mute and dirty. It is his disease of devil-worship that makes him thus.'

'He has passed the night in a dungeon, Uncle. We cannot blame him for it. But let us return to what vexes me most.'

Uncle sat back in his throne. She had his attention at least.

'Uncle, I simply cannot hear any more of your talk on this. It is too base and lewd. I am a lady and know little of the world beyond my eye.'

'Of course, my dear, I am sorry to have had to mention it. But I felt you must know his deed.'

'Undoubtedly. But if he has done what you claim and if he has been godless then it must never be discovered beyond our few. We will be destroyed, Uncle. I am not sure my marriage could survive such a scandal and then where will I be? Sent to the convent when my husband deserts me.'

'You see what you have done? Your sister's life as she knows it is over.'

Hortense perched against his desk, her back to him and facing me. 'You have done me a great injury, Brother. A stain on my reputation and that of all your kinsmen.'

'Sister, I am bereft.'

'Not as bereft as I when my husband abandons me and I am

left destitute and childless. And dear, dear Uncle.' She turned back to him. 'You, what is to become of *you?*'

'What of me? I serve my God. Rooting out depravity is his highest calling. I shall be rewarded for my steadfastness. The days of leniency in Languedoc are over. A new order has been pronounced.'

'Yes, and we shall all give praise for your vigilance and determination to purge this evil that my brother seems to harbour. You have been so tireless in God's work, dear Uncle.'

'It is my true calling.' Even for him, this was disingenuous. There seemed a side he was not showing.

'But Uncle, and I do hope you will not judge me unkindly on this, for I know you will not have thought it. While I know that you are not swayed by the offer of higher office and the matter of reputation, other than that before God, what of the men that have staked their own to support you? Can this be the rub? I am of course simply a niece, a sister, but will this awful sin not tarnish them by association?' She turned back to me. 'You see what you have done? Why are you so evil? What is your purpose?' She played a clever game.

'I could not say. Sister, please forgive me?'

'I cannot. My husband will never look on me again. And still childless, this will be my greatest sorrow.' She heaved a great sobbing noise into her hands.

'See what you have done to your sister? Look on her and know this is your work and worse to come.'

'I have nothing to say, only that I am sorry and she must know how I love her.'

'You cannot love her or you would not let her suffer in this way.'

Hortense let out a great wail and again wept into her hands and with great effect. She was magnificent. 'Oh, Uncle, you will be finished, we will both be. Kinship, lineage, alliance, all ruined, ruined and for what? A servant?'

For the first time, a look of doubt, panic even, passed across my uncle's face, though I could not tell if it was Hortense's wailing that gave him edge or some understanding that far from proving his worth before God and society, my entrapment may harm him.

But he was not so dumb. He must have known it. It occurred to me he had thought that to trap me and expose me would prove that he was himself unimpeachable. That he was hoping to gain favour with the newly pious Conti was clear, but he was so intent on being a good lapdog that he had not thought through the consequences – he simply hoped he would come out of it looking victorious. So impeccable was he that he would be willing to sacrifice his own nephew to do God's work. It would present well with the prince. Assuming he even noticed. But what of Clusy de Marcilliac? If this scandal came to the surface and Uncle had misjudged his sponsor, he too would be exposed – our name, our reputation as a family – and he would be cast aside in a cat's breath and quickly disappear from any public life and office. Hortense had let him see, if only for a moment, what might be the outcome if he had misunderstood the reach of his influence and commission. Conti's approval might be fleeting, whereas his sponsor had supported him for years and the damage could be permanent. My sly and beautiful sister had thrown the dice, exposed the gamble and with it the rich purse he might be squandering. With that moment of doubt came the hope of salvation.

'Now cease your crying, Hortense, I cannot think when there is such a clamour.'

'But I am bereft. Bereft and devastated. All of us ruined.' She sobbed again.

'There is, of course, a way out. Perhaps.'

'I can scarce imagine it, Uncle,' said Hortense.

He turned to me. 'You must denounce him, say that it was he who trapped you, that he was sent to trap you and extort favours, money, influence. He is a servant after all. A Dutch one. We will have him named as a Huguenot.'

I looked to Hortense. She had lifted her head from her hands to watch me. Time slowed a moment. The room seemed to fill and heave with heat and weight, crowding and staring. It was as if all the Baudelaire patriarchs, the line of name and inheritance, sat rigid and waiting. The obligation of my bloodline, my failure to assume the role of paterfamilias, cousins, uncles, fathers, all were there. The man who was not there was the foreigner without name or ancestry or household; he had no land nor armies to raise to defend himself and the one on whom these centuries rested. My beloved, even beyond death.

'I will not denounce him.'

'Jehan! Brother, what is wrong with you?'

'I will not send him to be slaughtered.'

'Oh, Brother, no.'

She had fought to save me, bravely, but she needed to fight for us both. What was freedom without the one you love? It would be meaningless.

My cards were shown. My naked heart exposed. 'And I should like to know, where is he? Is he even alive? He was taken from his cell and roughly beaten. Uncle?'

'He is well enough.' Our uncle looked for the first time despondent. 'God and all the saints, you are a fool, a *fool*, and we will all pay the price for you.'

'Brother, try to listen to reason. There may be a way.'

'There is no way. If he is to die, then I will go with him.'

'For what? For what?' Uncle Hippolyte was incandescent. 'You will betray your name, your blood, for an indulgence? What is the matter?'

'I love him.'

'Oh! I cannot hear it! I cannot. Stop in the name of God.' He was raging again. His composure retired with it. 'And he has done you no favours, he has called you the Devil and worse.'

'I know he has not.'

'How can you know? You saw him last being taken to me that I might hear his mind. You know nothing of what he has said, of the sins that he places at your door. He claims you paid him for his whorish ways, and that if he refused you would beat and expose him. I am sorry you have to hear it, Hortense.'

She sat with her head resting in her hand. She was weary. She had tried to save me and I had refused it. Her work in vain, she was now simply in despair.

'You are lying, Uncle.'

'How do you know?'

'I know it as I know my own name.'

'He has not only said it, he has signed a paper to prove it. It will be evidence in court. A servant abused by his master in the vilest way.'

'He has betrayed you, Brother, can you not hear it?'

'I do not believe either of you. He would not.'

'You should, I have it written. A full confession.'

'I should like to see it.'

'In time.'

'In time? You cannot produce it. I have sat here long enough to know it. Entrap your own blood and send them to death? And for what? Nothing.'

'Jehan, I do not think a sodomite has much sway over a man of God, do you?' He took a breath, to measure his temper. 'Denounce him. Listen to your poor and wounded sister. We can tear up his confession and replace it with one of your own. You should know that there are forces at work that have nothing to do with kinship and affection. This, all of this, is not my doing. You see me as its full agent, but it is not I alone who will see you die.'

'Who then? Why will you not say it?'

'I cannot.'

Hortense came quickly, 'You must, Uncle. You must say who controls his fate.'

He straightened. 'It is our cousin, Clusy de Marcilliac.'

'What?' I was up.

'Uncle, is it true?'

'Yes, Hortense. It is painfully and terribly true. And he will have his way. You see? You who are so naive? Having your way, indulging your whims and fancies and having no ear to my position? My place is tied to his favour.' He was near to tears of fury and frustration. 'It is he who will have you removed from this sphere that I may find my path, in which he is so heavily invested. And so it is my work to do it.'

'Oh, Uncle.' Hortense comforted him. 'The burden you have carried.'

He patted her and turned to me. 'Jehan, you must denounce him. It is the only other way. Conti will look favourably on us all for our decisive action. Without it, we will all be done for. Our cousin has no mercy for your transgression.'

Is that a decision to make in a moment? Can anyone be asked to choose between their lineage and the one true love they have ever known? Who was I without him? A name without a self, a bloodline without blood in his veins, a man with alliances but no connection. What is kinship without love? A single moment of transgression in their eyes would amount to more love, more passion, more honesty than they would know in all their lives.

I felt my eyes and throat begin to burn again.

'I will not. There is nothing to admit to other than what you have taken great and cruel pains to determine.'

'Not so. You may say he assaulted you.'

'He did not.' My voice was just about a whisper. 'Nor did I assault him. And that is the end.'

'I have witnesses that say he did.'

'No.'

'He assaulted and sodomised you, a servant, forced to flee his home for the very same offence.'

'What is this?' Hortense was roused.

'Ah.' His bile was back. 'That has piqued your interest. I have in my possession a letter written by one Edvard Hoost, cartographer. A letter of some interest, addressed to your dishonest servant.'

My stomach turned in on itself to hear that name, but it gave me back some vestige of energy. 'Not addressed to you. Did you steal it?'

'I am no thief. I simply arranged to have it intercepted. Young Kryk has not been receiving all his correspondence of late. His mother writes a dull missive, though, and hers were passed on to him once scrutinised. But this one,' he leant to retrieve a folded sheet, 'this one was most instructive. Shall I read it to you?'

'You will do what you wish.'

'Niece, you may find it troubling.'

'I doubt it. I have heard it all now.'

'Let me begin by reminding you, Jehan, that this proves he has a history of buggery, whereas you have none against your name and should you denounce him – he a servant and you a marquis, by name at least if not by bearing – you will most likely get no sanction and we can make amends to all who need it.'

'I will still be tarnished.'

'No, I can see to it that you are exonerated. The Dutchman will disappear, you will travel for a month and return to your bride.'

'My bride. I see. And your coronation no doubt.' I was so weary I could near feel myself spin. 'I will not do it.'

'You will. And this letter will tell you how.'

'Jehan. Hear our uncle. Let him continue. This may be a way. Perhaps your man is dishonest. You should hear it.' She was wavering from my cause.

'Here it is:

'*Joe, it has been more than a full year since I last saw you. Our parting was not good. But you know I had to flee. I still dream of you. I know that you might not like to read this from me, but I still consider you my best loved. If you will have me, then let me know if I may come to you. I could find employment near you. If you will have me, please send, for repayment, of course, some advance for travel. I know you are well-employed by your master and your mother tells me you keep her well. I would ask that you extend some of this kindness to your old friend. Yours in love, Edvard.*'

'It is a fabrication.' I knew it was not.

'I assure you it is not. It is imprudent to the point of stupidity I agree, but fabrication it is not.'

'This Edvard Hoost is trying to extort money. It is clear. He is down on his luck. He seeks commerce, not love.'

'Maybe. But remember this too, he was his bedfellow. He has done to him what you have done. The same workings.' He hissed it at me and just to hear it raised in me such ire and pain.

I closed my eyes. I knew Uncle was trying to sway me, but simply the mention of Edvard made me soften, just enough to doubt my choosing. Edvard who had touched Joe and coached him, chambering with him in a small house; the thin walls, the stairs, taking his virgin heart.

I was exhausted. I suddenly had the sense that I would

do anything only to make it all end, erase the room, Uncle, Hortense's misery, the night before, the horrible discovery, and now the ghost of my heart's rival, all of it. Endless layers of weight and evidence and interests that had nothing to do with me. I wished it would all evaporate before me.

'Remember this, Jehan. That boy has done this before. He has a history of complaint against him and his sins are many. This Edvard has had him. How many more? A man-whore who knows his ways and how to use them. And he finds you, wealthy, a man of reputation, inclined to the Devil, with everything to lose should your secret be exposed. If you cannot see that I am here to save you from this trap, then I cannot help you. He is a common criminal. That is all.'

The slightest grain of doubt begin to take root and nestle in my jealous heart.

As seemed to happen whenever I was unable to fully comprehend what was going on around me, or when a truth began to weigh too fully, I felt my head swim a little. I allowed myself to step behind myself for a moment; separate, protect my heart. I thought of Joe. I saw him when I gave him the ring. I thought of him, his confidence and the way he used his own body with mine. The learnt tricks of his hands, his mouth taking me in. I thought of him laughing with his friends in the alehouse, how he clung to me in the water, how he laughed when I read him a story he liked, his face as he slept, bathed in beauty; how in that same sleep he would thread his fingers through mine and close his hand around, and the night before when he had stood shaking and exposed, unable to stop weeping, so great was his fear. I opened my eyes full. I looked at my uncle – respectable, patrician, his face lined with the kind of dignity and weight a man of his office must bear – waiting for me to save them all from misery and myself from death by the most cruel and degrading method.

'I will never denounce him.'

'Then you will die.'

Hortense began to weep.

'Let me. Rather that than betray him.'

'You are a fool. A fool! And you will die as one, burn as one. And all for some sick-minded game and with a servant no less. A servant. There is no depth to your depravity.'

'There is no depravity in love.'

'It is not love, it is degrading lust and nothing more. I cannot hear any more, I am offended to my soul. You are to burn and it will be too good for you. You disgust me.'

'But Uncle—' I tried to go to him.

Hortense grabbed my hand as he pushed me away.

'No.' He was spitting. 'Stop where you are. I will not be touched by your impurity. You will burn. I will see to it. And both Conti and Clusy de Marcilliac will promote me for it.'

'Only if you betray me! My life is in your hands, you can save me.'

'I betray *you*? It is I who is the betrayer? You know it is a sin, an obscenity of the most blasphemous kind.'

'I know what the Church says.' I was loud with him. 'I have prayed daily and for years to find a different way. But I cannot.'

'You have chosen sin.'

'Uncle, you will never see it. I know what your God says, I am always in his service. But I question that it is God that you fear.'

'You are a man facing death and you choose impertinence as your defence?'

'I choose to ask for your pardon and I choose mercy as my defence. A man of God should know mercy as well as he knows judgement.'

'Jehan, you should mind your words. You have offered the worst insult to your God. Do you not fear him?'

'Fear God? You, Uncle, do not fear God. You fear your position, you fear exposure. You simper before Marcilliac.

'Ha, I fear no cousin of mine.'

'Then who? Who will you feed me to?'

'You fool. Enough!' His bureau thundered as his fist came down on it. 'This is Avignon.' He was hissing. 'We all answer to Rome.'

I broke. I was beaten. There was nothing more that could be said and suddenly death was in the room. 'Uncle . . .' I needed solace, reprieve.

'Cry all you like. A child's tears. It is too late. You will be punished with death.' He flicked his hand. Hortense came to me.

He would not find my eye.

'Uncle, will you not look at me? *With death?* You say this as if it were done, with no care, no catch to your voice. You were my father.'

'I was your guardian for a time. There are no sodomites in my family.'

Recounting all of this misery has raised in me such sorrow. My scribe feels it too. I can see she struggles for the words to make real to you all the true depth of my betrayal by my uncle. We both weep, for there is nothing more one can do in the face of such pitilessness. To deny the existence of love is to deny the existence of all hope and neither she nor I can hold such darkness without suffering.

I have felt today, reconstructing this for you, that perhaps I have done wrong – that I raise it more to satisfy my own need to exorcise it and expose the dishonesty of those involved and their ruthlessness. What possible reason can there be to relive such horrors? Must we record the cost of our love? We have hesitated to replay the detail of our degradation. But we should hope that you read too the resilience of devotion which until that day even I did not know I possessed. I confess to being a coward. I am vain, easily wounded, I cheat at games, drink to falling over, spend money on amusements and am reckless with my corporal needs. I am not a man whose *mémoire* should be written. But, in addition to my manifold failings, my greatest victory was a man of no standing, half-beaten in a prison cell because I loved him. He had nothing to offer other than his radiant, eternal self and I loved him more than I had ever known was possible. In more ways than the sky can shine at night, I found ways to love him and believe he could love me too. The light of all those stars placed adjacent to our degradations is reason enough to persist with this tale.

But I am weary and my scribe is hollowed out. Nearly four centuries and my heart breaks still.

10

Maurice Gathers Musketeers

I could offer Hortense no solace and Uncle was spitting his bile. We had reached an impasse and all I wished was to be let out of that close and swamping room that I might try to find Joe. That he might be needed as witness or scapegoat meant he would be kept alive, but any possibility of speaking to him was distant. Only, I needed to convey to him that I had not betrayed him.

There came a knock.

'Enter.'

A page poked his nose around. 'Monsieur, there is a man here. He is all noisy and mad and wishes to report that his master, the Marquis de Baudelaire, is missing, unless he is here. He speaks of kidnap and Calvinists. The maid saw devils too, white-faced and frightful. He has men-at-arms.'

'What? Who is this?'

'He is Benoit, Monsieur. He has been to every house to find his master. He has raised an alarm and then a footman from the Vicomte de Cherbonne arrived after him. The vicomte has also raised a party with arms to find the marquis. They request your assistance and as many men as you can spare. All Avignon will soon be seeking the Marquis de Baudelaire.'

Oh, a chink of light. And it should be caught in a glass before the door was closed again.

Before my uncle could speak, I said: 'But look, boy, you have found me yourself. You are quite the hero. I am the Marquis de Baudelaire.'

The page gave a little bow in my direction. 'Oh, oh, Monsieur, I will report to Benoit that you are found.'

'Do so at once. Say I am with my uncle. I am safe and well and they should prepare for my homecoming within the hour along with my valet Mister Kryk, who is also here with me. Monsieur Benoit will be most worried about him too.'

Uncle grimaced. 'Who is Benoit?'

The wind was in my sails once more. 'He runs my household. You know that. He was away visiting his mother last night, uncle, as you may now recall, but has returned early no doubt and fears for my safety. I have always been fond of his cakes. And his rabbit fricassee is exceptional.'

Uncle leaned into me and in low and awful voice, 'I should have left you in your cell to die. Now the boy has seen you and will report who was in the room.' He called out, 'Go, boy, tell Benoit his master is well. He need not fear for his safety.' The page left.

I eyed my uncle. 'Should Monsieur Benoit fear for my safety?'

'He should. Stupid man. Why did he come here? He should be with his mother or his pots. Idiot. I suppose you expect I should let you leave now. Your cook has come to call, with cakes and a rabbit fricassee, so you may walk away? Well, that is not possible. You are here on criminal charges and it is I who am responsible for holding you to account.'

'If you do not give me my liberty, questions will be asked. A search has already begun. Kidnapped by Calvinists. Even Maurice has raised musketeers. To deny my liberty would expose yet more questions. What was your plan exactly? To keep me indefinitely? Did you think no one would ask? I am due to play *lansquenet* with young Boutin-Valouse and his jolly sisters in a few hours. I should like to bathe before I am presented.'

'Your sister was to be sent to smooth things over, say you were unwell and required some isolation. This will still be necessary.'

I could tell that Hortense did not appreciate being assumed as a conspirator.

'If I let you go, I will have Clusy de Marcilliac to answer to. I cannot see you at liberty. Your freedom will destroy us all. You will remain here.'

'Uncle, if I might … ' Hortense as ever the voice of calm. 'What if he were allowed to go home, but promised to remain there.'

'You expect me to take his word that he will not abscond? This man of no conscience or morality?'

'Well, now that he understands what he has done and that even our esteemed cousin Monsieur Clusy de Marcilliac has concerns, I am sure he will comply. Will you not, Brother?' She was so careful in her register that even I could not glean her side. But I was never more grateful for her suggestion than then.

I fear my face may have betrayed the immediate fantasy I had of implementing the Parisian escape route, as Uncle chimed in quite readily. 'You seem to have forgotten, Hortense, that your brother is a criminal. I will consider it, but know the risk I run.' He ran his forefinger along the top of his desk as if looking for dust. 'Very well. You may return to your house. But you will have a guard at each and every door and exit, be it a pigeon roost in your roof or a tunnel of rats. Should you, Jehan, so much as open a window to breathe the air outside, I will personally bring down my vengeance on you. Do you understand? We will say that you were attacked and your man too. And that the guards are for your own safety. This arrangement will last while I decide what to do with you, given your refusal to do what is obvious and sensible and might I add, your God-given duty in your position of patrimony. You eschew God, lineage, reputation. You repulse me. Dear God, what have I done to deserve this misery?' He was weary, he rubbed his forehead with his palms. 'Clusy de Marcilliac returns tomorrow. By then I will have decided your fate. And *I* will decide it. You had your chance to walk free but you squandered it. You have chosen the pyre, Jehan. In the meantime, you will be watched every hour, day and night. Your man may not attend you.'

'That will not look right.'

'You will say he is unwell having been roundly beaten by your attackers.'

'Will I find him roundly beaten?'

'You will. And he deserved more.'

It took all that I had to hold my tongue. He was alive and I could return to my house. Once there I could think what to do next. I could try to convince Hortense to help us.

She was grey with misery. 'I cannot think of anything better. There is simply no good outcome to this. It seems a fair arrangement and soon we will all know our fates. Please, Uncle, do not yet tell my husband, not yet. I beg a few days to find a way to tell him myself, softly so that I might try to salvage something there before he hears it properly.'

'But he must know it, Hortense. As a wife, you must bear that consequence. I am sorry. There is nothing more I can offer you. Such is our predicament.'

'Yes. There will be that consequence.' She turned to me. She seemed about to speak to me but turned back to our uncle. 'If I may, I will visit my brother daily to be sure that he is complying. I am sure you will too. And this will give us a chance to work a plan that might avoid any trial, any public outing of our sorrows.'

'I cannot think of any. It will be the execution of us all.'

'Uncle, I am so eternally grateful for your kindness and the great and generous leniency you have shown my brother.' She kissed his hands. It made me sick to see it.

'Brother, you will leave now. With guards.' Her face was unsmiling.

'Where is my valet?'

Uncle flinched to hear me speak of him. 'He cannot accompany you.'

Hortense frowned and laid a careful hand on Uncle's sleeve.

'Dear Uncle, I fear his man must go too or there will be too much attention on us all. We cannot afford to have this cook and a household of maids stirring trouble with gossip or we will have men-at-arms to defend against as well. The valet will be kept well away, dispatched to his cot to recover and he will know to never speak a word, or he will be the first to die.'

My uncle pursed his lips. 'Do it then.'

11

Defeat

My *hôtel*, so elegant and discreet, was overrun with thugs. One at each door, down corridors, at each staircase, one in the *salon*, and if someone came into a room in which I sat unattended, they would be accompanied by a guard. My scribe is concerned that their odours infected my household too and she is correct. They were all both uncouth and unfragrant.

I consoled myself remembering that Molière himself had passed some time in a debtor's prison, after his rent for a *jeu de paume court* in Paris had not coincided with healthy ticket sales. How distant he and his players seemed to me now. Instead of their pretty flowers and hats, bright costumes, masks with feathers, florets and bells on stockings and shoes, I was cursed with my captors and their swamp-like colours. Against my beautiful rich cloth walls and bright decoration, their clothing was nasty and coarse. They were not in my uncle's livery – the same colours as mine – but differently appointed. Criminals for hire and no more. Pocked cheeks, language you have never heard. Still, even with the constant surveillance, being free from that cell gave me a sense that I might survive, and Joe too.

Monsieur Benoit, who received hearty thanks and great praise for his brave efforts to rally my paltry defences and come to rescue me, gathered the household in the hall. Pages, footmen, maids, cooks, lackeys, stable hands. As was custom,

Joe came to take his place in the front with lackeys and pages behind him. God in heaven, he was broken. His left eye was black and swollen near shut, and his lip too, bloodied and swollen into his cheek. He walked with difficulty. He stood with his head bowed low and made no move to look at me. Just to see him gave me both hope and fear all at once. That he had been so abused and I hardly at all was a wickedness. I wanted to ask him to forgive me, protect him from all his misery and fear.

He would have had been told that we were still under arrest, hence the presence of the guards, and he was to remain indoors at all times for some spurious reason that he alone had identified the attackers and would need to be kept safe from further reprisals. The fictions that were produced were enough to rival any of my own making. My disappearance in the middle of the night had been a failed attempt at abduction but my uncle's men-at-arms had come to my rescue. Joe had been beaten in the scuffle. It was a farce and a miserable one too.

And yet, as I stood in front of the assembly, it was I who sought solace. Even in his broken body, I knew Joe was stronger than I.

I completed my speech. Joe did not move throughout it. The maids were nervous, but some of the gardeners and the younger boys looked alive to be part of something so exciting. They were too young to know that these things, when true, were never exciting, only bloody and brutal. A short sword turned three times in one's belly was no good way to die.

There had to be a way to Joe. A chance meeting that I would engineer. What I did not know was how much the guards knew, who among them knew the truth and who were simply there to swell the ranks. It was unlikely they all knew our true predicament, that would be too great a risk. He moved about and I quickly surmised that one other guard without fixed post knew the circumstances of our imprisonment too. The rest were probably unaware and only charged with not letting anyone in or out of the house.

I had hoped Hortense would visit me that same day, but by the time the sun began to set she had not. I had placed her in an impossible position. Hortense could face ruin, but so too her husband. He would be forced, or perhaps would happily choose, to consider an annulment of the marriage, something their childless position already raised as a possibility. As kind as she was to him, so too he did her great service by his patience. Once annulled, her only options were to live with a family member who would have her – it may come to the Cherbonnes, whom I had lavished with great favour in an effort to help them gloss over their own numerous debts and indiscretions – or be forced to enter the convent. This was the burden I had placed on her. If she fought for my salvation and to avoid this scandal, it was as much to save herself and her marriage as it was to save her brother.

And for all that, I too had made my choice and Joe his. That beautiful man, Mister Jonathan Kryk of Amsterdam, who had arrived one afternoon before a game of *jeu de paume*, had watched as I had dishonestly tapped the ball across a chance line in front of a full gallery of spectators and the King's own cousin, and had concluded that he could love me.

That we found each other on that day in that court was fate and it was destiny. I believe it would have happened with or without our bidding and who was I to deny such forces as all the heavens combined?

On the third day, and still no visit from my sister, a letter arrived from my uncle. He did not deliver it himself nor come to read it, rather he had it sent in a sealed chest.

We were both to be tried and executed. Officers would be sent by the end of the day.

That was the word from Clusy de Marcilliac on his return

and from our uncle too. After three days of torturous confinement, still having not seen Joe other than that briefest
glimpse, this was the verdict. My refusal to denounce and
accuse him meant I had saved him from a charge of assault
but condemned us both to die.

There was nothing to be done. My sister had not come to
me and I would never see her again.

I reread the letter. I neither wept nor raged nor collapsed in
fear. Rather, I took to my bed. In a silence that was entirely of
its own temper, I removed my slippers, my banyan and all my
rings. I pulled the curtains around the bed, the covers across
my body and lay down. I felt no panic.

I tried to imagine Joe, lying too on his cot, alone and terrified. He had escaped prosecution and come halfway across the
continent only to find his death again.

All evidence of our acts would be read in detail, the witnesses called. Then to torture, the stocks, castration, possibly
disembowelment and then, whether still alive or not, to be
taken naked, meat dripping, and strapped to a burning pyre.
It was done.

I pulled the *tapis* over me, tight and close like a child might.
I tried, as a conjurer would or alchemist, to send my thoughts
to Joe. I imagined our foreheads pressed together as we had
on so many nights and I said over and over, 'I love you, I love
you, I love you, beyond death, beyond death, beyond death. I
love you.' And I let myself believe he heard me.

No one came. Every noise from the gate, or voice from one of
the guards, set my skin on edge. But no one came. After what
seemed an eternity, I fell asleep and woke to a new day, alone
and with nothing changed.

I did not for a moment believe we were pardoned. Rather,
I feared something worse. What, I could not say, only I knew

there could be no good end for us and this protracted lack of any action unnerved me further. I dared not leave my chamber and so after a time, a maid brought me a meal. She was young. I knew she was a sister of one of the stable boys. I decided that even with a man outside my chamber door, I might ask some questions of her – idle chatter, no more.

'Lucie?' I spoke most quietly and she seemed to return the courtesy.

'Monsieur?'

'How is it in the household? What is the weather?'

'We are afraid, Monsieur.'

'Of attack?'

'No, Monsieur. Of the guards.'

'Oh. Yes. I understand. I too am afraid.'

She smiled. A sweet maid.

'Lucie, how is my manservant?'

'He is very sad, Monsieur.'

'Sad how?'

'He weeps and lies curled on his cot. He will not eat.'

'He must eat. Will you tell him I command him to? Although do not let the guards hear you, they may be affronted that my man is upset by their presence, given that they saved us both from terrible misfortune.'

'Oh, I see, Monsieur.'

'In my experience, they might look fearsome, but they are, in truth, very emotional.'

She smiled again. She would be a good ally.

'Do not ever take one as a lover, Lucie. No end of trouble.'

She blushed. Poor creature.

'I will not, Monsieur.'

'Good. I am pleased. Now tell my valet he must eat and tell him too that I asked after him and was concerned for his wellbeing. He saved my life as you heard, defended me. And you may report these exact words to him, if you can remember them: I owe him a debt of gratitude for his defence, even beyond death. Might you remember that?'

'Yes, Monsieur. A debt of gratitude for his defence. Even beyond death. For he has saved your life.'

'Perfect. Relay that to him, quietly. And perhaps take him a meal, a good one and command him, in my name, to eat it all.'

'Yes, Monsieur. I will.'

'You are an angel.'

'Monsieur.'

'Thank you for my meal. If I am still here later, I would be happy to continue to eat in my chamber, rather than in the presence of the guards. Though you may hide a small cake and give it to the man at my door if you do not feel it would compromise you.'

'Yes, Monsieur.'

'Excellent. Thank you, Lucie. You may go now.'

The effort it had taken to force such levity near broke me. As she closed the door, my breath came in gulps once more. I held my hand tight across my mouth to stop myself from wailing and I had to fight to hold back my tears for I knew if they began there would be no end to them.

Joe was broken. It was unusual for him to be so lacking in agency. Typically, it was I who would become paralysed with indecision, emotion. He was a man of action. If something did not suit him, he would go about fixing it. That he was capsized on his cot was the worst news. So, I decided that if he was unable then I should prepare for our imprisonment. I called for water and bathed as best I could. In the absence of Joe, I shaved with the aid of a useless page boy and then set about tearing paper into small, neat squares. I hid in the innermost pocket of a warm doublet a small quill and a pouch of soot which I surmised I could mix with water to make some kind of ink. Also in that pocket, and in my boots and hose, I hid coins to offer as bribes. Somewhat indulgently, I also doused a kerchief in rose oil that I might inhale it if my lodgings were putrid. My night with the mice had been sobering. I found my bible, which I might be able to convince my guards was acceptable luggage, and placed between the pages those torn from my volumes of poetry. I would need solace.

It is true I had written too many fictions of damsels being locked up in towers and lusty musketeers being interned for their indiscretions. It was possible I had an unrealistic expectation of my future circumstances. Even as I was tucking the last sheet into the Book of Revelation, there came the cry of lackeys and the noise of hooves into my courtyard.

I could not see who came. There was the sound of posturing and arms and armour as the guards prepared to let open the gates for whoever it was. The clamour was ferocious, echoing up the stairs and through the gallery. I decided I would not wait. It was impossible to be taken without honour and so, near sick with fear, I opened my door, strode past my guard and stood at the top of the stairs. Below, my pages and a lackey had appeared. No Joe.

12

My Brother, The Toad

Along the gallery that led from the entrance, the sound of an approaching storm. I descended the stairs to be sure to meet whatever was coming with at least a modicum of dignity.

The clattering of arms.

Hortense. Behind her, in a demi-circle, her husband's men-at-arms. She looked like a warrior queen at the dawn of a great battle.

'Leave me.'

Nom de Dieu, what had she become? I was awestruck and terrified. She marched ahead of her now-marooned entourage and without so much as acknowledging the armed man at the door, she beckoned to me and disappeared into my *salon*.

'Hortense, will we die today? We received—'

'Brother, sit, please.' That she was vexed was clear. 'The rage I feel has finally tempered. I still cannot understand your insistence on this matter. I simply cannot fathom your determination to die. You have behaved with a selfishness I have never thought possible in my own brother. My own twin. You who are one half of who I am, and yet would send me to penury for your own pleasure.' She flushed to say it.

'Sister, you are always and forever my darling. It is not for pleasure, it is not. I cannot think how else to express it to you. It is for love. In as much as a husband might love a wife or a brother a sister, it is love, not mere lust nor base desire but only for love. How it is between us as two men is but the expression of that love. Outside of you, he is my dearest friend, he is my heart's natural intimate. He is as close an ally as I have ever had beside you.'

'Well,' she blinked slowly, carefully removing one glove and then the other. 'Then I envy you.'

'Sister?'

'Then you have found your soul's own marriage. Only, Jehan, it comes with punishment. It comes with death.'

'But you can see why I must take it? And he too. Our uncle, our cousin has tried and failed to make us turn. We are not criminals, Sister. We are not. And to reduce our purest affection to that is the truest crime.'

'I have passed these three days in their counsel. And my husband too.'

'He knows?'

'He had to. His position is affected because mine is. It was ever the worst night when I told him.'

'What has he said? Will he protect you?'

'He has done better.'

'He has? How and what?'

'You are unkind to him. But he has these days come to be for me,' her voice cracked, 'for all of us, a most exceptional man.'

'The Toad?'

'Jehan! On my life, you will *never* call him that again. Let me finish and when I have you will hang your head for shame and call him Brother.'

'I have offended you again.' I admit I was not behaving as I should. If my scribe could slap me, she would.

'He has conspired with me a plan that we have put to our uncle and cousin. It is not the best end that I had hoped for, it is not. But, Brother, I have come with the best that we can do.

And the man you call Toad advocated most strongly on your behalf, though he has much to lose from your indiscretions. He did it too out of love for me, and for that you owe him a great debt of respect and gratitude. He has done more for me in these three days to show his love than you have these last torturous months.' Her eyes flashed at me.

'You mortify me.'

'Let me continue. This plan is a good one. It is the only thing we can do for you now. I am offering it to you and it is as close to freedom as we can afford you.'

My impatience overwhelmed me. 'What is it, Sister? Tell me now.'

She took a deep breath and her eyes brimmed. 'You will be exiled to Jamaica, where you will live out your days.'

My mind was mute.

'We will give word that you have died at sea. And you will never be heard from again.'

'Jamaica?'

'Yes. It is in the Indies.'

'I know where it is, Sister. Jamaica. But I will travel alone?'

'Our cousin and uncle were eventually swayed. Mister Kryk will accompany you.'

I could feel my lungs begin to swell with hope for the first time in days. 'And in Jamaica we will be . . .?'

'You will be free men.'

'Sister!' I embraced and kissed her as ever I could and told her how much I loved her over and over.

'Do not kiss me. This will not be easy, there are constraints. You will travel freely but with our uncle's men-at-arms. There can be no thought of absconding. The men will be charged with delivering you on board. When you arrive in the Indies, you must report to an agent who will be charged with reporting that you have made land and have behaved in accordance with our agreement. Then you will both be at liberty. Only—'

'Only I may never see you again.'

'No. Nor write, nor ever return. You are banished, Jehan. You are both banished.'

'But I could write sister, I will assume a new name.'

'No. No. That is the condition. For your freedom, Jehan. For your life. You are exiled from your blood. We will announce that you and your manservant died at sea. And it is I who will arrange for your memorial.'

'Oh, my love.'

'Yes. I will bury you. Do you understand?

'I do. Does Joe know?'

'He does not. Uncle will tell you both together.'

'He will die from shock. He is terrified of the ocean.'

'I could, I suppose, warn him.'

'Could you? And explain it is the only option? Then he will be ready. To be alive and free. Hortense, you have done me the greatest and the best service. You have saved my life. Joe's too.'

'It was politic to do so. He is a witness. Our cousin would have him killed to bury what he knows. He was eventually convinced that his death and your sudden interest in merchant travel would be seen as irregular. It is the way. Uncle will come to tell you the same. I had thought it better that I forewarn you.'

'Where is my brother?'

'The Toad?' She allowed a small smile.

'My brother.'

'He has returned without me. He has pressing matters of estate and we have been awake these three days.'

'I owe him a great debt.'

'You owe him your life.'

'And you. I owe you all and more. I have asked too much of you.'

'You have asked me to prove my love for you. And it has stayed the course. But the worst is still to come. I fear I will not know my own self without you. I do not have a sense of my own boundary and edge in the world when you are not here. I cannot say where I begin and eternity ends because you were that for me. I am so afraid, Jehan, that I will cease to exist, with my one half cut from me. Who will I be without you?'

Hortense wept and I held her to me.

'You will be beautiful and brave and prosper in your life with my new brother.'

'I do not feel I will. And soon I will discover it.'

'We leave soon?'

'On the first ship that will sail for Jamaica. You will pay your passage and his as any other. Uncle suggests no more than three Lord's Days to pass before you leave. But it may be sooner.

'Dear God. I have hardly left Languedoc before.'

'And now you will sail for Port Royal, a merchant, hoping to advance his family's influence and fortune. How well it will look for our uncle. How jealous the other *grands* will be of the Baudelaires, so expansionist and brave.' She was cynical now. 'Your banishment and my grief will be well used, my love. Our patriarchs will make great capital of it. Do not think for a minute they did any of it for love. They are vipers. Jehan, the things I heard said I hope you never know.'

'And yet, I find myself in deep and abiding gratitude for what this journey allows.'

'As do I. Were it not for my husband, I might have succumbed to their pressure.'

'Sister, you have been brave as any man who went to war.

You have done me a great, great honour where I gave you none. I could not love you more.'

She let her eyes fill a little. 'I did not think I could be brave. I have been so afraid.'

'Yet see how you faced them? So boldly and with such wit and guile. You are magnificent.'

'I did not do it to be magnificent. I did it for you.'

'You are always and ever my truest.'

'Except for your servant, Mister Kryk. He apparently must take precedence.' She was still wounded. And would be I suppose forever.

'Sister,' I did hesitate. 'On that mention, when will you tell him? Might it be now? I have not seen him nor spoken to him at all. The maid tells me he has been in a very bad way. He will not eat nor stop weeping and he was badly beaten. And she reports he has had dreadful pain in his heart. I have asked so much of you but, if it is not too much, might you tell him soon? To see how he is.'

'Has he seen a physician?'

'I doubt it, but I cannot say. I am a prisoner. I know nothing and have no authority to help. I cannot see to him without arousing suspicion and I cannot tell what information the guards have been furnished with.'

She took a breath and rubbed her hand across her forehead as if to wake her mind and think more clear. She was so weary, I could tell in how she held herself.

'Come. You will accompany me. We will see him in your library. It is private and we may leave the guard at the door but speak in whispers.'

'You are perfection. I adore you.' I kissed her.

'Come. We must be quick. I do not know when Uncle arrives.'

To the library. Hortense simply told the guard he should

allow her an audience with myself and Joe and, astonishingly, without question he agreed. Seldom did men refuse her when she made demand. It came to her way of looking straight into their eyes and smiling with the innocence of a novice. I learnt this early on. Where other women would drop their heads in modesty, Hortense would lift her chin yet higher.

Hortense sat but I could not. I was so desperate to see Joe and yet knew that with my sister, decorum would be required. Shuffling footsteps approached. The guard said something I could not hear and the door opened.

Oh, heart, to see him. Grey with great black and yellow bruising all about his mouth and eye. His lip still swollen and the cut visible. He looked even worse than when I had seen him last. His cheeks had hollowed. He had the look of a man already dead.

'Joe, *pardieu.*' I could not help myself.

He did not seem to know where he was. He saw my sister before me and made to bow to her, though it clearly hurt him to do it. She stood quickly.

'Mister Kryk?' She went to his side and reached him as I did. Together we helped him to the chaise and lowered him onto it. He let out a groan. I grabbed his hand to me and held it. 'Mister Kryk, have you seen a physician?'

'No, Madame.'

'I will call one. My own private physician. I cannot be sure who will be sent and what will be their work if our uncle is charged with it.'

I looked at her in surprise. She let me know not to speak.

'Tell the guard to call my footman, Jehan. He will fetch the doctor to us. Tell him to be quick.' Even as I turned my back to them to call instruction, I heard Joe begin to weep.

'Come now, Mister Kryk, we will see that you are made well.'

He could not halt his misery even though a lady was present. He had ceased to care, for he had no more energy it seemed to even hold his manner or his bearing.

'Madame, for what? To die a healthy man?'

I returned to them and sat next to Joe and took his hand in mine to kiss it, then remembered myself and my sister. She glanced at me.

'No. To live as a healthy man.'

'My sister comes with news.'

'I have told my brother, Mister Kryk, that you are to accompany him on a voyage.' She paused and he looked at me, though he had the look of a man swimming through air. 'You will sail to Jamaica.'

He swallowed and frowned.

'Joe, we will not be executed, rather banished. It is the best choice and the only one. My sister has brokered for us this reprieve. She fought for us both. Will you take it with me?'

He seemed no longer in his own body, which was so broken and held none of his strut and beauty, only all his defeats and humiliations written in pools of blood trapped beneath the veil of his skin.

'We will be free. We will live as free men in the Indies. Turtles, Joe, magnificent shells, parrots in great flocks. Would I not look fine with a parrot at my shoulder? Will you take that reprieve?'

'Yes. I will take it.' His face had changed. He did not yet smile. 'Madame, I owe you my life. I am in your debt.'

'I am only sorry it has come to this end. You will travel under guard until you are on board but once you have come to Port Royal, you will be without sanction. It is a place of diabolic reputation, as you know. You will both find your way and, I suppose, create some livelihood.' She was careful how she spoke, though not unkind. She turned to me. 'You are to be allowed some income, though not extravagant. Now, I will see how long before my physician may arrive. I will leave you for a short while before returning.' She looked at us both with meaning, then took her leave. The door had hardly latched before I fell to my knees in front of him. 'Where is the pain?'

He put out his hand to touch my face. 'Everywhere.'

I hardly dared to kiss him. His face was so bruised.

'Those monsters, your beautiful face.'

'They said you accused me.'

'For shame, I never would.'

'And beat me to make me do the same. But I would not.'

'How were you beaten, do you think it is dire?'

'They kicked me so hard I spat blood.'

I held him as well as his pain would allow. 'And all for me. You will never be beaten again. Never.'

He clung to me. That he needed me so gave me such purpose. It had ever been he who set our mood and pace, he who had agency and courage, he who pinned my arms to the pillows as I lay beneath like a helpless, needing lamb.

'But we are together now and will be again. And once we are in Jamaica, we will be free, can you imagine it?'

'No.'

'You must. It will help you to heal. We may find sea porpoises too. And mermaids! Birds as we have never seen.'

I felt sick. It would not be an adventure. Not all ships that set sail ever arrived and of those that did, there were always casualties, mostly from disease, but profiteers and storms too. It was late in the year to be setting sail for the Indies. I did not dare mention pirates to Joe, he would flee in the night.

The physician found Joe in a bad way and suggested more rest and close attention for any change. He was to be attended in his cot and be allowed to sleep uninterrupted until his strength returned. He did not think anything broken nor any mortal danger, but told my sister that the pains in his chest may suggest some ague of the heart. Oh, that his heart had broken thinking he would not see me again was such a sweet sorrow. I should have been concerned, and I was, truly, only to know that his heart had broken for me was all the medicine I would ever need.

13

My Inheritors

The next weeks passed strangely. The number of men my uncle had sent reduced significantly but there was still no way to move about the residence unhindered and a vile thug sat all the while around the corner from Joe's cot, so that to get to see him was impossible. I once through sheer persistence glimpsed his shape asleep under blankets as I passed, but it was brief and only served to break my heart afresh, so that I too became convinced I suffered his ague.

Beyond that, I occupied the ground between elation at reprieve and trepidation at the potential adventure we faced. I scoured maps and books to gather what information I could on the Indies and then would roll up these pages into small *billets* and get my new ally, Lucie, to pass them to Joe when she took him his suppers. I would scratch notes in the margins of the pages or underline portions I thought he should focus on.

The household had been told that I would be travelling to Jamaica on matters of commercial enterprise and, as was usual, my valet would accompany me. While they were to expect my return, it would never come and so I had the strange task of arranging for my own death. My inheritances were all set and cast and having no heir made it somewhat more complicated. My name would die with me. There would be no more Baudelaires in our line and any remaining record of my family name – and my name – would be quietly but thoroughly expunged from all records both public and private. *I* would be eradicated from all record.

On and on went my administrative demise. My uncle would receive his patronage and attach his new lineage to my sister and her husband's name. They were still virtuous and good. They would be my inheritors after smaller amounts had been cast among staff and the household. I provided well for Monsieur Benoit of course. Hortense and her husband would retain their residences and of course attach my *hôtel* and the two other country estates as well as all the land, coffers and associated titles and privileges. A substantial coffer had to be left for Maurice Cherbonne, who, in the absence of my near-daily beneficence, would surely fall to ruin. My brother, The Toad, as an appendage to my sister, who was my true inheritor, would do well out of my demise. She, and by proxy he, would double their estates and carry the purse too. I made sure Hortense received a vulgar personal income. In the event that no children were forthcoming, it would not serve The Toad well to annul his marriage to my spectacularly wealthy sister. She was too fine and too courageous for the convent.

She came to see me on the day I was to sign the last of these deeds. So many were they that I could scarce remember which was what by the end.

'I bring some news that you might like. Or I think you will like it.' She looked so sweet and coy.

'You are being mysterious.'

'What is it?'

'I did think not to tell you, but on reflection, I think you will be better to hear it.'

'Tell it then.'

She leaned very close and whispered, 'I am with child.'

'Oh! It is wondrous!'

'Is it? It is for me. Though of course, I am not without anxiety.'

'Of course not, but this is the best news. When do you expect?' And even as I said it, I knew her answer would be a fresh cut.

'It will be, God-willing, in the spring.'

'Ah. Well, that is joyous and Avignon will have its most beautiful spring yet.' Try as I might, I could not stop the tears that suddenly began to overwhelm me.

'Oh, Brother.'

'No, Hortense, I am determined to give you your joy.'

'And yet your face is not very pretty for trying.'

We laughed and laughed as we had not done for months. It was blissful.

Monsieur Benoit was charged with making sure that not only was Joe healthy, but that he was prepared for the trip too. He was found new clothes that would be better suited to seafaring and hot climates and so forth. I was assured that letters had been written to his family and that Monsieur Benoit would forward on any further information as he received it – relating to our supposed demise, of course. Beyond that she would hear no more of her Joe. I had to ask Hortense to make provision for his mother. She was at first reluctant, but I appealed to her good and charitable heart and explained the difficulty of his mother's position. Hortense agreed eventually, her primary concern being that she was being dishonest. She would have to do so without her husband's knowledge.

My accomplice, Lucie, soon reported that Joe was much healed and had rejoined the household for most meals.

I had begun to assemble a collection of items for the journey: waxed cloths, multiple bottles of ink and oils. It was all fantasy, I had no notion of what life on board a ship was like and less still about what might await us once we arrived in Port Royal.

You will have heard it said that, at that time, the Church itself named Port Royal as 'the most wicked city on earth' – or certainly in Christendom, which was their main concern. It was overrun with buccaneers, private merchants and pirates; there was a brothel on every corner and it was reported that men would drink from early morning 'til late at night and have their way with strumpets under alleyways and behind inns where all was plain to see. Thieves, murderers and, apparently, sodomites roamed the streets in gangs and preyed on those new to the city.

Not that Jamaica was lawless. The Spanish were recently ousted but it was now an English jurisdiction. We would still be subject to scrutiny and accusation should we become complacent, but a degree of anonymity and a more secluded accommodation might be our friend. Once in Jamaica, I hoped we would find a position a distance away where we might, in my fantasy, establish a sort of domesticity. I would write and Joe would do what a man does when he is forced to retire from his employ. He could chart the island perhaps. We could expand our travels to yet newer lands. I imagined he could simply rest, sleep, dream, while I watched over him.

Eventually, news came. Our passage had been booked. We were to depart in fewer than ten days.

I received the note to that effect while sitting on the floor of my *jeu de paume court*, where I had spent an hour or so thinking – or perhaps reminiscing is more accurate a descriptor. I was guarded by a dunderhead, of course.

'Do you know the plays of Molière?' I asked him.

He only shook his head.

'A great pity. I dare say you would have derived much benefit.'

I stood, dusty and perhaps somewhat forlorn looking. The time for sentiment was done and there were preparations to be made.

Back in my private quarters, I wrote a small and secret note to my Joe, telling him of the date and encouraging him to be brave and prepare well for the journey. I wrote it in the margins of a page that I tore from the binding of a book on sea turtles and had Lucie deliver. Later that same day a note so small I had to squint to read it was returned with my wine. It read:

Damn them all to the Devil. We are Jamaica bound!

He was well again.

14

Hortense II

Today my scribe and I begin the work of relating my departure from Avignon. My scribe is already on the brink of tears before she has written a word, worrying about Hortense and myself.

What unfolded in the days before our departure was a farce. Cousins, endless cousins and acquaintances, all came to offer their wishes and greatest hopes for my safe arrival and, here is the bitter pill, prosperous acquisitions in the Indies. According to the news spread by my uncle and his cohort, I sought ambitious commercial enterprise and so they came, these simpering, empty sycophants, all of whom hoped to gain should I be successful. How they kissed me, such protestations of support for my noble self, my standing and enterprise! It was with muted amusement that I imagined myself leaning into these fawning vipers and whispering so close that they could feel my breath, 'I should point out, Monsieur, that you have just kissed a sodomite, condemned and banished for the upending delight he takes from being railed senseless by his manservant.'

I did not and regret it still.

I had no desire to see any of them again, not beyond a certain group of closer cousins.

I found that the one person I wished to tell of my departure was dear Bobo, my first and differently loved valet. I had sent word to him, at his place of retirement, as soon as I had a date for our departure.

Of immense regret among all the farewells was the last kiss from the Comtesse de Montmorency. It broke my heart.

She saw me privately in my *salon* two days before departure. I say privately, though we were fortunate to have the most discreet company of a snorting, nose-picking and heavily armed guard just outside the door.

'And what is he, pray tell?'

'Ah. I must apologise. He is my newest friend. Now that I am a commercial adventurer, I must keep more robust company.'

'Quite so.' She sat. 'I shall regret no longer being able to keep your company, Monsieur. Though you have been conspicuous by your absence.'

'I should like to explain.'

'I would prefer it if you did not.'

'If I may, you have been a most constant friend without whom I may often have fallen to despair.'

'How so?'

'You have been a great solace to me.'

'Have you required solace?'

'I have.'

'Indeed.' She bowed her head a moment then redirected her gaze to trap me. 'Now that you flee us, Monsieur, and the seas are so wide, I feel I owe you an honesty.'

'We are friends. I would expect nothing less.'

'I have loved you.'

'Comtesse?'

'I have loved you all these many years, Jehan.'

'I, I cannot think what to say only that I have held you in the highest esteem. More than that. Much more.' I tried to choose my words carefully. 'The highest esteem in which it has been possible for me to hold any woman. And I would call that love too.'

'Yes.'

I went to sit next to her. 'I have loved you as well as I could.'

For the first time in our years of acquaintance, I saw her eyes begin to brim. I felt my heart wrench to see it. 'I understand you. There is much I have understood. I have not always lived in Avignon.'

'Quite so. You are a woman of immense sophistication.'

'And yet I had still hoped you might see me.'

'Madame, I am overcome. I had no inkling.'

'It was ever thus. Doomed to love the one man who would not love me back. And trapped with one who cannot give me what I wish.' She took my face in her hands. So directly, as she had often done.

'Then I must send word from Jamaica and instruction on the best way to escape.'

She laughed. 'Ha! Will they have me there?'

'I will have you there. I will arrange a fine little hut for you. Made of grass and sticks.'

'How I have loved you.'

'May I kiss you?'

'Yes, Monsieur. I demand it.'

I kissed her and she took me to her as if to try to keep some piece of me. Then, she retreated and stood.

'Comtesse, I—'

But she was gone, and I knew that I had loved her too.

The day of our departure was barbaric in its finality. Joe, I knew, was well again. I had seen him through the door to the kitchen being given strict instructions from Monsieur Benoit, who was tapping a small pan and showing him a line of jars. It occurred to me that Joe was expected to cook for me. I cannot say what the jars contained but Joe looked utterly uninterested. Though I had not seen him to hear how he was, I had in my mind that if we could simply survive the journey, we would find freedom and happiness. Hortense, however, was a cause of such great worry that it felt closer to panic. Every last measure of me was welded to her and what I knew would come.

I had not slept the previous night. I cannot fully describe the sense I had. Each small sound, gesture, movement, took on the muted and slow quality of ritual. That dog I would never hear bark again, the starlings in the chestnut trees, the light as it fell across my desk; my cabinet, where I sat for over an hour so I could try to remember the exact arrangement of glasses and items, the smell of the panels, the feel of the chair under my hand as I moved my palm across the stitching.

Even Avignon looked beautiful to me. The place that had held so much censure and restraint and the final punishment, the place that had ultimately forced this exile. But with the light fading and casting long shadows across walls and trees, it all seemed suddenly bathed in the golden light of memory, even before I had departed. The sound of the maids sweeping, the click of the *salon* doors, the bellman, the night guards who were never as quiet as they should be, the horses kicking their stable doors, Monsieur Benoit yelling his orders to lackeys and lazy pages.

I had, stupidly, hoped that Bobo would appear so that I might embrace him once again and for the last time. But, of course, he did not. The journey would have been long and complicated, and it was possible his health was yet worse. All these sounds and half-scents and yearnings became things to pack away into a chest and carry with me.

The previous day had been long. Agents of my uncle and Clusy de Marcilliac had been with papers and orders and endless detailed instruction and warnings that if there were any indiscretions, death would await. As if by merely continuing to breathe, my presence was as brazen a threat as a sword tip to their throats. One of the agents demanded to see my luggage and went through it all as if he expected to find a Spaniard hiding among the quills and clothes. I was disappointed to see Monsieur Benoit had packed pewter plates and spoons but admit perhaps his practical-mindedness was more appropriate than elaborate table dressings. I did steal three pretty glasses and wrapped them twice in hose to protect them. Also two good cups and another small *tapis*, two more vials of oil and six more of pomatum. There is practicality and then there is misery and I was at pains to preserve the first but minimise the latter. I was and am a man of prodigious need.

The morning dawned as it always would. I should like to embellish this episode and instruct my scribe that there were clouds and storms brewing, that rain fell in torrents like God's own tears and with it my own heart broke. But it did not. It was cool and clear, the sky a pale cornflower blue. There was nothing to mark it out from any other day, such was the irrelevance of my departure from this corner of the universe. We like to think our lives are registered somewhere, in the heavens even, an astrologer's quill scratching our lives across a starscape. But in the end, we are mere seeds thrown to the furrows and whether some grow and some fail is of no great consequence to the plough come harvest time.

My Uncle Hippolyte arrived early and brought with him an ostentatious assortment of his household along with elder Cherbonnes, a minor Clusy de Marcilliac (no doubt invited that he might report back) and a few others. There was hardly room to move in the front courtyard. It occurred to me I should have bid farewell from my sister's house, but it was too many miles in the wrong direction and I could not face my new brother, The Toad. I had not seen him but had written him a lengthy treatise proclaiming his good name and my eternal shame and gratitude. Given what he stood to attach to his property and coffers as a result of my sister's imminent inheritance, a small note of acknowledgement might have been expected. None came.

Hortense was to travel with me in my carriage as far as Aix-en-Provence, where she would leave and go to stay a night with our cousins. It was a great comfort that I might be with her some of the way and yet I knew too it would make the parting even more painful.

I had again dressed with the aid of my page, masquerading as a second valet, and managed to affect at least some dignity by taking several deep breaths before stepping outside. I caught myself silently bidding my house farewell, just as I had as a child when we moved between residences throughout the year.

I saw Joe. He was loading a chest onto the back of the second carriage. I kept one eye on him, all the while afraid he might be left behind or try to flee when no one was paying him attention. There was such a throng that I could scarce keep him in my sights as he moved and ducked. I began to panic and feel an insistent terror begin to grow. My throat began to prickle and burn and then I spied little Lucie, who wept so hard she seemed to be choking. To distract myself from the torrent of grief I felt rising, and in a vulgar display of emotion, I embraced Monsieur Benoit and kissed his cake-and-pastry cheeks as well as I could, given his girth. He was immensely pleased, I could tell it, though clearly it surprised him.

As I released Monsieur Benoit, I turned to go to my uncle, whose face wore the weary disgust of a long-suffering warden of war. Behind him were assembled his household, his deputies, liveried and ready to wish me well on my adventure in enterprise. I could not see Hortense.

'Where is Hortense?'

My uncle indicated with a curt nod of the head that she waited for me in my carriage. I looked past him and could just make out her shape.

I saw Joe shake hands with the lackeys and pages and bow to Monsieur Benoit. Benoit rather kindly had moved along to wish Joe well and patted him on his shoulder and said something that made him smile. As Joe moved away from the group, he turned back to look for me. My fear subsided a jot.

With my entire household and some of his own assembled and waiting behind him, Uncle took my hands hard, crushing the bones, and leant in as if to kiss me. Then, when he was as close as could be, he spat in my face. He stayed close. I felt him like a musket, hot and murderous.

'You are less than rubbish.' His fury had whipped his eyes to red. 'Wipe your face. Make it look like tears.'

The shock of it I cannot recount. Somehow, despite all the punishment I had endured, this, at the final moment, was the worst. By the time I got to the carriage and Hortense, I felt I had been cut clean through with a cleaver.

We made our way along the streets and across the front walls of the Palais. I sat next to Hortense, my head on her shoulder and our hands entwined. I felt nothing but misery and, worse, foreboding.

Joe rode up front with the driver, who answered to my uncle. On the back were two prefects, or so we might call them, also appointed by my uncle's office and whose charge it was to get us onto the boat without incident. Behind followed another vehicle with our luggage and another two guards; another carriage behind that was to take Hortense back home once we had parted. All the men were armed and at least some, I was told, had instruction to kill us should we try and escape. To the passing world, they were the generous and stately send-off my

uncle had provided his favourite nephew as he embarked upon
a great adventure to expand the fortunes of the Baudelaires.

For a while, Hortense and I did not speak. I could think of
nothing I might say to her and only tried to remember each
moment as it passed and feel her closeness that I might remember that too. She wore her pearls. She had not done so for a
few weeks. In silence, I placed my hand on her belly and she
covered it in hers and looked to me.

'I will remember you to my child.'

'Will you be allowed to speak my name?'

'I will speak it.'

'Thank you, Sister.'

'And you must speak mine. That way you will remember me
and have me close.'

'I cannot think how I will survive without you.'

'Nor I you. But we must. It is all that remains.'

'You must prosper and be well. You will soon be a mother
and then you will find a new object for your affections.'

'You are always and forever my other half, my twin soul. No
one can replace that. Do not forget it.'

'I will not.'

'Will you be careful, my love? You never seem to heed me,
but I hope that this experience has at least chastened you
somewhat. Your freedom is conditional. It will always be thus.'

'Yes.'

'I had never thought it possible to say, but I believe Mister
Kryk will do well and look after you.'

'He is wiser than I, and more useful too.'

'That is a good thing. Someone to keep you sensible.'

A moment passed.

'Perhaps . . .' She did not complete her thought, only began
to weep. So great was her grief that it overwhelmed me too
and we held one another and cried as if we were still babes

from the womb, our mother just dead and no one to help us nor look to our care.

We followed the Rhône. There had been talk of taking a boat, surely a quicker passage, but there were problems with collapsed shores and sandbanks. Each year the river would change its shape entirely after yet another flood had rampaged through.

We reached the road for Aix much sooner than I had thought we would. We stopped outside the limits so that my sister could make her way to our cousin and we could continue without entering the town.

Hortense did not move for a moment. She straightened her dress and hair and made herself tall in her seat. She turned to me and kissed me once on each cheek, slowly, so slowly, her lips hardly touching my skin. I tried to speak but she placed her gloved fingers on my mouth and shook her head. Her lady's maid was at the carriage door and looked away, embarrassed to have witnessed such intimacy. Behind her was Joe.

Once outside the carriage, we stood between the horses and the wheels. Hortense would not look at me and I stood as a child might, mute.

'Louise, are you ready?' asked Hortense.

'Yes, Ma'am. I am.'

My sister paused for a moment then quickly turned to Joe.

'You too are my brother, Jonathan Kryk.'

He blinked a few times and suddenly his eyes filled, as did mine.

'Thank you, Madame.'

'Your mother is now under my personal protection. I will see to her.'

'Thank you, Madame.' Dear God, he was shaking all through to hold himself together. There seemed a moment of great quiet as Hortense simply looked at him as if she was trying to know him, as if by looking into his eyes she might know who it was that I loved so desperately that I would surrender my life for him.

With no more word, she turned from us and walked to her carriage and we knew not to follow, for even before she reached its door, she had let escape great sobs that seemed to take her over entirely. The cost of loving one is to break the heart of another and I knew that even to my death, I would never forgive myself for what I did to my sister.

15

Marseilles

Marseilles was yellow. It had the pallor of a city courting its next plague. The sky was long and flat against the sea and their jaundiced palette did nothing to recommend our arrival. We seemed to wind through endless nasty streets, filled with brutish townspeople and the most desperate-looking accommodations. The air was fetid and damp.

I expect, having discussed this with my scribe, that the odours of the time were of an entirely different order to those she might encounter now. But equally, she must endure atrocities of manner and a lack of decorum that I would find upsetting to the point of tears. She is distressed herself this morning, admitting that she dreads writing about ships, her doing so requiring a good deal of reading about and examining pictures of decks and masts, hulls and ropes. She sides with Joe (again) in finding that no good can come from a voyage at sea.

The harbour was immense. Beyond the break sat vessels and galleys of all sizes. They did not seem to move and looked as though they were wedged in sand. Their sails were down, save a few flags that hung listless on their staves. They were like sleeping beasts and yet I had seen the violence of their movement before and feared it.

Without wind, we would not be sailing. One of our guards

gave word of our arrival to the ship's captain, Wallace, and we were told to rest at an inn that lay to the side of all the noise and bustle of the port. When the weather permitted, we would be called to sail with cannon and gun. It would likely be a full day, possibly more.

On hearing this news, it was decided that two guards would remain with us and the rest return to Avignon. Most of our luggage was dispatched to our ship, the *Aurora*.

She was so much larger than I had imagined and yet so much smaller too. I could not imagine being confined there for eight weeks. Along the decks there seemed to be much activity, too much, loading and cleaning and sails being unfurled and rolled again. I could not quite fathom how many people it held and hoped that at least half would remain ashore.

I stood with Joe, my uncle's two guards – musketeers – a few paces behind. They would of course have their orders to get us on board no matter our protest, but did they know our precise crime? I prayed not, lest they intimate to the ship's captain that we should not be allowed proximity. I turned to my uncle's officer.

'Shall we find our lodgings? Do you leave us now?'

He took me aside.

'Baudelaire, you will be delivered safe to the *Aurora* and then on to Jamaica.'

'So I understand.'

'If you are not found to be on the ship you will be sought to the ends of the earth. Is that understood?'

'Quite so.'

'And him too.'

'Oh, he is certainly worth the effort.'

'These two have authority to kill anyone who waylays these arrangements.'

'Understood.'

And with that, he climbed back on board the carriage that had brought us here and departed. It was a strangely anticlimactic end to our journey. All these weeks of planning and threats, our lives in the balance, and in the end, I had the peculiar sensation of having been abandoned.

We were to repair for the night at least, the musketeers with us to prevent any escape, and be ready to leave the next day should the winds improve. Perhaps we should have fled. But where and how? Rather to be an exile and free than a fugitive forever. Eight weeks of ocean-bound penury seemed preferable to a life of fear.

'Is this our inn?' I glanced over my shoulder to one of the guardsmen. He nodded curtly.

'Yes, Monsieur.'

'Will you deal with the proprietor or should my man do it?' I may have been accused of a crime, but I did not think it appropriate that as added punishment I should have to arrange my own accommodations.

The musketeer, Baudin I think was his name, indicated that Joe should do it. Joe looked to me and I nodded. He was so tired and from the hollowing around his eyes, I could tell he was in some turmoil. He lifted the small bag we had for our short stay and disappeared through the low wooden doorway.

'No, wait. I will accompany you.' Baudin went in after Joe. I stayed with the other one, a brute with too many scars and an unkempt beard. I recall his name as Charron. He kept making unattractive noises with his nose and throat, which he seemed to have only just discovered were in some way connected. Marseilles was as putrid as it had always been. I was miserable.

After an undignified eternity, marooned outside the inn, Joe stuck his head around the door and waved us in.

The inn was pleasant enough. It was noisy and there was

a mixed lot of patrons as one would expect. The musketeers must have presented an unsettling entrance, as at least one table of lackeys and another occupied by some sailors looked up from their cards and flagons to make a pointed welcome. I had a momentary fantasy that they might all kill each other in the night and Joe and I could run away unguarded. The inn-woman came forward with the keys and led us through the arch to the stairs. Baudin and Charron climbed with us, one in front, one behind.

At the end of the corridor of rooms, she extended a hand through a doorway. 'This is yours, Monsieur.' It was small. Half of a half of my pantry, a slim monkish bed, but clean. 'Your man is here.' Joe was next door. That was something. 'We've only the one room that leads through.'

'Leads through?'

'You requested it, didn't you? A room with access from the next.'

I could have kissed her full on the mouth.

'Quite so.' I did not even allow a smile. 'I will require assistance.'

'You two.' She eyed up the men with her narrowed black eyes. 'You lot are down this way and I'm telling you now, and don't make me remind you with a branding iron and a whipping stick, no whores, no Huguenots, no sodomites. Gottit? I find a whore in here, you'll pay her first and then you'll pay me second for her keep. And then I'll get you beaten. Gottit?'

They looked appropriately contrite. Away and across the stairs that we had just ascended, there was a single door; she opened it and in there I spied two cots. 'No whores!' she crowed out again as she descended. I felt Joe grab my hand. 'Wait here,' he whispered, and he was gone along the slanted floorboards to the musketeers' door.

He put his head through and spoke with them

conspiratorially. Then he turned from them, looking back to me his, face lit with glee. He stopped at my door and bowed a little, I assumed so that his subservience might be witnessed, then came through and quickly bolted the door behind.

I enfolded him entirely. All my fortitude and forbearance suddenly left me. We could neither of us pull apart.

He managed to say, 'I don't think I can survive. Now I've seen the galleon, I don't think I can do it. We should rather flee.'

'You must manage. It is eight weeks, ten at the most, and then we will be free.'

'I thought you were dead and then that I would never see you again and now I see you and I think it might be worse.'

'On the contrary, it is perfection. And look? Here we are together. How did you manage it? You are so clever.' I kissed him hard. He was pleased.

'It was nothing I did. I had assumed they knew everything about us. But then the one who followed me offered me some coins and asked if they could sleep further away from you, and that I make it look as if those were the only rooms available.'

'But why?'

'The best and only reason.'

'Whores!'

'Yes, whores! They have no interest in watching us as long as they are not punished for their errancy. He warned me that they would get us on the ship no matter what, but in the meantime they would need to have some sport.'

'Oh, this is perfection.'

'I protested, feigning shock. On my oath! My master will be furious, nay, incandescent! So he added more coins and I said I would need to stay close to you for your suspicions would be aroused and you might report them to your uncle unless I managed the situation. It seems they know nothing of their commission other than they should get us on ship.'

'Uncle could not risk telling them. They are a loose-mouthed lot. He would not have left his reputation in their hands. But tell me how you are? This business has made a ghost of you.'

'First, let's be safe. I will tell the fellows that you would like to rest and will sup around six. This will hopefully send them off on errands of their own. They may return to eat and satisfy themselves that they are well-employed. Then, you will say you are weary and would like to write to your sister, and they will be more disposed to sneak off on their pursuits. Yes?'

'Yes, yes, give these poor men the whores they so richly deserve. You are so clever. That is exactly how it will be done.' I saw the colour return to his cheeks a little. He was about to leave then turned back to me and kissed me as if to perform some alchemy between our breath, life passing between us as he did. I wished it to be possible. I wished it desperately.

'I have died without you,' he said.

'We will survive, Joe.'

'How?'

'We must.'

'And if we do not? If one of us does not?'

'Pfft, the other will follow, a seamless reunion, even beyond death.' His courage was leaving him again. 'Go, go now and speak to your fellows.'

He left and even as the door shut, I felt my legs give out and the great blackness come raging over me. Tears came from me without bidding or restraint. Again, I could not take in air. My desolation near strangled me. The shame of discovery, the rank violation of the inquisitors, my uncle, the gaol and the cruel separation and then always and forever my sister. Her distress that lay beyond language. I rest my head on my scribe's shoulder as we write this. She encourages me to forge ahead with the story.

And she reminds me that to be reunited with Joe was a joy, a precious hope, a prayer. Of course I could not say to him how I was grieving, not when he was enduring all he was for me. When there is nothing left there is only love and to be denied that is intolerable. There is no soul who has known it and that can then survive its loss.

This telling has been costly. Despite her earlier encouragement, my tears are infectious. My scribe is exhausted. We will resume our story when we both have rested. For now, let it be enough to know that you cannot love another often enough and deeply enough in the time you have. Love them with immediacy and urgency. Announce it, tell them with word and look and tender touch. Love often and deeply. It is all there is to keep us from despair, from meaninglessness. I knew Hortense but twenty-four years and I have mourned her for near-on four centuries.

16

A New Twin

Joe came back with wine and a single glass.

'Charron and Baudin have gone. I returned some of the coins they gave me and charged them to buy unripe fruit and cake for you.' He must have interpreted my exhaustion as bafflement. 'For the journey. So that you will have something sweet to eat. Have you been weeping?'

'No, no, dust and weariness.'

'If you say.' He sat next to me on the little bed and swung his legs sideways over my knees. 'I gleaned some information about what lacks on board a ship from reading about the pirates.'

This made me smile. 'Quite correct. We must bring provisions of fruit and what else we can. We may be kidnapped by pirates, but we will at the least have plum cake.'

He smiled and shrugged. He was trying to be energetic. It was his salvation. He was nervous though and for a man who seldom spoke unless drunk or provoked, he was babbling like a cook's help. I loved him for it.

'They were most amenable. I suggested their effort would explain their absence from your guard.'

'I begin to think you are versed in espionage.'

As if to prove it, he jumped up and locked each door twice and dropped bags in front of it them too.

'That should be enough.'

'Come. Lie with me here. You must be so weary.'

He came to me.

'I have missed you,' I said.

'Your notes were very good.'

'They were insufficient, but there was nothing else I could think of.'

We lay facing, arms about each other. There was nothing to say. We could replay what had passed, the base brutishness of it all. But in the face of such misery, what can one say? Despite all expectation, we had not betrayed each other nor ever would. Even beyond death. I knew it clear as anything I have ever known.

The light came through the small window, casting a long shade over our bodies. The heavy pillow, the chair. It was as if this room, a common room shared by all who came and went, became our true wedding bed. We were as ordinary lovers. I had no name nor title nor standing. My family, estates and obligations were all gone. I had as much possession as he in the world. He would never be my servant again. Perhaps for pretence, for safety, but no more. We were one and the same.

I looked at him as carefully as I could, to remember this moment when I felt him finally become my other self, my new twin. There was no one else in the world to consider or love. Hortense was gone and here next to me, with his hand resting on my face, was my new everything.

Dark, dark eyes that dropped a little and gave him a doleful look even when joyous; his full mouth that I had yearned to kiss for so many months. He breathed out, a deep release of all the energy he had mustered to get us to this silence.

'Joe, have you any regrets?'

'No. You?'

'Never.'

'But . . .'

'What is it?'

'It's nothing. It's just . . .'

'What?'

'I'm . . . only, I . . .'

'Why will you not say?'

He sat up. 'I'm . . . No, I don't want to say.'

'You. Are. Yes . . .? *Pardieu*, are you with child?'

'Stop it! I'm serious.'

'What then?'

He paused. 'I'm so afraid, truly. I'm terror-struck.'

'Come closer.'

He buried his face in my neck to hide his shame. 'I don't want you to think poorly of me. But I am. The ship, the ocean, so many are lost from disease and drowning. Drowning. And even if we survive the crossing, what will we find there? You know it's a no-good place. It's full of the worst wickedness.'

'Come now, you know that it has been declared that *we* are the worst wickedness and there is none the matter with us. We'll find no trouble and my exquisite face alone is sufficient to quell any riot. We will be among our own sort. And you will not perish. You will not.'

He held himself over me. 'It's eight weeks, on that *thing*.' He smiled.

'You must not think of it as eight weeks, that is the path to madness. You think of it as one day. And then the next and the next and so forth. And see how well we have conspired this? We will be together. The manifest says the captain is Wallace, an Englishman. He does not know our crime, only that we seek adventure in the Indies. And once there, freedom, and with it, togetherness. That is the thing. That will give you fortitude. It does me.'

He lay back down and began to kiss and stroke, looking for

some solace. I too needed it more than air. The bliss of it. I felt
his heat was getting up, but with it a flash of terror came too.
I glanced at the door.

He let his eyes follow mine there. 'Dare we?' he asked.

'Yes. What will we lose?'

'Our lives.'

'Then we will be free too.' I kissed him again. 'I have already lost one life. You are what remains.'

There was not much space. I helped him out of his clothes
before mine. Sitting across me, he flinched a little as he pulled
his chemise over his head. Across his chest were bruises and a
long flay mark. I was nauseated to see them.

'Can you ever forgive me?'

'For what?'

'I had no idea you still were injured. Forgive me, forgive me.'
I leaned up to kiss him and then each bruise that showed itself
across his torso and shoulders. He was broken meat, purple,
black and yellow. I was careful where I ran my hands along his
back and instead held his waist to me.

'We must be quiet,' he said.

'Yes.' And yet I could feel myself begin to rage even before
we were joined. I wanted to have him all and let him hold
nothing back.

He sensed it and moved off a bit and covered my mouth with
his. 'No. No noise. Not a sound. Lie still, I will have you in.
Then I can restrain you and help my own comfort.' I caught
him glance to the door. It was early evening. The inn was busy.

'I don't want to hurt you.'

'You won't. Not like this.'

'Perhaps—'

'I know what I'm doing.'

Even into my stomach, I was burning. He used his mouth
to cover mine so that I did not call out as he made progress

with his hand and seat to have me. Even before I was full in, I
near finished, but he held me back to fill him all. He breathed
quick to have me and the full grip of him meant he had to
cover my mouth with his hands to stop me shouting out his
name. I could hardly breathe from the panic of ecstasy as he
moved himself over and over in perfect motion, so that I felt I
had begun to drown. When it came, I let my whole self rupture
into him so that I died twice and then again.

We were both wet from our effort as he kissed me and I him
and whispered to him my love and gratitude and again my
love for always.

Then, though I was spent all through, he was still needing
so I stayed beneath him and let him find his way into me and
make his own finish. He was desperate by then and it cost me
to have him. He was heavy and hard, pushing at me painfully
and deep so that I had to work to hold my voice. Then with one
more effort he crowned fast and all at once collapsed into my
arms and wept and wept as if he could not hold back the tide
of sorrow and desolation of those crucifying days.

We slept entwined. I had stroked him and soothed him until
he had fallen asleep. His tenderness had broken my heart. We
woke to the sound of barrels rolling in the streets below and
with it the setting sun and our appointment with our minders.

In the wine house below, our two companions were tardy
and had a look of great adventure about them. It would
appear to have been a lovesome afternoon for us all. They
brought cake and fruit for us, as instructed, and had a great
appetite as did we. Joe was subdued, but the inn-woman
made unexpectedly good food – though I chose not to ask
about the meat that filled the pie crust she served. I stabbed at
one piece and it did not budge and would not yield to chewing. It is strange to remember that meal, perhaps on account

of its finality before a journey that would have important consequence no matter the outcome. To leave your home is to leave yourself and know that you have yet to become what you will.

This night among the rabble and the noise of the Marseilles inn was the last I would call myself the Marquis de Baudelaire of Avignon. I was in pensive mood as we made our way back upstairs to pass the night talking and feeding each other cake and making preparation in anticipation of the next day.

'It is not as fine as Monsieur Benoit's cake.'

'I only ever ate it when we saved your story for your sister's salon. I still don't forgive you for sending me to my cot alone that night.'

'I have to confess with great modesty, yet again, that I was far too overcome by you.'

'I came to your door after.'

'You didn't?'

'I did. By the time you went up, I was outside of myself with, you know, everything. I resolved that I would enter the room, strip off my clothes, get into your bed and lie over you. If you wanted me, you would have to do the fucking.'

'I confess I might have died of fright. And your language is very base.'

'No, you would have loved it. And you love my language too.'

'Then I would have transformed into a comet of desire. And then died of fright.'

'But would you have done anything?'

'Indeed, I would. As you can attest, I was the very model of masculine confidence and amorous skill gained from my vast experience with multiple, devastating lovers.'

'At the very most you would have said how delighted you were for the company and then lain like an aged abbess.'

'Not so. You offend me.'

'No? What might you have done? Remembering I am now naked and panting.'

'What any other man tossed on the horns of love would do. In a rage of passion and unbearable yearning twixt my loins, I would have said: Mister Kryk, might I hold your hand? And, if you please, a kerchief each to better conceal our modesty.'

At this, we both laughed so hard we had to control ourselves for fear of attracting attention or waking the entire inn.

Joe slept in the bed as I perched myself at the window. How many nights had I lain awake, watching him sleep, his every breath another thread stitching him to me for eternity.

While there was still life in the candle, I dug for my pen and ink. On a single sheet, I wrote:

Hortense, Sister most Dear and Beloved. I will love you forever. Even beyonde death. J

I returned to the narrow bed and to Joe and tried to note each point at which his skin touched mine, how his head rested, how from deep in his dreams, he curled around me.

In the middle of the night, we were woken by a banging of boards. At first I thought it might be our lusty musketeers, but it was the window shutters. The wind was up. When we woke, we would set sail for Jamaica.

17

We Sail

It was early enough that the air still had a dampness to it, but the wind was brisk. To the right of where we stood, great slabs of stone and all about them five, maybe more, fish sellers; a rough crew, some bending over the catch, others bringing the baskets from the boats. I could hardly dare to think how they smelled. Their voices were hard as they scratched through their haul. They flayed the fish, lacerated their skins with blunted knives so that the rock was punctuated with little piles of silver scales. If they each could be counted to thirty scaly coins, there might have been some awful poetry to it. But there was none. Just the putrid waste of the sea.

Some of you will judge Joe for his fear of the voyage. You should not. As part of the warrants we had to sign, we promised that we would arrive in Jamaica and deliver ourselves to my uncle's agent notwithstanding 'pestilence, drowning and pyrates'. It was almost certain that we would encounter their ships, which were quick and quarrelsome, and we could only hope that as we did not carry great riches on this particular vessel, they would let us pass and wait for more rewarding plunders.

Pirates aside, the scene before us did not recommend itself to optimism. Barrel upon barrel was being laid onto boats, cutting their oars through the salty swill. Bales of hay, sacks of grain, boxes of vegetables, black pigs, chickens in small crates, noisy geese in larger ones. The men who did the work were rough, pocked and leathered, all the while shouting and spitting the foulest language. It occurred to me that they may have already plundered our trunks and helped themselves to the contents. We had also under our name a good deal of ale and claret for when the water ran out, as well as dried meat, fish and biscuits that looked as if they could break a man's tooth right off.

My most grave concern was for my reams and reams of paper, rolled tightly in a leather pouch to keep the damp from getting to it, as well as some ink resin and other necessities, two volumes of poetry and a small portrait of Hortense.

Wallace had, evidently, raised the question of our choosing a merchant ship, but safety and convenience were offered as reasonable excuses. He was to know nothing of our plight or he would either refuse to take us or shackle us in the hold along with the rest. Hortense had laboured hard; she had sat at my elbow as I paid for our passage. I admit it was most galling to have to pay for one's own exile, but there was nothing else to be done.

You may expect that I would be in more of a turmoil over these arrangements. I was not. I expected undiluted misery, but beyond that I had no specifics to which I could relate. I had to agree with Joe though, a boat is unnatural and the very fact of them invites illness, melancholy and pirates. The route we would take was under constant attack as plunderers helped themselves to cargos of sugar, gold and human lives as sure as the sun would rise.

We made our way to the boats, our guards with us. They had reported to Joe that they had had the best whores and wine they could find. The musketeers were now penniless, spent and most pleased, and told Joe how sorry they were that he had not been free to join them for his last night ashore.

Wallace's man greeted us and gave some pause when he saw the two musketeers we brought with us.

'They will be leaving.'

'I have no doubt that they will, Mister Baudelaire.'

I turned and gave them an indication that they could depart. They stood back but we were on the ship before we saw them turn away. I should mention that the journey from the shore to the great beast was not exactly pleasant. Horrible little boats battering around in the water. Joe's boots were wet even before we had spent a moment at sea. I was not pleased and Joe was visibly shaking as we were buffeted this way and that.

We eventually climbed onto the deck, an effort I hoped not to repeat too often. Wallace was there and afforded us a weary welcome, instructing one of his men to show us to our lodgings.

We descended a wooden ladder below the decks and were immediately required to bend right over in order to avoid hitting our heads on the ceiling. The air was stale and our proximity to the guns and cannons gave me pause for concern.

Along we went after a boy called Putt. *Pardieu*. Never did you see such a cupboard. A plank attached to the walls that ran between the decks and on it lay some sort of rolled-out mattress. The plank was about as wide as I was. It had two ropes through which one would need to climb to get on to it, presumably to hold one in once the ship began to sway about. Under it were stacked our chests, though we were informed these could be stowed once we had extracted what we wished. There was a table too, nailed to the wall, and on the floor beneath it, another mattress. I could scarce believe my eyes and it took me some minutes even to recognise the plank and rough mattress as a bed. What was to pass as a room was, thankfully, roughly panelled all around save for the portion through which one entered. This was covered over with a curtain that opened directly under a heavy beam. I was to share the cupboard with

Joe. The boy apologised that it wasn't bigger, but that Joe could sleep on the deck with a few of the other servants if I wished it.

I did not wish it.

Our tentative joy at being left together was immediately deflated. The curtain shut and the boy gone, I quickly stole a pretty kiss which resulted in us both hitting our heads on the cursed beams above us. I concluded, quite definitively, that a seafaring life was not for me, though Joe let fly a volley of the foulest language (always immensely arousing) which suggested that he may be more suited to being a sailor than he had thought.

And so it was that on that day, the guns were sounded and with great flurry and activity and an unspeakable noise as all on board began to shout and labour to lifted anchor, we set sail for Jamaica.

We would first sail south to rest on the correct latitude, and then set forth our line for the Indies.

Quite apart from the stale odour of the vessel, the most striking aspect was the noise of the thing. It was as if we were trapped on the back of a great and hungry beast whose innards and tempers never stopped coursing and grinding to keep it alive. The men seemed to shout instruction and hold normal conversation at the same pitch. So too the *Aurora*, who raised her voice in a discordant tone that never seemed to cease. The constant grind and creak of the wood and every metal fixture and bolt clanking its call all day and night made for a ferocious din. Barrels rolling across decks and the general mayhem of over 300 souls in a confined space was enough to drive a man half to distraction.

I will admit, however, there was a moment of thrill and adventure when first we stood on the deck and saw the sails full of wind and eager for the sea. Though he stood away from me, I could see Joe swelled by the moment, his face alight. The

Aurora thrust ahead, the sea supplicant beneath her. It was very fine and I could begin to fathom the passion men had for the ocean.

I will not detail every moment of life on board. It was tedious and hard and Joe was required to do a good deal of labour – lugging and finding and fixing. Early on, we established that we would need to escape the stale spaces below, climb up to the deck and there find fresh air and reasonable company. The nights were cool and the winds that propelled us steadily on brought with them a chill, but rather that than acrid confinement. We would find some fellows similarly inclined for freedom, light a pipe with them and play at dice and cards as the great sky opened up above us. The watch, stork-like in his nest, would be passed some spirits to keep him warm and in good temper. This was the best of it. We could sit with crew or captain, it made no difference, and in it there was a kind of acceptance that Joe, though not able to sit next to me at cards for example, would still be in common company and not dispatched to the kitchen or below decks.

At night we would huddle into our cupboard. Joe always had an ear for a bawdy joke and would relay whichever he had heard. He didn't like Wallace and would complain about him.

'He watches me.'

'It is his job to watch you. You have the look of a mutinous type.'

'How so?'

'You are friend to all. You are much liked and included. He might not like that.'

'But there is nothing mutinous in dice and ale.'

'And you are beautiful. The women passengers will mutiny first.'

'Stop it. He truly does mistrust me.'

'You forget he is English.'

Joe nodded. 'There's the rub.'

Often, I would read him the next portion of a story I had worked on for his amusement alone. We spoke in whisper, though in truth no one ever paid us any mind below deck. Each was entirely preoccupied with their own survival and the drudgery that accompanied it.

On yet other nights, long after all around us had fallen to sleep and I was strapped to my grim plank, he would sometimes get up from his mattress and come to stand next to me and stroke my face and allow himself a kiss. Often sympathetic, sometimes hungrier. His ardour gave me immense strength and happiness, but we knew we would never allow ourselves an indiscretion while on board.

The days were endless, empty and exhausting in equal part. After an evening of lawless rain and wind which had made us both weary and nervous, Joe leant over me and I saw something new in him I could not name.

'Are you well enough?' I whispered.

'Yes. Though my breast is very painful.'

I placed my hand on his heart and rubbed my palm across his chest. His skin was cool and the bones of his chest protruded much more than they had. 'There. I will heal it for you.'

'You do.' He might have kissed my hand and given it back to me, but that night he closed his eyes, breathing deeply, and allowed me to massage his tired heart.

I yearned to say, 'I love you,' only to hear it back, but knew he would not respond. It was not his nature. He showed it rather, by leaning through the ropes to kiss me, by bringing me an apple and carefully cutting pieces to feed to me as I lay there. Each night he tidied my hair, pulling through the comb with the most patient touch, no matter the tangle the devil wind had made and, wisely, never again repeating his suggestion that I allow him to crop it clean off.

'You don't need it any more.'

I resisted with impressive theatre – 'You insult the very core of my being!' – and followed it with such a protracted period of petulance that he knew better than to mention it again and, instead, continued to unravel the snarl.

In truth I cherished my hair. It was my last attachment to my lost station. My decline from my elegant *hôtel* to a plank in the belly of a sinkhole galleon had been swift and rude, and to allow me to keep my hair was, I thought, an entirely uncontroversial kindness. Perhaps it was base vanity but soon I began to cherish so desperately those moments of attention from Joe when we could be together. I perched on a low beam and he behind me muttering as he worked, relaying a story, worrying about pirates: this had been seen today and yesterday, three galleons in close formation. I forgot what he had said as soon as he had said it, but all was balm for my vain heart.

18

Filthy Swabber

By the time we had found our line to Jamaica, the weather had worsened and the sea changed colour. What had been deep and clear became striped through with black and foam. Where before it had a clarity, it now took on the flavour of pestilence. Wallace warned that we would soon sail straight through some of the worst storms the ocean could offer, but if he could time his vessel well, the winds that brought the storms would be the same that would spirit us through them with great expedience and we would be in Port Royal long before our food and water gave out. I was not inclined to trust him, for no other reason than I had heard of many a captain who had planned to sail one way and the next day was so thrown off course by inclement weather that he had landed far from his target and was soon seeing his crew and passengers die from hunger and disease.

I did not drink the water on board, which even from the start tasted as if spoiled, and told Joe he should not drink it either. Instead, we fast developed a taste for ale, which was good at quenching thirst, and took from our store of wine, though sparingly. The ship's cargo was claret so we had decided early on that if we looked in any peril, we would steal it for ourselves and drown in wine before we drowned in the ocean.

That day we saw, for the first time, porpoises. It is a small thing to record here, given the length of this tale, but I shall never forget the joyous sight and my scribe assures me that even now, readers will be pleased to hear about it. And with the storms ahead, their arrival was fortuitous and, we were told, did portend a safe and prosperous crossing.

I watched Joe stand with some other men and smaller boys to look at the porpoises that had again begun to gather around the boat. As a group of the creatures launched out of the sea together, the men raised a delighted cheer.

I would never admit it beyond our few, but my favoured time aboard was nighttime. I felt bold sitting on deck in the dark, none but ship's people for company and guzzling ale from a pewter cup. My life had 'til then been so conditional. I admired the swagger of the sailors, their robust and easy ways and invigorating language. Women, neither whorish nor novice, only quick and clever as any of the men with a cutting word or sideways look. I envied Joe, how easy he was among them, for he was not their natural ally – being the son of a cartographer, educated and professional – but to him it mattered none. That he lay naked with a marquis or drank to a standstill with a swabber was all the same.

He was still at a distance away, engaged in a game that required each one to take a turn balancing a full cup of ale on his head. One of the girls would demand a secret. The boys could answer truthfully or, if they refused, would be kissed by the girl and with it risk losing the cup from his head.

Even through my own rising intoxication, I could tell Joe was in no fit state to balance himself on his own two feet, let alone with a cup on his head. The sun had made his skin darker and his hair had grown more flaxen with each day at sea. He was in nothing more than his breeches and open chemise, not a care to hinder his posture. I was near breathless watching him, how light attached to his every profile so that he glowed like a golden-haired god descended from Ouranos itself.

He laughed himself sideways as his new friends failed the test – a tiny kiss, chaste and sweet on any boy's cheek, sent pewter cups flying. Some tried to blame the freshening breeze, others the ship's natural sway.

It was Joe's turn. One of the girls, black-haired and bold, stood.

'Now then our Joey, we'll all hear who you love or I'll kiss you 'til you lose your cup.' A cheer from the friends. 'Which is it?'

'Cup.'

'You won't tell us who you love?'

He shook his head. 'No, no, no.'

To calls of 'Cup!' and the bays and whoops of encouragement from the assembled, he made great show to balance the ale on his head and shut his eyes with arms out like a great seabird to steady himself.

The girl, seeing her chance, stepped in and without touching him, bypassed his waiting cheek and took him full on the mouth, her tongue parting his lips and he, *pardieu*, responded full with his own. The watching group erupted with shouts at the naughty spectacle and I, my loins on fire, near fainted with desire when to loud cries and the stomp of feet, the girl pulled away and he, the cup still balanced, had not spilled a single drop of ale.

The bold girl laughed yet more as he carefully removed the cup, took a triumphant swig and bowed to her with charm and gallantry. A great cheer rose up. All of the assembled were in love with him. He could have asked them to throw themselves into the water and they would have gladly done it.

I was transfixed. Knowing he could be both princely and utterly indecent in the same breath was hot sorcery.

When later Joe tumbled through the curtain into our cupboard, I near flung him up against the partition.

'Shh, no, no. Why so ravenous? I'm too drunk. Jehan, what
are you doing?'

'I need you. I am beyond refusal. Have mercy.'

'No. No.' He shook his head, more to clear it than to protest.
'No. We cannot.'

'Please, Joe. I beg you.'

'You beg me?'

'I do. I *beg* you.'

The absurdity and tragedy of it seeped through our ale-
addled brains at much the same moment and we both began
to laugh, even as we tried to stifle it. I still had him pinned up
against the makeshift wooden wall, my brow collapsed on his
as we shook with mirth.

'Jehan.'

'Yes?'

'Don't beg me. It's not elegant.'

'*Dieu*, I have become a whore.'

'Yes. Yes, I'm sorry to say that you have. Will you let me off
this beam now?'

As I stepped back, he, still ale-soaked, near toppled clean
over. I helped him to his mattress.

'You were magnificent at Cups.'

'I was. I was.'

Much later, when the world was all asleep, he must have
woken and come to stand at my side. From deep in my dreams,
I woke to find him kissing me and using his sweet hand to ease
my desperate longing.

My undignified begging was not my finest hour, but my scribe
assures me that as you have travelled a long road with me, it
will hardly have surprised you. She suggests that although I

may no longer have been the Marquis de Baudelaire, I was still my true self: as ever, an incautiously amorous drunkard.

By noon the next day, I recovered myself sufficiently to make an appearance. A plank can be surprisingly comfortable. I was, however, in thunderous mood. No sign of Joe, which was just as well.

Even before I was up, I could hear talk of inclement weather. The palpable change in the air gave me pause. I emerged above deck like a bear after winter and sat with my back to a beam, trying to recover some posture and balance. I saw Joe briefly as he helped a younger boy hoist a barrel out from below. He looked decidedly grey.

Impossibly, that night, there was again more merriment. It seemed the more likely the chance of poor weather and the threat of drowning, the greater the call for rowdiness. Unexpectedly, a few of us were invited to dine with Wallace. Rum, ale and wine were all uncorked and a goose was taken to roast. I was not in the mood for levity but the offer of goose and wine after so many days of increasingly meagre and gloomy meals was a good enticement. Joe would eat with the other men as usual.

Wallace's table was well-appointed given our circumstance and we ate readily. I made sure to offer him good praise and gratitude. When the meal was over, the others returned to their births with a measure of wine, sated for at least the night. Wallace invited me to stay, drink more and smoke.

From below and all around the noise began to rise. Shouts and songs, a fiddle, drums, all conspired to add yet another layer of madness over the already constant din of the vessel.

'Come, Baudelaire, let us repair to the chart room. I must see something there.'

The chart room was near enough to his quarters and as we braced against the growing wind to get there, the true wildness of the night unfolded below us. A mass of bodies all dancing and reeling, and jug after jug raised in roars of good cheer. They surprised me for their vigour.

'Is it usual to carouse so wildly on consecutive nights?'

'Yes, they must do it,' said Wallace.

'I had thought ships to rely on discipline and stricture. Though I am a virgin to this geography and mean it as no disrespect.'

'For the most part, but this exuberance,' he waved his free hand over his head, 'is essential to my commission.'

'How so?'

'For sanity. If they do not do it from time to time, they will either go mad or mutiny. Neither suits my purpose. And to-morrow late I will need them strong and willing.'

We found the chart room. I liked it well. 'You are wise, Captain Wallace.'

'I am old.' He drew breath on his pipe as if to test the air with it. 'I am not entirely sure of your business, Mister Baudelaire.'

'Meaning?'

'You are not the usual merchant adventurer. You lack, and I mean no disrespect either, the bloody-mindedness. You do not strike me as a man whose first interest is enterprise.'

'Ah. You have found me out.'

He raised a wary eyebrow.

'I am not a merchant. I am a writer. But my lack of an heir means I must, apparently, find other ways to prove my rep-utation and where breeding fails, fat coffers make adequate compensation.'

'Ah. Yes. I know it well.'

'I am expected to send word that I am King of Jamaica and all the Indies before the month is out.'

'What will you really do?'

'I will write and go in search of sea turtles and other creatures in which I find great interest.'

'But why Jamaica?' He ran a hand over his desk.

'My cousins, many of whom will doubtless follow me, have
a taste for sugar.'

He laughed at this. 'And you will find all kinds of it there.
Do not spend too long in Port Royal, Mister Baudelaire,' he
found my eye. 'The sugar there will kill you.'

'A good warning. But now to bed so that I might steer your
ship should your sailors be unfit for work tomorrow.'

'Fear not, they will be ready.'

'My gratitude for your hospitality.' I turned to go.

I had not been a convincing man of enterprise, which stung
me somewhat. But I was not entirely without guile and inge-
nuity, so perhaps I had convinced him with my secondary tale.
I could not afford to have him snoop about me, but surmised
that he had neither the energy nor the information to do so.

I left his chart room somewhat reluctantly for, along with
our dining table, it was the closest I had been to a warm and
well-appointed chamber in so many, many weeks.

'Mister Baudelaire, how is your manservant? Kryk, is it?'
he called after me. The hair on my neck rose up. There was
something in the way he spoke.

I turned, to show confidence. 'He does not like the ocean.
But I suppose he is well enough.'

'I have noted this.'

'His father was a cartographer. He died at sea.'

'Ha. They do, they do.' There was sport in his voice.
'Perhaps it would be helpful, well, might I ... invite him to the
chart room? He will see where we sail. It might put his mind
at ease.'

My stomach lurched.

I turned to him. 'But of course. He would like it well.'

'Good. Better to send him soon. We will find the weather has turned even in the next hour.'

'I will be sure to mention it to him. Though he has much that occupies him.'

'Of course. At your discretion. Though I think it will set his mind at ease.'

'Indeed.' I took my leave. What was his meaning? His questions were designed to find information. No captain cares a jot for the travel-sick worries of a servant, yet he had noted Joe's name and, furthermore, watched him closely. The servant of one passenger among a hundred. It was either a trap or, worse – my jealous heart – he had thirst for Joe.

I spent an eternity looking for Joe and eventually gave up. The merriment had died down as the weather had turned very quickly to something sinister.

As if from nowhere, the wind had quickened and came in heavy gusts so that one moment you might find yourself making good progress and the next near blasted off your feet. Sailors were huddled in smaller groups. I asked one what we should expect for the rest of the night and he brushed it off, saying it was nothing to worry about, but by the same time tomorrow we should expect something heavier. At first I thought he was joking. How could these swells and wind not cause alarm? But he returned to his cards, unfazed.

I found our cupboard but no sign of Joe there. All I could think of was Wallace and poor Joe trapped in his chart room, so I turned to creep back along the deck and out through the ladder. With great effort, I finally saw some light emitting from the captain's cabin. There had been none before.

There came through me the most violent rage. I was up the rails, across the upper decks and pounding on the captain's door in one swift move.

I could hear nothing but the roar and spray around the vessel. I pounded again and after the longest time, there came a body to the door. Wallace.

'What is it?'

'Ah.' My nerve failed me. 'I seek my valet.'

'Here?'

'I thought he went to look at charts and seeing your light . . .'

Wallace, reeking of rum, had a sneer to him that I did not favour. 'He was here.'

God in heaven. But I affected cool. 'Oh? And he has taken leave?'

'He has.'

'Very well then.' I wanted to demand what he had done, beat this stupid old boar-pig 'til he bled. 'I will seek him elsewhere.'

'Yes. You should.' His hair was tangled by the wind and made an unbecoming nest about him. 'He is a most sullen servant. You should find one better.'

'Oh? I do not take your meaning.'

'There is no meaning. Only that he is ungrateful.'

He narrowed his eyes, and I looked right into him to let him see I knew his heart and would kill him for it if I had to.

'I am sure he did not act unwell.'

Wallace was drunk. He kept his eye though. 'He is not just your servant, is he?'

The sea seemed to recede, the wind died and all of time and the darkest, darkest night sat silent over the whipping sails.

'He is ever my loyal servant. And only mine.'

'A pretty one.'

'A loyal one.'

'Ah, Baudelaire, you surprise me. You are being prudish.'

'No, Mister Wallace, you are being base. You insult me and my servant.'

'I know your way and I know too that you could give him to me. A loan.'

I near choked on his words. 'You do not understand me, Mister Wallace. Find yourself a filthy swabber.'

'I would pay you well for him.'

I grabbed his throat and pushed him hard against the timber frame. He reeked of spirits. 'Leave Mister Kryk be or you will find a short sword against your neck as you sleep tonight.'

'You are threatening me?'

'No more than you threaten me.' I pushed him back. 'You disgust me. You concern yourself with either Mister Kryk or me again and you will find more trouble than a few storms in a large sea, Mister Wallace.'

'It is Captain Wallace.'

'I doubt it has ever been thus.'

Mon Dieu. I had never been so bold nor brave and suddenly I felt my resolve give way. Wallace staggered back behind the door, which had been left open. I cared nothing and left as quickly as I had arrived. On my way, I saw the boatswain.

'The captain is drunk and strange. I do not like it.'

'He's always like that. Don't worry y'self. I do the captaining round here when he's under it.'

'He is under it now.'

'Praises be, for I'm captain again!' He laughed at this.

I suddenly felt chilled all through. For the first time, I understood what it was to live without protection, without the ability to call on one's kin, one's title, one's coffers if necessary, to find safe passage through the world.

I had to find Joe. Never was the ship larger nor more difficult to traverse. I seemed to be hindered at every turn.

By the time I managed to get back to our cupboard, he was there. Wide eyes and ashen-faced. I pulled the drape closed and hung the *tapis* over it as quickly as I could, nearly tipping over all the while as the quickening swells rocked us.

'Where have you been?' He hung onto me. 'You cannot imagine—'

I grabbed the beam overhead to stop from falling, my other arm supporting Joe.

'I can. I know.'

'How can you know?'

'I saw him. Wallace. I have sought you everywhere.'

'You knew?'

'Yes. No. He suggested and I tried to find you to warn you. But what has he done? Tell me you are well?'

Wallace had invited him to the chart room, saying I had suggested it. Joe accepted the invitation, but he was no sooner there than the door was shut and Wallace grabbed him. Joe had to fight him off and, being more sober and strong, managed his escape.

Joe whispered. 'He tried to kiss me, Jehan.' He paused. '*Dieu*, he is ancient. I would guess near as old as you are.'

Had there been more space I would have hit him hard across his head.

'Scoundrel! I have run across this confounded ship all night in the rain; I took that stinkard by the throat and threatened to run him through with a knife defending your honour and you insult me?'

Another lurch as Joe clung on. 'You took him by the throat? When did you ever take anyone by the throat?'

'Well, let me announce it: tonight will be the first.'

'And you threatened a knife?'

'At his throat, no less.'

I could tell Joe was mightily pleased with this, flushed and holding back his smile. So we stood, holding each other up, lurching this way and that in our nasty little cupboard between the decks, storms to come and coming soon. The *Aurora* was being buffeted about and as Joe clung to me even as we struggled to stand, I thought, on my life and all beyond, there is nowhere else in the world I would rather be.

19

Storms at Sea

The storms came. There was never a more terrifying moment in my life than seeing a wave so great that it rose up taller than the entire ship and reached over us thick and black. When it came down, it took a slice out of the upper deck and with it six seamen, a cook and a small boy. Decks were set to swimming. We had no sense of where the boat ended and sea began. Joe had heard from one of the seamen that when all took to crashing and drenching, we should not be between the decks for water might collect there, rushing in through the sides and deck boards and, the space being small, we might drown if we were trapped below.

Yet Joe refused to leave our cupboard.

'No.' He managed. 'Those men will push us overboard. They do it when there is a storm, to lessen the demand for food as rations deplete. They use the swells as cover.'

'I have never heard it and you must fix your eyes on the jugs of fresh ale and merriment that wait for us in Port Royal. A goose, cakes, a large pie, hot bread sunk in dripping.'

And with that we seemed to be hit all at once from the side, flinging us against the beams, and there came such a noise that I was sure the tempest was now squat cross our path.

'God be damned, we will die here.'

'I think, Joe, that we need to reappraise your language. Let us practise the words that befit our new place in the world together, to pass the time.'

My wretched, my beloved. His skin dirty and smudged from the day's labours; tears and dirt had made an awful mud across his cheeks.

'We will die. What is wrong with you?'

'We will not.' Though I had to shout it to have him hear me. 'I will not die at sea and nor will you. Repeat, please: *I will not die at sea!*' Another great crash threw him to the floor so that I had to grab him and pull him back up. 'You really must try to hold on better.'

He looked as if he might take his fist to my head. Which was preferable to the tears.

'No, I command you to say it: *I will not die at sea.*'

'I will not die at sea, but you might.'

'Again and a little louder, you know I cannot hear you over this rolling and rocking. To think I used to love the smell of the ocean. Again.'

'*I will kill you at sea!*' he bellowed at me.

'Bravo, that is much better. That will have to do for now. You are quite ungovernable and, for now, you may call me Monsieur again until you have learnt how best to behave when our lives are in peril.'

Eventually, he was persuaded to leave. He was ashen-faced and could barely walk. We were to wind rope around ourselves and attach ourselves to whatever solid railing we could find, as it was possible that the lower decks would become flooded with swill.

I could not say what was worse. To see the great waves coming or to feel your entire self and all about you disappear behind the bulwark of water. To feel it unleash its full weight on the decks was beyond the worst terror. Joe could not help himself. These storms were everything he feared about the ocean.

We were trying to get to where we could attach ourselves with some other men. A great wave came towards us and, quite against every natural instinct, Joe froze, unable to move. I had to grapple him back. This even before we were under the worst of the weather and the galleon could still be launched over the tops of the swells.

Then we found ourselves in a black and deep valley surrounded by briny battlements, so deep and wide that the *Aurora* was unable to carry us forward. When one of the terrible swells came over the side again, Joe, crouching and hanging on, fell, knocked clean over by the weight, and I saw him being washed away across the deck. He tumbled this way and that, a bobbin on a torrent.

He did nothing. He simply let himself be thrown. I called his name over and over to get him to respond. With all my strength, I tried to reach to him, but was thrown back on myself and even as I thought I had him caught, I felt his hand slip from mine.

Then, just as suddenly, he was washed back towards me again and I grabbed him with the help of a man holding on to the ropes next to me. We pulled him right. The man, the finest sort, then began tying Joe to safer railings. Joe had taken to shock and responded to no instruction shouted to him over the thundering wash, even as the fellow wound him round his waist with rope.

I tried to shout to him to hold on, but he did nothing and as I reached out to him to shake him back to life, a great cry rose up from the company. All faces turned up to hear a tremendous crack as the great mast tilted and then snapped like a twig underfoot.

My scribe suggests that I report these terrors too coolly. I do.

I cannot describe it any other way than to look on it as from some distance. There is no language nor experience I have ever had to compare to it. There was such chaos and confusion everywhere that I could not fix on anything and only had in mind to see where Joe was and try to make him safe. Even the seamen, practised and long-travelled, were at times on their knees, calling out to any gods who would listen to save their souls and carry them safely. It was only with the loud and violent encouragement from Wallace and the masters that they eventually moved to action.

I cannot say how long this continued; I tried over again to get Joe to wake from his dream. Shouting over the thunder.

'Can you hear me?'

He said nothing, blind and mute, racked with tremors. 'Joe?' I shook him and made him look at me, 'Joe?'

He gave nothing back, only carried on his shaking.

Somehow, we survived the passage of storms, which seemed to disappear as suddenly as they had arrived, and though there were still passing squalls they were nothing compared to what we had suffered. The *Aurora* had to be repaired and some passengers who were skilled in carpentry were conscripted to add their service.

We heard news that land would soon be in sight and if the wind held well, we would have sufficient drink even though we now ate nothing but mouldy biscuits, a few eggs, dried fish and other things that could be pulled from the sea. I would, on occasion, declare myself not in the mood for a meal and thus made sure that Joe would eat my rations too.

It was with some excitement that we were one night offered sea-turtles to eat. I can report that they are green and liverish to taste but very good. We looked forward to their next appearance. We were none of us fat and had begun to dream of feasting at a heavy table filled with mutton and fruit and pudding. Where before Joe and I had whispered of imaginary banquets in the quiet of our cupboard, by this time ever more elaborate fantasies about food became our preferred language of love when we were alone at night. On one occasion, Joe claimed his yard near spent in his breeches as I described to him a whole line of partridge roasting on a spit and dripping grease into the fire below. In the main, I dreamt of cool forest water rushing across moss-covered rocks.

With any luck, we would soon be in Jamaica. Putt informed us that on his previous crossing, they had been within sight of land when the wind had died and three days later, still with no wind, the currents had dragged them back whence they had come. Lack of water and food had put them in great peril. I could not bear to imagine it and caught myself praying for another storm if it meant we might be propelled swiftly forward to land.

Notwithstanding the food, tempers had begun to fray. Fights and arguments would erupt over nothing so that on any given day there were at least two fellows trapped in the stocks where Wallace and the full assembly could see them. We had avoided the captain with great care. Not difficult to do in the end, but it was with a wary eye that I made sure to know his every movement and his proximity to Joe. He watched us too; I would say obsessively. Until we were safely away from him, I would not be easy.

20

The Most Wicked
City on Earth

One morning, deep in the dawn before dawn and from the
bowels of the decks, we heard the men above shout out,
'Land Ahoy! Land Ahoy!', followed by a great and uproarious
cheer. We rushed to climb free from our cupboard and see
what was there.

Port Royal.

Turquoise as I had never imagined possible, light glancing
off the ocean surface and all around us the sails and flags of as
many ships and sloops as would make you feel you were one of
a multitude of swans. Where less than two years before most
of the flags would have been Spanish, now they were English.
Vessels sliced, some bobbed, some sat deep and low, everywhere the sense of life, expansion, hope. It was a dazzling sight
and the sound of voices carrying across the water from other
craft gave me such joy. We had survived and the end of it all
was laid out before us like a bright, pretty table.

How our own ship charted its way through I could not say,
only each vessel, all of different sizes, picked through and all
about we could hear the ships sounding.

After weeks at sea, it felt as if we could reach out and touch
the land, but in truth it was further off. It would be possible to

get there in a boat with the oars of a few men but impossible to swim, I'd have thought. Houses and buildings were barely visible through the sea haze and I am sure my mind inserted them into the scene, so deep was my yearning to be there.

Also in the bay were a multitude of small islands, more or less a sickle moon of them – though some were no bigger than a few rocks with a tree atop – but far apart and they disappeared into the far horizon as I squinted along the curved line of them from left to right. A small rowing boat might perhaps get you to them from the mainland if the seas were calm enough, but it would take a few men to pull through the swells in such a small vessel. Other islands, cays, were more substantial. From our deck, I could make out from the nearest that it was sandy with low bushes and various trees, tall and thick, and even a small amount of open land, good enough earth and grass growing on it. These larger cays were habitable though miserable, and one that was off to the fore of us seemed to have buildings. Spanish prisons and watch towers, said the boy Putt.

I looked across to Joe, who was mesmerised by what he saw. Still, he looked most weary. We were not ill, but neither were we well and Joe was very much thinner than ever I had known him.

Land in sight though and with it, freedom. In 1657, Port Royal was seething with lascivious drunkenness, profiteering, murder and women of, shall we say, a moist countenance. No one would pay us any mind.

The *Aurora* would tie up and we could walk away into the city, find ourselves a temporary lodging with a few coins and then later a place of safety and quiet. A small villa in a grove, trees alive with parrots and monkeys perhaps. There was surely a theatre. I could find employment there, write bawdy tales for the stage. Joe was certain that the New World would have at least one cartographer in need of an assistant to map the island's topography. Or if we failed at this then we would live on chicken eggs and whichever full fruits fell from the trees in our pretty orchard. At night we would pull our shutters closed and lock our door and live together as we were wont to do.

We were charged with collecting our goods together and, it was true, we would disembark with much less than when we left Marseilles, our stores long eaten or spoiled.

'What is next?' Joe was aglow with excitement, his eyes fixed on the shore and the ecstatic scene before him.

'Freedom.'

'Freedom.'

My sweet love had suffered. He must have felt me examine him for he turned and smiled at me. There was still such clarity in his gestures. How I adored him.

The boatswain approached us.

'You two, you're coming on the first shallop.'

'Are we? That is fine.'

Our departure was a strangely rushed and inelegant. There is no easy way to descend a rope into a small vessel that is being tossed alongside. I nearly lost my hat and cane into the sea at least twice. I was sure we had come all the way to Jamaica and survived the worst tempest ever whipped from Hades only to drown slipping twixt the ship and its boat. Just before we descended, Wallace appeared. I had said nothing. No salutations nor gratitude were due. He was a viper.

'Baudelaire.'

'Wallace.'

'Your sailing days are done.'

'This is my hope.'

'You may live to regret saying that.'

'How so?'

'I have all along known your charge.'

'Meaning what?'

He leaned into my ear. He was foul-smelling. 'I know you are a whoreson. And that pretty boy of yours too.'

I straightened.

'Your language offends me, Mister Wallace.'

'You offend me. I should have locked you in the hold like the devils you are.'

'Was that your commission?'

'It was. And more besides.'

I tried not to betray my shock. 'Well then. That you did not follow it cannot be laid at my door.'

'You should have let me have my sport.'

I could feel Joe bristling next to me. 'Then you are a devil too and no better than anyone.'

'You are rubbish, Baudelaire. I took pity when I should not have.'

Suddenly it all became clear, the strangeness of it all, the attention, the questions and his knowing. I had assumed he knew our crime simply from recognising his own. But he had more, a letter perhaps, something from my uncle and his agents. I had been naive. For all that had happened and all the cruel betrayals, I still could be caught.

'No, Mister Wallace. You took fancy to Mister Kryk and manufactured your proximity. It is not the same.'

'You are clever with your words. So clever. But your days of being clever will soon be ended.'

'Meaning?'

'I have had enough of you, Baudelaire.' He looked at Joe over my shoulder. 'You would have been a meaty catch.' He stepped away, calling out, 'Take them off.' And before we could bid the putrid vessel farewell, we were off and down, climbing our way to the shallop and with no help from the crew. We found below us the craft and tied to its aft, a smaller vessel with no sail nor oars and in it our three chests. We were seated in the middle and told not to move. After the weight and depth of the *Aurora*, we suddenly seemed to toss about with much more violence.

'Who else do we await?'

'No one,' came the voice of the crewman. It was Gibbons, the roughest sort. He would slit your throat in the night for a sip of ale if he thought it would prosper him.

'But there is space for more?'

'No, there ain't.'

Joe kept looking out the sides of the little craft to see how close the water came and how deep it was. Though it was clear and warm, it was impossible to tell how far to the ocean's floor. Up went the little sails and, with great speed, we set course for the harbour's mouth. Joe looked at me in question. I had no reply.

Something was amiss. A shallop with just two passengers and a boat that had room for more and yet carried just our trunks as it trailed through the foam behind us.

I tried to be open. 'What is our course, Mister Gibbons?'

'Never mind that.'

We could see the harbour ahead, clear enough that plumes of smoke were visible and the sounding guns grew clearer. All about us were the cays we had seen from the deck. Some were in lines like a great ant's footprints that led from the sweep of the ocean in towards the mainland. Our course, straight ahead, would take us to Port Royal.

The silence between Joe and I was unnatural and fraught, but just to feel him next to me on the little plank that was our seat brought me comfort. The spray drenching us was a relief, as the air was very warm. My felt hat began to feel most inappropriate for the clime and it was no longer fine, having lost its plumes and jewels early in the voyage.

Then, without warning or instruction between sailors, we swung about and turned sharp and quick to the right. Joe looked at me and I whipped around in my seat. Gibbons' face was steely. I quickly glanced over the water to see if he had taken action to avoid something – rocks, a creature even. There was nothing. The men did not speak and simply continued in their work. Quickly, the harbour fell away to our left and then was behind us. Instead, we made way through shallower water, but water for drowning in nonetheless. The little rocks and islands were all about but as we went, they began to thin to a few and then further beyond only one or two could be seen.

'Mister Gibbons, I must ask again: what is our course?'

'You will see.'

'Will I be pleased?'

He only shrugged.

Panic and horrible foreboding began to take root. I kept glancing at Joe. He had begun clenching and unclenching his fists and I could feel his breath was quickening.

He was preparing to fight.

Then, without warning, a shout, an arm about my neck and Joe fighting and kicking. A sack came over my head. A dreadful commotion. Joe was fighting. Then with horrible clarity I heard Gibbons' voice shout, 'Evil devils, sodomites!', and a body fell on my feet in the bottom of the shallop. I knew it was Joe.

Oh, God in heaven.

We were still weak from lack of solid meals and only ale to drink. I sat up and tried to get the sack from my head, only to feel a heavy blow come over me and then another.

I knew nothing.

I cannot tell you what occurred after this, only that at times I felt water cover me, or dreamt it. Felt myself being dragged, for my legs were hurt. I may have heard, 'Get the other one!', which gave me the briefest sense that Joe was still near. I tried to call out to him but then lost sense and feeling again.

21

The Place of My Dreams

I could see nothing. I could not move. Beneath my body, the ground felt damp and cold. It smelled not of the ocean but of earth. My first thought was that I had been washed up in a cave, that a tempest had carried me there. Then I remembered Gibbons and the boat and the way we changed direction. I lay, curled about myself like a babe still new from childbed, and shook. My voice was more of a whimper, a dog who had lain down on the floor to die. And as no noise would escape me, I repeated the only prayer I cared to remember: 'Joe.'

I drifted and dreamt as I always did when afraid, of tempests and islands, towers, long white shores. And even as I did, even through the veil of sleep, I recognised with the most terminal of dreads that I had reached the shores of my long-held fears. I knew that I had manifested my darkest nights of imagination into a place as real as the bones in my body. I knew exactly where I was.

I knew I was in one of the old Spanish towers that were built on many of the cays that dotted the bay. I knew that I was surrounded by a deep circle of stone. I understood that the smallest sense of light came from a window, a hole so high up that it might hardly catch the sun, and another at ground level, the size of half of a large folio, enough to see through, extend an arm, pass a cup of water, but no more.

I knew too that when I woke, the truth and the terrible dream would be exactly alike and that I was locked in the tower alone.

There was no way out. I knew that I had been put inside, the metal door locked, and huge stones lifted by the weight of six men placed in front of it to deny all and every escape.

How much time passed does not matter, only that I lay there in this tower, surrounded by nothing but an eternity of loneliness. I drifted between sleep and wakefulness.

But then, my ear began to attach to a small chink in the dark. The smallest hope began to penetrate my sleep. I tried to speak but was still buried in dream. I heard a voice not my own.

I heard Joe.

'Jehan? Are you there?' I could hear he was distressed, gulping at air and in tears. 'Say something, say something to me?' The voice was distant and had the texture of water. He was too far away. I tried to get my hands to feel about me but found only earth.

In my dream, I said, 'Joe?'

'Can you hear me?' he said.

'Joe. I can hear you.' I knew I could not speak it aloud.

'Come to the window. Come to the window.'

The window. There was no light, there could be no window.

'Jehan, you have to try, please, I need to know you live. Please. I beg you. Please.'

As if I knew the cry to be his last, his last effort to live, I knew I still had one last effort too. And so, with some summoning of the gods, that same eternal force that will make a dying animal fight and thrash even though the cleaver falls, I forced myself to come back to my body.

I bid myself and God to pull me back, stuff and fill my soul back into my sack of skin and skeleton. I felt my legs burn, a thundering around my head and ears. I gasped with such violent force that I near choked.

'Turn around, turn, I am here.' It was Joe. I could hear him clear and real.

'Where are you, where?'

'Behind you, turn.'

'I can't see.'

'There is a window, further down, on the ground.'

The window I had dreamt of for years and knew I would find.

I let my eyes focus and there I saw light. I could not understand where Joe was. I could not see him and felt I must still be asleep or in dream.

'I cannot find you.'

'Come to the light, to the window.'

On my hands and knees, I crawled forward, pulling apart the straw that seemed to be collected there.

'Joe?'

'I am here.'

I pulled away the last of the grass and behind it was the window. But too the worst and most lonely sight I have ever seen. Joe on the other side of a wall, through metal bars, and the wall deeper than the length of my forearm.

They had locked me in and left him out.

I pushed my head as close as I could. He seemed a lifetime away. His face was grazed and his eyes near swollen shut.

'Can you see me? I see you. What has happened? Where are we, can you say where we are?'

He began to weep. He crawled along on his belly and lay his face as close to the window as he could and put his arm through the gap. I grabbed what I could of him with my hand. We were connected, only just, and through the darkest window of hell.

'I thought they would kill me. And then they said they'd killed you. I begged them to kill me too.'

He was broken. And here was I, locked in a tower, close enough to touch his face and aware enough to know he had never been further away.

He lay with his face towards me like a fledgling fallen from its nest, waiting featherless for the hawk to bear it away as carrion.

We lay and said nothing, for there was nothing that could be said. We may have slept, I will suppose that we did. Beyond that I cannot say, nor how long we were there, only that the sun began to sink.

'Joe?'

He moved his fingers across my skin. I had forgotten his arms reached through to mine. It was the best comfort there was.

I lifted my head to see him through the frame. His eyes were swollen and red, closed nearly, and on the side of his face was a great swelling too.

'What has been your punishment?'

He did not respond.

'What has happened?'

He only shook his head.

'They have abused you.' He said nothing and I knew it to be true.

He tried to say something, but his voice was empty of life, as if his soul had already begun to take its leave.

'Can you ever forgive me?' I asked.

His eyes were brimming but he would not look directly at me. 'For what?'

'For loving you.'

He began to shake, great gales of sorrow and devastation, a soul abandoned to its own end. I wept too, not for myself but for him alone and the tortures he had suffered.

What I know now is that after our torturers had gone, he

crawled to the hem of the sea, lay himself down and let himself be sloughed clean by the eviscerating sting of the brine. That as he burned all through, he had the impulse, horrible and true, to push further out, to crawl deeper into the water, until it took him away and further still, until he could no longer find his way back to the shore. He would not be afraid of drowning. He would let go.

Perhaps he should have floated to his eternal freedom. I cannot say. But he did not. He found his way back towards my prison, half-blind as he was, and called my name through the window until I heard him through my slumbers.

My scribe weeps with me, we sit close and offer one another comfort. We have grown to love each other most dearly and she holds our sorrows as if they were her own. Her most earnest wish is that her transcription will move others to choose love over all else. But now, sorrows, for this is what our love cost us. This brutishness was the price for tenderness. Can you see where we were and where we were still to go? And all of this for loving one another with nothing more than kind words and utmost faith and the softest of hearts.

22

Even Beyond Death III

When next I woke, a brighter light was seeping through the little square opening near the ground. It was a new day.

I could hear Joe outside muttering to himself, trying to shuffle closer. A horrible groan gave me the first inkling of the agony he suffered as he moved slowly into view, holding in his hand the biggest leaf I had ever seen. It was waxy and very green, and he held it pinched at the top like a pocket.

'You have to be careful. You can't be greedy or we'll lose it.'

'What is it?'

'Put your hands through. You must not drop the top and keep it pointing up as you pull it through.'

Even as he passed it across with painful care, I started shaking, knowing what was coming.

Water, clean and cold, the best I have ever tasted. I had to employ every last forbearance to stop myself from spilling it as I gulped and lapped.

'Oh, it is nectar, is there any more?'

'Not much, but there's enough. If it rains it will replenish.'

He had found shallow pools in a long flat rock.

'What else did you see?'

'Trees, grass.'

'Nothing else?'

'No. I'll bring you more water. It's not far.'

With great effort, prefaced by a line of lurid language, he lifted himself up and hobbled out of view once more. I felt the misery of his departure even before it had fully occurred and remembered that this was a feeling so often rehearsed.

I tried to adjust my eyes for the dark. I could see very little.

The room, if you can call it that, was round and dense. The stone floor was covered in a mixture of sand and some straw, suggesting there had been another there before me. I tried to get a sense of its height and as I looked up, I felt in my stomach the most terrible sense of defeat. It was as high as two rooms and about eighteen feet across. The stones offered no vulnerability, no chink through which to burrow or chip.

And the tower was dark as Satan.

I began to walk around and around in my pen, like the bears I had once seen in Marseilles, rabid with fear and isolation. Round and round I went until, unbidden, a great and monstrous howl emerged from my body, racking my very soul from its seat as the spectre of my coming death raked its rancid nails across my skin. I fell to the floor, sobbing and wailing, pathetically pounding at the fortress with my fist.

After an eternity, I thought I heard Joe return. I pulled myself up, gasping for breath and trying to regulate myself. I pushed my hair back and wiped my face on my sleeve. He could never know my terror. I would protect him from it no matter what it cost me.

He had dragged a large bundle of branches and palms to the tower and dropped them and then he too collapsed, his back to me against the stone wall. He was exhausted.

'Jehan? Are you there?'

'I confess that I am.' I hoped he could not read my distress.

'I'm making us beds.'

'And I am exploring my quarters.'

'Anything?'

'No.'

Despite his injuries, Joe dug and chipped and heaved at the barriers that held me fast, that he might free me. He did this over and over again. He worked until his hands bled and for all of that, nothing gave way. This fortress would not break. This had been a calculated punishment. The decision to keep us alive but apart had been quantified as a crueller trick than killing us. It had been designed to slowly break our hearts.

When he had recovered from the effort, he went to find more palm fronds and fed through the window some smaller branches which I could use to make a dryer bed. The larger ones he placed on his side, so that he could sleep close to me.

As evening fell and having once again supped on nothing but a leafy pocket of fresh water, we lay facing each other through our porthole. We said nothing but sought ourselves in the other's eyes, each needing comfort. As ever I found my solace in him and he in me. The place in each of us where all striving ceased, if only for that moment. But it was enough that eventually we felt able to sleep.

I woke gasping, and with it a thick tarry expulsion from my throat. As it coursed out, I could not breathe. The panic it brought was hot and immediate.

I must have turned away from the opening while I slept, as I woke on my back. I swung back to the window. No Joe.

I felt as if I were drowning in a dark miasma. Eventually, I managed to spit the noxious tar out and the air came back to me in increments until the dreadful temper eased.

I knew the environment choked me. The most overwhelming sense I had of the tower was the fetid quality of the air.

I had the sensation of cobwebs having to stretch to accommodate me, a stickiness possessing an eternity of humid tendrils.

This misery was temporarily elevated by the joy of freshly cleaned linen. Joe had taken my battered garments to wash in the sea and let them dry in the sun. On their return, the clothes had a near-ecclesiastical feel.

I felt a chill and heat all at once and tried to lie as close to the window as possible that I might feel the sea breeze cleanse me.

There I lay, a fever about me.

'I have brought you gold,' Joe said.

'You are my most dear.'

Joe placed in front of me a handful of small brown fruits, one was split open to reveal a yellow flesh and a few little black seeds. 'I have tried it. It is very good and there are many more. They fall from a tree.'

I gorged myself on four or five before I even looked up. Joe handed me more and it was the most satisfying meal I have ever enjoyed.

When I drank my pocket of water afterwards, I thought I might expire from joy, the terror of my waking forgotten.

'I've brought you something else. Here, reach through. Some shells and a flower.'

The flower was the perfect proportion of pink and orange and bright. In the middle, a long sword. The bloom was bigger than my hand. I cannot express to you how wild the life in it seemed to me.

To be deprived of colour even for a few hours is the strangest thing.

'I am afraid it's not fragrant, but it's the only kind I found. There may be more another time.'

'It is flawless.'

'Do you like the shells?'

'I will get to them next. I want to spend some time on the flower. It feels so soft against my skin. I had forgotten the feel of silk. How soft it feels, and cool.'

Joe's face appeared at the window.

'What's wrong?' he asked. 'Lie closer.' He knew me too well. 'Bring your face here.'

He reached his arm across and placed his hand on my brow. He had to stretch.

'It is nothing. A passing chill.'

'I'm going to get more water.'

'Stay a while. I like to have you near. And you are so weary. How is the pain?'

He sat up with his back against the wall of the tower. 'Much the same. But, to pass the time, shall I sing for you? What would you like to hear? Jehan?'

It began as a pop of air in the throat and then I began to wheeze as both laughter and pain collided in my body at the same time. I began to shake and tears coursed down my cheeks as I tried to control my mirth, all the while fighting for breath.

'What is the matter? Can you breathe?' Joe was back peering through the low gap.

'Jonathan Kryk of Amsterdam, this may be the pertinent time to tell you—'

'Oh, heaven? Do you die?'

I was struggling to take sufficient breath through my gulps. 'Joe. If you sing to me now ... I will surely die.'

'What?'

'You cannot sing. You should not sing. And that I am now trapped in here and at the mercy of your tuneless carolling is perhaps the cruellest trick that has been played thus far.'

'Tuneless carolling?'

'Truly none worse. I would rather listen to cats coupling. Accompanied by a lute.'

He snorted once and again and then there came from him such reels of laughter as there had ever been and to join him in it was such medicine.

'If you were not locked in there, I would box your ears.'

I had laughed myself breathless and Joe, complaining that the laughter had not done well with his injuries, went quickly to find me more water, singing as loudly as he could, his voice both toneless and shrieking at once.

Even as his joyous din receded, I could feel the tide begin to rise.

My whole endurance relied on knowing his breath rose and fell just an arm's length away, and I was afraid that with the effort that had just passed, I might begin to choke once more.

I lay down and within moments of his parting, the fever returned.

How I longed for my soft, pretty bed, Joe enfolding me with his body to keep the cold away.

He returned later – maybe that day, maybe the next. I was no longer able to mark the passing of time. My descent was rapid and dazzling in its thoroughness.

Joe was feeding me water and as many of the little berries as he could find. He tore his sleeve from its shoulder and doused it in seawater over and over and handed it through the window so that I could wash my face, hair and neck.

Later, as he lay exhausted on his bed of palm, he reached his fingers through the bars to touch my salt-scrubbed face. Already beads of sweat were beginning to reappear across its brow. I kissed his fingers. His spirits were eviscerated.

'We'll die here, Jehan.'

'Yes. I expect we will. I fear I will not be able to cheat the chance line this time.'

How strange the foreign silence that held us there. The breeze, chirrups and trills of birds whose names we would never understand nor ever speak aloud, for who would hear them? We found ourselves beyond the reach of language. It could no longer contain our experience, for the place to which we had been delivered lay beyond all comprehension. All we had was the language we shared and in it we would write our private epitaph.

'Joe, tell me how first you kissed me.'

'I have told you so many times.'

'Tell it again.'

'Well, you were so still. I thought maybe you were asleep. Even as I asked you to turn your head you barely responded, so that I had to turn your face towards me with my hand.'

'I remember. As drowsy as a man who has supped full on plates of poppies.'

'I oiled your face. I loved to do it. It allowed me to touch you and feel you near.'

'You said, *Please, Monsieur, the other side now.*'

'You turned to me, still in a dream. Your mouth parted just a breath. I was dying of love and knew that to kiss you would give me back my life.'

'You ran your finger along my lip.'

'And I kissed you.'

'Yes. You kissed me.'

'I was out of bounds.'

'Oh, much more than that, you had stepped out of time, you had dared to throw the entire world off its course. My Joe. Your disobedient tendernesses upended all of history. And you did it not with galleons and armies, but with that sweet, seditious kiss.'

'And look where it has brought us. That kiss was the same as a sad farewell.'

'Yes. But has not untempered hope always been our most persistent heresy? I allowed the jester to live because you demanded it. Not because it could ever be true.'

I began to cough, another sharp chill scraping over me.

All the while, Joe simply lay on the ground on the other side of the bars and talked to me, saying I would be well again and he would find a way to break the tower's defences.

I slept. Where before I had always dreamt of the tower, now trapped in it I was able to dream of Avignon. Hortense, her fingers brushing her pearls, her sweet and dearest self, the light across my desk, the sound of restless horses. I dreamt I was in my salon taking everything out of my cabinet, the *maquettes*, jewels, each hidden stage and scene revealing another secret drawer where a new trinket was hidden. I was preparing to have it sent to me and soon all my pretty treasures would be returned to my waiting hands.

I cannot say how long I dreamt, only that eternities and moments became the same as the fever racked through me and each breath began to require a deeper effort.

The feeling of being filled with water became more acute and with it the sense of the approaching moon tide.

It was night. Joe had been watching me as I slept, as I had watched over him near every night he came to my bed. I knew it for the act of profound devotion that it was.

'Stay here with me until I fall asleep again. I feel so afraid tonight. If I can lie here and I know you lie here too, I can forget where I am. Just for the moment.'

'I'm here.' His hand stretched towards me.

I pressed myself closer to the opening so that he could stroke my cheek.

I said, 'You are all I have ever needed. And I am lying on feathers, linens too, clean and perfumed. Orange oil and cypress.'

'Pillows full of goose down?'

'Yes. How is your bed, Joe?'

'Jehan, please—'

'No tears, Mister Kryk, there will be time for that. Lie back now. Look up, tell me what you see that I may see it too.'

He rolled onto his back. I could see the light on his tear-damp face. How I adored his everything. He said, 'The moon is high.'

'It is?'

'Yes. It's full and white.'

'Keep gazing at it. You are ever my perfect Endymion. You lie on the slopes of Mount Latmus, caressed by the wanting moon.'

Shudders coursed through me at intervals. I hardly had breath. 'You sleep. You cannot be woken but know that as you dream, I am the moon that looks down on you. I am dumb-struck by your beauty. If you shut your eyes, you will feel me hover over you as you sleep.'

'I can.'

'Can you feel that I am kissing you?'

'Yes.'

'I kiss you forever.'

And just as he had been when he had kissed me, I too was outside of time.

I was moonlight and feather all at once, I was perfect love and such lovely intimacies as only the dark can offer.

I was loved and had loved and that was enough.

I could hear Joe and see him too, as I began to separate myself from my body.

He was calling. His hand, his cheek, were resting on the wall as if it was myself.

I thought I might try to claw back into myself, but from out here, above it all, I could finally see how thin he had become, how tired, but still so beautiful, *so* beautiful, and I knew I had to release him.

I knew that he would follow me, that his heart would break,

for it had already begun to and he soon would be released back to me.

'I love you,' he said, or perhaps it was I.

No matter.

We were always only one, and always will be, even beyond death.

Au Revoir

My dears,

Are you now drenched with grief? I confess this telling has been punishing. Even now, its cruelty boils and gurgles in my throat. It would be just and right to seek vengeance on these brutes, haunt them across eternal plains. They wished to turn us into beasts, nothing more than an assembly of pelt and bone, racked with fear and believing the worst they spoke of us.

But no. Are we not more eloquent souls than that? I would propose that we are and as such I would say to you as I said so often to my beloved:

Do we dare?

His answer, as you know, was always:

Yes.

So, let us be mutinous and instead turn ourselves to what we would rather profess, which is our unwavering faith in a blazing, roofless love. Love that cannot be tainted or turned nor given titles which do not describe it. Let us be rebellious in our laughter, revelling in heretical joy. Let us speak rather of watching your beloved sleep, speaking their name as if it were your one true prayer. Let us speak of a hand that seeks another from deep inside a dream and tears that fall to the self-same song.

Let us, rather, choose all of those as the comets and stars to which we will hitch our tails.

We two have lived together for centuries now. In 1657, we met and loved. We died at the high tide of that love and thus began our eternity together.

As I relay this to you now, you find me walking along the long arc of a beach. None can see the end. I walk, as is my custom, with my cane in my hand and my hat upon my head. Its plumes and jewels have been restored so that I am once more the devastatingly handsome man you have come to know and adore.

Ahead of me is the only man more beautiful than I. He is golden. His chemise is untucked, the sleeves rolled up past his elbows and he cartwheels out along the sand, laughing as he does. When he grows too giddy from the reeling, I hold him to me and kiss him until the spinning stops.

In the intervening years between 1657 and your reading, our earthbound lives have been multiple and yet more spool out ahead of us in an unbroken string. We follow our beloved scribe about for merriment and tinker with her heart; we have thrown a devastating Cupid's bow her way and laugh to watch her so entirely upended by love. From time to time, we choose once more to slip through the veil. On each occasion the stars align, the clocks chime one in unison and we find our way back together again, delighting in our corporeal joy, glutting ourselves on our love for each other.

You may question our reasoning, that we would trust our perfect and immortal souls to so crude and brutish a vehicle as life.

But, friends, looking back, has it not been so very, very beautiful?

I leave you for now, but know that we will return again and that I kiss you all for eternity.

Jehan de Baudelaire

Catalogue of Desire

This index has been arranged according to the express wishes of M. J. de Baudelaire to assist readers in their desire for a more intimate and satisfying enjoyment of his record.

Baudelaire, Jehan
Agile
Charm (masculine and otherwise)
Drunk on
  ale
  hippocras
  love
  wine
  vin de Dieu
Handsome
Prodigious yard
Poetic soul
Tedious marriage conversations
Tenez/jeu de paume; *court de*; winning
    at; skilled at; cheating at
Threatening to kill
  Edvard Hoost
  Footman
  Toad, The
  Uncle (Hippolyte)
  Wallace (Captain)
Verbal jousts won
  Marriage (multiple entries)

Verbal jousts lost
  Hortense (multiple entries)
  Marriage (multiple entries)
Virility
Writings:
  Endymion
  Endymion (lewd)
  Lonely Jester, The
  Etc.

Bears
Do I look like a

Bliss
Endless
Longed for
Promised

Despair
Loneliness (multiple entries)
Separation
  Hortense
  JK

Kisses
Aching
Chaste
Daring
Drunk
Heated/hungry
Longed for
Misjudged
Remembered
Teasing
Tender
Wicked

Kissing
Hortense
JB & JK
JK bold black-haired girl
M. Benoit
Mme. Benoit
The Toad

Kryk, Jonathan (Joe)
Beauty
Excess of wine/ale
Eyes
Face
Fear of drowning
   clear pools
   dry land
   sea
Impertinence
Kindness
Laugh
Livery
Mouth
Pliancy (and cartwheels)
Practised
Prodigious yard
Professionalism

Prowess
Skin
Sweetness
   to friends
   to kitchen girls
   to Monsieur
   to mother
Swimming
Thighs
   reassuring
   shapely

Languorous looks
JB (multiple entries)

Longing for
Escape
Kisses

Loins
Aching
Taut
   delightfully so
   hot and
   inconveniently so
Thundering

Love
Bliss of
Brotherly
Eternal
Filial
Longed for
Symptoms of
Tossed on the horns of

Melancholia
Related to loneliness

Acknowledgements

That Jo Unwin – we laughed and cried so many times over this book. She gave it everything, everything. I worry it took the last drop too, meaning she left publishing entirely to recover from her labours. She was my excellent agent but now I consider her my excellent friend.

My dear editor at Corsair, Sarah Castleton is a marvel of editorial subtlety and, honestly, the most forgiving editor there is, in ways that only she and I will understand. Thank you. Truly.

At Hachette, immense support from Alice Watkin, Lucy Martin, Lilly Cox and enlightening copy editing from Hannah Boursnell. Each of them has been patient, focused and excellent. The luscious cover was designed by Sophie Ellis. I love it. Thank you to all who do the essential, unseen jobs at Hachette: mailing, boxing, copying, tidying, all the things that make it all work at the start of each day.

This book has made me cry myself to sleep. A few times. Andrew Wille is my dearest friend, emotional support dog and first reader. Self-obsessed writers need someone to say 'pull yourself together!' And make them laugh until they can't breathe – and he is that to me.

Extra hugs and kisses for my sister, Fiona Swaffield, and Bea Millar, Michele Magwood, Angela Sacco and Sally Dufour.

Darling Maggie Melrose, my other emotional support dog, has helped me write every book. Sausage.

Another sweet hug and hot kiss for secret friends and lovers, because, as this book shows, everyone should have at least one.

Eternal love for my darlings Jehan Baudelaire and Jonathan Kryk for their story. I can't wait to kiss their handsome cheeks on the other side of the veil when I'm done here.